FRAMED

Ronnie O'Sullivan is widely regarded as the most gifted snooker player ever. In May 2012 he won the World Championship and announced his retirement. He then returned in May 2013, having not played for a year, to win the World Championship for the fifth time.

Framed is his first novel.

FRAMED

Ronnie O'Sullivan

An Orion paperback

First published in Great Britain in 2016
by Orion Books
This paperback edition published in 2017
by Orion Books,
an imprint of The Orion Publishing Group Ltd,
Carmelite House, 50 Victoria Embankment,
London EC4Y 0DZ

An Hachette UK company

3 5 7 9 10 8 6 4 2

A CIP catalogue record for this book
is available from the British Library.

ISBN 978 1 4091 5131 9

Typeset by Input Data Services Ltd, Somerset

Printed and bound by CPI Group (UK) Ltd, Croydon, CR0 4YY

www.orionbooks.co.uk

FRAMED

FRAMED

1

Frankie James watched the mystery blonde getting dressed at the end of his bed. Nice figure. Nice smile. A good sense of humour too, from what he could remember from last night.

He'd met her in the 100 Club on Oxford Street. Some new Mancunian band touted as the next big thing in Brit Pop had been in town. His best mate Spartak had been running the door and had let him in for free.

Frankie had spotted her halfway through the gig. Six foot in heels. Nearly as tall as him. She'd caught him checking her out. Hadn't even blinked. Just stared back. A challenge. He'd never been able to resist one of them.

He wracked his brains. Bollocks. What was her name? Michelle? Or Mary? Or even May? Christ. His head was throbbing. How much had he drunk? Bloody hell. He was slipping back into the bad old ways. Had been trying to cut down. Had screwed up again.

He glanced over at the crumpled up AA leaflet in the corner of his bedroom. He didn't even remember where he'd got it from. It had been there for weeks . . . months . . . He didn't believe in that group therapy shit. More willpower. That's how he'd kicked the coke, wasn't it? Just by saying no. But something still kept stopping him from binning that leaflet anyhow.

He buckled his belt over his pressed black suit trousers and took a dry-cleaned white shirt from his wardrobe and pulled it on. He stared at the girl.

'Stop gawping,' she warned him with a grin.

Hard not to. She was standing in just her black satin knickers and bra, with her hands on her hips.

'You seen the rest of my clothes?' she asked.

'In the lounge,' he said. 'At least, I think . . .'

That was where they'd started, wasn't it? He watched her sashay out through the door and down the short corridor. Blimey. She was a looker, all right. Fit. Maybe even a keeper, as his mum might have said. A couple of years back, Frankie would have made more of an effort. Cooked her a bacon sarnie. Asked her out for dinner. Got to know her properly. But he had way too much crapola on his plate for that now.

Narrowing his ice-blue eyes against the sun, he pulled up the blind and gazed down from the flat's second-floor window. It was just gone eight and hardly any of the shops, bars, delis or clubs in Poland Street were open. Didn't mean Soho was quiet though. Shopkeepers were busy moving the homeless from outside their doors. Junkies and wasted clubbers stumbled past. Commuters trudged miserably into work. In the distance, a siren wailed.

'Our kingdom.' That's what Frankie's dad had always told him. 'And don't let any other bastard ever tell you different.'

Frankie took his dad's watch from the bedside table and slipped it on. A Rolex, a real one, with the old man's name engraved on the back. Frankie loved how heavy it felt.

'Think of it like an insurance policy,' his dad had once said. 'Even if everything else in your life turns tits-up, right here you've still got something you can cash in to start over.'

Frankie clenched his fist – a boxer's fist, just like his dad's. Just like the rest of his family, going right back.

Frankie's granddad and great uncle had both been pros. 'The

Bloodthirsty James Boys', people had called them, though never to their faces. No one had ever had the bollocks for that.

Neither brother had ever made the big time. Not through lack of talent, mind, more a lack of the right promoter. Rumour had it they'd both ended up working as enforcers for the Richardson Gang back in the '50s.

Frankie's was a family some people round here were still wary of, not just because of who his granddads were, but because of what they said his father had done.

Frankie turned to see the blonde standing in the bedroom doorway, wearing the same little black dress and heels he'd relieved her of last night.

'I've written down my number,' she said, pulling on a thigh-length, fake fur coat.

She swiped a bright pink lipstick across her mouth and blew him a small kiss. Her accent was expensive, educated. He tried to remember if he'd asked her where she was from, but nothing concrete sprang to mind. Probably somewhere posh like Berkshire or Surrey. The kind of place where girls like her rode ponies while their mums and dads hunted foxes. Somewhere far from here.

He said, 'Thanks.'

She gave him that stare again. That challenge. What was she after? His number? He let the silence hang.

'I'll walk you out,' he said, fishing out a pair of silver dice cufflinks from the old wooden box on the windowsill, another leftover from when his dad had been living here.

'A bit formal for you, aren't they?' she said, amused, watching him thread them into his shirt cuffs.

He'd been wearing a designer T-shirt and jeans last night. Both fake. But work was different. If you wanted respect around here, you had to at least look the part. Especially when you'd just turned twenty-three and were half the age of every other club boss in town.

He pulled on his suit jacket and checked himself out in the mirror, combing his fingers back through his black hair. Italian ancestors, his mum had always claimed. All of them as crazy as the Emperor bleedin' Nero. So said his dad.

'You scrub up pretty well,' said the blonde.

Frankie turned to face her. Was she being sarcastic? No, she was smiling. A warm smile too. Not the flirty one she'd used last night to hook him in. This was something softer, more personal.

He half-smiled back, but it was more of a reflex. He needed her gone, needed his head space back so he could work out how the hell he was going to convince his landlord to give him more time to come up with the rent he owed on the club. Then there was the problem of how to deal with his kid brother. Bloody Jack. He'd called last night. Had got himself in hock at poker to the Chinese. A-bloody-gain.

'I'll just get my shoes,' he told her, walking past, knowing she was watching him every step of the way.

He scoured the debris in the lounge: a stacked ashtray, the remains of a bottle of red, two glasses, one with her lipstick tattooed onto its rim. A half-empty bottle of whisky too. He didn't even remember opening that.

He'd hit the gym later. Soon feel less guilty. That, and an early night tonight.

He found his shoes by the sofa. Loafers. Italian leather. An indulgence from a few months back when he'd been feeling more flush.

The blonde was waiting by the flat's reinforced front door. Didn't look in a hurry. He wondered what she did for a job. The way she looked and acted, she could have been anything from a fitness instructor to an ad exec. Whichever, it was too late to ask her now.

He pulled back the door's two deadlocks and its stainless steel bolt.

'Looks like you're expecting an army,' she said.

'Used to be my dad's place,' he told her. 'He was very . . . security-conscious . . .' Frankie didn't know how else to explain. 'Watch the steps,' he warned. 'They're stupid steep.'

He followed her downstairs, careful himself. He remembered how one of the old man's business associates had once taken a tumble here. Broke both his legs. Frankie had got back from Leicester Square Odeon with Jack to find the old man busy scrubbing bloodstains off the wall.

Two doors led off the small hallway at the bottom of the stairs. One into the club. The other onto the street. Frankie had to squeeze past the blonde to open the street door's triple lock. It was the first time they'd touched properly since last night. The contact made her giggle.

'Sorry,' he said.

'Don't be.' She threw him a knowing look. 'I think we've been a lot more intimate than that.'

He smiled. Couldn't help himself. Something contagious about the twinkle in her eyes.

They stepped out onto the street. The air was heavy with the stink of disinfectant, kebab wrappers and chips.

'Cigarette?' she said, sparking one up.

'No. Thanks.'

She raised an eyebrow. They must have chugged through a whole two packs between them last night. He could feel it in the shortness of his breath. Something else he was meant to be cutting right down on. Shit.

'So . . .' she said.

'So . . .'

A rock steady beat drifted down from a window up above. She was staring at him again, unblinking. Her expression said it all: *your move.*

'It's been . . .'

'Memorable?' she suggested.

'Yeah, memorable.'

'And fun?'

He smiled. 'Yeah, that too.'

'Memorably fun.' She said it like she was trying it on for size. 'I guess I can settle for that. But, you know, do feel free to call me as well . . .'

'Sure,' he said. 'I will.'

She kissed him then. Quickly. On the cheek. Then walked away. He watched her as far as the end of the street, until she faded into the crowd.

'Goodbye Martha, Megan, or Molly,' he said under his breath, wondering if he'd ever see her again, and almost stepping into the street after her – before walking back inside, sick at the thought that if he didn't play his cards right today, he was going to end up losing the club.

2

Frankie hadn't so much inherited the Ambassador Club, as had it thrown at him like a ticking bomb from a speeding car. At least that's what his dad's cousin, Kind Regards, had told him five years ago – and that's how it still felt today.

Hitting the light switch in the club's main hall, Frankie breathed in the stale smell of smoke, chalk and beer, as he listened to the *tink-tink* of the strip lights flickering into life above the twelve tables.

He sighed. The hall's worn carpet was scuffed and stained and its walls and ceiling were patchy with damp. Two of the frosted plate glass windows overlooking the street had been cracked by some passing pissheads a few weeks ago and he still hadn't got round to fixing them.

Drumming his fingers along the edges of the tables as he walked to the bar, he was almost glad his dad wasn't here to see it. After his dad had been banged up and Frankie had first taken over managing the club, he'd hoped to turn its fortunes round. Easier said than done.

He'd hit the same old chicken and egg problem the old man had. The only way to make enough money to tart the place up was to bring in more punters. But the only way to bring in more punters was to tart the fucking place up.

Frankie's dad, Bernie, had taken out a thirty-year lease on the club over ten years ago, back in '84, after winning big on the horses. His plan had been to put it on the map. Make it a hub for the game here in the West End. But he'd always come up short.

End result was that Frankie and his brother Jack had hung out here pretty much full time in their teens when they weren't in school, being babysat by staff, while their mum and dad had gone out doing other jobs to make ends meet: managing brewery pubs, or running van-loads of tax-free cigarettes and booze back on the ferries from France.

Not that Frankie had minded. None of the rented houses they'd lived in at the time had ever felt as much like home as here. Frankie loved it. Soho. The club. The people. The free lemonades and crisps. And of course the snooker. He'd got the bug for it the instant he'd picked up a cue. Hadn't been a day gone by since when he hadn't fitted in a few frames.

He checked his watch. Still too early to go cap in hand to Daniel Listerman about the rent. Listerman was Tommy Riley's lawyer and Riley was the big-time gangster bastard who owned the freehold on this building along with the rest of the street.

Listerman the Lawyer was an early riser. Some said he never slept at all. But turning up this early at his swanky Beak Street office would only make Frankie look even more desperate – and skint – than he was.

Might as well make himself useful here first. He changed out of his suit in the storeroom, coming back out in tatty blue overalls and black rubber boots, with earphones in, a Sony Discman clipped to his belt, and a bucket of warm soapy water and a mop in his fists.

He'd had to let the club's regular cleaner go a month back, not having enough money to pay her. It didn't bother him that much, to tell the truth. Apart from the khazis. Especially the gents. What the hell was wrong with blokes anyway? Why

8

couldn't a single bloody one of them manage to piss in a straight line?

He cleaned the bogs first to get them out the way, then the bar and the ashtrays, before starting on sweeping and mopping the floor. He worked his way round the tables in the same pattern he did every day. It somehow made it go faster, like doing circuits down the gym.

He hummed as he worked. A Northern Soul compilation. Everyone was into Blur and Oasis these days, but he reckoned the old tunes were still the best. His dad had been a proper mod back in the day. There was a signed Small Faces LP up above the bar. Used to be an old Bang & Olufsen record player and a stack of Al Wilson and Jimmy Radcliffe singles back there as well. But Jack had pilfered the lot on his nineteenth birthday two years ago and flogged them down Berwick Street market to pay for a night on the razz.

Frankie still hadn't forgiven him, the little shit. Him and Jack had used to listen to those records as kids, dancing and larking about. They should have meant more to him than just some quick cash. Frankie remembered coming down here one night late when his mum and dad had still been together and seeing them slow-dancing round the empty club. He couldn't believe how fucked up his family life had got since then.

His mum had gone missing in '88, just after Frankie had turned sixteen. A year after her and his dad had started living apart, her at their rented house and him here in the flat above the club. She'd just vanished when Frankie and Jack had both been at school. No sign of a struggle. Nothing. Just gone.

Everyone else – Frankie's father, Jack and the cops – all reckoned that Priscilla James wasn't just missing, she was dead. Why else wouldn't she have come back? Or at least contacted them? But Frankie didn't believe it. He felt it in his guts. He just fucking *knew* that one day he'd see her again.

He checked his watch. Ten to ten. Nearly time to open up already. Nearly time to go see Listerman too, just as soon as Slim the barman got here to do his shift. Frankie headed back to the storeroom to get changed. The red light on the answerphone winked at him from the bar. He took his earphones out and hit 'Play'.

'Frankie?' It was Jack, sounding well stressed. 'For fuck's sake, Frankie, pick up.' Was he wasted? He was slurring. 'I'm coming over . . . Fuck. I need you. I need help . . .' A whisper, a hiss. 'I'm coming over. *Now.*'

Frankie groaned. Hell's tits, not again. How many fucking times already this year? Jack doing too much gear. Getting himself in a paranoid mess. Jack needing a lift back from some godforsaken club in the middle of piggin' Essex. Jack running out of dosh and expecting Frankie to bail him out. Jack making the same stupid bloody mistakes over and over again.

Frankie's heart thundered. Just pretend you're not here. Don't answer the door. Fuck off back upstairs and turn up the radio and get in the shower.

But all he saw in his head was his mum. That last morning he'd seen her, as she'd handed him his packed lunch in the shitty little driveway of that rented Shepherd's Bush house.

'Go catch him up and make up,' she'd said.

She'd been talking about Jack. He'd just cycled off in a strop over some football sticker he'd nicked off Frankie the night before and which Frankie had just wrestled back off him.

'He thinks he can take care of himself, but he can't,' she'd said. 'You know that. And promise me, *promise me,*' she'd said, squeezing his wrist so hard he'd winced, 'you'll always be there for him. No matter what happens. To me or your dad, or to anyone else.'

Even then, it had sounded off. Had she known? He'd asked himself the same question a million times since. Had she known that by teatime she'd be gone?

Crack.

What the fuck?

He turned to face the club's front door. Someone had just given it an almighty smack.

3

Was it Jack? Already? He'd sounded so wasted on the phone. Could he really have got here that fast? Not like him to give the doors a leathering either. Debt collectors then? Had one of Frankie's hastily negotiated streams of credit just dried up?

He reached under the bar for the cue he kept clipped there out of sight. Maybe not as tasty as a lot of other weapons when it came to a fight, but a hell of a lot easier to explain to the cops.

He flicked on the cctv, watching its squat screen shimmer into life. Relief, of a sort, flooded him. Forget debt collectors. A smeary, black-and-white image of his little brother loomed into view.

Jack was dressed in a black leather jacket and jeans, with his slicked back hair tied back in a ponytail. *Smack*. The door shook again as he shoulder-charged it. He glared wide-eyed up into the centre of the camera lens, his mouth flapping open and closed like a fish out of water.

'Pack it in,' Frankie yelled, ditching the cue and running between the tables, as – *thump* – Jack charged the door again.

Jesus. What the fuck was he on? Frankie hadn't seen him for weeks. Apart from the call last night, hadn't heard from him either. Jack had been working nights the last six months, running club nights with a bunch of DJ mates. Was it the Chinese? Was that why he was here? Or something worse? What the fuck kind of bother had he got himself into now?

Frankie jerked the metal crossbar up and flipped the deadlock round. The door burst open, smashing hard into Frankie's head, sending him staggering back. Jack lurched in, slamming and locking the door behind him. He slumped down panting on the floor.

Frankie stared down at him, rubbing his head. Shit-a-brick. He was covered in fucking blood. Apart from his jacket . . . under his jacket . . . everywhere . . . His neck, hands, jaw and wrists were caked with the stuff. But not fresh. Dried.

'What the fuck is going on?'

Jack stared up, shuddering. He was unshaven and baggy-eyed, like he'd been up for days. He looked like Frankie had used to. Before he'd got his shit together. Or at least before he'd got his shit together more than *this*.

'It's not what you think,' Jack said.

The way he said it. The fucking guilt. 'Oh, Jesus. What have you done?'

'Nothing. I swear it, Frankie. I swear it had nothing to do with me.'

'What didn't?'

'It . . . *this* . . .' He was rubbing his hands together, spitting on them, trying to get them clean.

'If it's not yours,' Frankie said, 'then *whose*? Whose fucking blood is it?'

'I dunno.'

'How can you *not* know?'

'It was just there. All over my bed when I woke up. Smeared . . . all stuck to me . . . all over my duvet and sheets . . .'

'But how? How did it get there?'

Tears filled Jack's eyes. 'I don't know. All I remember is I was down the Albion, drinking with Mickey . . .'

'When?'

'Yesterday.'

'What time?'

'Afternoon . . .'

'And then?'

'Nothing. I don't remember anything.'

'What else?'

'What?' Jack was shaking, snot bubbling from his nostrils.

'What else were you fucking on? Apart from drink. Were you wasted? Is that why you can't remember?'

'I dunno.'

Jack started sobbing. Actually crying. Like a little kid.

But Jesus, even if he'd been totally off his head last night, how the hell could he have forgotten? Getting covered head to foot in someone else's blood? How the hell could he *just not know*?

'What about at your flat? When you woke up?'

'What about it?'

'Was there anything . . . I don't know . . . anything that can fucking explain *this*?'

'No. Nothing. It was just everywhere. All around me.'

'And you don't even remember getting home? Getting into bed?'

'No.'

'Do you even remember if you were on your own?'

'No. I don't know.'

'You sure?' He didn't sound it.

'There was something . . . this morning . . .'

'What?'

'A jonny.'

14

'A what?'

'A fucking condom.' Jack clawed his hands back through his hair. 'I trod on it next to the bed as I was running for the door. I got it stuck on my fucking foot . . .'

Frankie almost laughed. Apart from the blood. And how fucking much there was. Enough to maybe mean that someone somewhere was dead?

'And you really don't remember a thing?'

'I swear, Frankie. The whole fucking night, it's a blank.'

The condom . . . that meant someone must have gone back with him, right? Didn't it? But who? And was this their blood? Had Jack somehow ended up getting in a fight with them? With a woman? No. He was no fucking woman-beater. No matter how wasted he got.

Jack pulled out a pack of fags and jerkily tried sparking one up. But his lighter just sputtered. Didn't have enough gas. He crushed the cigarette in his fist and threw it away, gripping his head in his hands.

'You said you were running,' Frankie said. 'When you put your foot in it, you said you were running for the door.'

'Yeah.'

'Why?'

'Because of the call.'

'What call?'

'Someone rang.'

'Who?'

'A man.'

'What man?'

'I don't fucking know. I didn't recognise his voice.'

'What did he say?'

'He told me, you know . . . to get the fuck out . . .'

'Of the flat?'

'Yeah.'

'What did he actually say? What were his actual words?'

'That the cops were coming . . . That I had to get out of there. *Now*.'

The cops? Oh, Jesus. They were already on to this? Frankie felt sick.

'I asked him what the fuck he was talking about,' said Jack, 'and that's when I put on the light and looked round and saw all that blood . . .'

He started sobbing again.

'And then you ran?'

'If I hadn't done, they would have got me,' Jack said. 'The second I reached the end of the street, there they were: fucking cop cars everywhere, a riot van too, lights flashing, sirens screaming . . . screeching right up outside the building . . .'

Jack was making out that whoever had made the call had done him a favour, but that was bollocks. Why would anyone call him anonymously like that? And how the hell would they know the cops were coming and he had reason to run?

Running had made him look guilty as hell.

'Did anyone see you?' Frankie said. 'Leaving your building, I mean?'

'No.'

'You call anyone?'

'Just you. From the phone box down the tube station. Then I came over. As fast as I could.'

Frankie was already doing the maths. Anyone could have seen him on the way over here. Hard fucking not to with him looking like an extra out of *Halloween*. Anyone could have called the cops.

'We've got to get you out of here,' Frankie said. 'They'll come looking.'

Even if no one had seen Jack coming this way, it wouldn't take the cops long to work out where he'd gone. Both him and Frankie were well known. Because of the old man. The same went for the club. Once they realised Jack had split . . . once they'd seen all that blood at his flat . . . their next port of call would be here.

'Get up,' Frankie said.

He grabbed Jack by his collar and dragged him to his feet. Jack's flat was over on Warren Street. Only two stops away. Less than five minutes in a fast car or van.

'But can't you just hide me?' Jack pleaded. 'Tell them I'm not here?'

'They'll tear this fucking place apart.'

Jack looked down at his hands again, appalled. 'But I've got to get this off me . . . I've got to get myself clean.'

'We're getting you out of here. Now.'

Cleaning him up would help, but it wouldn't solve anything. Not with that same blood all over his flat. First things first. Frankie had to get him somewhere safe before the cops showed up. Had to buy them both time to figure out what the fuck was going on.

'Move.'

He dragged Jack quickly back through the club, checking the cctv monitor as he ducked behind the bar. The front of the club was still clear.

'How much money you got?' he asked, snatching the Small Faces LP down off the wall and quickly opening the safe behind.

'Nothing,' Jack said. 'My wallet. It was gone. I swear it was in my jacket last night, but it's not there now.'

First the condom and now this. Who the hell had Jack been with last night? And where the hell were they now?

Frankie took last night's takings out and shoved them into Jack's jacket pocket. He grabbed a cloth from the sink.

'Wipe your fucking face.'

Jack did as he was told, then reached out to hand it back.

'No,' Frankie said. 'In your pocket as well. If the pigs turn up here, I can't have them finding anything. Or whatever the fuck this is, I'll be in it right alongside you up to my neck.'

He marched Jack through to the back of the club and ducked into the storeroom and grabbed a set of overalls. He threw them at Jack to put on. A cop siren whooped outside the front of the club.

'No time. Quick.'

Frankie unlocked the club's back door and jerked it open. He checked up and down the service alley which ran along the back of the buildings. Just bins, graffiti and litter. No cops. Not yet. Didn't mean they wouldn't start funnelling down the alley any second.

'Which way?' Jack said.

'Up.'

Jack stared uncomprehendingly at Frankie, but then a smile crossed his face as he realised what Frankie meant.

The roof. A cast iron fire escape zigzagged up the red brick wall leading up to it. Reach the top and you could crawl along right to the end of the street.

It was a game Frankie and Jack had used to play together as kids, pretending they were in *The Great Escape*, each of them squabbling over who'd get to be Steve McQueen every time.

Keep out of sight and Jack could hide up there and bide his time, and wait for his chance to climb back down one of the other building's fire escapes and slip away into the crowd. It was either that or run down the alley now and risk running right into the arms of any cops already closing in.

A flash of determination glinted in Jack's dark eyes. Frankie gritted his teeth. Good. At least the little bastard still had some fight in him. He was going to need it.

'Once you get away, you're gonna have to lay low for a couple of days,' he told him. 'Then call Slim and tell him how we can get hold of you.'

Frankie's dad had inherited Slim with the club. He'd been running the bar here for over twenty years and had known both boys since they were kids. Frankie trusted him with him life.

Jack wiped his nose on the back of his sleeve. 'Thanks, bruv. I won't forget this.'

'You're damn fucking right. Now get the fuck out of here and don't you dare look back.'

4

Frankie stepped back inside and locked the door, quickly sticking the key on top of the doorframe out of sight.

Crack.

Sounded like a battering ram. Looked like one too. Frankie spotted two cops on the bar's cctv monitor taking another massive swing as he ran past.

Crack.

A whole squad of them out there. *Them*. The enemy. Rozzers, Five-oh, Babylon, flatfoots, Dibble, fuzz, plod, filth, pigs, the Old Bill . . . Didn't matter what you called them. They'd always spelt one thing for Frankie's family: fucking trouble.

'Those bastards aren't here to protect you,' was what his dad had always said. 'More like hurt you. Tell you what to do. Hassle you, rob you, trick you, cheat you. Try any way they can to break you and bend you till you snap.'

And worse than that too. Frankie grimaced. They could catch you. Catch you and arrest you and lock you up and try you. Like they did to the old man. They'd nicked him for armed robbery five years ago. He'd sworn to Frankie he was innocent and Frankie believed him. But a jury had found him guilty and they'd banged him up for life.

Frankie didn't have a fucking clue yet what was going on with Jack, or who'd put the cops on to him, or why he was covered in blood, or even whose blood it was, but he knew this: he wasn't going to lose him. Not if he'd done nothing wrong.

He opened the cctv recorder cupboard and flipped the eject button on the machine. Pulling out the tape, he tore at it, unspooling its guts, before shoving it deep down into the bottom of the bin under all the slops and fag butts.

Deep breath. He watched the front door shudder as the cops charged again. Right, let's fucking do this. He ran to the front of the building and flicked the locks off the door, setting his face to neutral, the same way his old man had used to make him and Jack practise whenever they'd played cards for matchsticks as kids.

He pulled the door open and stepped smartly back, as the two uniformed plod with the battering ram gripped between them came hurtling through and landed in a heap of twisted limbs on the floor.

Next in was a plainclothes. A wrinkly old bastard. Half a foot taller than Frankie. A thin black moustache and balding grey hair shaved down to a grade one buzz cut. Something spider-like about his long limbs. Nasty. Marched past Frankie like he owned the bloody joint.

'Get up, you pair of pricks,' he told the two uniforms groaning on the floor.

As they scrabbled up, two more plainclothes, ten years younger than the spider, made a beeline for Frankie, looking like they wanted to punch him in the face.

Frankie stood his ground. Tweedle-Dum and Tweedle-Fucking-Dee. Red-faced and tubby, they looked like a couple of Toby jugs brought horribly to life.

'Wrong brother. Leave him,' the tall man snapped, a length of spit at the corner of his mouth stretching and shrinking as he spoke.

Wrong brother? Frankie's eyes narrowed. Who the hell was

this? He tried placing him. There was something familiar about him, but he couldn't quite work out what.

'And who the fuck are you?' Frankie said. Might as well get on with winding him up. The longer he could keep them distracted here, the better chance Jack would have of giving the bastards the slip.

The tall man smiled, his teeth the colour of cheddar. 'Big words for a young lad.'

Frankie looked him slowly up and down the same way he did whenever he was thinking about refusing to serve some pisshead a drink late at night. Creased lilac shirt and purple tie. Expensive-looking blue suit. Two sizes too big. Baggy round his shoulders, like he'd recently lost a ton of weight, or had just taken a fancy to someone else's jacket and had nicked it from a club.

'I said, who are you?'

The spider took a step closer. 'Snaresby. DS Snaresby. Name ring a bell?'

'Nah.'

'Funny, that. Most people round here do know me. Particularly families like yours. Check the back,' he told Tweedle-Dum and Tweedle-Dee.

'You'll need a warrant for that.'

Frankie blocked their path.

'Will we now?' Snaresby checked his watch. A Breitling. Expensive. Looked nicked on this bloke, the same as the suit.

'So where is it?' Frankie said.

Snaresby's tongue flickered in the corner of his mouth. 'Being printed and signed even as we speak.'

'Yeah, well until that's done, you ain't allowed in here at all.'

'But we already *are* in here.' Snaresby stretched out his arms, his bony wrists sticking out of his jacket, making him look like a scarecrow. '*Quod erat demonstrandum,*' he said.

Frankie didn't budge.

'Unless you want my lawyer to go *veni*, *vidi*, *vici* on your arse, I suggest you get off my property now.'

Blood rushed to Tweedle-Dum's face. 'You want me to nick him, guv?'

But Snaresby just smiled thinly, his eyes locked on Frankie. 'Well, well, well,' he said. 'An educated James boy. Whatever next? A flying pig?'

'Only if you've brought a helicopter,' Frankie said.

'We haven't.'

Frankie turned to see a woman in her mid-twenties. He hadn't even noticed her come in. She was wearing a smart-looking grey business suit and buttoned up white blouse, with a black wedge haircut more suited to a club. Green eyes. Pretty eyes. Something about her he couldn't quite place either, something from way back in his past.

'Here you go, guv.' She handed Snaresby a computer printout.

'Perfect timing, love.'

She winced at the word, but Snaresby didn't notice. He shoved the piece of paper into Frankie's hand.

'Read it and weep.'

Frankie glanced down. A warrant.

'Got the alley at the back sealed off both ends, guv,' said the female plainclothes.

Frankie's heart sank. Was there any way Jack could have snuck out further down the street already and got away? He doubted it. More likely he was still hiding somewhere up top.

'Good work,' Snaresby told her. 'Now be a sport and go and see if you can rustle me up a nice cup of tea.'

Another wince. Maybe she thought her boss was as big a prick as Frankie did. Their eyes met for a second. He'd definitely seen her before. But where?

She marched back out of the club.

'Nice view,' said Snaresby, watching her go. 'Check the toilets,' he told Tweedle-Dee and Tweedle-Dum. 'The cellar too.'

He lit a cigarette with a well-polished brass Zippo.

'Smoke?' He offered Frankie the pack.

'I don't.'

'Then whose is that?' His slate grey eyes flicked towards the crumpled up cigarette Jack had left on the floor.

Frankie shrugged.

'I only ask because the rest of the floor looks so clean, see? Like it's only just been swept.' Snaresby crouched down, all knees and elbows. 'And just look at it. It's not even lit, like whoever was planning on smoking it was in a terrible hurry to leave.' His gaze returned to Frankie. 'Oh, and I couldn't help also noticing you've got a nasty little bruise right there on your head. Recent too. Had a run in with someone else already this morning, have you?'

'I walked into a door.'

'Ah, if I had a quid for every time someone's told me that . . .' Snaresby shot Frankie a lopsided yellow smile as he stood. 'Now, are you going to tell me where our secret smoker's hiding? Or am I going to have to get my boys to really start poking about?'

Frankie said nothing.

'Suit yourself,' Snaresby said.

He walked over to the bar and glanced at the open cctv machine cupboard. He opened it up and tutted at the lack of tape inside. He turned his attention to the open safe and peered inside.

'Oi, that's private,' Frankie said, following him.

'And empty. Someone made a recent withdrawal?'

Snaresby picked up the Small Faces LP from where Frankie had left it on top of the glass-washing machine. He turned it over in his hands as he stubbed his cigarette out in the sink.

'I hate music,' he said.

'What?'

'A waste of time. Fucking boring.'

Frankie didn't know what to say. What kind of a person said that?

'Oops,' Snaresby watched the record slip from its sleeve and land with a crack on the tiled floor.

Wanker. Frankie bit the word back. Snaresby was just trying to rattle him, to get him to lose his cool, and maybe give something away. Just ignore the bastard.

'I do hope it didn't have any sentimental value?' Snaresby said, looking down at the broken record. 'Didn't belong to anyone special, did it? You know, like your dad?'

Frankie's cheeks prickled. So he knew the old man? So what? What copper round here didn't? Didn't mean he knew anything else.

Tweedle-Dum reappeared at the top of the cellar steps, red-faced, panting and shaking his head.

Snaresby clicked his fingers at Frankie.

'Keys,' he said.

'What?'

'For the upstairs flat.'

'You'll need a warrant for that too,' Frankie said. 'A separate one.' It was a guess, but from the sour look on Snaresby's face, he'd guessed right.

Snaresby took a step towards him, so close that Frankie caught a whiff of his aftershave, something nasty from another decade. Aramis, Old Spice or Brut.

'Funny you haven't even asked me why I'm here,' Snaresby said.

Frankie swallowed, knowing he'd been caught out. He forced a grin.

'Why the fuck are you here?' he said.

'Because your nasty little brother's been running round my shiny nice town all covered in blood.'

'Bollocks,' Frankie said.

'Hard not to have blood on him, the way I see it. That bedroom of his was like an abattoir. Disgusting. Just as well your mum isn't around any more, eh? She'd have been ashamed.'

Frankie's hands curled into fists.

'Don't talk about my mother.'

Snaresby flashed him a smile, then slowly nodded, clicking his tongue. 'Fine. Let's talk about Susan Tilley instead.'

'Never heard of her.'

'No? Well, she's someone you're going to be very familiar with before too long.'

'And why's that?'

'Because she's the woman your brother's just killed.'

Sweet Jesus. They wanted Jack for murder?

'He's not killed anyone. There's no fucking way he'd—'

But Snaresby was already walking away. 'We'll see,' he said.

He stopped in front of the back door and stared at it, with his back to Frankie, before reaching up and taking the key from the top of the frame. Shit. Shit cubed. He must have noticed it glinting up there in the gloom.

'You really should find a better hiding place for this,' he said. 'Who knows who might find it?'

Unlocking the door, he opened it wide.

A uniformed cop was already standing outside.

'Anyone try and make a run for it up the alley?' Snaresby said.

'No, guv.'

'Good.' Snaresby stepped out and peered up at the cloudless blue sky. 'When I was round at your brother's shithole of a flat earlier,' he told Frankie, 'I couldn't help noticing that he also happens to be a smoker, much like myself, and that his poison of choice are Marlboro reds, much like that screwed up cigarette back there on the floor.'

'He's not been here.'

That smile flickered into life on Snaresby's face. 'Shall I tell you something else I find interesting? Just now, during the course of our little conversation, I couldn't help but notice you glance up at the ceiling three times.'

Frankie felt a jolt of alarm. Had he looked up? He didn't think so, but he couldn't be sure. 'So what?'

'So, as tempting as it is to mark you down as every bit as stupid as every other male in your family,' Snaresby said, 'I think you might be the smart one. In which case, I imagine that the second your naughty little brother turned up here begging you for help, you rightly guessed that me and my colleagues wouldn't be far behind.'

'I don't know what you're talking about.'

'Oh, I think you do,' Snaresby said. 'I think you probably also guessed that we'd leave no stone unturned in our quest to locate said brother, either in the club or the flat above. Meaning that, instead of hiding him here, you'd have rightly concluded that your best bet under the circumstances would be to get him clear of the property altogether.' Snaresby's smile was steadily widening, yellow as a crescent moon. 'And you wouldn't have slipped him out front, would you? Because that would have been too risky. And you wouldn't have sent him off up this alley either. Because you'd have been worried that we might have already been closing in. Which means there's only one way you could have sent him, really, isn't there?'

Frankie knew it then. This bastard had worked him out.

'And that,' Snaresby said, 'is up.'

5

'Search the roofs,' Snaresby ordered the uniform. 'And keep the ends of the alley covered. I'm not having this little weasel giving me the slip twice in one day.'

The uniform barked Snaresby's instructions into his radio, then repeated them to the three burly, uniformed male coppers standing to his right.

Frankie watched them scrambling, clanking up the fire escape. He felt like he'd just walked into a nightmare, like everything had turned fluid and was somehow slipping away.

Was Jack still up there? Fuckety-fuck. Frankie bit down the urge to shout out a warning. Or maybe Jack had already shinned down one of the drainpipes at the end of the alley and got away? Please, God. Yes.

He noticed Snaresby gazing at him through those glittering, grey shark's eyes, loving every fucking second.

'How did you know?' Frankie said, his voice trembling.

Snaresby raised and lowered his eyebrows. 'Like I told you: your body language gave you away.'

'No, I mean about Jack and his flat and all that blood you say you found. What made you go there looking for him today in the first place?'

'He did.'

'What?'

'He drove his own car to the crime scene last night.'

'What crime scene?'

'Susan Tilley's grandmother's house. A lovely place. Out in Royal Berkshire, no less. That's where the gardener found Susan Tilley lying in a pool of her own blood. So much blood. It looked like a video nasty, I can tell you. It's where they found her grandmother too.'

Her *grandmother*? Jesus. Frankie felt his stomach twist. They were after Jack for *two* murders? But how the hell did Jack know either of them? Or did he? Frankie wracked his brains. Jack had never mentioned them. He was fucking sure of it.

'We've got cctv of his car. Ran the plates as soon as we saw it,' Snaresby said. 'We've got him going in through the property gates at eight twenty-two pm and then out again at eight forty-one, right after he'd bludgeoned them.'

Bludgeoned?

'Jack didn't hurt anyone,' Frankie said. 'He wouldn't.'

'So why's he running?'

'Who said he is?'

'All right then, hiding . . .'

'You don't know that either.'

'We soon will,' said Snaresby, gazing unblinkingly up at the cops' progression over the final few rungs of the fire escape and onto the rooftops above. 'If your little brother is up there, I think even you'll have to admit that it looks somewhat suspicious. Or maybe you'll just tell me he's up there fixing the tiles?'

Shielding his eyes against the sun's glare, Frankie watched the cops split up, two of them edging left and two of them right along the rooftops, visible now only from their shoulders up.

He remembered the layout of the roofs from when he'd used to play up there with Jack. Each building was bordered by a waist-high, ornate Victorian façade, behind which was a flat gutter half a foot wide you could walk along. The roof tiles slanted up from there into peaks, some of them with skylights, through which him and Jack had used to spy while they'd practised smoking cigarettes.

But there weren't any places to hide . . . apart from crouching down out of sight behind the chimney stacks which rose up between the roofs of each building. The cops would have to be half-blind to miss anyone.

'Of course, all that blood's not exactly going to do him any favours either,' Snaresby said. 'My colleagues from forensics are camped out at your brother's flat this very minute and it's my firm belief that they'll very shortly be able to match what's there with samples taken from Susan Tilley and her gran. Furthermore, I'm guessing that once we do apprehend your brother, any blood discovered about his person will also prove a match.'

The cops spreading out across the rooftops reached the end of the Ambassador building and threaded their way between the chimney stacks onto the roofs of the buildings next door. Frankie stared along the alley to the left. The cops stationed there hadn't moved.

Again he saw Snaresby was watching him – again too late.

'Let's head this way, shall we?' Snaresby said, clasping his hands behind his back as he set off slowly down the alley to the left, keeping level with the cops searching the roofs above. 'There's a Shakespeare quote I've always been fond of,' he said. 'Who'd have thought he'd have so much blood in him?'

'*Macbeth*,' said Frankie.

Another smile from Snaresby. 'Didn't I say you were the smart one? Quite right,' he said. 'It's what Lady Macbeth says to her husband after he's killed the Scottish king.'

'Duncan,' said Frankie. That was the king's name. Frankie had been studying English, History and Art for A-level before he'd had to drop out of school and take over running the club because of what had happened to his dad.

'Most people don't know just how much blood's inside your average human body,' Snaresby said. 'Or realise what a hideous bloody mess it can make, excuse the pun. Not until they cut someone open. Or bludgeon them repeatedly with a blunt instrument until dead. As happened to poor Susan Tilley last night.' Snaresby shot Frankie a distasteful, almost squeamish look. 'Her face was caved in completely,' he said. 'Tenderised like steak.'

The wanker. Frankie hated Snaresby for enjoying this as much as he was.

'I don't blame you for looking shocked, sunshine,' Snaresby said, not breaking his stride. 'But wait till you hear this. It already seems possible the poor girl was sexually molested too. Her underwear had been literally torn off her. Bits of it – like the gusset, I believe – entirely gone. Taken like some sick souvenir.'

Frankie shivered in the sunlight, trying to force the image of the poor woman's battered corpse from his mind. What kind of a monster could do what Snaresby had just described? Jack? No fucking way. Frankie couldn't see it. Not in a million years.

'But that's not the worst of it,' Snaresby said. 'At least for someone like you, a local lad who's grown up round here the way that you have . . .'

Frankie knew he wasn't going to like what was coming next.

'Susan Tilley was meant to be getting married today,' said Snaresby. 'She was planning on taking her new husband's name. And can you guess what that name is?'

Snaresby stopped and stared deep into Frankie's eyes, clearly not wanting to miss a beat.

'Hamilton,' he said.

Hamilton? Snaresby couldn't possibly mean—

'That's right. Good lad. You get it,' Snaresby said. 'She was meant to be marrying Douglas Hamilton, Terence Hamilton's boy. Today. Her body was found barely fifty yards from the marquee they'd got set up on the old lady's front lawn.'

Only then did Snaresby blink, like a camera taking a snapshot to enjoy over and over again.

Frankie just gawped. Dougie Hamilton. As in *The* Hamiltons. A family every bit as fucking scary as Frankie's uncles had ever been, or Tommy Riley's mob were now. Terence was the boss, Dougie his only son. Frankie had only ever seen Dougie once. Jack had pointed him out in a bar. He'd been with his old man and a bunch of his thugs, but somehow quiet and not a part of it at all. Frankie only remembered him at all, because Jack had told him he was a lawyer. A gangster's son who'd trained to be a lawyer. Jack had thought that was one big fucking joke.

'The way I hear it,' Snaresby said, 'young Dougie's devastated. And who can blame him? One minute, he's living with his pretty little fiancée in their posh city apartment, with their whole future ahead of them. Then last night out he goes on his stag night with his old man and some pals. To that new place. Quaglino's. You been there? I hear the steak's off the clock . . .'

Frankie's mouth was so dry he could hardly move his tongue.

'And then this morning, he hears the bad news.' Snaresby tutted. 'Of course, Hamilton Senior's not taking any of this too well either. In fact, I'd go as far as to say that he's every bit as keen to get hold of your little brother as me.'

Frankie felt numb. Snaresby reached out and gripped his shoulder.

'Just as well we've got you out in this lovely morning sunshine now, isn't it?' Snaresby said. 'What with you suddenly looking so deathly pale.'

A shout rang out. Heart pounding, Frankie jerked back from Snaresby and shielded his eyes as the cops heading left on the rooftops surged out of sight. A scream went up. Then another.

Fuck. They'd got him. They'd caught Jack.

'But look on the bright side, eh?' Snaresby said, 'at least we got our hands on the little bastard first.'

6

'When can I see him? How do we get him out?'

Kind Regards stared back at Frankie through half-moon glasses, drumming his fingers on his green leather desktop. Pushing back his chair, he walked to his office window and looked out over Shepherd Market, running his hand over his lank brown hair.

Birdlike, that's how Frankie's mum had always described him. Always flitting around, never sitting still.

It was Frankie's dad who'd given him his nickname, on account of how formal he always was, right down to the way he signed off his Christmas cards. His real name was Alan Grant. He was Frankie's dad's cousin as well as his lawyer. They'd been good mates as kids and the two of them had lived together in their early twenties after Alan had left uni in Bristol and moved to London. More recently he'd worked on Frankie's dad's case and was now organising his latest appeal.

'Those are two very different questions,' he said.

'The first then.'

'When can you see him? That depends on when – *if*,' he quickly corrected himself, 'the police charge him. Until they do, I'm the only one allowed in.'

Six grim hours had gone by since Jack had been arrested. Kind Regards had been Frankie's first call. He'd taken the news calmly,

34

professionally, before heading over to the West End Central cop shop on Savile Row where Jack was being held. Frankie was lucky he hadn't ended up there himself. Snaresby had warned him not to skip town. If he'd been able to prove Frankie had helped Jack hide it would have been worse.

'The police have the right to keep him in custody for up to ninety-six hours.'

'And then?'

'They either charge him . . . or let him go.'

'But it's going to be the former?'

'I'm sorry, but yes.'

How could it fucking not be? If all that stuff Snaresby was saying about the blood was true. 'Take me through how you reckon it's going to play out,' Frankie said.

Sparking up a cigarette, Kind Regards perched on the edge of his desk and explained. He'd sat in on the cops' first interview with Jack and already, in their view, the evidence against him was overwhelming. Barring a miracle, they were going to charge him with the murder of Susan Tilley, along with the attempted murder of her grandmother. That was one thing at least. The old lady wasn't dead. Not yet. She wasn't much alive either, mind. On top of the horrendous injuries she'd sustained, she'd suffered a stroke and was now in intensive care. No one knew if she'd even make it through till tonight.

Bail was out of the question, because of the seriousness of the charges. And on account of the fact he'd run. Meaning Jack would be kept banged up on remand until his court hearing. He'd then be put back on remand until his trial began. Again with no chance of bail.

'The only good thing to come out of the interview,' said Kind Regards, 'other than him saying he'd not seen you earlier today . . .' Kind Regards peered at Frankie over his specs knowingly before going on '. . . is that at least Jack's been consistent with what he's said. He's denied everything. Being there. Doing it. The lot. He said someone must have nicked his car and that's why it was on the cctv. He told them he didn't even know who Susan Tilley or her gran were, let alone where they might live. He said he had no idea where the blood had come from or how it had got on him and all over his flat. He emphatically denied any wrongdoing at all.'

'What happened when they told him that this Tilley girl was engaged to Dougie Hamilton?'

'He looked genuinely shocked.'

'As in genuinely shocked like you believed him?'

Kind Regards ducked the question, lighting another cigarette. Frankie grimaced. What did it mean? That he didn't believe Jack? Or he didn't know whether he was lying or not?

'And the cops?' Frankie asked.

'It's their view that whether Jack actually knew her or not is immaterial. The fact that she was about to get married to Dougie Hamilton provides enough of a motive for Jack having killed her.'

'How so?' As far as Frankie knew, his little brother had never had any serious contact with Dougie Hamilton at all.

'They think this was a revenge killing.'

'For what?'

'One of Tommy Riley's boys – a certain Danny Kale – was killed last month, found dead in a back alley over on Charlotte Street . . .'

Frankie had read about it in the papers. Kale had been one of Tommy Riley's debt collectors, an enforcer. He'd been battered to death, then dumped outside one of Riley's bars.

'I still don't see how that puts Jack in the frame for this,' Frankie said.

'Danny Kale was bludgeoned to death,' said Kind Regards. 'The same as this poor girl . . . Leaving the cops thinking that maybe Tommy Riley had her killed as payback for Kale.'

Frankie's eyes narrowed. It made a certain kind of fucked-up sense. At least for the Rileys and Hamiltons of this world.

'And, of course, it's no secret that Jack's been working for Tommy Riley,' Kind Regards said.

Frankie felt heat flushing through his cheeks. He'd heard the same shit six months ago. How Jack was getting himself involved. Running errands. Doing a bit of driving. The bottom rung of the ladder, but one that could lead right to the top.

Frankie had had it out with him. Had told him to back the fuck out. Had even offered him a job down at the club. But Jack had told him no, had said he'd got something else lined up. The club promo stuff. That might have been the last real conversation that they'd had.

'He told me he'd stopped.'

'He lied.'

'Even if it is no secret,' Frankie said, 'it's still pretty fucking difficult to prove.'

'Not after that incident in the Atlantic. He's a known associate.'

Kind Regards meant the fight Jack had got into alongside some of Tommy Riley's boys after a Gunners game. The cops had been called. Jack had been nicked.

'That was just a ruck. All he got was a caution.'

'Maybe, but it's enough for the cops to see this – and him – as part of an on-going turf war.'

'Even if Riley did want to take out Dougie Hamilton's fiancée to get back at them for Kale's death, do you really think he'd have sent Jack? Even if he is a known associate of theirs, it's just for petty shit and helping make up the numbers in a brawl. He's no fucking hit man, is he? You know that as well as me.'

'I'm just telling you what the cops think. That maybe Jack did this under Riley's orders. Or off his own back. To impress his new boss.'

Frankie couldn't help sneering. Jack showing initiative? A fucking joke in itself. Jack had never been a leader, more like easily led.

'Yeah, well you know what I think? This is all bollocks. Fucking cops have been served Jack up on a platter and they're too lazy to bother looking for anyone else.'

'But even supposing that's right, it doesn't help us, does it?' Kind Regards pointed out. 'Not with the evidence they say they've got. And whatever else they might find out at the old woman's house. Which might be a lot. The killer made a right mess of the place. Even butchered the old girl's dog.'

Frankie slowly shook his head. How much more messed up could this get? How the fuck were they going to get Jack out?

'How is he?' he asked. 'I mean in himself?'

'Past the scared stage, if that's what you're worried about. Past angry too. He's slumped. You know. Low. It's to be expected. The pressure they've got him under.'

Frankie took a deep breath. Another.

'It will get better,' Kind Regards said. 'He'll feel better once he's in remand. That's when we can start to plan. How we're going to move forward.'

Move forward? Kind Regards wasn't fooling him for a minute. More like, prepare for the worst.

'And he still doesn't remember anything?' Frankie said. 'About last night?'

'No, not that he's saying.' There it was again, that note of doubt in his voice. 'And as you can imagine, the cops aren't exactly too happy about that. It looks bad, Frankie, him not even offering up any kind of plausible explanation. It makes him look like he's refusing to co-operate.'

'But how can he, if what he's saying is true?'

Kind Regards ducked the question, staring down at his fingernails instead.

'Snaresby . . .' Frankie said. '. . . the DS who came round the club . . .'

'What about him?'

'He knew who I was. Made out that he knew Mum and Dad too.'

'He grew up round here.'

'They were friends?'

'Not for a long time.'

What did that mean? If not friends now, then when? And what did that make them now? Enemies? Was that why Snaresby was enjoying this so much?

'The cctv footage he says he's got – placing Jack there at the old lady's house – you seen it yet?' Frankie asked.

'No.'

'So it might not show Jack at all? Just his car. If it even *is* his car . . .'

Kind Regards frowned. 'They said the plates match.'

'And what about the blood? They matched what they found on Jack and at his flat to Susan Tilley?'

'Not yet. But they're confident they will.'

'So that might be bullshit too. So why are you standing there looking at me like you've already given up?'

'We need to be realistic, Frankie. And focus on how we're going to play this . . . if the evidence does point towards him . . . if this does go to trial . . .'

'Even if it does,' Frankie said. 'I still won't believe he did it. Because there's no fucking way. And if that blood does match him, then it's because that's how someone wants it to look. Because he's being fucking set up, all right?'

'But by who?'

'That's what I'm gonna find out. There's so much of this shit that doesn't add up. Like how come he can't remember anything. Like, if he had done it, why would he be stupid enough to go home covered in all that blood and just go to sleep and make no effort to clear up?'

'It's the police's opinion that he could have been high at the time of the murder.'

Frankie could hardly believe what he was hearing. 'What? They think he did it because he was *high*?'

'No, not *because* he was high, *while* he was high. If it was a revenge killing . . . and if it was his first time, maybe he needed to get off his head to get the job done. It would explain the mess . . . the dog . . . the flat . . . all of it.'

'I still don't buy it. And you know what else doesn't make any sense? Who called Jack and told him to run? Someone did that because they wanted him to look guilty. I tell you: someone's fucking with him *and* fucking with the cops. And I'm gonna bloody well find out who . . .'

'And how exactly are you planning on doing that?'

'I don't know. Not yet. But I tell you this. I'm not going to just sit here on my arse and do nothing.'

'You want me to find you someone? A detective?'

'Round here? You having a laugh? The only people that people from round here will talk to are other people from round here. People like me.'

Kind Regards grimaced.

'I know how bad you're feeling, Frankie. But I've got to warn you, as your lawyer as well as your friend, that you don't want to go getting yourself involved in this. You're lucky Snaresby found Jack on top of the club, not in it. He's got his eye on you and the last thing we need is having both of you on the wrong side of the law.'

Frankie stared hard at Kind Regards. He knew the advice was meant well, but what other fucking choice did he have?

7

Frankie was still reeling when he got back to the club. He felt like he had when he'd first heard his dad had been sentenced to fifteen years. His brain hadn't been able to process the number, hadn't been able to grasp what it meant.

All he knew was he couldn't just wait for the law to run its course. The only one who could save Jack now was him.

The club was already open. Slim was stationed in his usual spot behind the bar, with his worn leather cowboy hat pulled down low over his brow and a smouldering B&H hanging below his bushy grey moustache.

Six punters were already in and playing. Life going on as normal. Just as well. The last thing Frankie needed was people steering clear of the place and leaving him even more financially screwed.

He needed to act normal too. No matter how churned up he felt. He had to show whoever was watching – cops, creditors, whoever – that he wasn't rattled. Jack had been wrongly accused. That's the signal he needed to be sending out right from the get-go. He'd been accused of a crime that he didn't commit.

Frankie nodded at the punters at the tables, all of them regulars. He didn't detect any sideways glances or awkwardness. News of Jack's arrest clearly hadn't got round everyone yet. Only a matter of time.

Slim was incredibly tall, even without the added height of his hat. He was dressed in a blue cheesecloth shirt, green moleskin waistcoat and piano tie. The height of fashion – for 1974, as Frankie's dad had always joked.

'How did it go?' he asked, his voice husky from decades of drink, smokes and staying out late playing cards.

'Good,' Frankie said. 'He's confident. *We're* confident that he's innocent, that we're going to be able to prove it, that we'll turn this all right around.'

He said this plenty loud enough for anyone eavesdropping to hear.

Slim had already poured Frankie a lager without asking. He slid it towards him across the bar.

'I know you're meant to be cutting back, but . . .'

Frankie took it and drank deep. Slim raised his whiskey and soda. He never drank neat before dark.

'To your brother,' he said. 'When you see him, you make sure they're feeding him properly? That's the worst thing about the clink, the food. Alongside the beatings and the buggery, of course.'

Frankie shook his head, smiling grimly. Life going on as normal. Yeah, Slim knew the form, all right.

'He'll be OK, don't you worry,' Slim said. 'But I do mean it about the food. It sucks.'

Slim had been banged up a couple of times. For nicking cars, something he'd once described as his hobby as well as his vice. He was a reformed man these days, mind. Had seen the error of his youthful ways.

'When did you last eat?' he said.

'Yesterday.'

'I thought as much.' He flipped on the Breville. 'I brought in some Jarlsberg. That's spelt with a "J". It's from Norway. A smooth texture with a nutty tang.'

The Breville was the only cooking appliance in the club and Slim made the best toasties Frankie had ever tasted. His stomach growled as Slim set to making a couple of rounds of Frankie's favourite: cheese and tomato. He took another swig of lager and stared at his hands. Why the fuck wasn't there someone older, someone wiser, who could sort this shit all out. Why did the buck always, fucking always, end up stopping with him?

'Ketchup or Mum's?' Slim asked.

'Mum's' was the mixture of mayonnaise, ketchup and Lee & Perrins that Frankie's mum claimed to have invented. Her and Slim had always got on. Partly because they both liked nothing more than sipping whiskey and eating toasties into the late hours, and partly because they both had the knack of making each other laugh.

Frankie and Slim ate in silence, watching the players on the nearest table. Normally Frankie could watch a couple of decent players like these two for hours. But not today. Everything, the whole fucking world, felt slow, out of whack. Do something. He had to do *something*. If he didn't, he'd go out of his mind.

'Beats the hell out of cheddar, eh?' said Slim as Frankie swallowed his last mouthful. 'And Norwegian, eh? Who'd have guessed. I didn't even know the Norwegians liked cheese.'

Frankie was staring at the door.

'You all right, son?' Slim asked.

'Sure. And thanks.' He got to his feet. 'I've just got to go see someone. A man about a dog.'

44

8

A dog about a man, more like. Mickey Flynn was a low-life, a drug dealer, and one of Jack's closest mates. The last person Jack remembered seeing last night. Frankie's only lead.

Frankie stuck to Soho's back alleys as he headed across town. Passing Morgan's wine bar, he checked over his shoulder. How many times now since he'd left the Ambassador? Twenty? More? He'd be doing his neck more favours getting wing mirrors taped to his head.

No harm in a bit of healthy paranoia, mind. The cops could be following him, seeing if he was mixed up in all this, interfering, warning him off. Then there were Hamilton's boys. Just because Frankie hadn't seen any of them since Jack's arrest, didn't mean they weren't around. He could feel it in the air, like one of them build-ups of pressure you got before a thunderstorm. Somewhere close, Terence Hamilton was about to fucking explode.

Frankie hoped he'd be able to avoid a ruck, but if it did come down to it, he'd be ready. He'd learned how to handle himself at an early age. The old man had seen to that, after this one time Frankie had been jumped by some prick in Islington as a teen. He'd lost his wallet, even though the only thing worth anything in it had been a passport snap of him with his first proper girlfriend, Rach. He'd lost his jacket too. Vintage Levi's. Keith

Moon's autograph in biro on the back. Bad luck for Frankie. It had belonged to his dad.

The old man had clipped him round the ear when he'd got back home. And worse. He hadn't given a shit about the mugger having a knife.

'Bollocks to what you hear on the telly about not fighting back,' he'd yelled. 'You never let anyone take fucking anything from you ever again.'

The old man had marched Frankie and Jack down the boxing gym and told his old trainer to toughen them up. Jack had stopped going a couple of weeks later, but Frankie had stuck with it until he'd turned sixteen, when he'd moved on to kickboxing, something he still did most weeks.

He slowed at the end of the alley and lit a smoke. A Rothmans. Punchy as. He hadn't been able to stop himself from picking up a pack. The stress. Fifty yards ahead was The Toucan pub off Soho Square. A bunch of early evening drinkers were soaking up the sun on the pavement outside. All of them harmless enough. No one he recognised. Advertising and new media types, over from the nearby film screening rooms and editing suites. Designer specs and trainers, no ties.

Frankie threaded his way past girls sipping Chardonnay and lads guzzling Guinness. Best pint of the black stuff in town, according to Potty-Mouth Pete, the manager, who nodded at Frankie now as he reached the bar.

'How the fuck you doing there, Frankie?' he said with a gap-toothed smile, his accent Belfast and broad.

'Not so good.'

'Why's that?'

Not a flicker of suspicion in his dark eyes. Meaning he hadn't yet heard about Jack?

'Nothing. Just parched,' said Frankie. 'Must be the sun.'

'Then you're in the right place.'

Pete had several pints of Guinness already lined up for punters. He topped one up and pushed it across the bar to Frankie. Frankie pulled out a twenty from his silver money clip. Pete waved it away.

'Keep it. You can spot me a couple of frames next time I'm in.'

'Fancy your luck again, do you?' Frankie had thrashed him seven frames to nil the last time they'd played.

Pete grinned again. 'What the fuck did luck ever have to do with sport? Next thing you'll be telling me you believe in friggin' pots of gold at the end of the rainbow and leprechauns too . . . you superstitious cunt . . .'

'On the subject of mythical creatures,' Frankie said, taking a long, cold swig, 'you seen young Michael?'

Young Michael. AKA Mickey Flynn.

'Happens that I have. The wee bastard's downstairs, getting shitfaced with one of his pals.'

'Cheers.'

Frankie drained his pint and pushed through the crowd, his hands balling into fists.

Mickey tried running the second he saw him, jumping up out of his chair like he'd just sat on a wasp. He nearly made it to the open fire escape too. But he was so pissed he tripped up and fell flat on his face. Trying to haul himself back up, he grabbed for the nearest solid object. Big mistake. Turned out to be the leg of a bull-necked geezer with 'Millwall F.C.' tattooed under a roaring lion on the back of his shaven head.

The giant kicked Mickey away. Mickey scrabbled back looking like he'd just shat himself. Made this horrible, high-pitched keening noise, like he'd just trapped his finger in a door.

'Ahs soh . . .'

Frankie reckoned this was probably Mickey's slurry attempt at saying, *I'm sorry*. But it sounded a lot like *arsehole* too.

'You fucking what?'

The giant glared down. Everyone waited to see what would happen. The last thing Frankie needed was Mickey in A&E with a broken jaw not able to talk. He had to control this shit now.

The skinhead looked down at his pint. It was full. Not a drop had been spilt. He held it out over Mickey's head, but just as he started to tip, Frankie stepped in, gripping him by the wrist.

'Steady, mate,' he said, smiling a smile that wasn't friendly at all.

The skinhead gawped at him, clearly not quite believing Frankie had dared to touch him, but Frankie ignored him. Letting go of him, he turned on Mickey instead.

'I've told you before. You're barred. Now get the fuck up.'

'Whuh?' Mickey stared in confusion.

'How many times already this week, you fucking wanker? When are you gonna get the message you're not welcome round here?' Frankie shook his head in disgust, glancing back wearily at the skinhead and shrugging as if to say, *What the fuck's a bloke to do?*

'You work here?' the skinhead asked, murder in his eyes.

'Yeah,' Frankie said. 'On the door. Just started my shift. Boss sent me down to kick this little weasel out. Now up,' he told Mickey. 'Before I let this gentleman behind me kick your rotten teeth into the middle of next week . . .'

A grunt of laughter. The skinhead. Phew. Might not now be a fight. Frankie jerked Mickey up by the scruff of his neck and steered him out through the fire escape into the gloomy beer delivery alley outside.

Sunshine streamed down through the metal grilles from the pavement above. You could see the soles of a dozen pairs of shoes up there and hear the chatter of the punters outside the front of the pub.

Frankie kicked the fire escape door shut behind him and slammed Mickey hard up against the brickwork.

'Right, you bastard, talk.'

There was nothing to him. A bag of bones in a dirty grey hoodie and stained jeans. Christ. He stank of vodka and vomit. What the hell was wrong with Jack? Why the fuck would he want to hang out with someone like this?

'I swear, Frankie, I swear it had nothing to do with me,' Mickey spluttered.

'*What* didn't?'

'Yesterday. Your brother.'

'Spill it. Everything. You hold anything back and I'll know.' Keeping Mickey pinned to the wall by his throat, Frankie spread the fingers of his right hand across Mickey's face, stretching his eyes wide open like he could stare right into his fucking soul. 'Everything,' he said. 'Right. Fucking. Now.'

'It was meant to be safe.'

'What was?'

'What I gave him.'

Frankie increased the pressure on Mickey's throat.

'What I *sold* him,' Mickey hurriedly corrected himself. 'The Billy. At least that's what it was meant to be. That's what the geezer said.'

Billy Whizz. Amp. Speed.

'What geezer?'

'Big Mo.'

'Who?'

'He meant Mo Bishara. Ran a caff on Tottenham Court Road.'

'Go on. What was wrong with it?'

'I don't know. It was cut weird. Blue.'

'You try it?'

'No. Ain't gonna either, not after—' Mickey welled up, his darting eyes glistening.

'After *what*?'

'What Jack did to that fucking girl . . .'

Frankie upped the pressure again. 'He did nothing. You hear me?'

'Yeah. I'm sorry. All right.'

'I hear you telling any cunt otherwise and you're dead.'

'I swear it. I won't say a fucking word.'

Frankie gritted his teeth so hard it hurt. He wanted to hit him. To fucking pay him back. For whatever part he'd played in all this. But what part *had* he played? Could Jack really have flipped out because of some shit he'd shoved up his nose? Flipped out enough to do what the cops said? No fucking way. Flipped out enough to not remember how he'd ended up covered in blood? Yeah, maybe that.

'You saw it happen?' he demanded. 'Him losing it? After you sold him it?'

Alarm flashed in Mickey's weasel eyes. 'No. He didn't take it with me.'

Backtracking. Covering his arse. The same as he would if the cops or anyone else ever asked. He'd deny fucking selling it too.

'He said he was gonna have it later. And he must have . . . 'cos just now, I heard how he went crazy . . . how he did . . . what they're saying he did . . .'

Just now? What was it Potty-Mouth Pete said up at the bar? That Mickey was downstairs drinking with some pal?

'And *who* exactly told you that?'

Mickey swallowed. Frankie felt it in his fist. 'Max. Max Winters. He's one of Hamilton's boys.'

So Mickey was playing both sides, the Hamiltons and the

Rileys. Frankie glanced back over his shoulder. Was Winters still in there? Had he seen him dragging Mickey out? Were more of Hamilton's boys already on their way? He stared back into Mickey's eyes. Squeezed his neck tighter to help him focus.

'Max said Jack had been arrested. Arrested all covered in blood.'

So they knew that as well. Means they'd know where he'd been arrested too. At Frankie's club.

'You got any left?' Frankie said.

'Of what?'

'The fucking gear.'

'No . . . I flushed it.'

Was he lying? Frankie couldn't tell. No point in shaking him down here either. Nasty he might be, stupid he wasn't. No way he'd be carrying it now. But what else did he know about what the fuck had gone down last night?

'How long were you there?'

'Where?'

'The fucking Albion. Yesterday. With Jack.'

'All afternoon. Into the evening.'

'With him?'

'No. He left. Around four.'

'And went where?'

'I dunno. He said something about meeting some bird . . . a new . . . You know how he was . . . *is* . . .'

'No. I don't. Spell it out.'

'Fresh . . . that's how he liked them. His hookers. New to the game. Just over from Poland or whatever . . . clean . . . before they'd been passed around.'

Frankie felt sick. What the fuck had Jack become? Why hadn't he noticed? Why hadn't be been there to stop it? He remembered the condom Jack had mentioned. The one on his floor. Was that

51

from him being with whoever this girl was? And when? Before Susan Tilley got murdered? Or after? Or even during? During would give Jack an alibi. During might get him off.

'But you've got no name? No idea where he went?'

'No.'

Frankie heard raised voices inside. The skinhead? Or Hamilton's boys? Time to make himself scarce. He let Mickey go and watched him slither down the wall like a stain.

'You hear anything – *anything* – and you call me.'

Mickey nodded. 'I swear it, Frankie. I swear I will.'

Frankie stepped over him and walked quickly up the gloomy brick steps into the blazing sunshine above.

9

Frankie turned onto Oxford Street and headed east through the crowd of shoppers back towards the Ambassador Club.

He needed to find out more about this blue speed. Pay Mo Bishara a visit. Find out who else he'd been selling to and if anyone had flipped out the way Mickey claimed Jack had. Or suffered the kind of memory loss Jack said he had.

He'd have to be careful, mind. Mo was higher up the food chain than Mickey. And what about Kind Regards? What would he make of it? Frankie didn't know whether to call him or not. Was this something he could use? Because finding out this gear made people flip was hardly going to help Jack's case, was it? More like back up the cops' theory that Jack had been high when he'd attacked Susan Tilley and her grandmother.

But the memory loss? That was different. If Frankie could somehow explain how this gear might have made Jack black out and forget, then at least it might prove he wasn't just deliberately not co-operating with the cops because he had something to hide.

It would make the possibility of Jack having spent the whole night blacked out and at his flat more credible too. Nowhere near the old woman's house. Because if this blue gear really was that strong, then how the hell was Jack meant to have driven anywhere, let alone done what they'd said?

Frankie stopped outside Top Shop, lighting another cigarette and having a quick look round to check no one was following him. What he really needed was to find the girl. Whoever Jack had gone to meet. Whoever he'd been with last night. Find her and he might still be able to prove that Jack hadn't attacked Susan Tilley and her grandmother at all.

Million dollar question was *how*?

He pressed on into Poland Street, seeing the club sign in the distance and hurrying towards it. He could still smell that scumbag Mickey on him from when he'd dragged him outside. He needed a shower and a change of clothes. Then what? Make a plan. About Mo Bishara. That and go see Listerman the Lawyer. About the rent. And about Jack too? Try and find out if he knew anything. Or was that just asking to get his teeth kicked in?

He heard a scream. A woman. He turned to see a sky blue Merc coupé roaring down the street towards him. What the fuck?

It drove right at him, swerving up onto the pavement, engine gunning. He threw himself hard to the right. Out onto the street. Got lucky. The Merc veered left, slamming into the metal grille of the newsagent next to the club. Glass exploded all around.

Jesus wept. Steam hissed up from the Merc's crumpled bonnet. The driver's door swung open. A man staggered out, half-collapsing. Early twenties, well-built, with blood all over his face.

'*You*,' he shouted, pointing at Frankie.

Frankie recognised him then, from that one time Jack had pointed him out. Dougie fucking Hamilton. Shit. Piss flaps. Fuckety-fuck.

He lurched towards Frankie. Then stumbled, looked like he might fall. Was he drunk? Or concussed from the crash? He righted himself and kept coming, shouting and swearing.

Frankie sidestepped. Just in time. Dougie's punch missed him by less than an inch.

Dougie spun and hit the floor. Got straight back up, his black suit trousers covered in muck and ripped at the knee. His dark eyes burned beneath his messed up, bloodied black fringe. He threw himself at Frankie again.

Frankie tensed as Dougie threw another punch. But it was weaker, slow. Frankie blocked it easily with a sideways sweep of his forearm. Dougie lined himself up for another, but Frankie took a couple of quick steps back, and again Dougie missed.

But what the fuck was he meant to do now? Defend himself properly? AKA take Dougie down? This was Terrence Hamilton's son, for fuck's sake. He was untouchable. Planting him on his arse here in public in front of a gawping crowd would land him in a whole new world of shit.

And chances were Dougie didn't even deserve it. He was meant to be a lawyer, for fuck's sake, not a crook. He was probably just out of his mind because of what had happened to his fiancée. Hardly deserved a beating for that.

Another punch, another block. This time Frankie stepped in behind Dougie. Pinioned the back of his neck with his left arm. Half-Nelsoned him with his right, twisting his hand hard back up against his wrist in a lock. Sorted.

Dougie froze, gasping in pain. Frankie offed the pressure a little, but the second Dougie sensed this, he started struggling again. Frankie had no choice. He tightened his grip again.

'You're dead. I'll fucking kill you,' Dougie hissed.

'I don't want to hurt you—'

'Dead.'

'. . . but unless you calm down—'

'Fuck *you*,' Dougie snarled.

'I know you think he done it,' Frankie said, 'that my brother—'

'He *murdered* her. That bastard. Your bastard brother. He fucking killed her . . . he's ruined everything that I had . . .'

The crowd was closing in. Fuck. How the hell was all this going to end?

'Murderer,' Dougie yelled. 'He's a fucking murderer.'

Jesus. People started backing off . . . They thought he meant Frankie, that Frankie had killed someone. A woman ran for the nearest phone box. Good. Call the cops. Let them bloody come. Frankie couldn't see any other way out. The second he let go of Dougie, he'd have at him again. Let the cops fucking deal with him instead.

A screech of tires. An engine roar. Frankie wheeled round, still holding Dougie. The crowd parted, as a black Bentley slowed to a halt barely three yards from where Frankie stood.

Private number plate: TH 1. Terence fucking Hamilton. Didn't need to be Columbo to work that out. Fuck, fuck, fuck. Four doors sprang open. Four blokes in dark suits stepped out.

Shit. One of them was Wilson. Shank Wilson. A Face. Maybe *the* Face in this part of town. More infamous even than his boss, Terence Hamilton. He was short and wiry with sharp ferrety cheekbones. A fucking killer through and through.

He stabbed a finger at his backup crew. Frankie braced himself, as Wilson waved them forward, but they stopped a yard from him, just staring as Wilson marched across the street to the phone box. Jerking the door open, he tore the receiver from the woman's grip and slammed it down onto its cradle.

'Fuck off,' he told her. 'And the rest of you,' he shouted at the crowd. 'Show's over. Get the fuck out of here. Now.'

They didn't need telling twice. They splintered left and right. Not that Shank even waited to see if they'd do as he said. He was already heading straight for Frankie. His face could have been carved out of flint.

'Put him fucking down.'

Frankie's heart was pounding. Shank was in his late fifties and grey and haggard with it. But Frankie knew his rep. You didn't fuck with him. No one did.

Frankie shoved Dougie forward, hard, trying to clear himself some space for whatever the fuck was going to happen next. Was Shank going to go for him here? With people still watching from further up the street? Frankie's fists were already up. Fuck, he wished he had a weapon. His cue. He glanced left. But the Ambassador Club door was too far. He'd never make it.

'Pick him up,' Shank snapped at his men.

They hauled Dougie up. He was gasping for breath. He tried pulling free, but Shank shook his head. Dougie purpled with fury and twisted round to look at Frankie.

'You're fucking dead,' he roared. 'Fucking dead.'

'Get him in the car,' Shank said, 'before the fucking pigs turn up . . .'

The men dragged Dougie over to the Bentley and shoved him inside. Then Frankie and Shank were alone.

'I didn't touch him,' Frankie said. 'That blood on his face, it's got nothing to do with—'

Shank stepped right up to him, all starched collars and cuffs and slicked back hair. He stared fearlessly up into Frankie's eyes, his hot breath stinking of aniseed.

'The best thing you can do right now, my friend, is fucking disappear,' he said, with a look in his eyes that told Frankie that he'd be just as pleased if he didn't and decided to make a fight of this instead.

Frankie opened his mouth, to tell Shank Wilson what he'd already tried telling Dougie: that Jack was innocent, that he hadn't killed Susan Tilley, that he hadn't done anything wrong.

But what was the point? Wilson had already made up his mind.

'You even think about pressing charges and I'll come back here and skin you,' Shank said, two long slanted veins throbbing on his forehead.

He stared at Frankie's fists with disdain.

'I'll see you around, cunt,' he said.

He crunched back across the broken glass to the front of the newsagent. Raj, the owner, was standing beside his wrecked shop grille, blinking like he'd just beamed down from another planet.

Wilson took his wallet out and stuffed a thick wedge of notes into Raj's shirt pocket. Didn't say a word. Then walked back to Dougie's mangled car and got in. He reversed it off the pavement with a squealing of tyres and stared out through the cracked windscreen at Frankie, his last words running through Frankie's mind. Not a threat. A fucking promise. Then he drove away.

The Bentley followed. Slow as a funeral hearse. Another face stared out at Frankie as it passed him by. Terence Hamilton. Like a block of fucking concrete, as his boy struggled and raged between the heavies in the back.

Frankie watched both cars to the end of the street, his heart pounding. He stared at the devastation all around him. It felt like the start of a fucking war.

10

Frankie's father, Bernie James, put the copy of the *Evening Standard* down on the chipped Formica table in Brixton prison's visitors' centre and smoothed it out with his clenched fist.

Susan Tilley's face stared up. Jack's name too. In block capitals. Above it the headline: 'REVENGE KILLING?'

The old man finally cleared his throat. 'What they're saying . . . about the drugs . . . Is it true?'

Frankie was sitting opposite him. He didn't answer. Force of habit. As kids, him and Jack had never grassed each other up.

'Fucking tell me, boy,' Bernie James warned. The same tone of voice he'd always used whenever he'd been about to belt Jack and Frankie as kids.

'All right,' said Frankie, 'some of it . . . but not like they're saying in there.'

'How so?'

'He's not a junkie.' The paper had run with what the cops must have fed them, about Jack being high on the night of the killing. Even had a quote off some anonymous source who claimed he'd seen Jack wasted in The Albion and named him as a known user. Better not be Mickey fucking Flynn. Frankie found out it was, and he'd pay.

'You sure about that?' asked the old man.

'Positive.'

But was he? After what Mickey had told him about the girls? The hookers. How Jack liked them. *Fresh*. Was that the Jack Frankie knew and loved? Hardly. He'd always been naughty. Cheeky. A handful. But never nasty. Never scummy like that. Frankie's fault. Not Jack's. He was his big brother. Should have been there to stop him taking a turn like this. Was going to sort it too. Put him back on the right fucking path. No matter what it took.

But it made him wonder as well . . . how right *were* the papers? About how big Jack was into the drugs? It would certainly explain how come he'd been keeping so much to himself these last few months, avoiding Frankie and not coming round the club. It would explain how shit he'd started looking too.

'You don't exactly look convinced,' the old man said.

Frankie tried staring him down. He didn't want him worrying, not until he'd found out himself how much of all this was true. But it was pointless. The old man just stared back. He'd never been one to back down. Not even at his trial. He'd not broken eye contact with anyone. Not the prosecution, judge, or jury.

'I don't know,' Frankie admitted.

The old man's cheeks flared red. 'Well why the fuck don't you? He's your little brother, for fuck's sake. It's your fucking job to know.'

Frankie's nails dug hard into his palms. Nothing ever fucking changed, did it? The old man had always held him responsible for Jack. Because he was older. Because right from the second they'd left the fucking womb, it had been Frankie's job to keep his little brother's nose clean as well as his own.

'And the rest of it?' said the old man. 'You'd better not be telling me he's mixed up in any of that shit too.'

He meant the gang connection. According to Kind Regards, the article had been written by the same hack who'd covered the murder of Riley's debt collector Danny Kale. He was ped-dling the same theory now, about an escalating turf war between Terence Hamilton's and Tommy Riley's gangs. An 'undisclosed source close to the investigation' had confirmed that the cops had not discounted the possibility that Susan Tilley had been battered to death in revenge for what had happened to Danny Kale.

'The way I hear it, he was driving,' Frankie said.

'You what? For who?'

'Tommy.'

The old man's expression darkened. Him and Riley went back, way back. Word was the old man had once even worked for him, or with him, some sort of association at least. Frankie had never dared ask. The old man and Riley hadn't spoken for years, even though Riley owned the building the club was in. All the dealings on the club's rent had always gone through Listerman. Frankie didn't know if they were outright enemies, but he sure looked like he wanted to kill him right now.

'He told me he'd stopped,' Frankie said.

'Well, you should have fucking checked.'

'I did.' But as soon as he said it, Frankie knew he should have done more. Not just accepted what Jack had told him about how he'd been making his money these last six months promoting club nights. He should have looked in on him. Seen who he was hanging out with. And fucking sorted him out if he'd caught him lying. Which according to Kind Regards, he would have. Because that whole time he'd been working for Tommy Riley instead.

'I'm sorry.'

The old man's breathing was coming hard. He lit another cigarette. 'He's gonna need protection,' he said. 'From cunts like these . . .'

He said these last words sharp and loud enough for every other fucker in the room to hear. A couple of the uniformed cons glanced across, but quickly looked back at their visitors when they saw who'd spoken. The same went for the guard, who stopped and looked over, before continuing his slow circuit around the room like nothing had happened. Respect. The old man had earned it on the outside. He'd done the same here.

'He's not gonna get sent down,' Frankie said.

'Says who?'

'Says me. He didn't do it.'

A bitter smile crossed the old man's lips. 'And that's supposed to make a difference, is it?'

'I mean it. I'm not gonna let it happen. Not again.' Frankie's eyes locked on the old man's. A promise.

The old man nodded. 'That's as may be,' he said. 'But hear this: Hamilton won't wait for the trial. He won't give a fuck about that. The second they've charged him . . . the second he's out of that cop shop and stuck in here or wherever else they stick him on remand . . . that's when they'll get him. They'll have him fucking battered and killed.'

Shank Wilson's leering face flashed into Frankie's mind. Word was, it was here he'd earned his nickname. Inside, during a ten-year stretch for manslaughter. He'd been the go-to man for slitting people's throats in the washrooms, or cutting their eyeballs clean out. And Hamilton would have other people, other Shanks, still in here now. To do his bidding. To cut his fucking throats.

The old man was right. Jack wouldn't stand a chance.

'What do I need to do?' Frankie said.

'Go to *him*.'

'Who?'

'Riley.'

62

Frankie's mouth turned dry. It wasn't just the obvious bad blood between the old man and Riley, or even Frankie owing Riley rent – though Christ knew that was all bad enough. But more than that, Frankie didn't want to even step foot into Riley's world. Ever since he'd been a kid, he'd seen what happened to people who did. Who got involved. In that side of London. The side that ate you up. They fucking changed. Like Jack. Or ended up in here where his dad was now. And Frankie wanted something else for his life. Not even better, just not this.

The old man said, 'You tell him I sent you. You tell him I need him to take care of my boy.'

The way he said it . . . it was like a demand, like he was owed. But for what?

'There's something else,' Frankie said.

'What?'

'The copper in charge. His name's Snaresby.'

The old man scratched irritably at the fresh scab on his cheek where he must have cut himself shaving. 'What of it?'

'Kind Regards said you knew him. Both you and Mum.'

'Not any more.'

'The way he was talking . . . the way he looked so fucking pleased when they got hold of Jack . . . it was like it was personal, Dad.'

'You just watch him. Don't fucking trust him. He's a bastard. The very worst fucking sort.'

'Time,' the guard called out.

'Yeah, we all got plenty of that,' Frankie's old man called back, looking round grinning, letting the whole world know he wasn't ruffled, that he was granite.

As chairs scraped across the floor and people got up around them, he leant in close to Frankie and quietly said, 'Jack's not the only one who's gonna need protection.'

'I can handle myself.'

The old man gripped his wrist. 'I know that, son,' he said, 'which is why I'm telling you that whoever comes at you might come at you twice as fucking hard, because they might know that too . . .'

'I'll be all right.'

The old man leant in even closer. 'You remember that new boiler we put in at the flat?'

'New?' Frankie couldn't help smiling. It was nearly ten years old.

'Have a little nosey round the back, eh? There's a couple of loose bricks that could do with some attention. You make sure you take care of that for me, will you, son? Just as soon as you can.'

11

The Ambassador Club was busy when Frankie got back, with all but one of the tables being used. Frankie was surprised, and pleased. People reacted funny round places the cops had raided. Sometimes shunned them for a bit, like whatever had caused it might be catching.

Slim was behind the bar, chatting to Ash Crowther and 'Sea Breeze' Strinati. Frankie ducked in beside him, eyeing the vodka optic thirstily, but pouring himself a Diet Coke instead. He drained it in one. It was still sweltering outside. Getting back from Brixton had been hell. And he was still knackered, dehydrated and hung-over from last night. Had needed a couple of drinks to calm himself after his run-in with Dougie Hamilton. More than a couple. He didn't even remember going to bed.

'How did it go with your dad?' Slim asked. Didn't bother keeping his voice down. Sea Breeze and Ash were old friends. Had been drinking here since way before even the old man's days in charge.

'Not good. He's gutted.'

'We all are,' said Sea Breeze.

'Nice kid, your brother,' said Ash. 'The papers have got it all wrong.'

'And the cops,' said Sea Breeze.

'Aye, and those wankers too.'

'Thanks,' Frankie said. He meant it. It felt good having people he knew and liked around him today.

'He'll be all right,' Ash said.

'Don't talk like that,' said Sea Breeze.

'Like what?'

'In that miserable tone of voice. Like he's already friggin' well doomed.'

'I wasn't.'

'Well, that's how it sounded.'

'Well, you should get your bloody ears syringed, you old git.'

Slim rolled his dark eyes at Frankie. Sea Breeze and Ash had been bickering for decades. It wasn't that they didn't like each other, more that they just really enjoyed rubbing each other up the wrong way. Particularly after a few drinks. Too much like each other, Slim reckoned. Both in their sixties and moody with it. Hearing them talking was like watching a monkey fight its own reflection, was how Slim had once summed it up.

Frankie poured another Diet Coke and drained that too. He pictured the rack of optics on the wall behind him and did his best to ignore the two beer taps in front. But hell's tits, it was tempting. To get totally hammered. Drink himself into a stupor like he had done last night. To forget. But then what? He'd have to sober up some time. And deal with what was going on. Because it sure as hell didn't look like anyone else was going to sort this shit out for him any time soon.

'Fancy a couple of quick frames?' asked Sea Breeze.

'Yeah,' Frankie said, 'why not?' Playing always helped him think, helped him relax.

But quick? Well that was a joke. Sea Breeze was without doubt the slowest player Frankie had ever met. *Glacially slow*, was how Ash always put it. *So slow you could pop out for curry between shots*. But slow was exactly what Frankie wanted right now. The rest of the last twenty-four hours had passed in a blur. This routine, this steady lining up of shots and potting of balls and building of breaks, and waiting for Sea Breeze to take his turn . . . Frankie sank back into it, feeling his whole body relax like he was sitting in a bath.

'So how's the tournament coming along?' Sea Breeze asked as he painstakingly returned the blue Frankie had just potted to its spot.

He meant The Soho Classic. The new tournament Frankie had been trying to get up and running. *His* tournament. One he wanted to launch here in the Ambassador to help really put it on the map. And boost membership, of course. Only last week, he'd finished putting together a loose affiliation of central London clubs and players who were keen to support it.

Only last week? For fuck's sake, it could have been a decade ago, so much had happened since. And when would he next get a chance to move the prize on?

'I'm still on the hunt for a sponsor,' he told Sea Breeze, as he stroked another red home, dropping himself nicely into position behind the black.

He'd met with one of the capital's biggest bookie chains two weeks ago. They'd sounded interested. Had wanted to hear more. He was meant to be seeing another potential backer next week. A hedge fund manager. Whatever the fuck that was. Some kind of City boy set-up. Loaded, according to his mate who'd put them in touch.

But what did any of that matter now? If they'd seen the article in the *Standard*, the chances of them returning his calls were zilch. The plain fact was that until all of this had blown over, until he'd got Jack's name cleared, he was going to have to put the whole tournament – along with the rest of his future – on ice.

'How big a prize you planning?'

'Depends on the sponsor . . . shit.'

Frankie stepped back from the table. He'd missed the black by a whisker.

'You planning on getting any pros in?' Sea Breeze asked, as he walked round the table and studied his options.

'Amateur for now. Though it would be nice to put on an exhibition match, eh? Maybe get a serious name in.'

'Someone like "The Rocket"?'

'Yeah, why not?' said Frankie. 'You never know. Though he might be a little bit too fast for you, eh?'

Sea Breeze smiled, getting the joke. Then went back to deciding on what shot to play next.

Frankie sparked up a Rothmans. His third pack that he could remember since the one he'd bought on his way over to see Mickey Flynn. Exhaling, he pictured his old man's expression when he'd found out Jack had been working for Riley. Loathing mixed with fear. His dad had wanted out of that life too. Still did. The tournament was something they'd talked about over and over again since he'd been inside. He was still snooker loopy. Just talking about how it might be, what players might one day show up, made his black eyes light up. Frankie desperately wanted to make it happen. For him as well as the club. He could see him here watching it so easily, smiling at what they'd built.

'Well, you know you can count on all of us here, everyone on the ladder, to support it,' Sea Breeze said.

'Thanks. It means a lot. It really does.'

Frankie looked him in the eyes when he said it. They both knew he wasn't just talking about the tournament. Sea Breeze, Ash, Slim, along with a few of the other regulars still took time to visit the old man. And not just out of duty either, but because they were mates and, well, because they all knew that this place just wasn't the same without him.

Frankie pictured the old man's face again, this time in the visitors' room when he'd mentioned Snaresby. He glanced up at the ceiling, wondering what the fuck might be waiting for him up there when he checked out that brickwork. Did he even want to find out?

'Oi, Frankie,' Slim shouted out across the bar.

'What?'

'Phone.'

'Who?' Frankie mouthed.

'Kind Regards.'

'Tell him to call me in the flat. Sorry,' he told Sea Breeze, 'I gotta go.'

12

Frankie hurried upstairs and grabbed the living-room phone on the third ring.

'I've got good news and bad news,' Kind Regards said.

'Bad news first.' Might as well get it over with.

'They've matched the blood found on Jack and at his flat to Susan Tilley. Hers and her grandmother's too.'

Shit-a-delic. Frankie sank down onto the sofa. He'd known this was coming, but still. Jesus. His shoulders slumped.

'And that's accurate, is it?' he said. 'Whatever tests they did. If they say it's someone's blood, then they're right? A hundred per cent. That's it?'

'Afraid so.'

Fuck . . . fuck, fuck. It was all Frankie could do not to throw the phone across the room.

'Still doesn't mean he did it, though, does it?' he finally said. 'Just because he's got it on him doesn't mean he got it on him when he was actually there doing what they said . . .'

Frankie knew he sounded like he was grasping at straws. But he still couldn't believe Jack had done it. There had to be another explanation. No matter how cut and dried it looked.

'No, but it doesn't look too good, either,' Kind Regards said. 'Particularly if he's got no other way to explain how it got there.'

The memory loss.

'I spoke to someone,' Frankie said. 'About that.'

'Who?'

'Doesn't matter.' He'd wanted to wait before telling Kind Regards about it, until he'd had a chance to track down Mo. 'The point is . . . there might be an explanation . . . something he took . . . that might have made him forget where he really was that night . . . Wherever the fuck he was that wasn't there . . .'

That might have made him violent too. Forget mentioning that. Keep him focussed on proving Jack's innocence, not worrying about his guilt.

'You mean drugs?'

'Yeah.'

'And you can prove that?'

'I'm working on it.' But was he? Frankie pictured himself this morning. Drenched in vodka sweats. Upturned takeaway tins on the floor. Chucking up in the sink. If anyone was a fucking mess, it was him.

'Like I advised you not to?' Kind Regards said.

'Yeah,' Frankie admitted. 'Exactly like that.'

A pause on the other end of the line. 'Well, if we could prove it was something he took . . . that might have affected him . . . his behaviour . . . maybe even his memory . . .'

He meant other behaviour – nasty behaviour – crazy shit that Jack might have thought, or done.

'. . . then I suppose . . .' he went on, 'and I'd need to talk to a barrister about this, mind you . . . but it might be possible we could enter a plea of temporary insanity . . . and claim that at the time of the crime he committed—'

'That he *didn't* commit,' Frankie corrected him sharply.

'Right, but listen, Frankie, you've also got to be realistic . . . the way the police case is shaping up now, it's possible that our best defence might end up being just this . . . to claim diminished responsibility, argue that Jack didn't appreciate the nature or wrongfulness of the acts he committed at the time because of the influence of the drug he was under . . . Because then we could go for manslaughter, not murder, you see.'

Frankie did see. But he didn't like it. Not one little bit.

'But even then,' warned Kind Regards, 'it'll be a stretch, particularly with the cops claiming his gang affiliation gave him a stone-cold sober motive anyway . . .'

A back-up plan. That's what Kind Regards meant. That's all he saw this as. They could use the fact that Jack might have been on some nasty, head-fuck of a drug that had caused his amnesia and whatever else as a back-up plan, if they didn't come up with anything else. Anything better. Anything that actually proved that Jack hadn't killed the girl at all.

They could use it to possibly reduce his sentence, but not keep him out.

What Frankie needed was the girl. Whoever it was Jack had gone off to meet. Whoever might have been there with him at his flat. Find her and they might not need an insanity plea at all.

'You said you had some good news too?'

'They've shown us the cctv footage.'

'And?'

'The car . . . it's Jack's all right.'

'How the fuck is that good?'

'You can see the driver.'

Frankie's stomach tensed. 'And?' If it was Jack on the cctv at the old lady's place, they were fucked.

'He . . . she . . . whoever . . . they were wearing a balaclava.'

Frankie was already on his feet. He punched the air. So that's why those bastards hadn't shown Kind Regards and Jack the footage the first time they'd interviewed him. Because they hadn't been able to ID the driver. They'd been hoping the mere threat of the footage would be enough to make Jack 'fess up.

But he hadn't.

Because he hadn't been there.

Because that driver wasn't bloody him.

Please let that be so. Please let that be why Jack kept on denying it. Because of that and not because of the horrible alternative – because he already knew the driver had been wearing a balaclava, because it had been him.

No. Not that. Frankie wouldn't, couldn't believe that.

'And what about the old lady?'

'She's still in intensive care, but alive.'

'Good.' And not just because she obviously didn't deserve it. 'Because if she comes round, she might still be able to say who her real attacker was. Because it wasn't Jack. In spite of that blood work. And you need to believe that too.'

'I will, Frankie,' he said. 'I mean, I do.'

'Good.'

'There's one more bit of bad news.'

Frankie's heart skipped a beat. 'What?'

'You know I'm happy to work *pro bono* on this . . .'

'And I appreciate it, you know that too.'

'Right, but like I said, your brother's going to need a barrister . . . unless some miracle turns up . . . now that this looks like it's going to trial . . .'

Frankie's cheeks prickled. 'Who? Like that overpaid ponce who took our money and didn't keep Dad out of jail?'

'I wouldn't be thinking of using him again, but to be fair—'

'Yeah, yeah,' Frankie said, knowing already how this sentence was likely to end: *but to be fair, I don't think anyone else could have kept your father at liberty either* . . . Not with the way he'd been stitched up by the cops.

'You find me the best that there is,' Frankie said.

'And the money to pay for it?'

'You let me worry about that.' He was going to have to do a hell of a lot more than just worry. He was going to have to be inventive. He was going to have to somehow conjure up that cash from thin air.

After he'd finished the call, he went over to the window and looked out. The sun was beating down on the street below. Tiny diamonds of glass left from Dougie Hamilton's crash still glittered like stars on the tarmac.

Frankie remembered Shank Wilson's face and his promise. And he remembered again what his old man had told him. About the brickwork. What if it wasn't something bad, but something good? Pissing hell . . . what if it was cash? What if right now in his hour of fucking need, the old man was about to come through?

He walked slowly through to the bathroom, a part of him still dreading what he might find. Martha, Megan, or Molly or May – the phone number she'd left him was still written in bright red lipstick on the mirror above the sink.

He ducked down and opened the airing cupboard door. Inside was the boiler and a couple of shelves of towels he hadn't even known were there. He shoved them aside and got down on his knees and peered in. He could see the exposed brickwork at the back, but none of it looked loose. He reached round the right side of the boiler and started pushing at the individual bricks.

It was only when he started working his way down the left side that he felt something shift. He peered in closer. Yeah, right there at the bottom. There were two bricks on top of one another with their mortar chipped out.

Adrenaline buzzed through him as he pulled them out one at

a time. There was a cavity behind. Something in it. A dull glow of metal. A box? He slid it out. Had to use the tips of his fingers to guide it. It was that close a fit. What the? It was a shoe-polish tin. Heavy too. When he tilted it over, something solid moved inside.

'Right,' he said out loud. 'Let's see what we've got.'

Still kneeling, he prised the lid off. Whatever was inside was swaddled in cloth. It had to be important. He knew that. Or the old man wouldn't have hidden it. It had to be something that could help him and help Jack too. But what?

He lifted it out and carefully unwrapped it, then nearly dropped it in surprise when he saw what it was. A gun. A revolver. Like something out of the old *Commando* comics him and Jack had used to love reading as kids. And something else too. Fucking hell. Six shiny bullets in a plastic ziplock bag.

13

Frankie woke up next morning feeling physically better than he had done in days. He'd hit the gym the night before, then had a microwaved spud, cheese and beans and an early night.

He took a shower and then put in a call to Tommy Riley's office. After being kept on hold for nearly five minutes, the girl who'd answered told him to come by Riley's office that evening at six.

Frankie pulled on a hoodie, jeans and trainers and picked up his car from the multi-storey over by the Raymond Revuebar. A jet black Ford Capri. Retro as hell. Like something out of *Minder*. And all the more gorgeous for it. His dad had won it in a bet when Frankie was sixteen. He'd been going to sell it, but Frankie had begged him not to. He'd loved it from the second he'd heard its V8 engine growling outside the club.

The old man had given it to him for his next birthday and he'd passed his test two weeks later. Frankie still had a photo of the two of them sitting here, him grinning like he'd just won the lottery, the first time he'd taken the old man out for a spin.

He slipped on his New York Yankees baseball cap and aviator shades and ripped it over to Tottenham Court Road, past the rows of cafés and discount electronic stores. Mo Bishara's place was called Sahara. A ground-floor restaurant with a golden metal sign out front glinting in the morning sun. Slim had snagged him the address off one of the Arab lads he played chess with. He'd not mentioned Frankie's name.

A couple of punters were sitting outside, smoking a hookah that smelt sweetly of rose water and apples. A young lad who couldn't have been more than fifteen was serving inside behind the bar. Frankie ordered a heavily sugared coffee and sat drinking it at a corner table, flicking through the paper. More stuff on Jack, but nothing new. Only made page four. The cops had nothing new to say. Not that they needed to. Not with them thinking they'd already bagged their man.

Frankie kept his baseball cap and shades on. He'd only ever met Mo once, in a bar off Piccadilly at a rammed party Jack had taken him to a year back. They'd shaken hands but hadn't spoken other than to say hello. Frankie was pretty confident Mo wouldn't know him from Adam even if he did clock him today. But no harm in doing his best to make sure.

About an hour later, just as Frankie was finishing his third cup of coffee, Mo came through from some private room hidden at the back of the restaurant. He wasn't alone. With him was a balding minder with a strawberry birthmark on his forehead who looked like he'd recently swallowed a hippo. Nearly six-and-a-half foot tall and a little less wide.

Mo was an altogether shorter proposition, but stocky with it, and in spite of the stifling heat was wearing a three-quarter-length leather coat with its collars turned up, the same shiny slick black colour as his hair. Frankie leant further forward with his head in his hands as they walked past and sat with their backs to him at the bar and ordered two espressos.

Mo's rep was a bad one. He was a fucking wolf, the kind of nasty bastard who'd eat most people alive. A ragtag of small-time street pimps and dealers answered to him. He dealt in hookers, rent, weed, coke, ketamine, heroin and pills – and, according to Mickey, this crazy blue shit too.

His sphere of influence extended from here to Warren Street in the north and Great Russell Street down south. The Rileys and the Hamiltons of this world might have been longer established and better organised, but much like Notting Hill, Chinatown and Brixton, round here was immigrant turf – the old cockney and Essex firms had long since surrendered.

Frankie had to be careful. He had no intention of talking to Mo today. Especially with that gorilla around. But when he did, he was aiming on putting the frighteners on him big style to make sure he didn't hold anything back. Which meant he'd need to somehow find a way of doing it without Mo seeing his face, or else he'd be hunted down.

His plan was to follow him today and find out where he lived, so he could then pay him a visit in private. Slim had already done some asking around. He'd not come up with a home address, but he'd found out Mo was recently divorced, meaning he might be living alone, which would make any home visit a whole lot fucking easier, of course.

Frankie tried earwigging, but Mo and his giant pal were talking Arabic and Frankie couldn't understand a word. Five minutes later another bloke came in. A white guy with a mottled complexion, a scraped-back black ponytail, shiny new suit and briefcase, and a spotless pair of white Reeboks. He gave Mo a hug and got a grin in return. He had a Manchester accent and Mo switched to speaking in English too. Frankie listened as they shot the breeze, talking about football mostly. Then the white guy said his goodbyes and left, leaving his briefcase behind on the floor.

A drop-off then. So what was in the case? Drugs? Or maybe cash? Enough to sort out Frankie's problems at the club? Stop it.

That was the trouble with sneaking around like this. You started thinking like a criminal too.

He pictured the gun where he'd hidden it inside his mattress. The bullets as well. Start carrying something like that and who knew how it might all end up? If he'd had it when Dougie had attacked him, would he have used it? Threatened him with it? Worse? Fuck knew. But if he had, he'd be inside just like Jack and then they'd both be screwed.

Two minutes later and Mo and his minder, or whoever the fuck this was, headed out, the fat lad carrying the case. Frankie stayed put, watching Mo shooting the breeze with the smokers on the pavement outside. Short he might be, but he still had a mean look about him that made passing pedestrians steer well clear.

He finally headed off. Frankie waited ten seconds before following, slapping a tenner down on the counter on his way out. He followed Mo, hanging twenty yards back. Not that he needed to. Mo didn't glance back once, clearly never suspecting he was being tailed, probably never thinking even for a second that anyone would fucking dare.

He took the next right and then a left after that, before ducking into a corner store for a pack of smokes and a bottle of full-fat Coke. Another ten yards and he turned right into an old cobbled Victorian mews, trailing his fingers lovingly along the powder blue paint of what must have been his Aston Martin, before taking out his keys to open the front door to his house.

Number nine.

Fucking gotcha.

Frankie would be paying Mo Bishara a visit very soon.

14

Tommy Riley gazed at Frankie, his eyes moving slowly over him like he was memorising every part of his face. He hauled in another lungful from the short, fat butt of his cigar, smoke funnelling from his nostrils and up towards the dark red ceiling of his office as he slowly exhaled.

'You look like him . . . like you father.'

His voice was low and gravelly, almost a whisper. The way he said the words – slowly, deliberately – it was like he'd never set eyes on Frankie before. Which was bollocks, of course. Because Riley had seen him plenty over the years, back in the early days of the Ambassador, when him and the old man had still been friends.

And more recently too, the occasional glance across a crowded room, when they'd ended up in the same bar late at night. But as for actual conversation? Well, Riley hadn't said a word to him in years. So long that Frankie couldn't remember him ever having spoken to him at all.

'Not like now, of course,' Riley continued. 'All fat and knackered and grey . . .'

He let his comment hang for a second, clearly waiting to see how Frankie might react to the insult. Well, fuck him. Frankie wasn't going to give him the pleasure. He stared instead out of the fifth-floor window of Riley's office across the rooftops of

Soho's red light district. No point in pissing Riley off, but he wasn't here to kiss his arse either. Riley wouldn't respect him for it. He'd just think he was weak.

'Just like the rest of us old boys these days, eh?' Riley finally said.

Frankie turned back to face him. A joke, but a warning too. For him not to underestimate who he was dealing with. Because Riley wasn't fat, or knackered, or even grey. He had a chest like a beer barrel, a tan like teak, and expensively cut, slicked-back hair as black as freshly poured tar. He was at the top of his game, at liberty and at large. He was nothing like Frankie's dad and they both fucking knew it.

'No, I mean how he was when he was your age . . .' Riley said. 'How we both were, with our whole lives stretching out before us. You remind me of him, you know, Frankie. You've got that same lean look of potential about you he once had. You've clearly found yourself a half decent tailor too.'

'Adam of London, Portobello Road,' Frankie said. He'd ditched his hoodie and jeans for something more business-like, a blue mohair suit.

'Him of the "Dog's Bollocks" fame,' Riley said.

Frankie nodded. Riley was talking about the sign in the shop's window which boasted how good their suits would make you look.

'I've not been there in a while,' said Riley. 'But fuck it, eh? You're not here to talk about whistles and flutes.'

'I'm here to talk about Jack.'

'I know.'

'He needs protection.' No point in fucking around. Just get to the point.

Riley got up and walked over to the far side of his office and pushed the corner of one of the wall's wooden panels. It gave with a click, revealing a short, gloomy carpeted corridor leading off the other side.

'Excuse the cloak and dagger,' he said. 'It's just that the Mrs would have my bollocks in a fucking sling if she knew . . . you know how women are . . .'

Riley disappeared through the doorway, beckoning Frankie to follow. Frankie ducked through after him. What the fuck? The corridor was actually a viewing gallery. A floor-to-ceiling two-way mirror ran the length of its left-hand wall. A brightly lit dressing room on the other side. A bunch of girls from the lap dancing club downstairs were getting dressed and undressed, clueless they were being watched.

'I like a nice view when I'm thinking,' Riley said.

Frankie stared.

'You can take your pick if you want.'

'Thanks, but no thanks. I'm fine.'

'Not a queer, are you?' Riley asked.

'No,' Frankie said.

Didn't look like Riley gave a shit either way. He just shrugged and watched appreciatively as one of the girls sat down topless right in front of him and gazed into the mirror as she started to put her make-up on.

'I heard Dougie Hamilton tried you run you down,' Riley said.

Frankie nodded at Riley's half-reflection in the glass, realising his host was no longer watching the girl, but watching him.

'He missed,' Frankie said.

'Missed with his punches too, the way I hear.'

'He was upset.'

Riley half-raised an eyebrow. 'Sounds like you're defending him?' he said, shooting him a curious look.

'He'd just lost his fiancée.'

'No fucking kidding. But that's not why he missed. He missed 'cos you were better. The better man. I heard you dealt with him and then stood your ground an' all when that ugly little fucker Wilson turned up.'

Riley was hard, all right, but Frankie wondered if even he'd say that to Shank Wilson's face.

'I'm always on the lookout for new talent,' Riley said.

'Like my brother?' The words were out before Frankie could stop them.

Riley sniffed. 'So you heard he was working for me?'

'I heard.'

'And don't much approve, by the sounds of it.'

Frankie said nothing. What could he say? That he'd rather Jack had done anything with his life instead of that.

'You think your brother done it?' Riley asked.

'No.'

'Me neither.'

Adrenaline buzzed through Frankie. What was Riley saying? Did he know something? Had he got proof? Frankie tried to read his face, but the older man was giving nothing away. He was watching the girl again.

'But someone certainly wants him to look guilty, eh?' Riley said. 'Probably whoever's really behind that poor girl's death.'

Frankie's nails dug into his palms. He had to be careful. What if – and God knew he didn't want to believe it – Jack really had been acting on Riley's behalf like the cops said? Or what if one of Riley's other goons was behind the killing and Jack had got somehow involved? Then Riley would try and steer Frankie off, make him think anyone else was to blame except him. Don't get sucked in by this guy. Just get what you came for.

'Dougie Hamilton told me Jack was as good as dead,' Frankie said.

'I heard he said the same to you.'

'I can look after myself, but—'

'Don't worry,' Riley said. 'I'll make sure your brother's got back-up. As soon as he's on remand. And after that too, if it gets to that. For no matter how long. I always look after my own.'

My own. The way he said it. Like Jack was a possession. Was *his*.

'What do you mean, *if* . . .?'

'Well, the way I hear it, Jack's got himself a guardian angel, hasn't he? Who's got it into his head to prove he's done nothing wrong. Which in my book means he'll have to prove who really did do the wicked deed instead.'

So he'd heard Frankie had been asking around. From who? Mickey? That wanker must have said something. Must have told Riley Frankie was on the warpath and was trying to get to the truth.

'Which of course is all well and dandy,' Riley continued, 'and completely understandable too, all things considered . . .' His dark eyes bored into Frankie's like drills. 'But there's another way of looking at it . . .'

What was this? Was Riley warning him off? In case he caused him even more trouble? Well, he could go fuck himself. No fucking way was Frankie backing off.

'I understand you not wanting to work for me . . . yet,' Riley said. He was staring hard at Frankie again. '. . . and wanting to keep your independence . . .'

Yet.

'But you proving your brother had nothing to do with this would certainly pull some heat off me and my organisation, as far as the filth are concerned. In fact, I'd see it as a favour – one I'd be inclined to look very kindly on indeed – particularly in regard to any outstanding debts you might owe . . .'

He meant the rent on the club.

'You'll help me then?'

He smiled. 'However I can. Backup if you need it. And anything else I hear, you'll be the first to know.'

Riley was using him. Frankie knew it. But there wasn't a damn thing he could do about it. If he wanted to get Jack out of this shit, he was going to need all the help he could get.

Riley's pager beeped. He took it out of his pocket, shielding it from Frankie as a red neon message scrolled across its screen.

'Technology, eh? Ain't it clever?' he said with a grin. 'I got a phone call I need to make. Come on, I'll show you out.'

He led Frankie back through to his office and on past his desk to the door.

One of his heavies was waiting outside. A big fucker who looked like he tortured kittens for fun.

'Take him downstairs, Arthur,' Riley said. 'And anything he fancies while he's down there, you let him have it on the house.'

He meant whiskey, women, the works.

Riley held out his hand for Frankie to shake. Frankie hesitated, but then took it. He still didn't trust him, not as far as he could spit. Didn't even trust him not to have had anything to do with the girl's killing yet. There might be some part of this game Riley was playing that Frankie didn't even yet understand.

15

Frankie meant to go straight home after his meeting with Tommy Riley. He failed. Too stressed. He ducked into De Hems off Chinatown. Drank two pints of Oranjeboom. Boom, boom. Just like that, letting the booze wash over him until his heart stopped hammering so hard.

It was Riley. He'd got right up under his skin. Frankie thought he'd held his own, had been treated as an equal, while he'd been in there with him. But now? He wasn't so sure.

Yet . . .

He couldn't get the way Riley had said the word out of his head. He'd gone there asking Riley for help, but Riley had somehow turned that around. Twisted it. Was that what had just happened? Was Frankie now working for him? Was that what he'd just agreed?

He lit a smoke and stared at his reflection in the chintzy mirror behind the bar. Once this business was over, he'd cut off all ties with that bastard for good. He'd seen what had happened to Jack, how quickly he'd been sucked in. And not just by the seedy glamour of it all, the drugs and the birds. No, what had kept him hooked had been that once you were in, bastards like Riley did everything in their power to stop you getting out.

Frankie ordered another pint. Crisps too. Wotsits. Carbs. He kept an eye on the door as he munched his way through them.

It was risky being here. Out in Soho. On his own. One of Hamilton's boys might spot him. Or some low-life dealer or snitch. It would take just one phone call and the whole Hamilton crew would be round here to finish off what Dougie had started in the street outside the club.

Well, let them try. Frankie cracked his knuckles. He was in the mood to hit someone. To take control. And yeah, fuck it, be what Tommy Riley wanted him to be. A fixer. A solver. It was time to sort this fucking mess out.

He tore the back off his cigarette pack and took a Ladbrokes pen out of his jacket pocket and wrote down 'Mo'. There. That was one decision he'd already made. To go see Mo and find out what he knew. But it was a long shot. That he *might* have some dodgy gear that drove people nuts and even made them black out and forget. That Kind Regards *might* – only *might*, mind – then be able to use this to help Jack cop an insanity plea and get his sentence reduced.

Frankie glared at his reflection in the mirror. Come on . . . think. You can do better than that. What else do you know? What else can you find out? What else can you *do*? He stared down at his pen, picturing Jack outside the club. All that blood. His terrified voice on the answerphone.

If Jack hadn't done what they said he had, then what the hell *had* gone down during those missing hours between him saying goodbye to Mickey Flynn and waking up in his bloodbath of a bed?

Frankie added 'The Girl' to the list. But who the hell was she? How the hell was he meant to track her down?

'Flat'. Frankie wrote that down too. The cops had already had a good snoop round, but it was high time he did the same.

'Personal?'. He added that to the list. What if someone had killed Susan Tilley for some reason that had nothing to do with the war being fought between Riley and Hamilton? What if it was some ex-boyfriend of hers? Or colleague? Some stalker or other nut? Were the cops even bothering to look into all that? Maybe. Or maybe not. Meaning maybe he should. Or shouldn't, because how likely was it really that someone like that would actually be able to frame Jack? How would they steal his car? And stitch him up like that in his flat? Wasn't it more likely that if someone really had framed Jack, they were connected. With know-how. A pro.

'Why Jack?' he wrote down. Because if Jack hadn't done it, then whoever had framed him had chosen him specifically.

But who?

And *why*?

Frankie just couldn't see it.

Not *yet*.

Frankie folded the piece of card into his back pocket and headed home, not calling in at the club on the way. He couldn't stop thinking about Jack's flat, about getting inside.

He got changed out of his suit in the bedroom. Fuck knows what state the cops would have left the flat in. Jesus, it might still be covered in blood. He pulled on his hoodie, jeans, baseball cap and trainers and checked himself out in the mirror. He looked anonymous, a nobody, perfect for slipping in and out.

Should he wait? Was it just the booze making him this impatient? No. Getting in there was the right move. Doing something, anything, everything he could.

He got himself a cold lager from the fridge and necked it. He'd handle all of this better after a couple more drinks. Take the edge off, right? Keep him calm. He thought about the pistol in his mattress. Maybe he should take that too? Just in case. No, he hadn't even worked out how to load it yet. Leave it here for now.

He fished out Jack's spare key from his cufflink box, but left his car keys behind. He was just about the right level of pissedness for breaking and entering, but too far gone to drive.

He flagged down a black cab outside the club and told the driver to take him to Warren Street tube station. He walked the rest of the way to the mansion block Jack's flat was in, pulling his cap down low before he got to the building, not knowing if the cops might still be working around, not wanting them to catch him out trying to snoop.

He let himself in through the main entrance downstairs. Didn't have to worry about any further security or being challenged by a concierge. This place was decrepit, run-down, with sticky, stained floor tiles and patches of damp on the walls.

Frankie reached Jack's door at the end of a dingy corridor on the third floor. It was covered with police tape, warning people not to enter. Bollocks to that. If they'd taped it up, then it meant there were none of them inside now, right? Anyway, it wasn't like he was really breaking and entering. He was family, for fuck's sake.

Pulling the tape aside, he slid Jack's key into the lock. The door opened with a creak. Hinges needed oiling. The lights were off inside, but it wasn't pitch black, just gloomy. The orange glow of streetlamps spilt in through a gap in the living-room curtains.

He stepped quickly inside and closed the door behind him. Jesus. He covered his mouth and nose. Something stank in here. Something stank bad.

He stayed put for a few seconds, letting his eyes get used to the gloom and listening. He heard nothing. Nobody here but him. He went through into the living room. Took a quick look out through a gap in the curtains. A couple of hoodies trudged past on the street below. Something else caught his eye. A flicker of light in a dark car parked opposite. There for just a second, and then gone.

Was someone watching the flat? Was someone in there lighting a smoke? Someone who had something to do with this mess? Some crim? Or a cop? Or was he just being paranoid? Too much booze. He kept watching. Didn't see that flicker again. Probably just a reflection of something else. Cool your jets. Stand down.

Drawing the curtains tight shut, he fumbled around the living-room sideboard for the lamp he knew was there. Found it. Flicked it on. A nice low wattage. Enough to see by, but hopefully not enough to let the whole of NW1 know he was here.

He shivered. The place was a tip, even worse than the last time he'd been round. The cops had clearly given it a thorough dusting and going over. Open drawers. Piles of papers on the carpet. God only knew what kind of contraband they'd found. A damp circle on the table beside the TV was all that was left of Jack's marijuana plant. Must have been seized as evidence. He wondered what else they'd found. Coke? Some of that speed?

And what should he be looking for? Coming here had felt like the right thing to do, but now he was actually here, he didn't have a clue where to start. He gazed round at Jack's scant possessions: the VCR, a broken guitar and his prized signed and framed Arsenal poster on the wall.

Just look. For something, anything unusual. Something that might make sense of Jack's story about waking up here and not knowing how the fuck he'd got home or who'd been with him when he had.

But nothing in the living room caught his eye. Everything looked familiar, looked normal. But should that really come as any surprise? Anything out of the ordinary, the cops would have already most likely taken. Was he wasting his fucking time?

He looked back to the door leading out into the entrance hall. The bedroom door stared back at him from the other side. In there. That's where the real mess was, according to Snaresby. Frankie couldn't face it yet. He went through to the kitchen instead.

The stink was ten times worse in here. The fridge-freezer door was wide open, gently humming, its light glowing eerily. Its drawers were sticking out. The cops had been through them. Looking for what? A murder weapon? Drugs? Something else?

A tub of melted vanilla Häagen-Dazs stood in the centre of the counter to the right of the fridge. Little bruv's favourite. Still had a teaspoon sticking up out of the melted goo from when Jack had probably returned it to the freezer mid-spliff. A half pack of shop-brand fish fingers and an emptied bag of frozen peas sat in the sink. Defrosted burgers. Over on the side of the counter was the remains of a takeaway curry. Bluebottles too gorged to even bother flying away walked in drunken, retching circles around it.

Frankie opened the window above the sink and sucked in fresh air. Sodding cops. Messy bastards. He picked up a half-empty bottle of vodka from beside the grease-stained microwave and took a deep swig. Then he set to, blurrily tidying up, grabbing a bin bag from an open drawer and scooping out the rotting food from the sink with his hands, clearing the surfaces, wiping them down.

He finally turned and looked back across the hallway at the bedroom door. He took another slug of booze. Just do it. Fucking get in there. You can't come here and then not.

Another stench hit him as soon as he stepped inside. Vomit. He covered his nose, pinching his nostrils. Saliva flooded his mouth. He flicked on the light switch and grimaced. Blood. It was everywhere.

Why the hell hadn't the cops cleared it up? Not their problem, but still . . . It was streaked across the bedroom furniture and doors. It would have been hard to make more of a mess with a bucket of paint. What the fuck had happened here? It looked like someone had slaughtered a cow. How was it Snaresby had put it: *it looked like an abattoir in there . . .*

There was blood smeared and daubed on the white walls in patches. Even on the wardrobe mirror. A thought hit him. Whoever had put it there would have had to look at their reflection as they did. Sick fucker. There was more on the bed. Something else too. Yellow and lumpy. Sick? It was smeared across the sheets. In a puddle on the floor.

Frankie tried to picture Jack standing here, mad-eyed and blood-drenched, the way the cops saw him. Jack the monster.

He could picture something else, though. What Jack had told him, panic-eyed and shaking in the Ambassador just before he'd been arrested. Someone had rung him on his home phone. Someone had tipped him off that the cops were coming and told him to run.

Frankie reached for the answerphone on the bedside table and pressed the playback button. 'No messages,' an electronic voice said. Probably already listened to and wiped off by the cops. He picked up the receiver and dialled 1471. A long shot, because whoever had called would surely have blocked their number.

Only they hadn't. The automatic operator dictated the phone number of the last caller to have rung Jack. It said what time the call had been made too. Frankie did the maths. Minutes before Jack ran.

This was it then. The number of whoever had called. Too drunk to remember it, Frankie rifled through the bedside drawers. A chewed biro, but nothing to write on. Bloody typical.

Bloody Jack. He hit 1471 again and scrawled the number on the inside of his wrist instead.

He punched the number into the phone and felt his heartbeat rise as a phone the other end started to ring. But it just kept on ringing. No answerphone. Nothing. Who the fuck didn't have an answerphone these days? It made no sense.

He remembered something else then and checked the floor. No sign of the condom. Must have already been bagged up by the cops.

He spent another couple of minutes looking round, under the bed, inside Jack's wardrobe. But nothing stood out. Still, at least he'd got the number. He'd been right to come here after all.

He walked back into the kitchen and looked around. Did the same in the living room. The bathroom too. Something felt wrong. But what? Then it hit him. No blood. But why? Because if, as the cops said, Jack had come back covered in the stuff, then why wasn't there any blood anywhere else apart from in the bedroom? Unless the cops had already for whatever reason decided to clean just some of it up, then how the hell could there be such a mess of it in the bedroom and yet none of it out here?

Jesus. He felt like his head was being twisted. None of this made sense. Tiredness washed over him. Time to get the fuck out. Go the fuck home. He grabbed the trash bag from the kitchen, switched out the lights and headed for the front door.

That's when he heard it. The soft squeak of the door handle starting to turn. Shit, he hadn't locked it. He stepped quickly back behind it. Not a second too soon. He shrank back flat against the wall as the door swung open.

A torch beam reached out into the darkness. But who the fuck was holding it? Frankie couldn't see. Whoever had been outside smoking in that car? A neighbour? The cops?

The torch beam probed left and then right, before picking out the bin bag that Frankie had been carrying and locking on it. Whoever was holding that torch knew it wasn't supposed to be there. Which meant they'd been here recently. Recently enough to have already guessed there was someone else in here too?

Frankie pushed off fast from the wall, driving his shoulder hard into the door, slamming it against whoever had just opened it. A grunt of pain. A gasp. The torch crashed to the floor.

Frankie stepped quickly sideways and grabbed at whoever was there. He missed. Shit. He stumbled, sensed movement. Below. Something hit him so hard in the bollocks he felt they'd just exploded out of the top of his head. His legs gave way. He sank to his knees.

Click. A switch. The hallway light glared down.

'Stay,' a voice barked.

He groaned, keeling over onto his side, wrapping his arms round his knees.

'You even think about getting up and whatever you're feeling now, it's going to be ten times worse.'

The voice . . . it was high pitched. What the fuck? A woman? Frankie slowly turned to look. But his eyes were too screwed up in pain. All he caught was a blurry glimpse. But it was definitely a woman, all right. The condom. Jesus. If Jack had been here with a woman that night, this might be her. This might be the girl who'd set him up. Or could prove he'd been here and not at Susan Tilley's grandmother's place at all.

Her face came more into focus. Green eyes. Fuck, they were beautiful. Short black hair . . . Shit, there was something about her . . . something he'd seen before.

He saw what she'd hit him with then. A baton, gripped in her left fist. One of them telescopic jobs you could hide in a jacket pocket – or a handbag. She reached into the little black leather number hooked over her shoulder with her free hand. For what?

Frankie tried rolling away, but couldn't. In too much fucking pain.

He looked up to see her holding a radio. Not a gun. Thank fuck. But not just any radio either. A cop radio. Triple crap. He remembered her now. Green eyes. She'd been there at the Ambassador Club. She'd brought Snaresby the warrant.

Not taking her eyes off him for a second, she switched on her radio. A crackle of static. Fuck, fuck, fuck. He'd been nicked. She was going to call him in.

'Please . . .' he said, pulling his hands away from his face and knocking his cap off as he did. 'Wait . . . I'm not a burglar . . . or whatever you think . . . I'm—'

'Jesus,' she said, her eyes widening. 'Frankie. I'm sorry. I didn't realise it was you.'

16

Frankie limped into the Starlight Café round the corner from Jack's building and waited while Sharon Granger ordered them both a coffee, his, milk with three sugars, hers as black as her wedge-cut hair.

Sharon bloody Granger. He shook his head. He'd only half-recognised her when he'd seen her at the Ambassador. Too stressed by everything going down. But he remembered her now, all right. School. The sixth form. Five years ago. Another fucking world.

'We'd better make this brief, all right?' she said, as they sat down at a quiet corner table not overlooked from the street. 'I could get in a lot of trouble just talking to you, do you understand?'

He got it. He was the brother of the prime suspect of a case she was working on. Fraternising with him could put a serious dent in her career. Maybe even write it off entirely.

'The same goes for not calling you in,' she said. 'But . . . well, you seemed in a lot of pain for one thing. I just wanted to check you were OK?'

He nodded, even though the truth was his bollocks still hurt like hell. She smiled, looking genuinely relieved.

'I know you're not a bad bloke, Frankie. And I don't want this to go any worse for you than it already has.'

'Thanks,' he said. 'I appreciate it.' He smiled.

'What?'

'Just who'd have thought it? You, of all people, becoming a cop.'

'Of *all* people?'

'Well, all right then . . . Of all people, apart from me.'

Schoolyard fixer, smoker, lad about town, Bernie James's son – no one at their East End Comp had ever expected Frankie James's life to run exactly smooth.

'You think I'd be better off doing something else?' She pulled a pack of Silk Cut from her handbag and struck a match.

He remembered the car across the street from Jack's flat, the hidden smoker inside. Had that been her? Had she watched him breaking in? Was that why she'd gone up to Jack's? Or had she been there for something else?

'Maybe,' he said.

'Why?'

'Three reasons. History, English and Art. You were a straight-A student. Could have done anything you liked.'

She still hadn't lit her cigarette. 'You remember what subjects I did for A-level?'

He felt himself blushing. Shit. Too much information. He took a swig of coffee, wincing as it burnt his throat on the way down. He was still a bit pissed. Time to sober up.

'Yeah, well I did English and History with you, didn't I?' he said. 'And I remember you doing Art, because old Mr Hayden was always giving you prizes in assembly. I always thought you'd end up working in a gallery or something, you know?'

'I remember you leaving,' she said, finally lighting her smoke. 'Before the end. Before we sat our exams.'

She didn't mention his dad. Didn't need to. It was obvious from her face she was thinking about it, what an enormous fucking deal it had been at school when the old man had first got nicked.

'You ever thought about going back? To school, I mean.'

'Nah.' He smiled. 'Mr Hayden says I'm too old. And besides, I don't think my uniform would fit any more.'

'Hah.' A proper smile. 'I mean it. You've never been tempted to finish off getting your qualifications? Because the way I remember it, you were pretty smart yourself.'

He shook his head. 'Too busy with the club.' He pictured himself cleaning the toilets. Her there with Snaresby during the raid. Him telling Sharon to fetch a cup of tea. Tweedle Dee and Tweedle Dum panting around, not even acknowledging she was there.

'All blokes, aren't they?' he said. 'Your colleagues. All of them lots older than you, as well.'

'That's just how the Met is. For now . . .'

'You sound like you're planning on changing it. Good for you.' Couldn't do a worse job than those bastards do now. He kept the thought to himself.

'I joined up as part of a fast-track graduate programme,' she said. 'Designed to rejuvenate and modernise the force. The pay's good. Decent pension. Not bad in a recession like the one we walked into after school. And a lot more exciting than working in an art gallery, I can tell you.'

Exciting. The way she said it . . . she'd obviously not exactly appreciated his guess at the kind of safe, arty career she'd been destined for after school. Fair enough too, judging from the way she'd just dealt with him up in Jack's flat.

She sipped her coffee. She was wearing a ring. A diamond set in gold. Not on her engagement finger, mind.

'Nice rock,' he said.

'Thanks.'

'Family heirloom?' It didn't look old enough, but he didn't want to come straight out and ask if it was from a bloke.

'No.'

So she was with someone then. Hardly surprising, but different to how she'd been at school. She'd been single. Famously so. Loads of his mates had tried chatting her up and they'd all crashed and burned. Geek, they'd called her out of earshot, because of the rejections. Or frigid. Or lezza, because of the way she'd worn her hair, even shorter then than she did now. He'd never bought into any of that shit, though. He'd seen something different in her. From the way she'd worked. Her focus. She'd just wanted out of there. He'd been the same, working hard, secretly, behind his mates' backs. Him and her . . . they'd not been so different back then.

'And what about you?' she said. 'Are you with someone? You always had a girl on your arm.'

He was surprised she'd even noticed. The way he remembered it, she'd never even looked at him. He stared back down at her ring.

'So who's the lucky fella?'

'Nathan.'

'Another cop?'

'Banker. We met at uni. Durham. He was doing a post-grad in economics. I was reading history.'

Durham Uni. One of the places Frankie tried hard not to think about. He'd gone there on an open day. A couple of months before everything had kicked off with his dad. If things had turned out different, he might even have studied there himself.

Her expression hardened as she stubbed out her cigarette. She reached into her handbag.

'Whoah.' He raised his hands in mock surrender. 'What else you got in there? A pistol? Pepper spray? A pack of Rottweilers?'

Another smile. 'I already said I'm sorry. For hurting you. If I'd known it was you, I wouldn't have hit you. Well, not so hard, anyway.'

'Try telling that to the kids I'll never have.'

She took out a pack of gum and slipped a piece into her mouth. She pushed her fringe back from her forehead, giving him the first full glimpse of her face in quite a while. More memories hit him of her at school. He'd noticed her right from year one. Her in the art room, the refectory, sometimes even glancing back at him from the passenger seat of her dad's silver Volvo, as him and Jack had set out on the bike ride home on their busted up BMXs. Or maybe that had all just been in his head.

'Listen, you're not to go in there again, Frankie, all right? Not until you're told. It's still a crime scene.'

'Sure.' He said it, didn't mean it.

'I know you were probably just in there trying to make sense out of everything that's—'

'Yeah,' he said, suddenly flaring, suddenly remembering Jack and the noise he'd made on that roof, suddenly remembering why he was here, 'that's exactly what I was doing. Because right now, what *you* lot are doing – what you're thinking – it doesn't make any sense at all.'

'I know this is difficult for you, Frankie. But you've got to trust us—'

'Tell me something,' he said, leaning forward. He was trying to keep his voice down, trying not to shout.

'What?'

'The blood . . .'

'What about it?'

'If it got there because of Jack, because he was covered in it when he got home – like you say – then why did he leave it? Why didn't he clear it up?'

'Because, well, because he was high on something . . .'

'You say that like it's a question.'

'No. It's the only thing that—'

'Makes sense?'

'Yes. That's logical. That fits. Your brother's a known user, Frankie, you must know that. We found coke in his apartment . . . weed . . .'

'Anything else?' He meant the blue speed.

'No.'

No. Leaving Mo. Frankie would still be the only one looking into that.

'Listen,' Sharon said, 'you've got to understand . . . the people your brother's been hanging out with . . . the things they might have got him involved in . . . he could have just ended up out of his depth. He could have done this because he had no choice . . .'

The same line Kind Regards had told him the police were peddling. Believable. Just. But not fucking true.

'Or he could have not done it at all.' Frankie forced himself to breathe in. 'You don't remember my little brother, do you?' he said. 'From school?'

'No. I mean, I remember his face, but he was two years younger. I didn't actually know him.'

'Right, well let me tell you something about him. He was a show-off, OK? Right from the start. From when we were little. A clown. Funny, you know? An attention-seeker. And, yeah, sometimes he'd do stupid things to make people laugh. But he was a lovely kid too. He used to look out for other kids. Littler kids. He never bullied anyone. Any joke he ever made, he was always the butt of it himself. And he was a good brother too. All those shit years we had. After Mum. After Dad. We stuck close. He kept on smiling. No matter how shit it got. He kept me smiling too. Right up until recently. And even then . . . even if something inside him did change these last few months . . .' He meant the drugs, the girls, what Mickey had said. '. . . no one changes that much, not from who he was as a kid into the kind of monster you want him to be now.'

'It's not what we want, Frankie. It's just how it is.'

'No. You want this case solved. And that's what Jack does. That's what that blood does. It solves it. As neat as can be. And that's why it's bullshit. Because it's too fucking easy. Because it's not fucking true.'

'You've got to face facts,' she said, counting them off her fingers. 'We've got the cctv of him driving to the house . . .'

'No. You've got footage of *someone* driving his car, *someone* who I'm telling you isn't him.'

'. . . we've got the blood all over him and all over his flat . . . and no, we can't prove *why* he did it, but I promise you this, Frankie: we will.'

'If he was so wasted when he got back from killing Susan Tilley like you say, then how come he didn't get blood smeared all over the rest of the flat too? Why just the bedroom?'

'What?'

'Because that's true, isn't it?' It was just a hunch, but he knew already he was right. 'None of your lot cleared it up, did they? Blood in the hallway, or the kitchen or the living room? Because there wasn't any there. And I bet there wasn't even any on the front door handle, was there?'

'No, but he could have wiped whatever was on the front door handle off. Or started cleaning up the rest of the flat, but then crashed out. They found a bucket in the bathroom. Bottles of bleach. Traces of blood in the drain.'

'Have you ever got high, Sharon? I don't mean the odd cheeky drag of a joint at a party. I'm talking totally off your fucking head on class As?'

'No.'

'Well, let me tell you something. If you ever do, I can guarantee you this: the last fucking thing you're gonna want to do is go straight to bed and sleep.'

She broke eye contact with him. But it was too late. He'd already seen the flash of alarm – of doubt – in her eyes.

Silence. He let it run.

'There *was* blood on the front door,' she finally said. 'But only on the inside handle . . .'

Frankie sneered, couldn't help it. 'Which could have got there in the morning,' he said. 'On his way out. When he was leaving, when he was running. *Not* the night before, *not* on his way in.'

'You really don't believe he did it, do you?'

'I think he's been set up.'

'But how?'

'I don't know yet. Not how, or why. But you know what?'

'What?'

'I know there's a part of you that thinks the same, that thinks this case isn't quite so open and shut as you claim. I think that's what you were doing coming back here tonight. On your own. In the dark. Without backup. Without Snaresby and whoever else it is out there who wants this all tied up in a neat little bundle, with my little brother taking the rap.'

He remembered the way Snaresby had patronised her and the anger that had blazed in her eyes when he had. He remembered too what Kind Regards had said, about Snaresby once being friends with his parents, before he became a cop. He remembered the look on the old man's face when he'd told him it was Snaresby who was bossing this case.

'Yeah, Snaresby,' he said, 'you don't like him any more than I do.'

She said nothing.

'You know damn well he made up his mind about my brother being guilty the second he heard that he'd run . . . regardless of why he might have . . . or who might have made him.'

Her jaw clenched. 'I don't know that at all. And neither do you.' She stood up. 'I knew this was a bad idea. I shouldn't have come here. We shouldn't be talking. Not about the case. And not about my boss.' She stared at him, her eyes dark with anger. 'But I tell you this, Frankie: no matter what you think about Snaresby, or cops in general, I'm not one of the bad guys. I'm just trying to do my job. I'm just trying to do the right thing.'

'Wait,' he said.

But she didn't. She headed for the door. He hurried after her, catching her up on the pavement outside.

'I'm sorry,' he said, grabbing her arm.

She stared down at it until he let go.

'I didn't mean all cops were bent,' he said, 'or that you were bent, or shit at your job. It's just . . . I do mean what I said, about him, about Jack not having done it . . . about there being more to all this than meets the eye.'

'And I meant what I said about us not talking about this any more.'

'And we won't.'

Try that and he knew she'd never speak to him again. And he didn't want that. Because he believed her. She really wasn't like those other bastards. She really did give a shit.

'No more talk about the case. I promise. But, here . . .' he waved down a taxi '. . . let me at least get you a cab. To say thanks, for the coffee, and for not calling me in. Unless you drove here?'

'No. But I'll pay my own way, thanks,' she said, getting in.

She slammed the door and said something to the driver. Her

window buzzed down and she reached out, handing him a business card.

'I'm not saying that you should,' she said. 'In fact, I'm telling you that you shouldn't. But if you do find anything out, you let me know.'

She didn't wait for an answer, just turned and nodded at the driver. Then the cab pulled away and she was gone.

17

The pink neon Ambassador Club sign fifty yards ahead was looking well blurry by the time Frankie spotted it. Those last two Jack Daniels in the Pillars of Hercules might have been a mistake. Shit, he wished he was already in bed. Asleep.

His head was hurting from too much thinking. He had a bad case of Sharon Granger on his mind. Kept picturing her driving off in that cab. She hadn't looked back, not like he remembered her doing at school. Meaning what? That was it? He'd probably never see her again?

After she'd gone, he'd walked back down the road to Jack's building. Her saying she hadn't driven there had left him wondering again what she'd been doing going back there in the dark on her own. When he'd asked her in the caff, she'd not answered him, had she? But she'd not denied either that she hadn't got doubts.

He'd also been left wondering, if she hadn't driven there, then who the fuck had been in that car opposite? He'd gone looking, but it had already vanished by the time he'd got there. There'd been ten cigarette butts in the gutter next to the space where he'd seen it parked. Like whoever had been in it had been waiting there for hours.

'Sorry, mate,' he half-said, half-slurred, nearly tripping over some homeless guy's feet.

A muffled response came from the nest of cardboard and blankets. Frankie walked on, then thought better of it. Digging into his pocket, he backed up and knelt down.

'Here,' he said, proffering a tenner.

A pale, skinny hand reached out from beneath a grey blanket and took the cash. More muffled words. Could have been thanks or piss off. Frankie glimpsed a pale face peeping out at him from a black hoodie. A bloke or a bird? Hard to tell. Young, though. Fucking tragically so.

'I got a club,' Frankie said. 'The Ambassador. See? Just down the road from here. You ever need somewhere to shelter, you know, if it's pissing down or whatever . . . then you just come and knock, all right?'

No reply. The eyes watched him in silence.

'All right, mate. You go well.' Frankie patted the pile of blankets goodbye, before getting unsteadily to his feet.

Shit, he was pissed. But fuck it. He was nearly home. Up ahead the club's glowing sign pointed out into the street and he smiled, remembering Vegas, and that first time, way back, when he'd gone there with his folks. Must have been '82, '83. Before his mum and dad had split. Just before the old man had started running the club.

They'd come into a shitload of money somehow. Some big property deal the old man had helped out on. It was the first time in their lives they'd been properly flush. There'd been no more cheap hop-on-a-train-at-the-drop-of-a-hat day trips down to Skeggie and Brighton. The family James had started tootling off on posh European 'City Breaks' instead, to Barcelona, Paris and Rome. And further afield. The States. New York and Vegas.

Good times. And the holidays weren't the only changes Frankie remembered. His mum had stopped worrying about how much water they used in the bath and had started buying

Heinz and Smirnoff, instead of Tesco's and Asda's own brands. The old man had ditched his grubby jeans and T-shirts, for Paul Smith, Ben Sherman and Ray-Bans. He'd taken out the lease on the Ambassador Club too. For 'a bit of fun'. Frankie remembered the phrase. Like it was just a lark, a whim, something he was doing just because he could.

Frankie's mum had changed too. Always beautiful, the kind of natural stunner you could have dressed in rags and she'd still have drawn looks, she'd turned into a proper show-stopper. All designer clothes and hairdos. He remembered other geezers, geezers who weren't his dad, really noticing her. And he remembered the old man noticing them. Even then he'd known that things wouldn't fucking last.

He sighed, finally reaching the club, feeling suddenly flat, feeling knackered. He fumbled for his keys. But then something caught his eye. The lights inside were off.

Hell's tits, what time was it? He checked his watch – the old man's watch, just about the only thing left of any value from his family's glory days – and saw that it was already half-past-midnight. Bollocks. He'd told Slim he'd be back by eleven.

He saw something was wrong the second he reached the side entrance for the flat upstairs. It was the cctv camera that gave it away. It was pointing the wrong way. Someone had twisted it round, so that it now faced upwards. Someone strong. The camera wasn't designed to be pointed that way. Its bracket had been bent out of shape. The door's lock had been forced as well.

He hurried back down the street to the club's main door. His heartbeat spiked the second he tried it. It wasn't locked. But why not? Fuck. Slim always locked it, whenever he closed up himself.

He leaned in, took a closer look at the door. But it hadn't been forced. Meaning maybe that whoever had gone in through the side entrance might have come out through here and already left?

But who the hell would be doing that? Certainly not Slim.

Should he call someone? The cops? No. Sod that. He didn't want them back here. Didn't want to be on their radar any more than he already was. Especially if whoever had broken in was now gone.

Easy does it. He edged the door open and stepped inside. Didn't reach for the light switch just there to the right. Not yet. Just listened. He knew this place better than the back of his hand. He could hear the clock ticking above the bar, the distant hissing sound of the leaking toilet cistern. But nothing else. Nothing wrong.

His eyes began to adjust to the dim light filtering in from outside. He heard no one, saw no one. A car drove past outside, its headlights sweeping across the room through the cracked windows, casting long shadows across the tables, but not picking out anyone lurking inside.

The middle of the bar where the till was. His eyes locked on it as he moved slowly forwards, letting the door hiss shut behind him. Had Slim remembered to put the takings in the safe? Yes, of course he would have. A few steps more and he'd see.

But then – fuck, he stumbled, nearly tripped. He thudded into one of the tables. Bollocks. Stupid drunk twat. His rubbed at his eyes. They were watering. The whole room looked blurry. He sniffed. Jesus, he could even smell Jack Daniels on his breath.

He still couldn't see. He reached for the lighter in his pocket. Didn't want to risk turning on the lights. Not yet. His thumb found the wheel and started stroking it into life.

Then stopped. Because – oh, shit, oh bollocks, oh fuck – it wasn't Jack Daniels he could smell. Something much more fucking deadly that that. *Petrol*. A shiver chased up and down his

109

spine. Jesus, yes, that's why his eyes were watering. He had to get the fuck out of here. Now.

Softly, slowly, he backed up to the door. Gently, ever so gently, he felt for the handle and turned it. He slowly pushed the door open and took off his jacket and used it to wedge it. He let the cool night air flood in.

He saw it then. In the wide shaft of amber streetlight now stretching across the room. There. On the table in the centre of the room. A five-gallon jerry can. Deep breath. Go. His stomach twisted with nerves, as he walked slowly back towards it. Was it open? Yes. Fuck. Its lid was off. Right there on the table. And something else. What the fuck? A piece of paper. Something on top of it. A solitary match.

A message typed in black ink underneath it read:

One match. That's all it takes. Back off. While you can.

18

Frankie had no choice but to keep the club shut the next morning. He glanced at his reflection in the old Guinness mirror on the wall by the club's front door and tried not to retch. Not just because last night's Jack Daniels seemed determined to put in a reappearance, but because of the stink. Because he couldn't clean it up. Not until the piggin' cops arrived.

He'd been sitting here, suited and booted, two aspirins and one bacon sarnie down, waiting for his hangover to clear, for nearly two hours, since eight a.m. He'd reckoned on them being here by now. First thing. He'd called them last night and reported what had gone down. He'd expected them round right away, but they'd fobbed him off.

He was now half-wishing he hadn't called them at all. Because they were obviously just enjoying messing with him and keeping him waiting. Maybe he should call them back? Tell them to forget it? To sod off? So he could clean this shit up instead? Or not. He stared at the jerry can on the table, still wanting to punch something . . . someone. But part of him wanted the cops to nail these bastards.

He groaned softly. This was another reason why he hated drinking, why he hated *him* drinking, not just because he made bad decisions *while* he was drunk, but because it affected his decision-making so badly the next day too.

Slim, who was sitting next to him on the worn leather sofa, said he hardly ever got hangovers. One of the benefits of being a fully fledged alcoholic, he claimed, though Frankie reckoned it was probably more to do with the fact that most weeks Slim never really sobered up fully at all.

The windows looking out onto the street were wide open on their hinges. Bright sunlight glared in, bringing with it a whiff of drains and hot tarmac from where council workers down the street were filling in potholes. But none of it was strong enough to totally drown out the stink of petrol inside.

'If I ever find out who did this . . .' Frankie said.

'Then you'll leave it well alone,' said Slim, sipping on his coffee and brandy, or *carajillo*, as he called it, something he said every adult in Spain had with their Weetabix or whatever they ate every morning, like it was something cultural, instead of just another early morning fix.

'No, I won't. I'll bloody well . . .' Drag them down the petrol station and jam a pump nozzle down their throats and fill them up like balloons. That's what he wanted to do. Just another in a seemingly unlimited variation of vigilante revenge fantasies his brain had been cooking up since he'd gone to bed last night, some involving snooker cues and places to insert them, others, more lurid, involving emptying whatever petrol was left inside that jerry can over whoever had brought it here, before holding up a lighted match to their faces just for the joy of watching them squeal.

But fuck it. What was the point? The reality was he had no way of tracking these pricks down. On top of killing the side-door camera, they'd swiped the cctv tapes from behind the bar. They were pros. But still, he had to hope. Maybe the cops might find something, eh? Prints on the jerry can. Or the match. Or the note. If the lazy toe-rags ever got here, that was.

'Fuck it. I'm gonna call them again,' he said, getting up. He couldn't sit here any more.

'Don't waste your time,' said Slim.

He had a point. Frankie had called the cops six times already. Each time the answer had been the same: they'd be here as fast as they could.

'If this was some posh mansion in Chelsea . . .'

'But it's not. It's here . . . and . . .'

Slim didn't need to say it: *And it's you.*

Meaning not Frankie James, the citizen who had the same rights as any other citizen, but *that* Frankie James, the son of Bernie James and the brother of Jack, just another set of bad genes from a family used to living on the wrong side of the law.

'I'm half tempted to march down the station.'

'Stay put. They'll come. When they're good and ready,' Slim added. 'When they know they've left you to sweat long enough and get you properly pissed off. Then they'll turn up, just to see the look on your face.'

He was right, of course.

'You know what gets me most?' Frankie said, walking over to the table. He glared down at the jerry can, still there on the table where he'd left it for fear of contaminating it with his own prints.

'What?'

'Whoever did this, right? They'd have done it because they were told to . . . because they were following orders . . .' From whatever gangster scumbag they worked for. Terence Hamilton, was Frankie's guess. 'To send out a warning, yeah?' To warn him off playing detective. To stop him trying to prove Jack wasn't behind any of this shit. 'But this isn't just a warning, is it? This is actual damage. Deliberate, that they must have known was gonna cost.'

113

The drenched baize around the base of the can was ruined. The sodden, petrol-soaked cushions would now need reupholstering. Whatever bastard was responsible had clearly walked round the whole table, pouring as they did, pissing all over his property like a fucking dog.

But what really stuck in his gullet was what they'd left right there in the centre of the table. He hadn't seen it last night, but couldn't stop looking at it now. The framed photo of his mum and dad which they'd taken from the wall, the last one he had of them before they'd separated, before she'd vanished, and before the old man had been put away. It had been spattered with petrol. Parts of it had already faded away.

Personal. They'd made this fucking personal. Whoever had done this had loved every second of it. And for that he wanted to ruin their fucking lives.

He read the note again. How it was phrased. Whoever had typed it knew he was snooping around. Had Mickey Flynn been shooting his mouth off again? Had word reached Terence Hamilton's mob the same way it had reached Riley? Or had there really been someone sitting in that car last night watching Jack's flat? Someone who'd now fingered Frankie for what he'd been doing? Was that what was behind this? And if it was, then what else had they seen? Him and Sharon leaving together? Sweet fucking Jesus. What the hell might they have made of that? At least she was plainclothes. They might not even have known she was a cop.

A knock at the door. Frankie went over to open it. It was ten o'clock. Opening time. Most likely a punter, rather than a pig. He'd already decided what he'd tell them. That they'd had a leak in the upstairs flat and had the plumbers coming round. Didn't want them knowing the truth. Plenty of other places they could play instead of here.

114

But when he opened the door, it was bloody Snaresby he saw standing there. King Pig. With his dirty yellow fucking smile.

'I understand you've suffered some kind of a threat?' He said it cheerily, like in his mind this might somehow actually be good news. The prick.

'What's that got to do with you? They told me at the station that an Officer Klein would be coming round.'

'Yes, but I was in the neighbourhood, so I thought I'd save him the trip.' Snaresby walked past Frankie without asking. 'I noticed your cctv unit was mangled outside. I take it you didn't get any footage of the people who did it?'

'Nothing. They took the tapes.'

Again, that smile. 'Oh, you do keep tapes in there sometimes, do you? It's just I wondered after the other day when I came round.'

A warning. Frankie had to be careful. Snaresby was no mug. Frankie remembered him checking the machine when he'd come round looking for Jack. He must have guessed that Jack had been there right from the start and that Frankie had ditched the tape.

He walked over to the table and stared down at the piece of A4.

'Now what could that mean?' he said. 'Back off? Back off from what?' He poked his tongue into the corner of his mouth, like he had a piece of food stuck there he was trying to dislodge. 'Don't tell me you've been putting your nose somewhere it doesn't belong?'

'I don't know what it fucking means,' Frankie said. 'But I want to know who fucking done it and I want them nicked.'

'Ah . . . so us poor coppers can be useful sometimes, can we?' He sniffed loudly. 'Computer printout,' he said, looking back down at the piece of A4.

'They teach you that at detective school, do they? To point out the obvious? Glad to see my tax money's being well spent.'

'I'm surprised you're paying any taxes at all, son,' Snaresby said, looking around at the empty tables. 'What with it being so, well, deathly quiet in here. You might even have a case to apply for charitable status,' he added, before nodding down at the piece of paper. 'No,' he said, 'you see, the point I'm trying to make here is that anyone could have printed this out. Even you.'

'What,' Frankie scoffed, 'I'd threaten to torch my own place?'

Snaresby picked at his teeth again, then examined his fingertip with a smile, before wiping it on his trouser leg. 'Well you may laugh,' he said, 'but a note like this might make a nice little cover story if you *were* planning on torching the place yourself . . . You know the thing . . . making out you'd been threatened in order to put yourself out of the picture – foreshadowing, I believe writers call it – before burning it all to the ground a couple of weeks from now and claiming the insurance.'

'So now you're accusing me of arson?'

'And fraud,' Snaresby pointed out in a horribly helpful tone, as if Frankie might have missed the point. 'But only theoretically, of course. Not in reality. At least, I don't think?' Again that smile. 'No, son, you see I'm merely pointing out that you would not be the first owner of an obviously failing business to try and pull off this kind of a stunt.'

Enough of this fucking around. 'Are you gonna get someone down here to check for prints, or not?' Frankie said.

Snaresby ignored him. He walked to the far end of the table and gazed down at the photograph of Frankie's parents.

'I seem to recall that was up on the wall before. Am I right?' He didn't wait for an answer. 'A shame that. The loving couple, all messed up like that. Disrespectful, you know? Not at all nice.'

The way he said it . . . the *knowingness* . . . Frankie knew he was just trying to rile him. To taunt him with having known them. Like it was some kind of secret. But there was more to it than that. Frankie could sense it. What were they to Snaresby? Why the fuck did he care?

Snaresby waited for him to speak. Frankie said nothing.

'Right you are,' Snaresby then said. 'I'll put a call in to forensics. Get them to pop over and see what they can find. But between you and me, I'm guessing it's not going to be much. Whoever did this looks like they did a nice tidy job.'

'When?' Frankie said.

'Ah, well that's the thing. It's easier said than done. Particularly at this time of year, with people on holiday and limited resources. Might be as late as this evening. Even tomorrow. Even – dare I say it? – after the weekend.'

'Forget it,' Frankie said. 'I can't keep the place shut until then.'

'Ah, but you might have to. Because, you see, officially this is now a crime scene. Now that you've called it in. Now that I'm here.'

The tosser. He knew damn well Frankie couldn't afford to just leave this crap sitting here until then. The longer the club stayed shut, the worse it would look. The last thing he needed was word getting out about this, making punters think the Ambassador was no longer a safe place to play.

'Or then again,' said Snaresby, 'I could of course speed things up. Pull a few strings. Maybe get forensics down here, say, in the next half hour? So that it would have as little impact as possible on your business and you could just get on with the rest of your day?'

A favour, then? But why? For what? Because he felt sorry for him? Because somewhere under that slimy exterior, there was actually a decent human being trying to get out? Fat chance. Why else then? Because maybe Snaresby wanted this kept quiet too? Because he didn't want rumours of a gang war being stirred up even more than they already were?

'After all,' Snaresby continued, a sudden look of warning in his eyes, 'that really is what you *should* be doing, isn't it? Concentrating on *your* business, not *mine*.'

Frankie felt his mouth turn dry. So Snaresby wanted the same as whoever had done this. For Frankie to back off from looking into Jack's case. But how did he even know that Frankie *had* been looking? Just because of this note? Or because someone else had been talking? Mickey. Or Riley? Or Hamilton? Or Sharon? Snaresby took out his shiny Zippo and pack of cigarettes, but then thought better of it, sniffing the air. Frankie again remembered that spark of flame last night inside that car. Had that been him? Had he gone to her? Had she told him they'd talked? Could she really have done that?

'You need to leave this to the professionals,' Snaresby said. 'Like the note says. Back off, son, before you get fucking hurt.'

19

Frankie was busy working behind the bar in the Ambassador Club the next day, one eye on the phone, the other on the windows. Sheet lightning flickered. Thunder rumbled. It was hammering down outside, raining cats and fucking dogs.

All good for business, mind. Snooker was the perfect wet weather sport and plenty of punters had ducked in earlier and stayed put now the heavens had opened up. All the tables were full. Except for the one that was missing, of course.

Frankie had got Taffy to pick it up and get it across to his workshop in Kensal Rise first thing this morning to see what could be done about getting it cleaned and reupholstered.

Of course Taffy had wanted to know – as he'd inspected it and loaded it with his boys onto the back of his flatbed – what the fuck had happened. How in God's holy name could a table have got so badly soaked like that with fuel?

Frankie should have had a story prepared, but he hadn't and, when pressed, he'd drawn a blank and had ended up telling Taffy some bollocks about having left a petrol can on it himself because his car had broken down.

It hadn't made an ounce of sense and now he felt like a right twat for having lied and done it so badly too. But it was better than the truth, wasn't it? Better than telling Taffy he'd been targeted by some psycho. Taffy had a gob like Tom Jones and

Frankie wanted all this kept well schtum. Apart from Slim and Snaresby and Co., no one knew a thing about the threat of arson hanging over the club.

Snaresby had been as good as his word, getting his people in and out sharpish early yesterday afternoon, so that Frankie had been able to open up again this morning as soon as Taffy had sodded off. But why exactly was Snaresby helping? Frankie was still wondering about that. Why was he so intent on Frankie backing off? Just because he was a cop and he didn't want some amateur poking around? Or because he didn't want his nice little open-and-shut case starting to leak? Or because of something else? Because of something he didn't want Frankie to find out?

More lightning. One of the punters started whistling *The Twilight Zone* theme. Frankie shook his head. Could be the theme tune to his life these last few days. He took another swig of coffee. Had to keep his shit together today. Things would spiral out of control pretty fucking fast if he didn't, with what he had planned for later on.

After Snaresby's goons had buggered off yesterday with their cameras and swabs and print kits, a couple of drinks down and all Frankie had wanted was to get out there amongst it. Amongst them. Amongst whoever might have been behind all this.

Hamilton's boys. They'd been right up there. Top of his list. Why? Because they had plenty of reason, didn't they? They wanted Jack kept inside. Didn't want Frankie rocking the boat. Would be happy seeing Frankie frightened off. His reaction? He'd wanted to get hold of one of them. Give them a proper hiding. Find out if they'd done it or knew who did this. Fight fucking fire with fire.

But something had stopped him. And not just his general decency and love for his fellow man. Or Snaresby either. Snaresby could stick his sodding warnings up his arse. No, what had stopped Frankie heading out on the warpath was something Slim had said: *Why would anyone bother warning you off at all unless they had something to hide?*

Frankie had actually listened. He'd tipped the lager he was halfway through and had gone upstairs and fixed himself some food to sober up. He'd decided he needed to be more careful, smarter, like a real detective. And stop all this bullshit of trying to look into what had happened to Susan Tilley in such a haphazard, pissed-up, way.

He'd gone back to his piece of card. Those words he'd written down. His leads. And he'd made a bigger plan too. About how he was going to go about it. To tell no one what he was doing. Not even the people he trusted. Not Jack, Kind Regards, Slim or the old man. Because someone *had* been watching him, hadn't they? Or listening in. Someone with something to hide, someone capable of breaking in here and threatening his livelihood as well as his life. Meaning he had to be careful. Make it look like he'd listened to the warning. Because whoever it was who'd been watching him before, you could bet your arse they were still watching him now.

No one was in earshot. He tried the phone again. The same number he'd been calling all day, the one he'd copied down in Jack's house before Sharon had knocked him flat.

Sharon. He'd woken up thinking about her this morning. But not how she was now, as a cop. And him different too, younger. The two of them at school, just before he'd dropped out. He'd remembered that the day his dad had been arrested had been the day he'd been going to ask her out. He shook his head. He'd totally forgotten about that. All these years. She'd dropped out of his life, but now she was back. And guess what? His whole life was messed up again.

He counted the rings. Last time he'd tried he'd got to thirty before hanging up. But this time halfway through the first ring, someone picked up. Silence. No . . . breathing. He could hear breathing. Someone was definitely there.

'Hello?' he said.

'Yes?' A man.

Fuck-a-de-do. This could be them. The fucker who'd tipped Jack off to run. Keep it calm. Don't scare them off.

'This is going to sound a bit strange . . .' he said. *But who are you? And did you call my brother?*

He never got a chance to ask.

'Listen,' said the voice, 'I don't know who this is, but I'm trying to make a call.'

'You what?' said Frankie.

'A call. And whoever you're trying to get hold of, they're not here. The box was empty when I got here.'

'What box?'

'This one. The phone box. The one I'm standing in now.'

A phone box? 'A public phone box?' Frankie said. 'Is that where you're telling me you are?'

'Yes, and if you don't mind, I'm trying to—'

'Where exactly?' said Frankie.

'What?'

'Where exactly is the box that you're in?'

'Er . . . Look, who is this? And what possible business is it of yours where—'

'Someone called me,' Frankie said. 'From this number. Someone called me and . . .'

Fuck. There was no way he could explain the real reason. But he had to stop this bloke hanging up. Be nice. *Sound* nice. He forced himself to smile. He'd read somewhere that doing that made your voice sound kind of fucking smiley too.

'Listen, mate, I just need to know where it was they called

me from, OK? It's a bit complicated to explain, but yeah, if you could just humour me, I would really appreciate it if you could just help me out.'

'Soho,' the man said.

'Which bit? What street? I mean, if you don't mind, mate . . .'

'Um, well . . . I'm not exactly sure of the name . . . The rain, you see. I was walking down Oxford Street and then I spotted this and . . .'

Oxford Street. Jesus. Well close to here. Less than a mile from Jack's place too.

'What can you see?'

A pause. Come on. Come on. Frankie pictured whoever it was on the other end of the line peering out through the phone box's rain-spattered glass.

'Um, well, hang on, yes, there is something . . . A big grey building with a blue sign out the front . . . Er . . . it looks like a police station, actually, I think . . .'

A fucking *cop shop*?

'Which one?'

'The sign. It's too blurry. I can't read it from here.'

Then bloody get out there. Bloody look. Calm. Keep calm. Think. There were only two round there.

'Can you describe it, mate? The front of the building. Is it old or new?'

'Old, definitely . . . stone . . .'

Frankie didn't need to hear any more.

'Cheers, mate. You're a gent,' he said, hanging up.

He stared at the phone. The only old cop shop round here was West End Central Police Station. Where they were holding Jack. Where Snaresby worked. Jesus. Jack's tip-off had come from there? What did it mean? Something? Nothing? Everything? Could a cop have made that call? Snuck out there just before the raid on Jack's? Some bent fucker on some bastard's payroll? Even Snaresby himself? To make Jack look more guilty? To make him run? Or had the call come from someone else? Someone trying to help him? Some kind of accomplice? But on whose orders? Who'd called the shots?

Frankie pictured Sharon's face. Christ alive. She was based there too. Was she somehow mixed up in this? Was that why she'd just happened to turn up there at Jack's flat at the same time as him? Not a coincidence, but because she or whoever she was working with had somehow known he'd be there? What if it had been her who'd been sitting in that car with someone else who'd then driven off? No. Piss off. Bollocks. Not her. No way.

The hiss of the rain ramped up a notch as the club's front door swung open. Frankie watched Kind Regards dripping in his trilby and mac, shutting up his umbrella and tapping its point on the doorstep to shake off the worst of the weather.

'Oi, Slim,' Frankie called out. 'You mind keeping an eye on the bar for ten minutes?'

'Yeah, yeah. No problem.'

Slim wandered over from where he'd been flicking through a paper on the sofa. Frankie went over and shook hands with Kind Regards. He tried reading his expression. It didn't look good.

'Come on,' he said, 'let's talk upstairs. It's quieter there.'

Kind Regards followed him in silence across the hall and up to the flat. Frankie took his wet coat and hat and hung them on the antique hat stand his mum had bought the old man for their fifteenth wedding anniversary. Kind Regards smiled, seeing his trilby next to Frankie's dad's.

'I remember the first time he wore that,' he said. 'Cheltenham Gold Cup. He was only twenty-three and everyone took the piss. Told him he looked like some kind of bloody spy out of a Cold War flick. Not that he gave a toss.'

The old man had loved that hat. Even now, years into his sentence, it still gave Frankie the odd pang, seeing it hanging there like the old man had just popped out down the shops and would be back any minute with a takeaway and a vid to sit in front of while they ate. Good times, those, when him and Jack had used to crash here weekends after their parents had first split. They'd been more like three brothers, instead of a father and two sons.

'I tried calling,' said Kind Regards, as Frankie stuck the kettle on in the kitchen, 'but your phone's been engaged all morning.'

Frankie told him about the public phone box next to the cop shop while he fixed him a cup of tea. The two of them sat down opposite one another at the small kitchen table.

'Interesting, but it's hardly proof of anything,' Kind Regards said.

'Maybe not. But it doesn't look good either. Not to me. It's not just that it might have been a cop who put that call in to make Jack run. It's why they did it. It's who they might have been working for.'

Whoever had wanted Susan Tilley and her grandmother dead. But the only people Frankie could think of were Tommy Riley's mob. For revenge. But then why frame one of his own people? Why frame Jack for that? Unless the cops other theory was correct? That Jack had been involved, but had made a fucking mess of it. Had become a liability. But even then, would they really have given him up for that? Because why risk it? What if he talked? Wouldn't it have been safer to just kill him as well?

'My offer to find you a professional detective to help still stands,' Kind Regards said.

'As does my lack of money to pay for one.' Plus, he wouldn't trust one. The only detectives he'd ever heard of round here were ex-cops. And he wouldn't trust one of them as far as he could spit.

Kind Regards put down his mug and leaned forward. 'There's something else we need to talk about.'

The way he said it . . . like Jack already being under arrest for murder wasn't the real problem . . . like there was something much, much worse . . . Frankie swallowed. Shit. Here we bloody well go.

'There's a witness,' said Kind Regards.

'You what?'

'Someone who says they saw it all.'

'What do you mean *all*?'

'Everything. What happened at the Tilley place. The cops – Snaresby – he says he's got someone who was there that night at the grandmother's house and saw the killer, covered in blood. They say they watched him remove his balaclava. They say they saw his face.'

Oh, Jesus. Frankie couldn't bring himself to ask. He already knew what the answer would be. He fucking prayed he was wrong.

'The witness says it was Jack. ID'd him in a line up. It happened this afternoon.'

Frankie couldn't believe what he was hearing. Was Jack lying? Had he really murdered Susan Tilley and beaten her grandmother half to death? He shook his head, feeling faint. No. Fuck that. What if Jack wasn't lying? Yeah, spin this shit on its head. If Jack *wasn't* lying then that meant this witness *was*.

'Then they're a fucking liar,' he said. 'Who are they? Who is this wanker? I will fucking kill them. I will tear them apart.'

To get them to recant. To tell the truth. But who were they? Why were they lying? *Why*?

Kind Regards shrugged. 'Your guess is as good as mine. They've already been granted an investigation anonymity order. Which means the police aren't releasing their identity and won't have to. Right up until the trial. To protect them. From whoever else might be involved. Whatever criminal elements the police think Jack was working with. In case they try to get at the witness before the trial in order to intimidate them, or worse. It's even possible they'll be granted a trial anonymity order too.'

Frankie's hands were shaking. 'So what? We've just got to wait, have we? We can't talk to this bastard at all?'

Kind Regards looked paler than Frankie had even known him. 'Once we've appointed a barrister, we'll be able to find out more . . . put more pressure on . . .'

In Frankie's mind all he could see was some faceless, lying bastard, right here with their lying neck gripped between his fists. Another thought hit him.

'But what if they did it?'

'Who?'

'This so-called witness. What if the reason they're saying Jack did it is because they did it themselves?'

'The prosecution say this person, whoever they are . . . they're watertight, completely credible. Their story checks out. Which is why they're formally charging Jack. They're putting him on remand.'

'That mean I can see him?' No matter how bad this news was, this might be one good thing at least.

'Yes. I'll sort it for you as soon as I can.'

'I still don't buy, it, though. This witness. I bloody tell you. Because what if the cops are wrong? Like they are about bloody most things? Or what if they're worse than wrong? What if they're in this as well?'

'Just don't do anything stupid, all right?' Kind Regards said.

'I won't,' Frankie said. 'How can I? I don't even know who this lying sack of shit is. At least not yet,' he added under his breath, but not quietly enough.

'Not yet?' Kind Regards frowned. 'Those are the kind of words a man uses when he's planning on doing something . . . something he might live to regret . . .'

'I'm not planning on doing anything,' Frankie said, staring down at the floor.

Not now.

Not yet.

Not at least until tonight.

20

Frankie sat parked in his Capri opposite the entrance to Mohammed Bishara's mews. He'd been here since six and it was now coming up for nine. Starting to get dark. Still no sign of Mo, though.

He kept thinking back to his conversation with Kind Regards earlier on. Whoever this witness was, they'd do for Jack unless Frankie got hold of them first. But how the hell was he meant to do that?

The only idea he'd come up with so far was a pretty dumb one that might well land him in jail. To somehow put pressure on Snaresby. To get him to spill the witness's name.

But what kind of pressure? How far would Frankie have to take it? Snaresby wasn't just a bastard, he was a hard bastard. Even if Frankie did come up with some way of putting the frighteners on him, there was no guarantee he'd crack. And if Frankie played it wrong, well, he'd end up as screwed as Jack, wouldn't he?

Then there was Sharon. He'd got over his panic that she might somehow be in with whatever bent cop might have made that call to Jack. Her doing that, it just didn't fit. *Did* it? She was too . . . well, she was too nice. Too fucking decent. Even if she was a cop. But not just decent. There was something else about her. The same something that had drawn him to her at school. He liked her, always had. Always wished he'd somehow got round to telling her. And he believed her when she'd said she wanted to do the right thing.

He still believed she had her doubts about Jack's guilt too. He kept remembering that look in her eyes when they'd talked about how come the blood was just in his bedroom. But even so, how much was she realistically likely to rock the boat, without some kind of proof to back her up? This was her career. And he was just somebody she used to know.

His eyes narrowed. A short, stout figure came into view fifty yards down the street. He felt his heartbeat rise. Mo. In the same three-quarter-length leather coat as before.

Frankie sank down lower into his seat as Mo passed on the other side of the road and turned into the mews. Phew. He hadn't spotted him. Frankie lit a smoke and then another. He chugged down three in total while he kept watch in case Mo was expecting company. Then he moved. Time to get in there and do this.

He parked the car a block away, then threaded on his gloves and pulled a rolled-up black balaclava he'd picked up from an army surplus store down onto his head, so that it looked like a Benny hat. He checked the street, before sliding the pistol from the glove compartment and zipping it up inside the left pocket of his hoodie. Fuck, it felt heavy. His stomach lurched. Get stopped by a cop with this and he'd be doing time.

Should he leave the gun behind? No, fuck that. Mo was a pro. This would tell him loud and clear he was dealing with another pro too. He took the knife out of the compartment as well. It was wicked – curved and sharp. He slid it carefully into his right pocket, tucking its handle up out of sight under his top. Better not fucking trip. Or he'd slice his bollocks off.

The less time he spent out on the street, the better. He fetched the old pizza box from the boot and pulled his hoodie up, then jogged back to the mews and on past Mo's Aston Martin. He hoped to fuck Mo hadn't headed out during the few minutes he'd not had the mews in his sight. A waste of his whole frigging night if he had.

He pressed the door buzzer, once, twice, then shouted, 'All right, mate. Pizza,' through the polished brass letterbox. Nice and friendly, like.

In case Mo looked out, he made sure the pizza box was showing at the door's peephole. Footsteps. Then silence. He kept the box up. The door's chain was taken off its latch. Frankie pulled the front of his balaclava down, concealing his face.

'Listen, pal,' said Mo Bishara tetchily, opening up, 'I didn't order any bloody—'

Frankie didn't fuck around. Bish, bash, bosh. He smashed the door hard into Mo, bundling in after and flattening the bastard up against the wall with it. Nice. Smack. He did it again. Got a good hold of him. Punched him in the gut. Again for luck. Kicking the door shut behind him, he stepped in sharpish behind Mo, hooking one arm tight round his neck. He flashed the knife blade right before his eyes. Gave him a good fucking look. Then pressed it flat to his windpipe.

'Anyone else here?' Frankie hissed, watching the living-room door and the stairs leading upstairs.

Mo made a horrible little strangling noise.

'I. Said. Anyone. Else. Fucking. Here?'

If Mo answered yes, then Frankie was planning on getting the fuck out of here. Pronto. Particularly if it was Mo's monster bodyguard. The same if he'd got some family member here or one of his kids. He wasn't here to hurt anyone like that. Just Mo. Just to make him talk.

'No,' Mo grunted.

'Right fucking answer.'

Mo's shoulders tensed, like he was planning a move. Frankie twisted the knife's blade around so Mo got a good, close feel of it on his neck.

'Do you know who I f-f-fucking am?' Mo said.

'Wrong fucking answer.' Frankie slammed Mo's head against the wall. Mo wasn't going to say shit until he knew Frankie was for real.

Again with the knife. Tight to the right of his carotid artery this time. Close enough to let him know that whoever had a hold of him knew exactly what they were about.

Mo froze.

'Easy, brother,' he said. It felt to Frankie like any second he might explode. 'Don't do anything you're gonna regret.'

'Don't tell me what to fucking do,' Frankie told him. 'You try anything like that again and I'll slit your fucking throat.'

Mo swallowed. 'You looking for money, I don't keep it here. The same goes for drugs.'

'Tell me about the blue speed,' Frankie said.

'The what?'

'That shit you've been peddling. The amps.'

'I don't know wh—'

'Liar.'

Frankie pressed the blade tighter. Any more and Mo would bleed.

'Who are you?' said Mo.

'I'm asking the questions. Now fucking answer.'

'OK. I had a batch of it. But it's gone.'

'Where?'

'I don't know. I don't keep fucking accounts.'

What the fuck? Was that meant to be some kind of a fucking joke? Crack. Frankie smacked his head against the wall again.

'All right, all right, I sold it,' Mo said.

Bang went Frankie's last-resort idea about maybe getting hold of some of this gear to test it to help with Kind Regards' temporary insanity plea.

'What does it do?' Frankie asked.

'What do you mean?' Mo sounded genuinely confused.

'Just tell me,' Frankie snapped.

'It just . . . it just gets you fucking high . . .'

'What else?'

'Nothing.'

'You sure?'

'Positive.'

'What about Jack James?' Frankie said.

'Who?'

'Jack. James.'

'I don't know anyone ca—'

'Liar.'

Frankie let the knife do its work. Just skin deep. Mo gasped. Blood trickled down the blade onto the knuckle of Frankie's glove.

'You're fucking dead,' Mo hissed.

'No, wanker. That's you. The next lie you tell me, I'll fucking do you.'

'OK, OK,' Mo said, 'he bought some.'

'Off who?'

'Mickey. Mickey fucking Flynn.'

OK. The truth. What else did he know?

'And you reckon it might have been that shit that made him do what he did? Go mental. Go round to that girl's granny's house and batter them fucking in?'

'No. Why would it? It's just fucking speed.'

So much for the cops' theory that whatever Jack was on might have led to him making such a fucking mess of the hit.

'What about memory loss?' he said.

'You what?'

'You heard. Fucking amnesia. Is that one of the side-effects? Can this shit cause that?'

'No . . . No, I swear it.'

No . . .

'Please . . . Please, I've got kids . . . Please, just let me go . . .'

Scumbag. The crap he'd sold Jack might not have messed him up enough to do what the cops reckoned, but that didn't change who Mo was. Frankie forced him face down onto the floor. Kneeling on his back, he twisted his head round and gave him a long, good fucking look at the barrel of the pistol as he pushed it against his face.

'I'm gonna leave now,' he told him, 'but you're gonna stay exactly where you are. You're gonna count to five hundred, nice and loud. I hear you stop just once, or even fucking stutter, and I'm gonna show you what a crack fucking shot I am. Gottit?'

'Please,' Mo said. 'Yes, please, I understand . . .'

'Get counting. Now.'

Mo started mumbling under his breath.

'Louder,' Frankie snapped.

'Four, five . . .' Mo shouted out, his whole body shivering.

Frankie backed up slowly to the door and opened it. He checked outside. All clear. Pocketing the pistol – which he still didn't have a clue how to load or fire – he walked quickly down the mews towards the road, keying Mo's nice shiny car boot to bonnet just for good measure.

Rolling up his balaclava from his face and pulling his hood down, he jogged out onto the street, gritting his teeth, his mind buzzing. Because if that gear Mickey had sold Jack hadn't caused his amnesia, then what the hell had? Or *was* Jack lying? Had he really not forgotten anything at all?

21

Frankie got back to the Ambassador at just gone ten. He was drenched. Another storm. It had blown up out of nowhere and he'd got caught up in it halfway here after dropping the Capri off in Poland Street.

He peeled off his sodden hoodie and baseball cap and hung them on the door, keeping his gym bag on him with the gun inside. There were only five tables being used. Sheet lightning flashed at the windows.

'Young Frankenstein, I presume?' Slim called over from the bar with a grin as another crash of thunder shook the air.

'Yeah, looks like Halloween's come early this year,' Frankie said, walking over to join him.

It was hot, in spite of the rain, and Frankie was gasping for a drink, half from thirst, half just to steady himself after what he'd just put Mo Bishara through. Monsoon weather – that's what Frankie's mum would have called this. She'd once gone travelling to India in the '70s, just before she'd met the old man. 'Following in the steps of the Beatles,' she'd always claimed. 'More like getting stoned off your tits,' the old man had always joked back with a wink.

'So what happened to your face?' asked Slim, pouring Frankie a lager.

'You what?'

Frankie checked out his reflection in the mirror beneath the optics. Blood. A smear of it. Just below his hairline. How the fuck had he missed that when he'd just cleaned up in the car? Careless. He couldn't afford to go making mistakes like that. The kind of thing that got you nicked. He licked his forefinger and smeared the blood off.

'Ketchup. From some chips I had earlier,' he told Slim.

Slim said nothing. He ran a cloth under the tap and handed it over. Anyone working in bars, they all knew blood when they saw it. Especially round here.

Frankie took a deep swig of his lager and wiped his face clean. He'd already ditched the balaclava, gloves and knife in three separate bins. He needed to hide the pistol now and quick. Just in case Mo had somehow sussed it was him and had called the cops or was planning on paying Frankie a return home visit himself. Frankie doubted it, mind. Mo hadn't seen his face. Didn't know him anyway. The only thing that might have given him away was him asking about Jack. Mo might have put two and two together and made Frankie.

He drained his pint. It hadn't even touched the sides. Didn't perk him up either. He was too knackered. But he couldn't crash yet. Being here was giving him a good alibi. He waited for Slim to go for a piss and then wedged his bag into the safe and locked it. He'd tuck it up safely inside his mattress later on.

He had a couple more drinks with Slim over the next half hour, as the rain hammered down outside and Slim talked world politics – something he always had plenty to say about, on account of him being a pisshead insomniac who listened to Radio 4 all night.

Frankie kept one eye on the door, telling himself to stop worrying and that Mo and a bunch of his boys weren't about to come barging in.

At just gone half-ten – with Israel, Palestine and Colonel Gaddafi now put to rights – Sea Breeze Strinati tipped up with a couple of drenched mates, all three of them a little unsteady on their feet. Slim served them and then wandered off to join them for a few frames, leaving Frankie alone at the bar.

He was in a slump, his adrenaline from earlier all burned off. He couldn't stop thinking about Mo and what he'd said about that gear. Frankie needed to see Jack and ask him up front again if he really was telling the truth about not remembering. Frankie needed to look him right in the fucking eyes when he did. He'd still be able to tell, wouldn't he? If Jack was lying? But he wasn't lying, was he? In which case Frankie had to somehow get to the bottom of what the fuck else might have fried his brain that night?

He called Kind Regards and left another message, telling him to find out when the hell he could see Jack. It couldn't be soon enough. Then he finished his drink and told himself he wasn't going to have another. He was in the clear, right? No show from Mo. He half-smiled. Wasn't likely any bloody arsonists would be popping over either. Hardly their kind of weather, was it, for burning places down?

The club's front door opened with a bang. What the hell? Frankie felt his muscles tense, as a tall, hooded figure walked in. Shit-a-brick. Had Mo somehow sussed it was him?

But even as he was reaching for his cue from under the counter, he saw that this was no hired thug, more like a junkie, just standing there, shivering and gawping. The last bloody thing he needed, some moon-skinned muppet barging in here with a mind to nick something to pay for their next fix.

'Get the fuck out,' he shouted.

They didn't move. Not a muscle. Just stood there dripping on the carpet as the door banged shut in the wind behind them.

Frankie marched forward, slapping the cue with deliberate menace against the palm of his hand.

No reaction. Nothing. He stopped less than three feet from whoever this was. The punters stared, like townsfolk in some fucking spaghetti Western waiting for two gunslingers to draw.

'Out. Now,' Frankie said. 'Before I bloody throw you out.'

The face staring out at him from the hoodie was like a black-and-white photo. Bloodless. Still. For all the good it was doing him, Frankie might as well have been talking to a ghost.

'Last fucking warning,' he said.

He took a quick step forward, hoping this would be enough to scare them into flight. No such luck. They didn't budge. Right, sod this. Frankie walked right up and shoved his face right up into theirs.

Finally: a reaction.

'You said I could . . .'

Frankie screwed up his face. 'I said what?'

'Last night . . .'

What the fuck was this chimp talking about. 'Take off your hood,' Frankie told them. 'Do it now.'

They stepped back, did as they were told. Frankie shook his head. Christ on a bike. It was just a kid. Well, a youth. A teen. Whatever. Couldn't have been anything north of eighteen. A girl? If he had to bet on it, he'd say so. Hard to tell, though. All skin and bone and short cropped hair sticking up.

But, hang on . . . yeah . . . there was something about her . . . about her eyes . . . He clawed back through his memories from last night, but all he got was fistfuls of Jack Daniels-flavoured fog.

'You gave me this,' the girl said. Reaching into her hoodie pocket, she pulled out a tenner. 'You said if I needed somewhere to go, if the weather turned bad . . .' Her eyes blazed as she pointed at the rain battering the window.

Fuck-a-duck. Yes. He remembered her then. On his way home. The bundle of cardboard and blankets with two blue eyes in its centre.

Oh, Jesus. What the fuck had he done now?

22

The Patron Saint of Lost Causes.

After Frankie had told the girl she could stay – just for one night, until the storm blew over – that's what Slim had called him. Or accused him of being, anyhow. Because he obviously thought he was being a total mug.

Her name was 'Xandra with an X'. That's pretty much all he'd learned about her since last night. That and the fact she was half-starved, as witnessed by the three cheese and tomato toasties she'd polished off at the bar, much to Slim's annoyance, who'd pointed out that the cheese had been a superb aged Gouda, fresh from Borough Market, and therefore something to be savoured, not gobbled up like ruddy Cracker Barrel.

'It smells like socks, but thanks anyway, mate,' was all Xandra had said.

She was Irish. From Belfast, Frankie reckoned from her accent – something else that had got on Slim's wick, not because he had any particular prejudice against the Micks, more because he'd lost over a grand on an Irish horse five years ago and had been blaming the useless beast's country of birth ever since.

From where Frankie was sitting in the living room, he could hear the hum of the water heater and the rattle of pipes. Xandra had slept the night on the sofa and had asked when she'd woken up if she could have a wash. She'd been in there now for nearly two hours. He'd been sitting here for the same time, making a show of watching TV, but really just in case Slim was right about this total stranger robbing him for anything she could get her mitts on the second his back was turned.

He flicked through the channels, but couldn't concentrate. It was all crap anyway these days. He preferred movies. Old ones. Westerns and war films. The ones he'd grown up watching with his dad. Had a billion VHSs stacked up either side of the box.

The phone rang. He picked it up.

'Morning, it's me,' said Kind Regards.

'You got word?' Frankie asked. 'On when I can see him?'

'Yeah, and it'll be soon . . .'

'How soon?' Frankie was already up, heading for his room to get his wallet. He'd have to get rid of the girl before going to see Jack. But how? He couldn't just kick her out.

'There's been a delay.'

'But you said they were charging him. What? Has something happened?'

Frankie stopped walking. His head buzzed. Had someone come forward? Had the witness gone back on what they'd said? Or had the cops turned up some new evidence? Something that pointed to someone who wasn't Jack?

'Sorry, Frankie. Nothing like that. It's to do with where they're going to put him on remand. Because of overcrowding. Not enough spaces. This country, I tell you, it's going to the dogs.'

'Tell me it's not going to be outside of London . . .'

'Hopefully not.'

'When will we know?'

'Possibly later today. Or tomorrow. I'm doing everything I can, I promise.'

'It's all right. I know you are.'

'Just sit tight, all right? I'll let you know as soon as it's sorted.'

'OK.' Frankie walked back into the living room and sat down. 'Any word on the old lady?' He still couldn't get her out of his mind.

'Nothing. No change.'

'Good. But you'll still let me know if there is?'

'The second I hear. And another thing . . .' Kind Regards said.

'What?'

'We're going to need to put that money down . . . the retainer for the brief . . .'

'By when?'

'Well, as soon as . . . Time's ticking, Frankie. The prosecution, they're already working on this. We need to be doing the same.'

'How much?'

Kind Regards told him. Frankie swallowed. Hard.

'All right,' he said. 'Don't worry. I'll fix it. I'll fix it and call you back.'

He put down the phone. Shit. The water heater was still humming, the pipes clanging. The fucking pressure of it all. Bloody hell. He rubbed at his face. He couldn't stop thinking of Jack as a kid. All those nightmares he'd had. Frankie had used to have to keep the light on for him and tell him stupid stories just to stop him from blubbing and waking up their folks.

Jack being there all alone made Frankie want to puke.

'Keep it together,' he told himself.

He clenched his fists. If they were going to trial – unless he somehow stopped that from happening – he had to do everything he could to make sure they piggin' well won. He flicked through his little black Filofax. He went to 'S'. For Straight Eddie. The loan shark. Frankie already owed him, but he'd been paying him back regular, so who knew, maybe Eddie might come through for him again?

He'd need some kind of collateral, mind. Proof he could pay the new loan back. He dug out a couple of copies of *Exchange & Mart* and *Auto Trader* from the pile next to the sofa. Both had Capris for sale. Going for good money too. With all this Britpop shit going down, it looked like retro was well in. None of them were in as good nick as his either. He tore out the pages with the sales enquiries numbers on them and reached for the phone.

The bathroom door lock clicked. Xandra walked out into the living room, red-faced and dressed in clean jeans and a hoodie and carrying the bag she'd arrived with last night.

Christ, she was skinny. But not junkie skinny, mind. Frankie saw enough of that on the streets round here to tell the difference. She didn't have that magpie look about her like she'd pilfer anything sparkly and shiny she saw.

He forced a smile. Didn't want her feeling unwelcome or thinking that him sitting here with a face like a slapped arse had anything to do with her.

'Feel better?' he asked.

She certainly looked it. The clothes were down to him. He'd popped round the market earlier that morning while she'd still been asleep and had picked her up some stuff.

'Yeah, thanks,' she told him. 'And look . . .' she pulled the back of her collar sideways so he could see it '. . . they've even got real price tags on. Not even from down the charity shop, eh?'

'No.'

It all looked a bit baggy, truth be told, but it would do. Christ, she needed feeding up.

'What size shoes do you take?' he asked. Her feet were bare and raw-looking. He'd chucked her old boots out. They'd been filthy rotten.

'Eights.'

'I'll pick you up some trainers.'

'Really?'

'Yeah.'

For the first time, she smiled. It made her look even younger.

'Only make sure they're Nikes or Adidas, right? None of that cheap Reebok crap, OK?'

'No problem,' he said, smiling back.

She stood there awkwardly, rocking on her heels. 'Seriously, though. You've been kind enough. I'll get out of your hair just as soon as I've dried mine.'

He nodded at the window. It was still pissing it down outside. 'Into that?'

'I'm used to it.'

'Yeah, well you don't have to.'

'And how's that?'

If Slim was here, he'd tell him to shut the fuck up. But he wasn't, so screw it. No one had done him any favours recently. He might as well do one for somebody else.

'I need some help round here.'

She looked round the room, a twinkle in her eyes. 'Well, it is a bit messy . . .'

'Hah-hah. No, I mean down in the club.'

'You're offering me a job?'

'Well, I wouldn't go as far as to say that. Not yet. But, yeah, there's a few odd jobs that need doing . . .'

'I'll do anything,' she said. 'Cleaning. Washing up. I'm a hard worker. Or I was, anyhow. Last time I got a chance.'

'I'll pay you properly,' he said. 'And something else.'

'What?' She looked wary.

'You can stay too.' Shit. Slim was going to have his guts for garters for this.

'Oh, come on. Really?' Another smile. Crooked this time. Unsure. She thought she'd misunderstood. Or he was winding her up. 'You're saying I can just move in? With you? No strings attached?'

'I don't mean like that.'

'No?'

'No.'

She looked him over. 'A good thing too. Because you're not my type. Not even the right gender, if you know what I mean.'

'You can still stay,' he said.

'What, even though I'm gay?'

'Even then.'

She put her hands on her hips, her fingertips nearly meeting in the middle, and stared at him, frowning, still trying to puzzle him out.

'And how would that work, then?'

'There's a storeroom downstairs.

'Ah, so I've been demoted.' She feigned looking sad.

'It's just a storeroom now, but it can be cleaned up. Made nice. You can fix it up how you want.'

'You are serious, aren't you?' Her smile was gone. Something much hungrier was there instead.

'There's a shower room next door to it, with a toilet and wash basin. It's full of junk right now, but—'

'It can be cleaned up too?'

Frankie nodded. 'Slim, the guy you met last night . . . he used to stay over here when he started working the bar . . . way back before this flat got done up and my old man started living here on site.'

'Right . . .'

'So anyway, yeah, downstairs . . . it's yours if you want it. You know, just for a bit. See how it goes. We can get a new bed in there and what not, until you get back on your feet.'

'In my nice new trainers?'

'Exactly. Your Nikes.'

'And why would you be doing this for me?' She was looking dead serious again.

'You just look like you need a break. And I guess I'm just in the right mood to give you one.'

Was he being an idiot? Shit. Only time would tell. What was the worst that could happen? She'd try and nick something. But what? The balls. The cues. Nothing else of much value down there at all. Not unless you happened to have a JCB with you to pick the tables up.

She stood there watching him.

'One rule, mind,' he said.

'What?'

'No taking the piss.'

'Meaning what?'

'I dunno.' He didn't want to spell it out. 'Just don't make me regret it, that's all.'

She sniffed, looking round. Shit. He nearly laughed. What had he just done? And *was* he going to regret it? He breathed out. Well, it was too late to back out now. And besides, he didn't want to. It felt right. It felt good. In fact, in a weird fucking way, it felt like all this might somehow have just changed his luck.

'Right, well I guess we'd better get down there and take a look at that storage room,' he said.

'You're on,' she told him, barely able to conceal her smile. 'After you, boss. Lead the way.'

23

'Let me guess. This is a coincidence? You just happening to bump into me like this?'

'You took the words right out of my mouth,' said Frankie.

'Yeah?' said Sharon. 'Well, I'm not buying it.'

They were walking fast along the pavement with the commuter crowd. It was the end of the day, people were heading for their cars, bus stops, the tube and home.

'Please stop,' he said. 'Just for a minute.'

'I already told you. We shouldn't be talking.'

He hurried after her, across the road. A car horn blared, a white van just missing running him down. He was half-tempted to grab her by the elbow, to try and slow her down. Forget it. She'd probably just deck him like she had done at the flat. She was kind of unpredictable like that.

'It's nothing about the case, I swear,' he said. A lie. Of course.

She stepped sideways.

'Shit. Ouch.'

Bollocks. He twisted round. He'd just walked bang into a bloody lamp post. He rubbed furiously at his arm.

She was a couple of yards ahead again already, glancing back over her shoulder at him, trying not to laugh.

'Oh, and I suppose you think that's funny, do you?'

She strode on, her shoulders shaking. He finally caught up.

'On what?' she asked, still trying and failing to keep a straight face.

'Eh?'

'You swear *on what*?'

'Oh . . . Er . . . I don't know.' *On my mother's life.* He nearly said it. Didn't. Hated it whenever Jack did. Felt it might somehow jinx her ever coming back. 'You know, on everything . . . whatever . . .'

'Everything? Whatever?' Sharon mimicked. She kept walking. The tube station was only ten yards ahead. Must be where she was going. He could hardly follow her down there, could he? She'd probably arrest him for stalking.

'I don't know,' he said. 'Everything. Everything I care about.'

'Like what?'

'Like . . . I don't know . . .' Say something, you muppet. Anything. Just get her to bloody stand still. 'Like . . . you.' The word was out before he could stop it.

She stopped too. So did he. She stared right into his eyes, unblinking as the crowd rushed past.

'Very funny.'

He swallowed. What the hell had he just said? That he *cared* about her? For fuck's sake. What a knob.

'Made you stop, though, didn't it?' he said, grinning, trying to make a joke of it.

'Fine.' She opened her handbag and pulled out a pack of smokes. 'Whatever it is you've got to say, I'll give you as long as it takes me to smoke one cigarette. But that's it, OK?'

'Sure.'

'And not here.'

Where they might get seen by one of her colleagues. He got it. Fair enough. He could hardly blame her for being wary. He was lucky she was still risking talking to him at all.

He followed her through the crowd and down a quiet leafy road to the right of the tube station. Leaning against a wall, she sparked up a cigarette and took a long, slow drag. She looked like she'd had a tough day and would rather be anywhere but here. With him. It was good seeing her, though. No point denying it. And not just because he did want to talk to her about Jack. Just because.

'So . . . what is it you wanted to ask?'

Just get the conversation started. Get her to relax. Drop her guard. Maybe then they could talk about Jack. Xandra. He thought about Xandra. Yeah, ask her about Xandra. Because he really could do with some advice.

'There's a girl,' he said. 'Homeless. She's nineteen. I've let her move into a room downstairs at the club . . . you know, until she gets herself back on her feet . . .'

'Very admirable,' said Sharon. But not sarcastically. Like she meant it. 'Though I don't see what that's got to do with me.'

'I don't know any other cops, so I thought, you know, I'd ask . . .' he said, '. . . see if you knew anyone she could talk to. About her future. Getting herself off the streets for good. That kind of thing.'

'It's a social worker you need. Not the police. I'll get you a number. You should try and find out if she's got family too, though. Someone might be looking for her.'

'I will,' he said. 'I'll ask. Yeah. Right. Cool. Thanks.'

She took another drag on her cigarette, almost done with it already. Shit. Tick-tock, tick-tock. He was running out of time.

'Well?' she said, seeing him staring.

'Look . . .'

'You didn't really want to ask me about your homeless girl at all, did you?'

He felt himself blushing. She saw it too.

149

'No.'

'So what's the real question you want to ask . . . the reason you rang up the station and pretended to be my boyfriend so you'd know what time I was knocking off work.'

'Busted,' he admitted. He'd stood there waiting outside the cop shop for her for over an hour. Had even gone into that phone box for a couple of minutes. Had just stood there. Like it might speak to him. Like a fucking mug.

'How about first I buy you dinner?'

There. He'd said it. Something else he'd been thinking about. The whole walk over here from Soho. Not just Jack. Her.

Her turn to blush. 'Dinner?'

'Yeah, you know, knives and forks and plates and food.'

Screw it. Why not? He'd already made a complete dick of himself, blurting out that he *cared* about her. Why not go the whole hog? She was probably about to walk away and never speak to him again anyhow. What had he got to lose?

'What?' she said. 'To soften me up so I'll tell you everything you want to know, is that what you want?'

'Well, of course that,' he said, 'but also because I'm starving and I know a killer little Italian just round the corner. That's got a little table in an alcove at the back, so you won't have to worry about any of your colleagues seeing us. And I thought, well, it might be nice to spend a bit of time together. You know, without you having to beat the shit out of me first.'

'You do remember I've got a boyfriend, right?' she said, waggling her ring at him.

'Yes. I remember.' Remember and don't care.

'And how do you think he'd feel about me going out for dinner with a strange man?'

'I'm not that strange.'

'A strang*er*, then.'

'I'm not that either. I'm an old friend.'

'Really? Is that what you are?' She ground her cigarette out with her heel. 'Because I don't remember us ever being friends. Just school mates. Or not even mates. Just at the same school.'

'Yeah, but maybe we should have been,' he said. 'Would have been.' He thought back again to what he'd remembered. About how he'd nearly once asked her out back in school. 'Maybe that's what I'm trying to do now. Make up for lost time.'

She looked him slowly up and down, before finally nodding. 'All right,' she said, 'but this Italian . . . it better be bloody good.'

No worries there. The restaurant he took her to had been his mum's favourite. He'd been going there for as far back as he could remember. Old school. Red-and-white chequered table-cloths. Way too much parmesan over your food. Black pepper deluged from a grinder as tall as the Post Office Tower.

Him and Sharon made small talk to begin with. He asked about her family, even though he'd never known them. Turned out she was an only child whose father had been a soldier. He'd died in the Falklands, a member of 2 Para shot dead at Goose Green by Argentine conscripts who'd first raised a flag of sur-render and had then opened fire. Her mum had never remarried and now taught part-time at a primary school down in Brighton. She'd been diagnosed with Parkinson's a couple of years ago. It worried Sharon sick.

She told him a bit about her boyfriend too. Six years older. A broker. Now away in Hong Kong for six weeks, setting up a trad-ing desk. Did she miss him? Yes. No hesitation. Had she been out to visit? No. Which made him wonder a bit. They'd been friends to being with. Had only really started going out just over a year ago, a relationship stat that surprised him, considering the size of that bloody ring.

The most expensive present Frankie had ever given a girl was a silver necklace Slim had been shifting a job lot of, which had turned out to be tin and had given the girl a rash. Did that make him rubbish? Or this bloke of Sharon's, this Nathan, was he just so rich that a ring like hers didn't mean anything at all?

It wasn't till the end of the meal that they got talking about Jack. And not because he brought it up. He didn't. He was happy talking about other stuff, about her. Truth was, he'd forgotten about Jack entirely for the first time since he'd thrown himself screaming at the club's front door. It was Sharon who brought him up. Just after the waiter had topped up their glasses with the last of their bottle of red.

'And so, this question of yours,' she said. 'I'm thinking you'd better ask it now before we drink any more.'

'I actually have two. And they're both about Jack.'

'I guessed they would be.'

'You don't have to answer . . . not if it's going to compromise you . . .'

'I won't.' She sat back in her chair and lit a cigarette. 'So go on then. Shoot. Let's hear what you've got to say.'

24

'What if I told you that the tip-off that Jack got the morning they arrested him – the anonymous call that made him run—'

'Came from a public phone box right outside the police station?'

He just stared.

'That *is* what you were about to say, isn't it?' she asked.

Had Kind Regards said something? During some conversation with the cops he hadn't told Frankie about? Was that how she knew? Or was it what he'd dreaded? That she *was* somehow mixed up in this too? That she knew who'd made that call?

'We're not complete idiots, Frankie,' she said. 'We checked the records against Jack's statement. And, yes, there was a call from a phone box. And, yes, it was just before the raid on Jack's flat took place.'

'Then you've got to admit—'

'What, Frankie? That someone at the station made that call? Maybe even me?'

He swallowed hard, embarrassed at how transparent she obviously found him.

'No, not you,' he said. 'It was a man who called. Jack said—'

'DI Snaresby, then? Is that who you'd like it to be?'

'It's not about what I'd like,' Frankie snapped. But was that true? Because he didn't trust Snaresby, did he? Especially after what his old man had said, after that look he'd seen on his face. 'And I'm not saying it even had to be a cop,' he said, hating the look of scorn on Sharon's face now and wanting to wipe it away. 'Just someone who knew one. Someone who might have been in the station that morning. Someone who knew that the raid was about to happen. Perhaps someone who knows something about who set my brother up.'

'It's a public booth,' said Sharon. 'Anyone could have rung him from there. Even deliberately. To make it look like the police might be involved. To add some confusion to the mix.'

'Like who?' Frankie said.

'I don't know. Any more than I *know* what that call was about.'

'I already told you. Someone called Jack because they wanted him to run.'

'We've only got Jack's word for that.'

'Which is good enough for me.'

Her look said it all. But not good enough for her. Not good enough for the cops, or the court.

'If Jack did kill Susan Tilley as part of a gang war, then might it not be possible that one of his accomplices called? That they didn't do so anonymously at all, but because they got a tip-off that we were on to him? Because they were worried after the state he was in the night before that he might not have had the wherewithal to clean his flat up?'

'*If*,' Frankie said. 'He *didn't*. And as for whoever made that call . . . Did you even dust it for prints? The booth, I mean?'

'Seriously?'

'Do I look like I'm laughing?'

'Have you any idea how many prints there must be in that phone box? Or how much time and resources it would take to attempt to discount them all? Even if the prints of whoever made that call hadn't already been smudged or wiped away? And don't you think that anyone devious enough to have tried to help set your brother up or who was working with him might also have been smart enough to wear gloves? Especially if they were police.'

As stupid as he felt, at least she'd said it too. Right there at the end. That a cop might have somehow been involved. Even if it was one smart enough not to get caught.

'Who else are you looking at?' he asked.

'What?'

'For the murder.'

She said nothing.

'No one, I bet,' he said. 'But the thing is, if it's not Jack. Which it's *not*. Then it has to be someone else.'

'Again,' she said, '*if* . . .'

'You've checked Susan Tilley's colleagues? Her exes?'

'Yes, but there's nothing. There's no one who looks remotely likely to have—'

'Well, I don't know, maybe some stalker then. Some nut job. Someone she lived near or used to know.'

'We've been very thorough. I promise you, Frankie.'

'What about someone who knew her *and* knew my brother and that's why they decided to frame him. Someone who knew them both personally, not just because of their connections to gangs.'

'Like who?' Sharon said.

'I don't know.' He'd wracked his brains, trying to make a connection himself. But Jack and Susan had no friends in common that he knew of and Kind Regards had already asked Jack the same thing too and had drawn a blank. There was no one whose name had stood out.

'What about Dougie himself then? What if she'd been, I don't know, shagging someone else? What if he decided to—'

'They were happy, Frankie.' She caught the waiter's eye and waved for the bill. 'Properly happy. Or hadn't you noticed? They were getting married the next day.'

'Not everyone's happy when they get married. Behind closed doors, things aren't always what you'd think.' He meant his own parents. How perfect it had all looked, right up to the day they'd split up. Maybe that's how it was with Susan Tilley and Dougie Hamilton too.

'We have talked to people,' Sharon said. 'Lots of people who knew them. And they – all of them – every one said they were completely in love.'

Frankie thought back to Dougie Hamilton attacking him the way he had. There'd been nothing fake about that. He'd been fucking gutted. Gutted enough to have beaten Frankie to a pulp, if he'd only been given the chance.

'And this wasn't a crime of passion,' Sharon said. 'Done in the heat of the moment. They're messy. Whereas this, it was premeditated.'

'This wasn't messy? Give me a break,' Frankie said. 'There was blood everywhere. And I don't just mean on Jack, in his room. I mean at the old lady's house. Snaresby told me it looked like a video nasty.'

'But no fingerprints,' she said. 'No DNA at the scene of the crime. In fact, your brother would have got away with it entirely if it wasn't for the cctv camera recording his car.'

'And your witness, of course,' he said, watching her closely now.

Her cheeks darkened. Maybe she'd thought he'd not yet been told. 'You know I can't talk about that.'

Who are they? That's what he wanted to ask her, even though he knew she'd just tell him to piss off. Who was this fucking liar?

Who was this wanker set on putting Jack away?

'Whoever it is, you know they're lying, don't you?' he said. 'Or they're somehow involved. Or they bloody killed Susan Tilley themselves.'

'I don't know that, no, Frankie. And neither do you. They're credible. Their story checks out. They've got no reason to lie.'

They. She was being careful, not even giving away if it was a woman or man.

She opened her mouth to speak, then clamped it shut. She didn't need to say the words. He'd guessed them anyway. Not like your brother, she'd been about to say.

'Frankie, you've got to trust in the process of law.'

Like with the old man? Forget that.

'Please. I know this is hard on you,' she said, 'but you need to trust us – to trust me,' she corrected herself, 'to do my job.'

He stared up at the ceiling. His mind was a mess. He had to have faith in Jack. But he could still trust her too, couldn't he? If he got her anything – anything at all – that could prove Jack's innocence. To do the right thing. To act on it and not bury it or look the other away.

'Look,' she said, 'can we just . . .'

'What?'

'Stop talking. About this.'

The waiter came back.

'Mine,' he told her, taking the bill. 'I mean, my treat,' he said, trying to soften his tone.

He paid in cash.

'Thank you.' She raised her glass to him. 'It was every bit as good as you said it would be.' She looked at the waiter and smiled. 'I'll be coming back.'

With him? Frankie wondered. With Nathan. Was that what she meant?

She finished her drink and got up, pulling on her jacket. He followed suit, then followed her outside. Rush hour was over. The evening was warm. A few people were smoking and drinking outside a little pub down the road, but other than that the world was still.

'I'll wave you down a cab,' he said.

'Or we could just walk.'

He looked at her, confused. 'Really?' he asked. 'Where to?'

'You can keep me company back to mine.'

He didn't even know where she lived. Was it close? 'I thought you were heading for the tube station before?' he said.

'No, just the street next to it. The same one we talked in. That's where my flat is.'

My flat. Interesting. Not *our.* Not hers and his. Meaning maybe things between her and Nathan weren't actually as fully advanced as all that after all.

'All right,' he said, resisting the urge to slip his arm through hers like . . . like *what* exactly? A couple? Hah. Who was he kidding? He must have had too much plonk.

They chatted about nothing much of anything as they walked. About school. Kids they'd both known, wondering where they were now. Not Jack.

After only a few minutes, they entered the same nice quiet street of white Georgian town houses as before. She stopped outside one halfway along and Frankie walked with her up to the top of the stoop. On the wall by the door were a bunch of buzzers with the names of the flat owners below them. He saw her surname there. No one else's beside it. Not like the other couples on display.

'I'm not going to invite you in, you know,' she said, turning her key in the lock.

'I know. You've got a boyfriend.'

'Exactly.'

'Meaning that if you didn't, then you would?'

'What?'

'Ask me in.'

She opened the door and stood there holding it. 'Now you're putting words in my mouth.'

'I'm just saying it takes two, that's all.'

'To do what?' she laughed. 'Tango?'

'To think what I'm thinking. When I look at you now.'

There . . . he'd done it again. Let it all out.

She didn't answer. Didn't shut the door either. Not the front door to the building, as he followed her inside. Or the door to her flat on the first floor, which he closed behind them. Or the door to her bedroom, which she left open for him too.

She reached the bed and turned to face him. Just do it. He walked up to her and kissed her. He'd wanted to do it all night.

25

'B e outside in ten minutes,' a man's voice said.

'Eh?' Frankie rubbed his eyes and sat up.

He dropped the phone. What? Bloody hell. He was still half-asleep. This wasn't his bed. Shit. Where was he? Right. The living room. What was he doing here? He leant forward off the sofa and picked up the phone. But it was already dead. He checked his watch and groaned. Quarter past eleven.

He peered blurrily at the table. No bottles. What he normally saw when he woke up here. No hangover either. He felt . . . *great*. So what the fuck *had* happened last night? Oh yeah. Blimey. He'd been at Sharon's. With her. In bed. Nice . . .

Or not. Because . . . Shit. She'd kicked him out, hadn't she? She'd woken him up at just gone six with a coffee and had told him she was off for a run and that he should get dressed and be on his way too. He'd tried getting her back into bed. Of course. Why wouldn't he have? They'd had a great time. But she'd been having none of it. Embarrassed? Was that it? Or guilty? Because of her boyfriend? Or because of her work? Because of the line they'd just crossed?

'What's the matter?' he'd said.

'Nothing. I just . . .'

'What?'

'I just hadn't expected to . . . I don't think this was . . .'

Right. A good idea. He didn't need her to say it. Had worked it out for himself. She'd not planned what had happened between them. It had been a mistake.

'So that's it then?' he said. 'You're just kicking me out?'

'It's not like that.'

'Like what?'

'Like you're making it sound. Like a one night stand.'

'Isn't it?'

'No.'

'So there'll be another?'

'No . . .'

'Ah, so it's not like that either.' Fine. He'd got up and pulled on his jeans.

'Listen,' she said. 'I don't know . . . last night, we'd both had a drink . . .'

'A drink. But not drunk,' he said. 'Neither of us were.'

'I'm not saying I didn't have a good time, Frankie. Because I did. But I've got a boyfriend. Who I love.'

Love. The word hurt. A lot more than he thought it would have.

He'd lashed out. 'Yeah? Well, it wasn't his name you were calling out last night.'

Idiot. He wished he hadn't said it.

'No, I don't suppose it was . . .' she said. 'But that's why I don't think we should—'

'Save it,' he'd said, buttoning up his shirt.

That was the last thing they'd said to each other. He'd let himself out.

His phone trilled again. He thought about letting it ring out, but whoever had just called had sounded pretty urgent. Maybe it was Kind Regards? He snatched it up and answered, 'Yeah?'

'Outside. Nine minutes,' the voice said.

Nine? 'Who the fuck is this?' said Frankie.

'Mackenzie. Grew.'

Frankie didn't exactly gulp, but he wasn't far off. He sat up straighter. Grew worked for Tommy Riley.

'Tommy wants to see you,' he said.

'Now?'

'No, next year, that's why he's sending round a car in eight minutes to pick you up.'

'But—'

'But nothing. Don't be fucking late. I'm driving round to get you myself.'

Shit. The line went dead. Frankie stared at the receiver. Then he was moving. Fast. No time for a shower. He got dressed. Splashed cold water on his face. Shoved a fingertip of toothpaste into his gob and swilled it round and spat.

He'd been going to call Tommy Riley today anyway. Because he needed help. He was all out of leads. He needed Riley to help him reach someone he could never get to on his own.

But why the fuck was Riley calling him in? That was more of a worry. About the rent he still owed? Had he changed his mind about going easy on him on all that while this shit with Jack was going down? Or was that what this was about? Was he calling him in because he'd totally fucking failed to help Jack and so hadn't pulled any heat off Riley at all?

He hurried downstairs and into the club. Good. Slim was already there, pulling the covers off the tables.

'I've got to go out,' Frankie said. 'To see Tommy Riley.' Probably no bad thing having someone else know. Just in case he didn't come back.

'No problem,' Slim said. 'We'll be fine holding the fort.'

'We?'

A clattering and swearing out back. Ah, yes. Xandra. In there sorting out the storeroom.

'All going OK between you two?'

'I'm keeping an eye on her,' Slim said.

'Good.'

'*And* on the till,' Slim added.

'Fair enough.' He was probably right, of course. To be wary. But Frankie still had a good feeling about her.

'But seeing as she is going to be around . . . I could do with a bit more help around the rest of the business,' Slim said, folding the heavy cover over onto itself.

Meaning maybe he was prepared to give her a chance as well? Bloody hell. Who said leopards couldn't change their spots?

'All right,' Frankie said. 'I hear you. Let's see what we can do.'

He checked his watch. How long did he have? Five minutes? Tops. He walked quickly through the storeroom. Xandra was halfway up a ladder, covered in paint. She'd cleared a lot of the crap out of here already and was now busy decorating. She'd got paint in her hair and all over her T-shirt. Her bare feet were spattered with it too, but he was pleased to see she'd already stashed the Nikes he'd bought her safely and in pride of place up on the window sill.

'Morning,' he said. 'How's it all going?'

'How does it look?'

'Funny?'

'Right.' She grinned. 'That'll cover it. It's going funnily. Thanks for asking, boss. Don't suppose you fancy giving me a hand?'

'I've got to go out. But listen . . . There's something we need to talk about.'

'Yeah?'

'About you . . . about you being here . . .'

Her expression crumpled. 'What? Have I done something wrong?'

'No,' he told her quickly, 'not a bit of it.'

'Then what?' She looked embarrassed at having jumped to the conclusion that whatever he'd been about to say had been bad.

'I was just wondering, if you'd . . . you know, once you've fixed your place up . . .'

Your. She smiled at the word.

'It's just I've been talking to Slim,' he said, 'and well, between you and me, he's not getting any younger, and while it's going to be great you helping out with odd jobs and cleaning and that, I'm thinking that maybe you could help him a bit too. Let him train you up. You know, on more front-of-house stuff. How to deal with customers. A bit of waitressing. Maintaining the tables. That kind of thing.'

She looked surprised, but only for a moment.

'No problem. I'll do it,' she said.

'Great, and of course I'll pay,' he added. 'The same rate as for the odd jobs. But I'll stick you on an hourly. We'll sort out some shifts.'

'Deal,' she told him. Grinning, she came down the ladder and held out her hand towards him, before seeing it was covered in paint. 'Or perhaps we'd better just shake on it later?' she said.

He remembered then. What Sharon had said. What he'd been too dumb and insensitive to think of himself.

He said, 'There's something else I've been meaning to ask.'

'What?'

'It's probably none of my business and I don't want to pry, but . . .'

Right there, something about her changed. A darkening in her eyes. Christ, how many times must people have said something like this to her before? Bollocks. Just cut to the chase.

'It's about your family,' he said.

'I haven't got one.'

'All right, then . . . your people.'

'My people?' She tried to make a joke of it. 'I'm not the fucking queen.'

'You know what I mean.'

She just stared blankly at him. 'Nope.'

'What I'm saying is . . .' he said '. . . is that . . . if there is anyone out there . . . anyone at all, anyone decent, that you ever cared about . . . or who cares about you . . .'

'There's not.'

'Yeah, but if there is . . . then I'm just saying that if you want to call them . . . or you want me to call them . . . just to let them know that you're O—'

'I am OK. I'm fine.' She picked up her paintbrush. 'So . . . if it's OK with you . . .?'

She turned her back on him and climbed back up the ladder.

He sighed.

Fuck it. At least he'd tried.

26

'You're late.'

Mackenzie Grew glared at him from inside the sparkling red Jag. A flash of white teeth, a pop of central locking. Frankie got in the back. Mackenzie turned round and glared.

'Do I look like a fucking chauffeur?' he said. 'Now shift your arse into the front before I sling you back out.'

He was big enough to as well. Frankie did as he was told, feeling a right fucking plonker.

'Clunk-click. Buckle up,' Mackenzie warned him. 'Don't want the fucking rozzers pulling us over, do we?'

Frankie fastened his seatbelt and Mackenzie Grew pulled out into the street.

'Cigarette?' he asked.

Frankie took it. He could smell bacon on Mackenzie's breath as he held out a silver lighter in the shape of a German Luger pistol.

'You've got nice clear skin, son,' he said, glancing over at him. 'Nothing like your brother. Been working out too, I see. Good man. Tommy wasn't wrong when he said that one day you might come in handy, should you ever see the light.'

Clear skin? What the fuck? Was he coming on to him? Jesus. That's all he needed today. And as for *the light?* More like the life. His way of life. The fucking gangster way. The life that got you patent snakeskin shoes, a powder blue Italian suit and a forty-thousand-pound fucking classic motor. Just like Grew.

'How is the snooker business going, by the way?' he asked.

'All right,' said Frankie. He took a long, soothing drag of the smoke. He hit the window button, wound it down. The smell of bacon was making him sick.

'I should pop in some time,' said Mackenzie. 'Have a few frames with you. Just like in the old days, eh?'

The old days? Nights, more like. Yeah, yeah. Frankie remembered, all right. Mackenzie was fucking hard to forget. He'd been a regular for a while, just after Frankie's dad had taken over the club. Him and a bunch of Riley's other boys had used to call in once or twice a week. Always around closing time, after the pubs had shut. A good place for a lock-in and a few more drinks. That had been the Ambassador's rep. Frankie remembered one night when there'd been a scuffle, loud enough to have woken him and Jack upstairs.

Worried for his dad, Frankie had run down and opened the door through to the club. But the old man had been nowhere to be seen. No one had. Next day he'd told Frankie he'd got it all wrong. There'd been no fight. Just some drunken misunderstanding. No one had got hurt. It had all just sounded a lot worse than it really was.

'Must be tough, mind,' said Mackenzie, 'making enough money to keep a place like that going. Especially in a recession and with the way kids' tastes are changing these days. Scruffy buggers in baggy jeans. No idea how to dress. Probably don't even go out at all. Rather take pills and get twatted at home these days, eh? Sitting there playing their fucking Game Boys and whatnots. Got no bloody class. Probably wouldn't even know what a snooker hall was. Makes you wonder,' he flashed Frankie that bright white smile again, 'whether a property like the one you're leasing off of Tommy might not be better off being used for something else. A restaurant, for example. Or an office.'

Frankie said nothing. So this, today, it was about the money. Or a warning about what Frankie owed, anyhow.

'Tommy's looking forward to hearing all about it,' Mackenzie said. 'Your investigation. He's hoping you might have some good news and I'm certainly hoping so too. Because we're all rooting for him, your brother,' he added, as he pulled the Jag smoothly over in a posh-looking street in St James. 'What with him being one of our own.'

Investigation? *One of our own*? What the fuck had Frankie got himself into? This shit storm was going from bad to worse by the second.

'*Et voilà*. Your destination,' Mackenzie said. 'Number twelve.' He lit another smoke and stared dead ahead.

'You not coming?'

'Not really my kind of place.' Mackenzie looked him slowly over again, the same way he had done earlier when he'd lit his cigarette. 'And, who knows, maybe not yours either, eh?'

'What do you mean?'

'You'll see.' Mackenzie tapped his watch – another Breitling, the exact same model Snaresby had been wearing. 'You'd better get your arse in there. He don't like to be kept waiting. And here . . .' he pulled an embossed white business card from his pocket with a flourish '. . . Tommy told me to give you this. My number. In case you need any helping out.'

Helping out? What did that cover? What didn't it? From the bruises on Mackenzie's knuckles, it probably meant trouble for someone. That much was for sure.

27

Frankie stared up at the sandblasted stone building. Wealth. The stonework practically screamed it. Wealth and privilege. Very fucking tasty indeed.

He stared down at the pavement too. At his feet. No point in kidding himself. He was about to cross another bloody line. 'WITNESS'. He'd written it in red ink on the torn scrap of fag packet in his jacket pocket. The second Sharon had confirmed that the cops were convinced this witness of theirs was credible, he'd known it was going to have to be him, not them, who'd have to dig up the truth and find out what this fucker was really about.

Who were they? Why were they lying? Because they were involved themselves? Because they'd murdered Susan Tilley? Or had helped? First things first. He had to find them. Make them talk. And if his little visit to Mo hadn't brought him any nearer to discovering what had really happened to Jack that night, it had taught him this: he could frighten people. Into talking. And *would* frighten them too. No matter who the hell they were. If that's what it took.

Right. Let's do this. He smoothed down his suit, adjusted his tie and walked up the steps and hit the buzzer. Just the one button. Meaning someone owned the whole house. In this part of town, that meant someone filthy rich.

Was this Riley's home? Not likely. People like Riley tended to keep their business activities hidden, off radar, away from the law. And totally separate from their families. The way the old man told it, neither of his great uncles' wives had ever had a clue about what it was they really did for a living. They'd thought their husbands had worked over in Smithfield's for one of the meat supply companies. Which was how come they'd always had so many bloodstains on their knuckles after work.

A crackle of intercom static.

'Hello. How can I help you? Have you got an appointment?' a woman's voice asked.

The soft whir of an electric motor. Frankie glanced up to see a sparkling new cctv camera pivoting on its bracket and focussing in on him.

He said, 'I'm here to see Tommy Riley. His driver just dropped me off.'

Silence. Three seconds, five, ten. Frankie wondered if he might have somehow got the wrong building, and was about to step back onto the pavement to check out the two either side, when the door lock finally buzzed. He pulled the door open. Spotted a whole bunch of bolts retracted in the frame. Electronic. State-of-the-art.

He walked through into a black-and-white chequered hallway. Plush. Light and airy. Very tasty indeed. Bunches of tall fresh flowers – lilies, his mum's favourite – stood on even taller marble plinths either side of a black stone staircase which spiralled up out of sight. It smelt good in here. Not just of flowers. Some kind of expensive perfume or cologne.

Not the only tempting thing here either. A pretty girl, aged nineteen or twenty, dressed in a slim-fitting grey business suit, was sitting at a polished antique mahogany desk.

He smiled. Couldn't help himself. She was that good-looking.

He got a funny little pang of guilt, mind. About Sharon. But she had a boyfriend, right? She'd kicked him out.

He walked up to the desk. 'Hello,' he said, trying on another smile for good measure.

She wasn't impressed. Gave him the same kind of look his bank manager did whenever he tried extending his overdraft.

'And you would be . . .?' She left the word hanging in the air.

'James,' he said, spotting another cctv camera watching him from the corner of the ceiling. 'Frankie James.'

She checked the leather-bound book on the desk. She had a silver padlock hanging from a black velvet choker tied round her pale throat. She caught him staring. Something flashed in her hard brown eyes. Annoyance? Or maybe amusement? Maybe she didn't find him so repellent after all?

'And how about you?' he said. 'What's your name?'

'Chloe.'

'Nice.'

A flicker of a smile. 'Have you visited with us before?'

Visited *with* us? What the hell was that meant to mean? On the surface, her voice was pure Home Counties, but beneath it he detected something rougher, an accent she'd probably spent years working hard to disguise and smooth over, something much more like his own from the streets.

'No.'

'Very well. If you follow the stairs up to the greeting room and make yourself comfortable, one of the girls will come to collect you.'

Greeting room? Girls? OK. Now he got it. What this place was. What Mackenzie had said outside. The need for all the bloody locks and cctv. His thoughts must have shown on his face. Chloe slowly raised an eyebrow at him. Invitingly? Disdainfully? Hard to tell.

'No need to leave a credit card,' she said. 'Today you're here as Mister Riley's guest. I do hope you'll enjoy your stay.'

'Right.'

Something in her expression seemed to be inviting him to say more. Or maybe she was just messing with him. If he'd been in a bar, he'd have bought her a drink. Or asked for her number. But not here. Not with that camera looking down. Just get upstairs. Stop making a dick of yourself. He wasn't here for pleasure. Time to get his game face on.

'Thanks,' he said, turning his back on her and heading up the stairs, the Blakey's on his shoes clicking out an echo with each step. He could feel her watching him. Wanted to turn to see if she was. Managed to resist.

The staircase opened up into a massive, dimly lit room with heavy drapes covering its windows and tapestries hanging off its walls. A bunch of red and black velvet and leather sofas had been placed at different angles, with polished glass and chrome tables in between. Three arched doorways led off to the left, right and centre, each guarded by heavy, beaded curtains.

There was some kind of bar in the middle of the room, covered in glinting bottles, crystal decanters and tumblers. He sat down on a sofa to the left of it. No matter what other people came here for, he was here on business. Might be in trouble too. He needed to remember that. So no getting hammered.

The smell of perfume was even stronger up here. It was warm as well. Muggy. It reminded him of being abroad. Night times here, he reckoned, if you were wrecked enough, you might even end up believing you'd blinked and woken up in Marbella or Greece. Or had even died and gone to heaven. It was that fucking nice.

He heard footsteps. The bead curtains covering the arched doorway opposite hissed aside as two girls came in. The first was tall and Asian-looking. Dazzling green eyes. The other was Latina, with dark curly hair piled up high on top of her head. Both of them were dressed in shimmering long white gowns. Like something off the cover of *Vogue*.

'Hello,' they said in unison, flashing him wide, white smiles.

'Er, hi,' he said.

The Latina sat down next to him. As in right next to him. Pressing her thigh up against his, she stroked her hand across his shoulders. What the . . .? He flinched, making her giggle. He tried shifting away from her a little, but she just moved closer still, working her hand slowly down his arm, gently massaging as she went.

'I like strong men,' she told him.

'What would you like to drink?' asked the Asian girl, pouring herself a whiskey and taking a sip.

'I'm fine,' Frankie said.

She flashed him another smile. 'Tut, tut. You know you really shouldn't ever leave a girl to drink on her own.'

'Or two girls,' said the Latina.

'That's right,' said the Asian girl, 'and whatever the reason for your visit with us today, you must make certain to include us both.'

Finishing her drink, she iced a tumbler and brought it over to Frankie, along with the bottle of whiskey.

'You sure I can't tempt you?' she asked, sitting beside him.

What the hell. He could smell the whiskey on her breath. Maybe just the one. Where was the harm in that?

'Go on then, twist my rubber arm.'

He watched her pour. Then downed it in one, loving the burn of it hitting his empty stomach. Jesus. What time was it? Talk about an early liquid lunch.

She sat down beside him and poured him another. 'There, I think you're now feeling much more homely.'

'You what?'

'She means at home,' said the Latina.

'Yes, Mister Riley said we were to make you feel perfectly at home,' the Asian girl purred in his ear. 'So how do you think is the best way for us to do that?'

Well, there was one easy answer. Stick him in front of a sink full of dirty dishes and a doormat piled high with unpaid bills. That would work a treat. He smiled, but didn't bother sharing the joke.

'And just exactly where is Mister Riley and when's he planning on—' he started to say, before feeling the admittedly not altogether unpleasant sensation of the Asian girl darting her hand down in between his legs. He grabbed her wrist. 'Thanks, but not now, love,' he said.

Not *now*? Charming. Not *ever*, he'd meant. Hookers. All this. Whatever this was. It wasn't his thing, no matter how seductive it all might look. He thought again about what Mickey had said about Jack. About him liking them fresh. All this was just a fucking illusion. Just gangster shit, all covered in gloss.

Another swish of beads, this time from his right.

'Good to see you're making yourself comfortable,' Tommy Riley said. 'And thanks for coming in.'

28

It's not how it looks, Frankie wanted to say. But how *was* it, exactly? He was here, wasn't he? Sitting with them. He pushed the girl's hand away, ignoring her pouting look, as she sat back away from him and sparked up a cigarette.

The Latina girl walked over to Riley and snaked her arms round his neck.

'Maybe later, love,' he said. 'Me and young Frankie here have got some business to discuss first.'

'Why can't you both stay here with us?' she said.

'Patience, patience,' he told her. 'I'm sure Frankie's looking forward to spending some more time with you afterwards too.'

'Probably not, in fact,' said Frankie, getting up.

'Oh?'

'There's things I need to be doing. As soon as we're finished talking, I'll have to be off.'

'And there was me thinking you were having a bit of fun.' He shot the Asian girl on the sofa a sour look.

'This way,' he told Frankie, setting off back through the archway he'd just come through.

Frankie followed him, down a long corridor covered with dark wallpaper and a series of closed, numbered doors.

'You own this place?' he asked.

'Let's just say I'm a shareholder.'

'The lap dance club not big enough for you?'

'Different kind of business. That's public. All about looking. This is different. About doing.'

'A brothel,' Frankie said.

Riley wagged his finger, continuing to walk. 'Ah-ah. That would be illegal. The girls who live here, they're just renting rooms . . . like in a nice big house share, as far as I know . . .'

No doubt as far as the law knew too. Not that they'd stick their noses in round here anyway. Apart from for fringe benefits. Riley had probably paid the bastards off handsomely to keep officially away.

'They certainly all seem to enjoy being here,' Riley said. 'Right from the reception up . . .'

The way he said it. Had it been him looking down that cctv lens at Frankie in reception just now?

'Them two back there not to your liking, then?' Riley asked, pushing through another beaded curtain at the end of the corridor.

'No, it's not that . . .' Frankie joined him in another lounge area, much smaller than the first, with two sofas either side of a brass pole running from the floor to the ceiling. 'I just don't. With them.'

'With who? With ladies?' A note of surprise in Riley's voice.

'No, with hookers.'

'Careful, son,' Riley warned, sitting down on one of the sofas and pointing at the other where Frankie should sit. 'The girls here are escorts, not hookers. Hookers are what you get sucking off blokes round the backs of pubs for a fix. Don't let any of these girls here catch you calling them that, or they'll scratch your fucking eyes out.'

'I'll bear that in mind.'

'You've never been with a pro before then?'

'Never needed to,' Frankie said.

'Needed to what?' Riley asked.

Frankie drained the last of the whiskey from the glass he'd brought with him. 'Pay.'

'It's not about need, son,' Riley said. 'More want. I don't *need* to pay for skirt. There's plenty of women out there who'd let me do God only knows what to them simply for the pleasure of my company, because of who I *am* and what they think being close to me might get them. No, this,' he waved his hand, 'is about *wanting*, wanting something you can't get just anywhere, off just anyone, skills of a professional nature, with the kind of women you normally only see in glossy fucking mags. And I promise you this,' he said, 'once you get a taste for it, you never look back. But who knows? Perhaps we'll yet find something to tickle your fancy after all . . .'

Frankie let the comment go. He hadn't come here for a moral debate. Riley finished his drink and pressed a brass button on the table.

'Hello?' A female voice came through the speaker.

'A bottle of whiskey and some ice for the red room. Oh, and some gear as well. I fancy a toot.' He looked up at Frankie. 'Tell Chloe to bring it up.'

The girl from reception.

'Chloe?' the voice checked.

'Yeah, that's right.' Riley sniffed. He sat back.

'So why did you want to see me?' Frankie said. No point yet in giving away how desperate he was and that he'd been planning on seeing Riley anyway.

'To find how everything's progressing,' Riley said.

'Not good.' No point in lying. 'But not bad either. I think I can see a way forward, but I'm going to need some help.'

Help: the magic word. It worked like a spell on Riley. A spark of satisfaction flashed inside his dark eyes.

'There's a witness.' Frankie said.

'So I hear.'

Frankie wondered again about Snaresby, about the make and model of his watch. Was he in Riley's pocket? Was that how Riley knew? But if he was, then why was he pursuing nailing Jack so hard? Because he had no choice? Because the evidence against him was already so fucking well sewn up?

'A solid one, an' all,' Riley said.

'That's what they say, but I don't fucking believe it.'

'The cops are taking him seriously enough.'

'Him?' Did Riley know that for sure? That the witness was a bloke?

Riley smiled, reading Frankie's mind. 'Her. It. No way of knowing, they've got them wrapped up so tight.'

Was he telling the truth? If he had a source close enough to the police investigation to know that there was a witness, perhaps they were embedded deep enough to be able to identify who that witness was, too.

'I need to know,' Frankie said.

'Just know?'

'To find them.'

A hiss of beads. Frankie turned to see Chloe walking in carrying a silver tray loaded with fresh glasses, a silver ice bucket and a bottle of whiskey, uncapped. She smiled warmly at Riley, but not at Frankie at all. She fixed them both a drink in silence. Then turned to go.

'Wait,' Riley said.

Chloe turned and waited.

'Put on some music,' he said. 'Something nice and mellow.'

She walked over to a stereo system in the corner and put on a CD. Chill-out music. Ibiza style. Elevator jams.

'Now rack us both up a nice fat line, will you?' Riley said.

She picked up the wrap that had been placed discreetly beside the ice bucket and unfolded it.

'Not for me,' Frankie said. 'I don't.'

'Don't any more, more like,' Riley said. 'At least that's what I've heard.'

Off who? When? Looked like Riley had been conducting his own little investigation. Into Frankie's past.

'Same difference,' Frankie said. 'But no thanks,' he told Chloe. 'Not for me.'

'Suit yourself,' Riley said. 'But at least you still like a drink.' He sloshed another slug into Frankie's glass, before nodding at Chloe, who chopped him out a long fat line on the table.

'Cheers, love. Now scoot,' he told her. 'Me and Frankie here, we need to have a private chat.'

Frankie watched her go. Riley hoovered up the gear with a rolled-up fifty.

'Phwoar, fucking lovely,' he said, wiping his glistening eyes, before leaning in towards Frankie. 'Now this person you're keen to meet,' he said. 'It might be possible to discover where they are.'

Frankie waited. His pulse began to race.

'But there'll be a cost,' Riley said.

'I thought you said you'd help me . . . That proving Jack's innocence and getting the cops off your back was in your interest too.'

'I did and it is and I will, but this is different. Doing this particular favour for you now, I'm personally putting my own neck on the line.'

Was this about money? About how much the information was going to cost? 'How much?' Frankie said. However much it was, he'd find it.

Riley laughed. 'No, no, no, son. I don't need your money. Particularly,' he added, 'when you ain't even got enough to pay your rent on the club.'

'Yeah, about that . . .' Frankie started to say.

Riley cut him off with a wave of his hand. 'We can talk about that when this is over. But back to this favour: when I say cost, I don't mean money. I'll cover that part myself.'

'Then what is it you want?' Frankie said.

'You.' Riley stared at him,

'Me?'

'Your time. Not all of it. I do hear you when you tell me that you're not ready to work for me.'

Ready. Another dangerous word. Every bit as bad as *yet*. Riley was pretty fucking sure of himself, wasn't he? That one day Frankie would change his mind.

'A favour, Frankie,' he explained. 'Me doing this for you now means you're going to owe me a favour, and one day – and I don't even yet know myself when it'll be – but one day I'm going to call it in. So . . .' he said, looking Frankie over. 'How about it, son? Have we got a deal?'

He leant forward across the table and stuck his hand out. Again Frankie hesitated, but again he took it. And shook. What other fucking choice did he have?

They talked a while longer. Both had another whiskey. Riley did another line. Frankie told him about the petrol and the note left at the club. Riley seemed genuinely surprised, angry even, which rather muddied Frankie's theory about Snaresby maybe being in his pocket, because he'd have already told him, surely, if he was. It left him wondering too, if it wasn't Snaresby who'd be getting him information about this witness, then who the hell was it, and how?

Finally, Riley walked Frankie back to the top of the stairs and sent him on his way. As Frankie walked back down to reception, he became aware of Chloe watching him. She got up from behind her desk and walked over to join him at the front door.

'It was nice meeting you,' she said, shaking him professionally by the hand.

He'd not been expecting that. Looking down, he saw she'd palmed him something, a folded up piece of paper.

He said, 'Thanks. You too.'

'I don't work here like the rest of them, you know,' she said. 'Not in *that* way.'

She meant she wasn't a pro.

He told her, 'Right.'

'But you don't seem interested in, well, that kind of girl either.'

'I'm not.'

She smiled. Seemed genuine. Nothing like the business one she'd given him before.

'So maybe I'll see you around,' she said.

A question? A promise? Shit. He couldn't tell.

'Yeah,' he said. 'Sure. Why not?'

She opened the door for him. He stepped out blinking into the sunlight, suddenly feeling the whiskey, wondering what else he should say. But by the time he turned back round, the door was already shutting, and she was nowhere to be seen.

As he walked up the street back towards Soho, he unfolded the piece of paper she'd given him. It had her phone number on it.

He pictured Sharon, how she'd been last night, lying there afterwards, asleep in the moonlit bed beside him. He remembered gently pushing away a lock of her hair from her face before spooning up close behind her, and how she'd sighed so deeply and that had been the last sound he'd heard before he'd slept.

But he remembered her this morning too. How she'd looked when they'd said goodbye. More like how she hadn't really looked at him at all. And when he drew level a few seconds later with a Borough of Westminster bin set into the curved cast-iron railing of a private garden square, instead of chucking Chloe's number into it, he folded it up and put it back in his pocket to keep.

29

A prisoner on remand is allowed three one-hour visits a week. That's what Kind Regards had told Frankie when he'd told him the good news that Jack was being put on remand here in London. Didn't sound like a lot. That's what Frankie had reckoned sitting there in Kind Regards' snug little office when he'd first heard it. But sitting here now in the Wandsworth Visitors' Centre waiting for Jack to turn up, it felt like an eternity.

Doing time. Not a cliché at all. He'd learned that all right, the last ten minutes he'd been sat here, sipping this piss-awful, sand-flavoured coffee. More like a truism. Which, if his memory from his aborted English A-level served him correctly, meant a phrase that captured the very essence of something and couldn't be improved on, no matter how many times it was used.

Time here passed evilly slow. Slower than on a deserted railway platform when you were wasted and tying to get home. Slower than watching an empty driveway for your mum to come home. Slower than it took for a jury to return a verdict at a trial.

He looked round the faces of the other prisoners and their visitors. It wasn't shame you saw in here. Or guilt or resentment or hate. It was just fucking unhappiness. Sadness. Of a mum for a son she still remembered as a school kid in shorts. Of a girlfriend for her man who she wanted back home. Of poor people divided because of desperation, stupid mistakes and miscarriages of justice. The same horrible sick sadness Frankie felt for the old man but had never had the guts to say out loud whenever he'd visited him, in case it had embarrassed him and made him look like a twat.

He'd hoped Jack and the old man might have ended up in the same prison. He'd pictured them together at meal times, or watching films in some echoing, flickering communal hall, or reading well-thumbed books in a dusty library – all fucking clichés, of course, culled out of *Shawshank*, which he'd watched in the Odeon in Leicester Square only last year with Jack. That's how he'd seen them. Like Morgan Freeman and Tim Robbins, uniting together to get through this shit, unbeaten and defiant to the end. But he was glad now that they were apart. Because no matter what he said, the old man would hate it. Seeing his boy here, not as a visitor, but on the same side of the bars as him.

He looked up from the table, hearing the door buzz. It was Jack. Pissing hell, he looked like shit. His skin was sallow and there were dark rings around his eyes. Withdrawal. From booze as well as drugs.

Frankie's stomach churned. This was all so fucking wrong. This was his little brother, but now he was dressed like their dad. For an awful instant Frankie thought he might burst into tears, just start blubbing and not be able to stop.

He forced a smile. Don't do it. He knew Jack too well. He took his cue from other people. If he saw panic in Frankie's eyes, he'd panic too. Frankie had to show him confidence instead.

'All right,' Jack said, sitting down opposite him, grinning at him like he didn't mean it, like he'd just been told to for a photo when he wasn't in the mood.

'Yeah, you?'

'Bearing up.'

He didn't look it. He looked like hell. At least he didn't have any bruises on him, though. Either from the pigs or from here inside.

'I brought you something,' Frankie said.

Jack grinned, seeing what Frankie had just pushed across the table to him. It was good to see him smiling.

'A KitKat?' he said.

'It was either that or a Snickers, mate,' Frankie said, nodding over at the near-empty vending machine in the corner of the room up against the scuffed lemon yellow wall. 'But you know how peanuts make you fart.'

'I was rather hoping for a cake.'

'Yeah? Let me guess: with a file inside.'

'Nah,' said Jack, 'the walls here are way too thick. But I'd have settled for a bag of draw.'

He meant it too. It wasn't just his skin that looked like death. His eyes were shot to shit, like he'd been pricking them with needles.

'I would if I could,' Frankie said. He meant it. Didn't matter how much he hated Jack being into drugs as much as he was. Anything to distract him in here would be better than nothing at all.

'They search you on the way in?'

'Same rules as with visiting Dad.'

'Yeah, only I'm not fucking guilty.'

'Don't ever fucking say that.'

'But I'm not,' Jack protested.

'I don't mean that. I mean what you're implying. About him. About Dad. He's not fucking guilty either, OK?'

'I know that, but—'

'But nothing. He. Did. Not. Do. It.'

A mantra Frankie had spelt out to Jack a thousand times. Still hadn't sunk in. Frankie believed his dad, believed him with all his soul that he'd not been part of the gang that had done that robbery. But Jack was different. Even back then, during the trial, he'd always treated their father's protestations of innocence with a pinch of salt. Like it was all part of some elaborate game where no one really believed a word of what the old man was saying, but you had to pretend you did and keep on showing a united front, because that was the story he was trying to sell to the jury. Frankie had even caught Jack boasting once, about how the old man had committed plenty more crimes he'd never been caught for. He'd dragged him out of the pub they'd been in and had given him a right talking-to. It had taken all his strength not to slap him down, he'd been that pissed off.

'I didn't mean it that way,' Jack said. 'I meant that I've not even been found guilty yet by a court. I've not even been tried and here I still am being treated like this. I'm telling you, Frankie, it's not fucking right.'

'I'm doing all I can.'

'Like what?' The way he said it, it was like an accusation.

'Like getting you a decent brief. The best money can buy.'

'How are you paying for it?'

'Don't you worry about that.' The advert for the car was running in next week's *Exchange & Mart* and *Auto Trader*. With any luck Frankie would make enough off it to pay Straight Eddie back before the interest piled up too high on the loan. As for the rest of the money he needed to pay the brief's fees, God only knew where he was going to get that. But get it he would. Even if it meant losing the club and selling off everything that he owned.

'And what good's that gonna do?' said Jack. 'The cops say I'm fucked, Frankie. Say I haven't got a chance.'

Frankie thought about Sharon. Had she been there at the station when Jack was interviewed? Had she interviewed him herself? He thought about telling Jack about her, but didn't. He'd fly off the handle if he knew they'd got close. Maybe even say something and get her in the shit. And besides, what did it matter now, when they weren't going to be seeing each other any more?

'Yeah, well I'm gonna prove them wrong,' Frankie said.

'How?'

'By finding out what really happened.'

'But the blood . . .'

'Forget the blood. Someone put that on you. The same bastard who nicked your car.' Frankie still wanted to believe this was true, but he made sure to watch Jack's face damn close as he told him, praying it wouldn't tell him otherwise.

'I tried telling them that,' Jack said. 'The cops. I tried telling them that's what must have happened.'

'You any idea who?' He knew Kind Regards had gone over this with him already, but he thought he might as well ask again.

'I don't know. It could be . . . it could be all sorts of people . . .'

All sorts of people that Jack had pissed off.

'I mean someone clever enough to have done it. Someone who wanted Susan Tilley and her grandma dead. Someone who for whatever reason fancied fitting you up for it too.'

'No. There's no one I know who knows her. No one at all.' An idea flashed in his eyes. 'What about my car? Have they found it? Maybe whoever took it, they've still got it and that will prove what they did . . .'

'Maybe.' Or maybe not. Because whoever had been smart enough to set Jack up like this would have been smart enough not to link themselves to his car.

'I will get you out,' Frankie said.

'You promise?' Jack's voice wavered as he said it. He was looking at Frankie like a little kid, like Frankie just by virtue of being his big brother had the power to make anything happen, to sort out a bully at school, to take him for a ride on his brand new bike, to get him out of prison and give him his old life back, that all he had to do was say the word.

Frankie told him, 'Yes.'

And there, the second he said it, he saw the tension draining from Jack's shoulders. He was going to be all right, that's what he was thinking. His big brother Frankie was going to make this all go away. He smiled, not like the smile he'd given Frankie when he'd got here. A real smile this time. One from the heart, not front. He picked up the KitKat and slipped off the red-and-white paper wrapper. He smoothed out the tinfoil before running the nail of his forefinger down the centre of the bar and snapping it cleanly in two.

'Brothers,' he said, handing one half to Frankie.

'Brothers,' Frankie nodded. It was something they'd been doing for as far back as he could remember.

They ate in silence for a moment. Then Frankie went and got them both a can of Coke.

'You got a cell mate?' he asked, sitting back down.

'Yes, mate. It measures exactly ten foot cubed.'

'Hah bloody hah,' Frankie said. 'I mean it. Who you in with?'

'Don't worry, they're not called Bubba, if that's what you're worrying about,' Jack said. 'Nah, I've lucked out, to tell you the truth. I was in with a bit of a prick the first night I was here. A right wanker, to tell you the truth. Covered in cuts all over his arms. Kept telling me he had a Stanley knife hidden somewhere in the cell.'

Frankie felt his hackles rising. 'Did he threaten you?'

'Not really. He was more mad, like. But it doesn't matter now anyway.'

'Yeah, and why's that?'

'He took a tumble down a set of stairs yesterday morning. Slipped and broke three ribs and his ankle too. Gonna be laid up in a hospital for months, they reckon. Honestly, would you believe it? It's like I've got a guardian angel watching over me or something. And even better than that, guess who's moved in instead of him?'

'Who?'

'Stanley Lomax. Remember him? Got done for GBH two years ago.'

Frankie remembered him all right. A huge bastard. One of Riley's boys. Meaning Riley was keeping his end of the bargain on this much at least. Jack now had a guard hard enough to take on any of Hamilton's boys here on the inside who might think about making a move. They'd maybe even done for the bloke in the hospital too.

'And you know what else?' Jack said. 'Even better than that, Stanley told me Riley said to say hi. Like, personally, you know? Told me not to worry. I said he was all right, didn't I? Back when you were slagging me off for working for him? I knew he wouldn't let me down.'

He said it with a level of pride that got right up Frankie's nose. Self-justification too. He'd not learned his lesson at all. Still worshipped the ground Tommy Riley walked on. Still wanted to be one of his boys.

'I want to talk to you about the night it all happened,' Frankie said.

'But I already told you, I don't remember . . .'

Frankie nodded, watching him closely now. 'Mickey said he sold you something in the Albion.'

'He did?'

'Speed. Do you remember that?'

Jack's face scrunched up. 'Yeah. I think I do now. Something weird about the way it looked.'

'It was blue.

A flash of recognition in Jack's eyes. 'That's right . . . Hey . . . hang on . . .' He clenched his fists. 'You don't think that had anything to do with—'

'You blacking out and not remembering? No, I don't. In fact, I already checked.'

'But how? With who?'

'Mo.'

'Mo Bishara?'

'Keep your fucking voice down,' Frankie said. Mo was enough of a face to have connections in here, just the same as Riley and Hamilton.

Jack nodded nervously.

'I went to see him. And you keep that to your fucking self all right, because I wasn't very nice and I was wearing a mask.'

What little colour there was, drained from Jack's face.

'And that shit of his that Mickey sold you, it doesn't cause amnesia or anything like what happened to you, and it doesn't make people go Norman fucking Bates either in case you're worried about that.'

'So it couldn't have made me do anything that I'd later forget?'

'No. And you've never had any blackouts before, have you?'

'Never. I mean, sure, the odd hour if I've drunk too much, but never anything like this. Not a whole bloody night.'

'And you promise me. You fucking promise me that's the truth. You still remember nothing. Nothing at all?' Frankie watched his face, his eyes again.

'Nothing.'

Not a wrinkle. Not a flicker of doubt in his eyes.

'Right. Which is why I'm thinking that some other bastard

slipped you something else. It's the only explanation there can be.'

'But who? When?'

'That condom on your floor . . . Mickey said after you were drinking with him in the Albion he thought you might have been heading off to meet someone – some girl.' The kind of new girl on the block you liked helping break in. Frankie shivered with revulsion. No point in bringing that up now, though. Neither the time nor the place. He'd fucking have words with him when he got back home.

Something about Jack's expression, it had changed.

'What is it?' Frankie asked. 'You remember something?'

'Yeah. I think so. But . . .'

'What?'

Jack growled, clawing at his hair, like he might somehow drag the facts from his head by force.

'It's so fucking hazy, but Stav . . . I think it might have had something to do with Stav . . . I can almost see his face . . . yeah, I reckon I might have gone over to his . . .'

Stav Christoforou. One of Jack's newer associates. Frankie had had the dubious pleasure of meeting him a couple of times when Jack had brought him into the Ambassador.

'He work for Riley?' Frankie asked, doubting it. Riley at least had standards. He liked his boys to dress smart. Whereas Stav Christoforou was a scruffy bastard, all trainers and hoodies and always in shades, whatever the weather, no matter if he was inside or out.

Jack said, 'No . . .'

But he looked evasive, like something was up.

'So who does he work for?' Frankie asked.

'Mo.'

'Mo Bishara?'

Jack nodded.

'Doing what?' Frankie asked. 'Dealing?

'Yeah, out at his mother's old place. He runs a kind of a club. You know. A shebeen.'

'And that's where you reckon you might have gone, is it? After leaving the Albion.'

'I dunno. But yeah. It's possible. I mean, I think so. I think earlier on, that afternoon . . . he might have rung me. Said he had some bird he wanted me to meet.'

Not just dealing then, pimping.

'But Jesus, Frankie, I can't even remember if I even went there or not.'

He went quiet then. Just sat there. A horrible, pained look on his face. That was it. Frankie knew it. That was all he had to give.

'The old woman,' he then said, looking up, his lip trembling, 'is she . . .? Has she come round?'

'No.'

'Fuck.'

Frankie heard Jack's knuckles crack, he was bunching his fists so hard.

'It's not your fault,' Frankie told him. 'She might still be OK.'

'It's not that,' he said. 'I don't give a fuck about her. I mean, I do. Of course I bloody do. But . . .'

'But what?'

'But if she woke up, then she might be able to tell them. That I didn't do it. To finger whoever the bastard was that did.'

Frankie was still hoping the same thing too.

'Well, let's just keep out fingers crossed that she does, all right,' he said. 'And, in the meantime, I'm gonna go and have a chat with your mate, Stav.'

30

A quick call to Mackenzie Grew had pointed Frankie in Stav's direction. At the end of their little chat, Mackenzie had cracked some joke about how quickly Frankie had lowered his standards. Frankie hadn't got it at the time. He did now.

The basement of Stav's place off Portobello Road was a prize-winning shit pit. A world-a-bloody-part from Riley's bordello over on St James. Mackenzie had told Frankie this was the same house where Stav had grown up. Where his strict, rich Greek Orthodox mum had lived out a saintly existence, before carking it from cancer a couple of years back.

Well, bloody hell. The old bird would be turning in her grave if she could see it now. Or smell it. It reeked. And not of anything so traditional and tasty as moussaka or kleftico. More like the sour death stench of crack, hash and piss. Smoke curled and candles flickered, casting twisting shadows on the mildewed walls.

Tip-fucking-toe. Frankie trod carefully, as he headed for the back of the room. Christ knew how many needles were lying around. Junkies and caners were muttering and tweaking all over the shop, rolling, cutting, burning, toking and snorting, draped over tattered, stained sofas and chairs, or just lying plain fucked-up and passed out on the floor.

Spliffs and pipes crackled and glowed. Faces peered out at him like ghouls. Thank God for the thrum of drum and bass. Meant he could ignore the voices calling out to him, begging him for fuck knows what. He pulled his hood down lower over his brow. Good job he'd worn his trackie, not a suit. These wasters would have skinned him alive.

He moved on into a short, stinking corridor, passing gaping dark doorways on his left and right. A shit-spattered toilet. A well-monged couple fucking in a bath. A half-naked geezer unconscious in a corner, vomit hanging from his chin.

A bare bulb lit the stairs leading up at the end of the corridor. Frankie took them two at a time, hairs standing up on the back of his neck, shivering at what he'd left down there behind him. Don't you run, you fucking pussy. But, fuck, it was tempting. Felt like he sometimes had as a kid late at night, terrified on the way back from the khazi that a witch might be racing up behind him to scrag him with her claws.

A gum-chewing heavy stood watch with a radio and a three-foot-long South African baton-torch by the reinforced steel door at the top of the stairs. Frankie lowered his hood. Let the fucker see his face: filth-free and clean-shaven, skin that had seen a vitamin in the past year, not like those yoghurt-skinned ghosts downstairs.

'You friend of Mr Riley, yes?' Accent was Russian or something. Looked like he could handle himself. A brick shithouse with bloodshot eyes.

'Yeah, that's right.'

Was what he'd told the goon on the door outside, who must have radioed ahead. His connection with Riley . . . Frankie figured it would give him some protection at least. Even if Stav worked for Mo and not Tommy, he'd still not cross him, not unless he was given no choice.

'We have no weapons policy. To make sure no trouble. Yes?'

Was this geezer going to finish every fucking sentence with the word *yes*?

'Yeah, sure. Whatever,' Frankie said.

He let the fucker frisk him down. Speedy. Professional. Like a cop. Probably what he'd once been back in whatever country he'd come from.

'Second door on the right, yes?' said the gorilla.

'Cheers.'

Frankie walked on past him into another corridor. Better lit. Actual electrics instead of bloody candle power. Less of a stink too. Thank god. Cleaner as well, but not much. What had probably once been lush thick red carpets were stained and patterned with cigarette burns and what he hoped were just food stains. Gang tags littered the flowery wallpaper. A spray of blood too. Weirdly almost the exact same shape as Italy. Quality.

Beats. A hubbub of voices. First door he passed on the right was the shebeen Jack had mentioned. A bar, people getting hammered. A classier version of what was happening downstairs.

The second door on the right led into a big ground-floor living room with a bay window. Hard to guess whether it was at the front or back of the building. A bunch of welded stainless steel panels blocked the view.

Spliff smoke hung heavy in the air. A motley crew of scowling hoodies and hard-looking girls sprawled on sofas and chairs in front of a giant TV. Sonic the Hedgehog was chiming his way through a maze of rings. Most of the girls were transfixed. The guys, though, they watched Frankie. Clear from their nasty little piggy eyes that they already knew who he was. Why he was here. Because of Jack.

Stav. He was slouched on a sofa a little apart from the rest of his crew, a copy of the *Racing Post* spread out on his lap.

'You,' he said, staring at Frankie from behind a pair of Ray-Bans.

Shades. At night. What a dick. Had lost weight since Frankie had last seen him. Too much fucking coke.

'Yeah, me,' Frankie said.

'So I hear you're rolling with Riley now? That how it is?'

'Something like that.'

'Sorry to hear about your brother.'

The way he said it. Like Jack was dead. He didn't look sorry. Didn't look like he gave a shit. Frankie felt the urge to just pick him up and lay into him. Use his boots and fists to find out what he needed to know.

Forget it. Keep calm. Stav might be a dick, but this was his place. Mess with him here and Frankie doubted he'd make it out alive. Who knew what kind of weaponry these toe-rags were packing? Or that Russian outside. Fact was, he had to play this smart. Even threatening Stav could get him in all kinds of grief.

'He doing all right?' Stav asked.

'Holding up just fine.' He scoped the room again. Two of Stav's boys were up on their feet, still watching him. 'He used to like it round here, didn't he?' Frankie said.

'Sometimes . . .'

Frankie let the silence hang. See if Stav would give anything away. Like, had Jack come here that night? And for what? To meet some girl? But all Stav did was smile.

'So what can I do you for?' he said.

'I'm looking for a girl.'

'Ah.' Another smile, stickier somehow. 'Then you're in the right place.' He stretched out his long, tattooed arms along the back of the sofa, palms up, in some kind of cheesy *mi casa es tu casa* gesture he must have pilfered off some gangster show on TV. Meaning what? That all the women in here were for hire? *Were* they all pros? Hard to tell. Another difference between Riley's place and this. The girls here were wasted. Half of them looked sick too, with God knows what. Had Jack really come here? For that? How could he have been so fucking stupid? Frankie kicked himself again for not having kept a closer eye on him. His responsibility. He'd let him down. Fucking wouldn't again when he got him out. Would get him back to who he was. The nice kid he'd once been.

'Oi, you. New skank. Keira,' Stav shouted across at the last girl Frankie had looked at.

'What?' She turned round, a cigarette drooping from her mouth.

'Show him your fucking tits.'

'Ha, ha.' She shot him a look of disgust, chewing hard on her gum, taking a drag on her cigarette and funnelling smoke in his direction.

'Do I look like I'm fucking joking?'

Stav's hand darted into a takeaway tin on the sofa beside him. He snatched out a pork ball or something horrible like that and chucked it at her, just missing her head. She hissed something under her breath.

'It's all right,' Frankie said. 'I don't— '

'No, it's not fucking all right.' Stav was already up. 'Fucking do it, bitch,' he said.

For a second, she looked like she was about to tell him to fuck off. But then something in her just wilted away. She started to pull up her T-shirt.

'With a fucking smile, skank, like you fucking mean it,' Stav told her.

She smiled at him like she wanted him dead.

'Not me, you fucking slag,' he snapped. 'Him. The guy who's about to decide whether he's gonna take you upstairs and fuck your brains out or not.'

She turned her dead smile on Frankie. Her eyes were dead too, black make-up making them look like the sockets of a skull. She pulled her T-shirt up all the way up to her neck. Tattoos. No bra. The hoodie standing next to her reached round and gave her a good, hard squeeze. Stav laughed like it was the funniest joke in the world.

'What do you reckon, then?' he asked Frankie, sniffing, sitting back down, and taking a slurp from his bottle of Sol.

'It's a particular girl I'm after,' Frankie said.

'Oh, yeah?'

The T-shirt girl rolled her eyes and pulled her top back down, before slumping on the sofa and staring vacant-eyed up at the screen.

'The last time my brother was here . . . the night he got arrested?'

Stav's face gave nothing away.

'. . . it was to see one of your girls . . .'

'Says who?'

'Says him. He told me you called him. Told him there was a new girl he might like. Fresh . . .'

The first sign of surprise on Stav's face. He tried to cover it up by lighting a cigarette.

He mumbled, 'So?'

So he *had* called Jack. Meaning Jack probably *had* come here.

'So who was she?' Frankie said.

Stav shrugged. 'Just some bitch. I don't even remember her name.'

You fucking liar. Frankie looked around. 'She here now? Don't worry,' he added, pulling out his silver billfold and leafing through the notes, 'I'm happy to pay for her time.' Nice and loud, so everyone could hear.

'Nah. She moved on.'

Moved on or was sent on? 'Where?' asked Frankie, still slowly flicked through the bills. ''Cos I'm happy to pay for that information too.'

'How should I fucking know?' snapped Stav. 'Or fucking care? I don't remember your brother being here that night. I don't remember nothing like that at all. Now, you spying or buying, bruv?' he said. 'Because this here's a place of business and if you got no real business being here then it's time you were moving on.'

Finally, he took his shades off and stared at Frankie. Had eyes like piss-holes in the snow.

'No, *bruv*,' Frankie said. 'I'm done.'

31

Instead of heading for Ladbroke Grove tube, Frankie crossed over into Portobello Road. The pink evening sky was darkening into blood. A reek of rotting fruit and veg. The pavements were slippery with it. Bins overflowed with polystyrene and cardboard packaging. The last of the market stallholders were packing up and the tourists and shoppers were traipsing back up towards Notting Hill. Taking their places were drinkers, dealers, and teenage gangsters, criss-crossing between the pubs, hissing past on BMXs, running errands between the bookies, bars and estates.

Time for some neck oil. Then some grub. He couldn't remember the last time he'd eaten. His stomach growled as he passed the S&M café, which served up sausage, mash and gravy in a hundred different ways. Tasty. A quality joint. Maybe later. A drink first. Or three. To calm himself down. Let himself think.

He thought back to Stav's, to those people, those ghosts, as good as dead al-fucking-ready, down in that basement. He glanced back over his shoulder, suddenly getting the idea he was being followed. But the only people he saw were a couple of dealers standing sentry outside a barber shop and a hooker silhouetted in the piss-yellow light of a streetlamp.

Paranoia. No one who looked like Stav or his heavies. No one who might have followed him from Stav's with thoughts of giving him a shoeing to warn him off, or relieve him of his wedge.

But something back there was fucked up, all right. Because for a lowlife heel like Stav to turn down money in exchange for information, well – Frankie couldn't help thinking, as that Russian gorilla had marched him back out onto the street – it meant someone was either paying Stav to button his lip, or else had put the frighteners on him. Big style.

But why? If Jack had gone there that night to meet a girl, then why was Stav pretending he hadn't? Because he didn't want his business getting mixed up in some murder enquiry? Fair enough. Or because he, or some other wanker he knew, had been involved in helping set Jack up?

Frankie ducked into the First Floor bar, an old haunt. Him and some of his old mates had used to come here drinking and hanging out and scoring dope off street dealers when they'd still been at school. Had ended up being ripped off more often than not. He remembered how he'd once bought an eighth of 'Moroccan squidgy', only to discover when him and his mates had tried smoking it that it was Branston fucking pickle. What a tool.

The First Floor had been tarted up since his last visit, mind. A posher clientele in here tonight. Notting Hillbillies. Even a couple of yanks if his ears weren't deceiving him. The old Notting Hill melting pot, eh? That much at least hadn't changed.

He ordered a pint. Then another. Passed the time of day with the barman, who recognised him from back in the day. But other than that he was glad to see there was no one else here he knew. Just as well. Not in the mood for idle chitchat. Couldn't stop thinking about what he'd just found out. Or *not* found out, which was probably a whole lot nearer the truth. He still didn't know where this girl Stav had put Jack in touch with was. Didn't even have a name.

Stav *must* know. So get hold of him on his own, like he had done Mo? Have a word. Make him talk. Or not. Because there was a big problem, wasn't there? Stav's connection to Mo. Pull the same masked vigilante stunt on him and the chances of the two of them not putting two and two together and making Frankie were pretty fucking slim. Sooner or later they'd work out they'd been attacked by the same man. Demanding the same fucking information about what had happened to Jack. And after Frankie's unmasked visit to Stav just now demanding the same, only a matter of time before they pinned it on him.

So if terrifying the girl's name out of Stav wasn't an option, what was? Should he call Sharon? Tell her that Stav had put Jack in touch with some girl? Maybe the same girl who might have been the cause of that condom on Jack's floor? But what would be the point? What would that prove?

He drained his pint and headed back outside. Set his sights on the next pub along Portobello Road. Another old favourite. The Castle. Nearly empty inside. Still scruffy as fuck. Nada gentrification in here. Just a couple of lads playing darts. A girl on her own at the bar. She gave him a smile as he ordered another pint and a whiskey chaser. She was dressed down, scruffy, but when she asked him for a light, her accent gave her away.

He smiled back, watching her inhale. He'd once gone out with a girl like her, a trustafarian called Devina who'd lived in a house in Chelsea. A whole fucking house to herself, mind, that her banker daddy had bought her. They'd not gone out for long. She'd just been slumming it. Had liked the idea of him being a convicted gangster's son more than she'd liked him for himself. He'd heard she'd since married an army officer and was living in Dubai.

Been there, done that. He left the girl at the bar. Took his pint over to a quiet table in the corner. The girl's eyes followed him, but he gazed past her and out through the pub's open door at the people walking by and the stars coming out in the night sky.

Then he spotted her. Not the rich girl. The opposite. The kind of girl the rich girl wanted to look like, so she could fit in round here, but whose lifestyle she'd not be able to hack for a day.

The girl who walked in now was the skull-faced girl from Stav's, the one who'd stripped off her top at Stav's command. She sat down on one of the knackered leather stools at the bar and fished a packet of cigarettes out of her torn denim bag.

She looked slowly around, everywhere apart from where he was sitting. But he wasn't buying it. No way was this a coincidence. What was the line from that *Casablanca* film that the old man always liked watching at Christmas? *Of all the gin joints, in all the towns, in all the world, she walks into mine.* Frankie necked his drink. That feeling he'd had someone had been following him earlier on. He'd been bang on right.

'What you drinking, love?' he said, standing next to her. *Keira.* Yeah, Keira. That's what Stav had called her, right?

The trustafarian girl shot Frankie a look that clearly said, *So what's she got that I haven't?*

A nasty black eye for one thing. Keira's sludge of dark make-up wasn't just a fashion choice. Her right eye was cut on the brow. Bruised beneath. Not fresh. Perhaps a week old. She'd been hit and hit hard. Either a present from a punter. Or that scumbag, Stav.

'You still paying?' she asked.

She didn't just mean for her drink. For information. What he'd said he'd pay for back at Stav's.

'Sure.'

'Double vodka then. Straight up.' She was English. Northern.

He bought himself another pint and took her back to his table.

'How much?' she said.

'A hundred. If I like what I hear . . .'

'Make it two,' she said, sparking up a fag and blowing smoke hard at him, letting him know he didn't scare her one bit.

'One fifty.'

'Two, or I walk.'

'All right,' he said. 'Done.' He just had been.

'But whatever I tell you, you don't fucking tell Stav, OK? Or he'll fucking kill me.'

'Fine.'

'Star,' she said.

'What?'

'Her name. The girl you're looking for. The one who went with him . . . with your brother that night at Stav's . . . she's called Star.'

So Jack *was* there. At Stav's. His addled memory hadn't served him wrong. Fuck. Frankie felt his heartbeat race. This could be it. The alibi he was after. What if Jack had still been at Stav's at the same time he was meant to have been killing Susan Tilley? Then he might not even need to find this Star. If Keira had seen him there with this Star, then she could provide an alibi too. The two of them could put him in the clear.

'How long was he there with her? What time did he get there? And leave?'

She shrugged.

'Dunno. I mean, most blokes, when they come there, they go upstairs, don't they? Or hang about in the bar a bit first and then head up. But her and your brother . . . that night, they went off somewhere else.'

'Where?'

'I don't know.'

Bollocks. 'What time?'

'I don't know. Evening.'

204

'But when exactly?' He stared hard into her eyes. 'Please,' he said. 'It's important.'

'I'd tell you if I could, but . . . it's fucking hard to tell in there, isn't it? The way all the windows are blocked. You can't even see if it's still light outside. And look,' she said, showing him her skinny wrists, 'I've got no watch.'

Calm. Keep calm. Think. All right. So Keira wasn't going to provide him with any kind of alibi about where Jack was. But there was still this other girl. This Star. Who'd gone off with him. To somewhere else. Her place, if she had one? What if she'd been with Jack when he was meant to have been at Tilley's grandmother's? What if he could get her to talk? Then he still had his alibi.

But . . . fuck . . . what if she was in deeper in this? Deeper than just a trick? What if she was somehow *involved*? What if she'd gone back with Jack to his place, not just to fuck him, but for something else? Something to do with all that blood?

'And this . . . Star . . .' he said.

Keira smiled. 'I know. Stupid name, right?' Her smile faded. 'But she wasn't stupid. She was sweet. Or at least used to be. Until Stav bought her.'

'*Bought* her?' What the fuck?

'He owned her,' she explained.

'Owned?'

'Her previous guy. He owed Stav money. Last week. He gave Star to Stav until she paid off his debt. Me and her both.'

'You knew her before then? Before she started working for him?'

'Yeah, but not like what you saw tonight – not there – we used to work hotel bars . . .'

Classier, she meant. Probably safer too.

'. . . before she got so bad with what she was taking.'

'Which was?' he asked.

'You name it. H. Es. Ketamine. Coke. She had this new contact who could get her anything: GHB, Temazepan, MDMA, you name it.'

What the fuck had this girl been playing at? Drugs Scrabble? Frankie had done his fair share of recreational narcs over the years, particularly a couple of years back when it had all got a little out of hand, but he'd never even heard of half of these. That was the trouble with the drugs world. You turned your back on it for a second and it moved on without you. He felt like a fucking amateur now.

'That night with my brother, did you see her and him taking anything together?'

'No. But she's always been sneaky like that. Keeps her gear hidden. Worried cunts like Stav'll nick it. But lately with me an' all. Like her new dealer – she won't even share his number with me – pretends like she's not allowed.'

'D'you talk to her? About my brother? After what happened that night?'

'No.'

'Why not?' No way she wouldn't have tried, it being splashed all over the papers. It had obviously been big news round at Stav's as well.

'Haven't seen her,' Keira said.

'What? Why not?'

'Not been answering her phone. I've checked at her place too, but no one's seen her. Like she's vanished off the face of the earth.'

Frankie's heartbeat started spiking again

'Why didn't you tell the cops? After you found out what my brother did – what they *said* he did?'

She looked for a second like she might laugh, like she couldn't believe how stupid he was even to ask.

'Because they wouldn't have believed me,' she said. 'Because Stav would have killed me if I got him involved. How many reasons do you need?'

Anger burned through him. Don't show it. Don't shout. Shout, and she'll leave.

'But the cops knowing she'd been with my brother that night,' he said, 'it could have helped him. Still could. Her being with him then and maybe later . . . who knows, maybe all night that might give him an alibi to help him prove he wasn't where the cops said he was at the time that girl got killed.'

'Or maybe it wouldn't,' she said. 'You ever think about that? That the reason my friend's gone missing might be because of your sodding brother as well?'

What was she saying? That Jack might have harmed Star as well? That was bullshit. Total fucking bullshit. 'You're well out of order,' he said.

'Maybe. Or maybe if your brother is innocent in all this, then whatever he got himself caught up in, she got caught up in it too.'

Find her. He had to find Star. Find her and he'd find the truth.

'What else can you remember about that night? Did she say anything to you? About him? About my brother? Anything at all before the two of them headed off.'

'Just that she'd call. Only she never did.'

'Her address. Write it down,' he said, tearing the back off a new packet of cigarettes.

'She won't talk to you. Even if you do find her.'

No doubt for the same reason that Keira hadn't called the cops. Because she was afraid.

'Just do it.'

She wrote it down.

'And what about family? Friends?' Frankie asked. 'Anyone she might be staying with?'

'I'm the only friend she's got.'

'Her real name then?'

'Star not good enough for you?'

'No.' Too cutesy. Had to be a working name.

'Tara. Tara Stevens.'

Made sense. Tara . . . stara . . . star.

'And you?'

'Forget it.'

'But what if I need to find you?'

'Then you already know where to look. Trust me, I ain't going nowhere anytime soon.'

He nodded. No point pressuring her any more. She was used to dealing with a lot nastier bastards than him and no fucking way was she going to go tell any of this to the cops.

He reached into his pocket and took out his billfold. Peeled off the ten twenties he owed. She took them off him and counted them fast.

'Thanks,' he said, getting up.

'Likewise.' She folded the cash and tucked it down inside her skirt.

'And for what it's worth,' he said, 'he wouldn't have done it. My brother. Hurt her. Hurt Star. Any more than he would have Susan Tilley. And if I find her – your Star – I'll do my best to make sure that nobody hurts her either.'

32

Frankie walked past the next pub, the one after that too. Had been planning on visiting them both, but now he'd met the girl he'd changed his mind. Had something concrete to go on.

First, though, food. He needed some ballast to soak up all the booze. Luckily, the kind of culinary Nirvana he was after was right there ahead of him at the top of the hill. George's fish bar. Best chippie in London. No question.

'Cod, chips, salt 'n' vinegar, bread and butter, mushy peas . . . and a saveloy,' Frankie said, as he reached the counter.

He slumped down in an aluminium chair to wait. A TV blared in the corner. Football round-up. Nice. Arsenal had won. Him and Jack and his dad . . . how many great days out had they had watching them play?

He reached for the pile of newspapers and fliers on the table next to him, and leafed through them, reading about new bands he'd not heard of and new club nights he'd not been to. He'd used to be well into the live music scene, much more than his occasional trips now to West End venues like the 100 Club. He'd used to know exactly who was who and what was what and who was over and what was in. Funny to think of it all still going on. He'd got no time for it any more. Too busy dealing with the club, keeping everything a-fucking-float. He felt like an old man now when he read this kind of shit.

He picked up a copy of the *Sun*. Straightaway wished he hadn't. His stomach lurched like he'd been punched. Susan Tilley's name was plastered across the front page. A photo too. Her eyes bored into his. A squirt of ketchup had been smeared across the words beneath. He wiped it away with the back of his hand.

Fuck. Bollocks. Shit. It said she'd been pregnant when she'd been killed. Pregnant? Jesus. How much more horrific could this get? Whatever hell Dougie Hamilton was going through before, it would be even more hideous now.

There was other stuff too, about how her parents had been killed in a car crash when she'd been a kid, about how the old lady, her grandma, had brought her up ever since. It said how she'd met Dougie at uni here in London, doing law. There was even a quote from an aunty of Susan's who lived in America, saying how her and Dougie had been planning on heading out there to work.

One bit of good news. Or a hint of it, at least. Word was the old lady might live. No details on the extent of her recovery. Was she talking yet? Was she well enough to be interviewed? His heart raced. Was it possible she might yet be able to put Jack in the clear?

He got up and lurched past the counter, ignoring the shout from the guy serving, telling him his food was ready. He wedged himself into the phone box across the street and fumbled in his pockets for some change and Sharon's card.

He rubbed his thumb over its embossed contact details. Was that all he was to her? Business? A part of a jigsaw she was trying to solve?

He dialled.

'Hmmm?' she answered sleepily on the seventh ring.

'It's me,' he said. 'Frankie.'

210

'What time is it?'

'It doesn't matter.'

'It does to me.'

'The old woman . . . I just read in the papers that she's better.'

'Frankie, you know I—'

'Just bloody tell me.'

He heard her growl. Actually growl. Like a fucking dog. 'She's getting better. Hopefully . . . it's not yet a hundred per—'

'What's she said?'

'Nothing. Yet. Her jaw's too swollen and her tongue's too lacerated from where she bit it when she was hit.'

'But she will,' Frankie said. 'She'll clear him. I fucking know she will . . .'

'We don't know what she saw, or what she'll remember, if anything. It's possible, Frankie, that she might identify your brother as—'

'No. No, it's not,' he snapped. 'And I want to know what she fucking says. I want you to call me the second she—'

'Frankie? Have you been drinking?'

Fuck. Was he slurring? Or shouting? Shit. He glanced across the road. A couple of people standing eating outside of George's were staring right at him.

'I'll talk to you later.' He slammed down the phone.

She'd see. As soon as that old lady came round, she'd put the finger on someone else and Sharon would have to eat her words. *If* . . . if she remembered . . . if she'd seen who'd done it. Sharon was right about that much at least. No fucking guarantee of anything yet.

He clocked a cab pulling up at the end of Golborne Road. A drunken couple half fell into the gutter, her in a big fake fur coat and seemingly not much else. Frankie ran for it. Tara. Star. Yeah, why wait till tomorrow? He had the address, didn't he? Why not

211

track her down now? No point holding off for the old lady to start talking. Might never happen. The ball was still in his court. Had to grab the fucker by the throat.

He reached the cab just before it pulled away from the kerb. Got in the back and ferreted through his pocket for the piece of card Keira had written Star's address on.

He told the cabbie the name of her street. Less than two miles away. Fucking fate. Should only take a few minutes to get there. The cabbie tried making conversation, but Frankie wasn't listening. He pulled his hoodie tighter round his head and stared out the window at the blur of buildings passing by.

Was this a dumb move? Tipping up in the middle of the night. Half-cut. Maybe. Might spook the shit out of Star if she was at home. Or not. Who knew if a girl like Star was even awake enough to answer the bloody door? Fuck it. He had to find her. Find out what she knew. Had to be careful too. Because, yeah, she'd been with Jack, but he still didn't know what for. Just for sex, then she'd not be such a danger. But if she was in this deeper, if she had somehow helped set him up, he was going to have to watch his back.

The sign for her street flashed past. The cab started to slow.

'Which number, mate?' asked the driver.

'Keep going,' Frankie said. 'Right to the end. Drop me round the corner.'

He kept an eye on the building numbers. Clocked Star's building on the left as they passed. A geezer in a black tracksuit and a baseball cap was heading in through its reinforced glass double doors, carrying something. Delivery bloke, looked like.

Her building was an old council block. Half its windows boarded up. Dim lights glowed behind tatty, lopsided curtains in a bunch of the others. Trellick Tower and the Westway reared up behind. Someone had once told him at the Notting Hill Carnival that there was a cop shop at the top of Trellick, that they controlled all the traffic from up there during Carnival. He couldn't help imagining them now peering down at him through binoculars, watching him, waiting for an opportunity to pounce.

He paid the cabbie and got out. Stumbled as he walked away. Fuck, fuck, fuck. *Was* he too drunk for this? Should he go home? No, sod it. He watched the cab leave. He went into the 24-hour garage on the corner. Gloves. He needed gloves, because if she wasn't there, then he was going to break in. He grabbed a couple of disposable ones from the dispenser by the petrol pump, then walked back down the street to her block.

Time to crack fucking on. He tried the building's main door. Locked. He couldn't just kick it open. There was an offie across the street. Some bastard might see. He made a show of pretending to look for his keys instead. Then stepped back into the shadows. Leant up against the wall. Lit a cigarette.

Softly, softly, catchee monkey. He didn't have long to wait. A few minutes later, the door to Star's block opened and a woman stepped out. Luckily she didn't look back as she walked away. Frankie got to the door just before it clicked shut.

He slipped through into the twilight of the lobby. A scuffed concrete floor. A buzzing strip light hung at an angle from the ceiling. Wires exposed. The air stank of rot. Christ, what a dump.

He checked the piece of paper Keira had given him. Flat 17. An 'OUT OF ORDER' sign hung on the closed lift doors. Typical. He took the stairs. Two flights up and halfway along the dank, deserted corridor, he found the door he was looking for. The '7' of '17' was hanging upside down with one of its screws missing. And then, the oddest thing . . . he saw a glistening yellow flower petal there on the grimy lino floor.

Pulling on the gloves, he reached out to knock. Then stopped. Think. Make a plan. Decide what you're gonna say. If she answered, if she seemed all right . . . then fine, he'd keep his hands behind his back and slip the gloves off while he explained himself. Tell her who he was. Let her know he meant her no harm.

But if she didn't answer? Well, then, fuck it. He'd break in. But then? Once he did? What was he hoping to find? Something to tell him where she might have gone. An address book? Phone numbers. Some kind of fucking clue.

He took a deep breath. Dib dib dib. Be prepared. If she *was* here, but just not answering, then who fucking knew? She might be high as a kite, or slumped, or manic, or with some other junkie, or her dealer, or Lord knew what? All sorts of danger might be lurking the other side of this door. Expect the worst and hope for the best. Now just do it.

He reached out again to knock. Stopped again. Fuck. The door wasn't even properly shut. It was open. Just a sliver. He nudged it with his toecap, opened it a little wider. Nice and quiet. No squeak. Good fucking karma, or what? He pushed it even wider, revealing a slice of tacky brown carpet and a bare bulb glaring down from a nicotine-brown Artex ceiling above.

He froze. Muffled voices inside. He waited, ready to back off, but then the voices gave way to music. What the hell? Ah. A theme tune. A TV show. Meaning good news. She might actually be in. Might not be off her head, either. Or at least not high. No one ever watched TV when they were properly wrecked. Only on a downer. Or even straight. Good news too. Easier to handle that way.

'Hello?' he called out. Didn't want to spook her by just marching right in on her.

The theme music tailed off. An advert kicked in. Opera music from that Cornetto spoof ad for Boddingtons. Fucking funny, that. Only not now. He checked the door locks. Three of them.

Heavy duty. What was the point of all that when you forgot to even shut your door?

'Hello?' he called again, louder this time. 'Your front door . . . it was open, so . . .'

No answer. He stepped right inside. More of them yellow petals and what looked like a florist's business card lying there beside them up against the wall. Right, sod this. He walked towards the sound of the TV. A Fosters advert now. He peered into a small box bedroom on his right. A shambles. Dresses, underwear, crumpled sheets and a litter of crack-smoking paraphernalia on saucers and plates beside the mattress on the floor. No one there. He checked the shower and toilet cubicle on his left. Empty too.

Only one door left. Dead ahead. Half-open. A single red high-heeled shoe on the floor outside. More yellow petals led up to it like a trail. *Follow the fucking Yellow Brick Road.* Closer up, he saw the flickering lights of the TV dancing across a white-tiled kitchenette floor as another advert kicked in. Levi's. Some old blues number.

'Star?' he called out again. 'Tara? Tara Stevens? I'm a friend of Keira's. She gave me your address . . .'

Nothing. His nostrils twitched. Perfume. He could smell perfume. No, not perfume. Fresh flowers. Whatever those yellow petals had come from.

Another theme tune kicked in. Bloody *Beadle's About*. He hated that twat. But what about Star? Maybe she had gone out and forgotten to lock the front door behind her, the dozy mare. What then? Wait? It would probably freak her out even more, her turning back up here and finding him.

'Hello?' he said, reaching the door and pushing it open.

He stepped inside. The light was off, but the TV was enough to see by. A big one. Looked brand new and well out of place on the kitchen sideboard beside the piled-up sink of dirty crockery.

A huge bunch of flowers on the kitchen table, wrapped in brown paper, a deliveryman's roster beside them. A plate of beans on toast beside it. Steam still rising off it. Must have just been made – but by who?

Oh, Jesus . . . Frankie saw her then. On the floor. Looking like she was somehow underwater in the writhing shadows cast down by the TV. Curled up on her side like a fucking baby with one red shoe on, the other foot bare.

Her face was split open. Fuck. Was she dead? He took another step forward and saw movement. Jesus. Her blood. It was creeping slowly out across the tiles from the side of her head. Like some kind of fucking cartoon speech bubble that was about to reveal her thoughts.

Then the thought hit him slowly . . . *too* slowly . . . If her blood was still moving, then it meant she'd only just been attacked . . . and that meant that . . .

Oh, fuck.

He turned. Too late. A grunt. A flash of dark blue. His whole world turned black.

33

*W*hugh? Darkness. Darkness all around. Where the fuck was he? Move. Just move. Which way was he facing? Christ, which way was even up? Was he on his back? Shit, was this a dream? Frankie started to panic. Felt like he was spinning. In oil, in ink, in black fucking tar.

Calm. Calm the fuck down. It's OK. You're breathing. Yes. Fast. Faster than a fucking piston. He reached out. Felt something. Something soft. Like what? Like leaves? No, cloth. Yes. He grabbed. Wouldn't let go.

Light . . . grey light . . . there, just there . . . a grey fuzziness coming into focus . . . shuddering, like interference on a TV screen.

Shit. The pain. It smacked him. His head. It felt like it was exploding. Oh, Jesus . . . White light exploded in his skull. Hit. He'd been hit. He'd been in enough fights to know.

Bang-bang-bang. Memories. A dark basement. Junkies lurking, watching. Then fresh air. A starlit sky. Portobello. Drink. Talk. Drink. The smell of chips. A taxi ride. Yellow petals on the floor.

A face. Right here. Wherever the fuck this was, this fuzzy, twitching gloom. He saw a face forming in the shimmering, growing light. Something fucking wrong about it . . . colour seeping into its blurry features, washing away the grey . . . first rose, then pink, then red . . . Blood. Oh, shit. The face was covered in blood.

Frankie let go of whatever he'd been gripping. Her dress. The blood-soaked woman's dress. She wasn't moving. Fuck. What did it mean? Did it mean she was dead?

He twisted onto his side. Ceiling. Floors. Cupboards. All shuddering in and out of focus. Pissing hell, his head hurt. Look. Look, dammit. Are they here? Whoever done this to you? Shit, are they still here? Gonna finish you off?

No one. Alone. Apart from her. He forced himself to look. A name. Star. Yes, he remembered her. He remembered everything then. Why he'd come here. To talk to her. Get her to admit she'd been with Jack that night. At what time? That's what he'd wanted to find out. Only . . . Jesus, this was hard; he pushed himself up onto his elbows and knees . . . she'd already been dead – been dying? – when he'd got here.

And whoever the hell had done that to her, they'd still been here as well. A blur of material. He remembered that too. Just before he'd blacked out. Someone had been here. What else? Flowers. Brown paper. A man entering the building when he'd first driven past. A florist's card. Whoever had delivered them, they'd done this. Done *her*. Attacked Star, then him. Left him here for dead? And her? *Was* she?

Her eyes. Dead eyes. Staring up at the fucking ceiling. Wide open, but dark. Without a spark. Finished. Done. And look. Her blood. So much. It had been moving when he'd first seen it, but now . . . now it had stopped. Thickened. *Congealed*.

Sirens. Faint. Now louder. Incoming. What the soldiers in all them Yank Vietnam movies always said. Imminent. About to happen. Nasty shit coming right at him. Fuck. Get out of here. Fast.

But what about her? What if she's . . .? Do it. Check her. You can't just leave her like this. He reached out to touch her hair, to push it back from her brow, like that might make a difference . . . Sweet Jesus. The top half of her head was caved in. Crumpled like a tin. What kind of fucker could do something like this? To another human being?

She had to be dead. Right? He touched her neck. Felt for a pulse. The right place? Fuck, he didn't know. Didn't know if he was doing this right. Should he take off his gloves? No. Prints. He'd leave prints if he did.

Sharon. Yes, Sharon. He pictured her. Standing right here like a fucking traffic warden, telling him he couldn't park, telling him if he did he'd get a ticket. Swabs. Fingerprints. All this and more could damn him.

Shit. Was that what was happening to him? Was he being framed just like Jack? Whoever had done this to him and her . . . had they known he wasn't dead, just out? What if they'd called the cops? Knowing he'd be found here? Knowing he'd then take the blame?

More sirens. Louder. Oh, fuck. They really were coming. Here. To this flat. To this room. He had to get the fuck out of here. Now.

Run. He pushed himself up. Felt his stomach contract like he was going to puke. *Don't do it*. Bile burst into his mouth, He swallowed it back down. Sharon's face leapt into his head again. *Don't leave DNA*.

He lurched for the door. Caught a half-glimpse of himself in the mirror on the wall. Hoodie. His hood was still up. Was he bleeding? Had whatever cunt who'd done this to him hit him so hard that he'd bled?

He half-turned, stared back down at the tiles. No blood where he'd been. No smears. He touched the back of his head again. More white pain. But just bruising? Maybe. Meaning maybe there'd be no DNA for them to trace him. Maybe he still had a chance.

He ran down the hallway, remembering coming in the other way. The petals were still there, but the florist's business card had gone. Nothing to say there'd ever been anyone else here.

The front door was open. He burst out onto the landing. No other doors open. Or – wait – maybe one? Across the hall. Had it just clicked softly shut? Bollocks. Had someone just seen him?

No time to find out. The sirens were screaming. Horribly fucking close. Cops must have pulled up outside. Forget going out the front of the building. They'd catch him for sure.

Had to be another way. He replayed the taxi journey though his mind. Hadn't there been an alley to the right of the building? Far enough away from where the cops would have already pulled up?

But which way was right? He turned, trying to work it the fuck out. That way? Here's fucking hoping. He ran across the hall and into another corridor, sprinting past a whole bunch of doorways, until he hit the fire escape at the end of the corridor. He snapped back the security bar and tore it open.

A blast of cold air hit him. He'd come out the right side of the building. A dark alley below. No one in it. Yet. Sirens shrieking. Blue lights flickering at the end of the alley. A cast-iron double metal ladder led down, but not all the way. Shit. No, that would have been too fucking easy, eh? It didn't reach the ground, not by a long fucking stretch.

He tried the locking mechanism that would release the second half of the ladder and let it rattle down. Jammed. Fucking rusted. Shitty council skinflint bastards. What the hell was he meant to do now? Climb down that and jump? How fucking long a drop was it? Shit. Might not be able to walk again, let alone run.

'Just do it.'

He said it out loud. Moved as he did. What other choice did he have? Stay here and he was screwed. Just get out onto the ladder. Don't think about the rust. Tits. Arse. Piss flaps. He grabbed hold of the top rung and started climbing down. Ignore it – the clanking, the fucking swaying.

He'd got almost the whole way down when he heard the shout. His eyes flicked to the end of the alley. Crap. A uniform. Had he spotted him? Yeah, the bastard was staring right at him. Frankie scrambled down the rest of the ladder. A fifteen-foot drop yawned below.

The cop shouted something that got lost in the wail of the sirens. Hardly mattered. Hardly like he'd be asking him out on a date. Frankie lowered himself quick off the end of the ladder. Till only his hands were gripping the rungs and his feet were hanging in mid-air. The cop was running hard up the alley now. At him. Frankie took a deep breath, then . . . just let fucking go . . .

34

O *of.*

Fucking *ouch.*

Hard to tell who got the bigger shock, Frankie or the cop he landed on. Pretty obvious who got hurt the most, though. All thirteen-and-a-half stone of Frankie hit the cop hard. Without warning. Knocked the stuffing out of him. Frankie rolled off him, leaving him crumpled in a wheezing heap on the ground.

Frankie scrambled to his feet. Shit-a-brick. He felt all right. Nothing broken. Biggest favour a cop had ever done him in his life. Move it. Now. Don't look round. Don't look back up that alley. Who knew who was already pounding down it after him? Don't give those bastards a look at your face.

He locked his eyes on the opposite end of the alley from where the cop had come – and ran. Only looked back when he got there. Couldn't help himself. Regretted it. Not just one cop after him now, but three. Two blokes and a woman. They'd already reached their mate, who was up on his knees now and pointing in Frankie's direction.

He ran on, bursting out the end of the alley, knocking some kid flying off his skateboard. Unlucky, kid. Brightly lit shop fronts stretched out into the distance left and right. Hardly any arsing pedestrians. Crap. He'd get spotted the second the cops reached the end of the alley.

Had to keep going. Try and get some distance between them. Find somewhere to lay low. He cut a left. Ran thirty yards down the pavement. Slalomed across the street, nearly getting mown down by a black Range Rover pumping out bass.

Risked another quick glance back as he reached the opposite pavement. Only two cops still chasing. Across the street. Less than twenty yards behind. They darted out into the street. Darted back, a night bus roaring past, horn blaring, nearly turning them both into mush.

Frankie kept running. Might only be two cops now. Soon be more. Not just on foot. In motors. Then he'd be royally screwed. He spotted a side road up ahead. Raced into it. He reached the end and saw the open gates of some kind of industrial estate. Nice. A whole lot worse lit than the streets.

He raced through the gates. Come on, you fucker. You can do this. All that time down the gym. Here's where it finally pays off. And no more bloody smoking, if you make it through in one piece. And cut back down on the boozing. He was going to make his body a fucking temple. All it had to do was not let him down.

How far ahead of those cops was he now? Had they seen him ducking in here? Here's hoping not. If they got hold of him now, he was super-screwed. That was the trouble with running. The same as with Jack, he'd look guilty as hell. They'd pin that Star girl's murder on him for sure.

He ducked into a thin alleyway running between two rows of high-sided corrugated iron warehouses. He heard shouts. Behind. Bollocks. They'd followed him into the estate. He was starting to cramp, getting a stitch. Shit, shit, shit. How far had he just run? His trainers were scuffing hard on the concrete with every step – loud enough for the cops to hear? How far were they behind?

He looked back. No one charging down the alley after him. What did it mean? Had he got away? Or were they circling round, trying to cut him off? When he hit the end of the alley in a couple of seconds, were they going to be already there?

He slowed to a halt, slowly peered out. Another empty bit of road. Shitly lit. A couple of parked-up fork lift trucks. Nothing moved. Across the road was another alley running between more warehouses. A dark hole. A mouth that would swallow him up. Reach that without being seen and he might still have a chance. Had to get the fuck clear before they called in backup. A chopper would do for him. Those bastards had infra-red.

Now. He threw himself forwards. The bit of road was ten yards wide. Had to get across fast. Eight yards. Five. Four . . . Three . . . Two . . . Yes, fucking one. He hit the alley still running hard as he could, but stumbling now, losing it, out of adrenaline.

No shouts behind him, mind. No pounding boots. Fucking yes. Go on, son. One more push. Don't stop now. He made it to the end. Breathless, weakening. From the drink or being hit, or just not being bloody fit enough. He lurched out into the road beyond without stopping. Slumped down next to a bin to catch his breath. Hands on his knees, he checked right, then left to the end of the buildings he'd just sprinted between.

Nothing. The street was empty. Relief burst inside him. Too fucking soon. A bloody cop. Fifty yards to his right. Ran out into the road. Turning. Looking. Jabbering into his radio. Frankie didn't move. Made like a shadow. Just crouched there panting. Quiet as he bloody well could. What now? Triple shit. He was out of juice. Couldn't outrun a tortoise. And triple bollocks. That cop was walking towards him. All purposeful. Like any second now he was about to break into a run. Had he seen him? More chattering into his radio. More crackling radio static. Was he calling Frankie's position in?

But no. The fucker stopped. He turned his back on Frankie. Ran in the other direction.

Get in. Frankie didn't know what to make of it. Didn't fucking care. He slowly stood. Steadied himself against the black bin. Black, the same colour as his clothes and his hood. Was that what had just saved him? Or had someone else got it wrong? Did they think they'd spotted him somewhere else?

Who gave a shit? Time to ride his luck. Just like the old man had always taught him. He stumbled on. Further west. Keep going. Don't you quit. Lungs burning, muscles tightening, seizing up from lactic acid. *Keep On Movin'* . . . The Soul II Soul song chanted in his head.

He reached the fence. High. Wire. He quickly worked his way along it, searching for a way through. In his head he saw that flash of material again. That blur of motion just before he'd got knocked out. A face? And what about her? What about Star? Not just the fact she'd been murdered, but *how* she'd been murdered. Hideously beaten by some sicko who'd clearly enjoyed every second of it. Beaten like Susan Tilley. Bludgeoned to death.

Then there, behind a stack of pallets, he spotted a gap, a tear in the fence. He slipped through, breathless, into a quiet residential street on the other side. Hood up, he limped away slowly. On foot. Didn't let up. No cabs. No buses. No witnesses the cops could later talk to.

He headed south for Hyde Park.

Then Soho.

Then home.

35

Frankie woke in a sweat. Still dark. Christ on a bike, what time was it? He sat bolt upright, hung-over, confused. Someone was pounding on the door. Only not the door downstairs which led out onto the street. Closer. Shit. The door leading into his flat.

Hamilton? Was it him? Either of them? Terence or Dougie? Or Shank Wilson too? Had they got wind of him poking around? Or Mo or Stav? Had they worked him out?

He scrambled out of bed. Onto his knees. Delved inside the slit he'd made in the mattress for the pistol.

Then stopped.

Shouting. A woman. But who? Cops? Bollocks. You fucking muppet. How could he have forgotten? Where he'd been last night . . . Blacked out, that's why. Yeah, the tell-tale bottle of voddie by the bed. Smirnoff red.

Only . . . no, not *last* night. *To*night. He checked his Sony digicube alarm clock on the bedside table. It was half one in the morning.

Fuck-a-duck. He stuffed the tin containing the pistol back deep inside his mattress. Wedged the sheets in tight. He remembered everything now in hideous detail. Star's flat. His escape. The sound of that fucking copper in the alley when he'd landed on his head.

He pulled on his dressing-gown over his boxer shorts. Grabbed his baseball cap from where he'd hooked it on the bed post. That lump on the back of his head. He had to hide it. He pulled the cap down. Winced. Christ, it hurt.

More shouting. Yeah, definitely a woman and definitely his name she was calling. Keep your shit together. Whoever it is . . . whatever they want . . . you weren't fucking there. You've been in here all night.

He hurried to the front door and opened it. Blimey. Sharon. He almost smiled. But not with that look of bloody fury on her face. She was in an overcoat and buttoned-down shirt. Here on business.

Xandra was with her. In an old Cure T-shirt and trackie bottoms. Looked like she'd just been torn from her bed. Sharon must have gone for the club's front door first. Xandra must have let her in.

'I'm sorry, Frankie,' Xandra said.

Forget her. Not her fault. Just deal with Sharon. Whatever this is, just front it out.

'You'd better have a fucking good reason for calling round this late,' he said.

'And you'd better have a fucking good explanation for where the fuck you've been tonight.'

'Yeah, I've—' He was going to say he'd been in on his own watching TV. Or a film. Yeah. Tell her *Ben Hur*. He had it on the shelf. Went on for bloody hours.

But Xandra cut in, 'He was here with me,' she said.

Sharon turned on her. 'What?'

'Downstairs,' said Xandra. 'He was helping me decorate.'

Sharon looked like she was about to call her a liar. But Xandra kept her cool. Held up her hands, palms out. Splodges of white paint all over them.

'And what about you, Frankie?' She grabbed his hands, looked them over. Nothing. Not even a spot.

'I had a shower.'

'I want to talk to you,' she said. 'Alone.'

Didn't wait for him to ask her in. Just pushed past. He took a shufti downstairs. No more cops in the stairwell. Thank fuck. She was here on her own.

'Thanks,' he mouthed at Xandra.

He owed her one. Couldn't believe she'd just lied for him like that.

She nodded. Turned her back on him. Walked downstairs.

Sharon was waiting for him in the living room. The first time she'd been here. The place was a pigsty. This wasn't a fucking social call, but he still felt a prickle of embarrassment. Oh, Jesus. It stank as well. As well as picking up a bottle of vodka, he'd got a kebab. Its grisly remains were splayed out on its greasy wrapper on the floor.

'Was it you?' she said.

'What?'

'Who called the station?' she said.

'About what?'

'About a girl. Last night. Was it you who made the anonymous call from a phone box just the other side of Hyde Park from here?'

He shook his head, then felt his pulse race. Bugger. His hoodie. Right there in full view where he'd tossed it over the top of the bathroom door. Covered in filth from that alley he'd fallen into. Idiot. He should have bunged it in the washing machine, like he'd done with the rest of his clothes before he'd showered.

He reached for a tinnie, one of two left of the four-pack on the table. He'd got stuck into them before switching to vodka.

'Want one?' he asked.

'No.'

'Suit yourself.' He cracked it open and took a long swig.

'The girl at the flat . . . she was murdered,' Sharon said.

'I'm sorry to hear that.' Keep your gob shut. Don't say anything. Because *you* don't know anything about being there. And neither does she. She'd have brought it up already if she did. And she wouldn't have fucking come here alone.

'Her name was Tara Stevens,' she said. 'Also known as Star.'

'Never heard of her.'

Her cheeks darkened. 'The person who called in with the tip-off told us her DNA might match the condom found at your brother's flat,' she said.

Look surprised. 'What are you saying?' he said. 'That someone was with Jack at his flat? That night? When he was meant to be out murdering Susan Tilley?'

Her hands screwed into fists. 'As I think I've already made perfectly clear, that's part of an ongoing investigation and none of your business. What I want to know, Frankie, is if you made that call?'

Push back. Don't let her see you're rattled. And remember: you need answers too. 'None of my fucking business?' he said. 'And how do you work that out? Because if there *was* some girl there with him, screwing him, then that means he couldn't have been anywhere else, could he? Which gives him a fucking alibi, right?'

'There's no such thing as a dead alibi,' she said.

'What?'

'An alibi has to be alive to give evidence.'

And Star was now dead.

'Fine, then. Proof. Whatever. That condom . . . if it's got her DNA on it, then it proves she was there. With him. Right?'

'No, Frankie, it doesn't.'

'Why not?'

'Because even if we do get a match for her DNA and the DNA on the condom, all that proves is she had sex with him.'

'In his flat,' Frankie said. 'Because that's where this condom was found. On the night he was meant to be murdering Susan Tilley. And you should bloody well sweep the rest of his flat for her DNA. Because she might not have just gone back there to shag him. She might have gone back there to help set the poor fucker up.'

'For someone who knows nothing about this anonymous call last night, you sure as hell seem to have all its implications worked out.'

Careful. Because, yeah, he *had* made that fucking call. To-night. On the way home. From the exact same Hyde Park phone box she'd said. One nowhere near any fucking cctv. Muffling his voice through his hoodie's sleeve. Because how the fuck else were the cops going to be able to make the link between Jack and Star?

'He could have had sex with her somewhere else and just kept that condom,' Sharon said.

'You what?' Frankie scoffed.

'To make us *think* he'd been there in his flat with someone that night. To try and put himself in the clear.'

'You're out of your mind.'

But she was right, wasn't she? The cops could see it that way if they chose. Should he tell her? Admit he went to Stav's? Tell her what Keira said – that Star *had* been with Jack that evening? Tell her that and then they might question Keira. But question her and she might tell them she'd given Frankie Star's address. Which of course would leave him fucked and suspect numero uno in her murder.

'Even if he did have sex with her there . . .' Sharon said.

'Yeah?'

'There's no proof of *when* that happened. It could have been earlier that afternoon. Or even minutes before he drove across to Susan Tilley's grandmother's house.'

Sharon was still watching him, trying to read him.

'Did you make the call to the station?' she asked again. 'I need to know, Frankie.'

'No.'

'Well, answer me this: who the fuck else would want to tip us off that your brother might have an alibi? The only one who believes that he's innocent is you.'

'I already told you: it wasn't me.'

'Where were you this evening? When you rang me? Earlier on, to ask me whether Susan Tilley's grandmother had said anything?' She glared at the beer can in his hand. 'When you rang me up drunk? I can find out you know,' she said. 'I can find out where you called me from.'

Could she? Shit. He'd forgotten about calling her from outside George's. Did him having done that contradict Xandra having just said he was here? No. He could still say he was there in Portobello when he made that call and then came back here to help decorate. That would still put him out of the picture for having been at Star's.

'Portobello,' he said. Not too near Star's flat, thank God.

'Doing what?'

'This.' He held up his can like he was toasting her.

'Who with?'

'Seeing some old friends.' The barman in the First Floor Bar. He could say he'd been drinking with him.

'And you've never been there?'

'Where?'

He'd said it too quick, too obviously carelessly.

231

'Don't play fucking stupid, Frankie. Her flat. Star's flat? That wasn't you scarpering off down that back alley the second the cops arrived? Because the description I got, whoever the hell it was, they were the same height and build as you.'

Meaning they'd not seen his face. 'I didn't have anything to do with what happened to her . . .' A mistake. He knew it as soon as he said it. He'd been too specific. He should have just answered no.

'And just what did happen to her?' Sharon asked.

'I don't know. Whatever they did. However she was killed. That's what you just told me just now. That she was murdered.'

'I should haul you in,' she said. 'For fingerprinting and testing.'

'So do,' he gambled. 'I've got nothing to hide.' A punt. He'd had gloves on. Didn't mean they wouldn't find something else. Hair. Skin. Christ. Even blood. The bruise on his head. Hadn't looked like a cut when he'd checked it last night. Just a bloody great welt. But who fucking knew?

He saw doubt flicker in her eyes. Was he finally winning her round?

'Why the hell would I hurt her?' he said. 'If she really could give my brother an alibi, I'd have wanted her alive.'

She did the maths.

'Maybe . . . or maybe not, because of what you've already told me, because you reckon she equally might have had something to do with setting Jack up . . . because then you might have wanted to make her talk . . .'

'What? And lost my temper? And murdered her? Is that what you're saying?'

She looked deep into his eyes. 'No, I don't believe that. But I do think you care enough about your brother to have gone round there. You'd just better hope there's no footage of you near her block.'

There wasn't. Not without his hoodie up, the one that was less than three feet behind her right now. The one he'd be incinerating the first chance he got.

'No witnesses either . . .' she said.

He thought about the door shutting in the communal hallway outside Star's flat. Had someone been there? Had someone seen his face?

'I want to believe you, Frankie. But I swear to God, if it does turn out you were there, whether you had anything to do with what happened to that girl or not, I'll do my job. I'll throw the fucking book at you myself.'

36

Frankie kept a low profile the next day. He did exactly what he'd told Sharon he'd done the night before. He worked with Xandra on finishing painting her room.

Slim helped too, before the punters started arriving. He seemed to be warming to their guest. A bit. In spite of his earlier reservations. She made him laugh, the same as she did Frankie. Slim was still watching her, mind. Frankie had spotted that too. Maybe not so obviously as before, but still doing it all the same. Clearly still didn't fully trust her. Not yet. Xandra would have to earn that. No different to anyone else.

Frankie felt watched too. Not by Slim. By Xandra, as the two of them kept on at the painting late into the afternoon. Because of how he'd lied to Sharon in front of her. Because of how Xandra had backed him up.

He tried bringing it up with her when they were having a fag break in the afternoon. Just the two of them alone. But she cut him off. 'You don't have to explain,' was all she said. 'Why ever you did it, I'm sure you've got a good reason, and the way I hear it, your brother's innocent too.'

It must have been Slim who'd told her that about Jack. Or she'd overheard something. Maybe Slim talking to Sea Breeze or one of the other old boys. She was hardly one for watching TV or reading the papers, so Frankie doubted she'd got it from there, and Frankie hadn't said shit to her about it.

He was glad she knew now, though. It meant him and Slim could talk more openly. Not just about how Frankie had another visit lined up with Jack the next day – one he couldn't wait for, on account of everything he'd learned about Star – but how everything else was heating up, the war between Riley and Hamilton.

There'd been another killing. A nasty one. Another of Tommy Riley's foot soldiers had been found. Beaten to death. Left by a bin just like Danny Kale a month ago. Kale's was the murder that the cops reckoned had led to the revenge killing of Susan Tilley. So what fresh hell was this new one going to lead to now?

The same dickhead journalist as before was stoking the headlines. With an added lurid twist. The new dead man, a street pimp affiliated to Riley, had been found with a torn pair of women's knickers rammed down his throat. In revenge for the way Susan Tilley's body had been left? For the underwear that had been torn off her and taken? This was the grubby little question the newspaper hack had left hanging in the air.

Frankie turned in early that night. Was shattered. Relieved, mind, that Sharon and the cops hadn't turned up. Maybe it meant he really was in the clear for having been there at Star's. He'd gone the whole day without a drink. Needed the break. Still couldn't believe the shit storm he'd walked into half-drunk at Star's last night. Another of his fucking nine lives gone.

Lying in bed, he thought about Sharon. Didn't want to. Couldn't help himself. About how she'd been here. In his home. About how angry she'd been. Could his life get any more fucking complicated? He doubted it.

*

His appointment at Wandsworth Visitors' Centre was for ten a.m. He got up early. Hit the gym. Knackered himself out good and proper. Left with his whole body aching. He was fucking unfit. For him. Had sussed that much as he'd run through that industrial estate. Needed to sort it out. More regular exercise. Less regular booze. No fucking smokes. Get his life back on track.

Jack's eyes were burning bright when Frankie sat down opposite him in the Visitors' Centre. Obvious why. Must have already got wind of Susan Tilley's grandmother regaining consciousness.

Frankie had picked up a copy of the *News of the Screws* on the way over. Had spotted it on a newsstand outside the tube station. No more details than what he'd already wheeled out of Sharon, though. Nothing about whether the old lady was yet fit enough to be interviewed. Or what she might have already said.

Good to see some hope in Jack's eyes, mind. More proof he was innocent, wasn't it? Because if he was guilty, he'd have been shitting it about the old lady coming round, in case she ID'd him, right? Yeah, screw you, Sharon. You think the old bird's going to point the finger at Jack? Think again.

'So is it true then?' said Jack. 'The grandmother . . . she's on the mend?'

'That's what the papers say.'

'That's what I heard on the grapevine in here as well. I got a good feeling, bruv. I reckon she's gonna put me in the clear.'

Frankie nodded. He hoped to fuck he was right.

'How's it been?' he asked.

Jack cracked a grin. 'Perfect. The facilities here are marvellous. Second to none. Gourmet grub and first class accommodation. And as for the staff . . . well, what can I say?' He nodded at one of the hulking great guards walking between the tables the prisoners were sitting at. 'They're attentive to the point of distraction. The Ritz has got nothing on this.'

'Very witty,' said Frankie. 'But I don't mean this shithole. I mean you.' He meant Riley – was the protection he'd promised still in place? Any more nutters with Stanley knives taking tumbles down flights of stairs? Any more shenanigans like that?

'I'm in the pink of health,' Jack said.

He looked it too. A lot fucking better than the last time he'd see him. The puffy bags under his eyes had shrunk and his sallow skin had faded. The whites of his eyes were, well, white, not bloodshot, better than in years. Looked like the enforced detox was doing him good.

'I've even started working out,' Jack said.

Frankie's turn to smile. The amount of times Jack had taken the piss out of him for going down the gym instead of the boozer.

'With Stan Lomax,' Jack added.

Riley's boy, now Jack's minder.

'He still keeping an eye on you?'

'Sticking to me like glue.'

'Good. And have you needed him?'

'What?'

'Any of Hamilton's boys been on to you?'

'No.'

'Nothing?'

'Not so much as a fucking sideways glance.'

Good news. But surprising. They wanted vengeance so bad, then why the hell hadn't they at least tried something on? Had to be biding their time. Waiting for the right time to strike.

'You just make sure you keep Lomax close to you, eh?' he said. 'Don't go dropping your guard. Those fuckers are still out there, OK?'

'It's like I told you before, bruv,' said Jack. 'Tommy Riley looks after his own.'

His own . . . The way he smirked when he said it . . . something inside Frankie flared right up.

'You know he doesn't fucking own you, right?' he said.

Jack's smile faded. 'It's just an expression.'

'Fine.'

But it *wasn't* fine. Nothing like fucking fine. Not for Jack and not for him either. He remembered his promise to Riley, the favour he'd one day have to pay him back. But only if Riley delivered. Only if the fucker gave him something on that witness. And he'd come up with sweet FA yet.

'Anyhow,' said Jack, 'the way I see it, I'm safer off in here than out there on the streets, the way things are going . . .'

'You mean Riley's boy?' The dealer. The one found dead with the knickers in his mouth. Hamilton couldn't have sent out a harder message to Riley if he'd tried. God only knew what reply he'd get back.

'No, not just him,' Jack said. He looked downcast. 'I mean Mickey.'

'Mickey Flynn?'

'You not heard?'

No. Not a peep. Nothing in the papers. 'What happened? When?'

'Late last night . . . he got done over. One of the screws told Stan this morning.'

'How bad?'

'He's in St Mary's now. They reckon he's going lose his left eye.'

'Jesus . . . They know who done it?'

'The Hamiltons.'

'But why?' Mickey might be officially affiliated to Riley, but he'd not exactly been exclusive, had he? He'd been drinking with one of Hamilton's boys when Frankie had gone round and collared him in The Toucan.

There was no love lost between Frankie and that little weasel, but shit, was this because of *him*? Because Hamilton had found out Frankie had gone there to see him the morning Jack was nicked? Because he'd worked out that meant he might have known something about who'd killed Dougie's girl? Or might even have been somehow involved in it himself?

Not good. Mickey was a pussy. He'd coughed up everything he knew to Frankie after he'd just slammed him up against a wall. What the fuck else would he have spilled when someone like Hamilton got hold of him? He'd have told him what he'd told Frankie. About the speed. He'd have told him about Mo.

'Word is it's not just any old fucking Hamilton who did him either,' Jack said.

'The old man himself?' Frankie could see it. Some goon – some nasty fucker like Shank – holding skinny little Mickey down, while Terrence set about him with a wrench.

'Nah.' Jack still looked revolted, because Mickey was his mate. But he looked excited too, buzzing, as if keeping this titbit to himself was too much to bear. 'Dougie,' he said.

Seriously? Not that Dougie didn't have the nerve for it. Frankie had seen that. The fucker was fearless. But that had been right when it had been raw, when he'd just found out about her, when he'd clearly been out of his mind.

'At least that's what they're saying in here,' Jack said.

'But he's a lawyer.'

'A lawyer with a knife.'

Frankie remembered him again outside the club. Had Dougie been carrying then? Was it only them being in broad daylight that had stopped him pulling a blade on him? Or was this something new? Was *Dougie* someone new? Had all this terrible shit that had happened turned him into somebody else? Someone much more like his old man?

'Has he been arrested?'

Jack laughed. 'Has he fuck. What? You think Mickey grassed to the pigs? He's not stupid. Well, not that stupid anyway, the poor prick. The way I heard it, whatever he told them . . . maybe how he'd been with me the day she got killed . . . and whatever else . . . and after, what I heard he got told was that if he ever showed his face west of fucking Bristol again, he'd have it cut right off. Who knows why they didn't kill him. Maybe some fucker he knew spoke up for him. Wasn't the fact he worked for Riley, though . . . Dougie didn't give a shit . . .'

Meaning the cops' worst fears had already come true. A turf war. But not just about territory and market share. Personal. About revenge. Tit-for-tat. About the Hamiltons running roughshod over anyone who got in their way. And Riley likewise.

'I meant what I said about Stan Lomax,' he said. 'You keep him well close.'

'I hear you,' Jack said.

It wasn't just Jack who should watch his back. The old man's pistol. Frankie pictured it there in his mattress. The Hamiltons might have another crack at him as well. He'd still not even loaded it. Wasn't even sure that ammunition inside the box still worked.

'There's something else,' said Frankie. He felt his heartbeat spike.

'What?'

'This . . .' He took a passport-sized, black-and-white newspaper clipping from his jacket. A photo of a girl. He put it down on the table. 'You recognise her?'

Jack picked it up, his eyes narrowing.

'I don't know . . . there's something . . . but . . .'

'It was taken a while ago. Her hair . . .' Frankie remembered

Tara lying there dead on the kitchen floor. 'Her hair would have been cut short more recently . . .'

Jack was still staring. He held the photo now in both hands.

'Yeah, I think I . . .'

'Go on.'

'I don't know when, but I think I . . . you know, with her . . . but I just can't . . . who the fuck is she, Frankie?'

'Tara,' he said. 'Tara Stevens.'

Jack shook his head and put the photo back down, but his eyes wouldn't leave it alone.

Frankie told him, 'You might have known her as Star.'

'Christ,' Jack said. 'It was her, wasn't it? Who I was with that night. I remember now. Round at Stav's. I remember heading out with her down Notting Hill to get wasted . . . but . . .'

'And then?' Come on, you wanker. Remember.

'I think . . . I think we—'

'Yeah?' Frankie wanted to shake it out of him. 'Come on. Go on.'

Jack looked up. 'I think we went back . . . back to mine . . . I think we ended up partying there . . .'

Partying. A fucking euphemism. For getting off their knockers. For fucking each other blind.

'You sure about that?'

'Yeah. I mean, I think . . .'

'For how long? All night?' While Susan Tilley was being killed?

Jack's expression crumpled. 'I dunno.' He pinched the clipping tight between his forefingers and thumbs, like he could somehow wring the answer out of it. 'I'm not sure . . . the rest of it . . . it's all still a blur . . .' His eyes flashed at Frankie. 'Where is she? Can she help? Have you found her?'

'I did,' Frankie said, 'and maybe she could've . . . but I was too late . . .'

He took out another piece of paper from his pocket: page five of today's *Daily Mail*. He smoothed it out on the table beside the snapshot. It detailed Tara's death, how she'd been found surrounded by petals in her kitchen. The empty square in the article was where he'd cut her photo from. He'd not wanted Jack to see the article first. Had wanted him to make up his own mind if he'd ever seen her before.

Tears welled up in Jack's eyes. All his earlier Mr-fucking-Cool was gone. 'Whoever did this . . . whoever did this to me . . . whoever put me here . . . they did that to her . . .'

'I know.'

'And now she's gone,' he said. 'And without her say-so, we can't prove shit, can we? Without her, I'm fucked. I'm gonna be stuck in here for the rest of my life.'

'No. Don't give up,' Frankie said. 'There's still the old lady. She might still put the finger on somebody else.' The old lady and the witness. If Riley ever came through.

Jack's lip curled. 'And if she doesn't?'

'Then we'll just keep trying, won't we? We'll do whatever it takes.'

And not just the old lady and Riley. Keira too. With Star now dead, maybe if Keira did know something more about that night, she'd be prepared to talk. Maybe she'd even be frightened enough to want whoever was doing this stopped. And women confided in each other, didn't they? Star might have told Keira something else, something that could help. Making Keira Frankie's next port of call.

Time to track her down again and really turn the screw.

242

37

Frankie waited until it was dark before heading over to Porto-bello Road. Neither Stav or anyone working for him would be conscious much before then.

The same motley crew of junkies and low-lifes were in the basement as before. The same smell of death. The same Russian heavy stood guarding the stairs. Part of the fucking brickwork.

'Remember me? I came round the other night,' Frankie said.

'I remember.'

Frankie moved towards the door. The Russian didn't step aside.

'Stav said not to let you in.'

'He did?'

The heavy just chewed his gum.

'And why's that?' Frankie asked.

The heavy shrugged. Kept chewing. His fist stayed locked round the same heavy South African baton-torch as before.

'I'm looking for Keira,' said Frankie. 'She here?'

The Russian shook his head. Was he lying? His eyes gave nothing away.

'Do. You. Know. Where. She. Is?'

The Russian smiled. 'The morgue.'

'You what?'

'Dead.'

'No,' said Frankie. This dumb fucker was confused. 'Not Star. I mean, Keira. The other girl. Her friend.'

'Dead.'

'Keira's dead?'

'Both dead.'

Frankie mouth ran dry. 'But . . . but how?'

'Drowned. In the river. This morning. By Hammersmith.' He said it like it was a suburb of Moscow.

'But she can't have . . . just fucking drowned.'

Another shrug. 'Junkies OD all the time.'

Frankie couldn't believe what he was hearing. Or seeing. This wanker. He was grinning. Frankie's hands balled into fists. But what was the point? This guy was a psychopath. He didn't give a shit. He'd probably enjoy getting hit. He'd enjoy caving Frankie's head in with that torch even more.

Frankie shut himself inside the phone booth on Ladbroke Grove. It smelt of piss and its grimy windows were a gallery of call girls advertising their wares. Jesus. Keira was dead? Was it true? Why wouldn't it be? That prick had no reason to lie.

He took out Sharon's work card and dialled her number that was on it. The receiver stank of someone else's breath and he held it at an angle away from his mouth as he counted the rings. Eight, nine, ten . . . Just fucking be in. Fucking pick up.

'Yeah?' a voice answered. Not Sharon's, some bloke's.

Frankie felt a prickle of . . . *what*? Surprise? Curiosity? *Jealousy*? It was half ten. Could be anyone. A friend. A relative. But it wasn't, was it? It was *him*. Her boyfriend.

'Is Sharon there?'

'Er, yeah. Sure. Who's calling?'

'A colleague.'

A lie. A stupid one. She was sure to have introduced him to some of the people she worked with. But he lucked out. The bloke – Nathan Witherspoon, wasn't that his sodding name? – didn't even ask.

'Janey,' he called out.

Janey? Who the fuck was Janey? Shit. Had he dialled the wrong number? But no. He couldn't have. He'd just said clear as day it was Sharon he wanted to talk to.

'Someone for you,' shouted the bloke. 'A *colleague*.'

The way he said the word . . . it was obvious he'd found it odd after all. Frankie cringed. Idiot. He should have hung up the second he'd answered. A crackle on the line. The receiver changing hands.

'Hello,' Sharon said. 'Who is it?'

'Frankie.'

'Oh, right . . . Er, hi, Dave,' she said.

'We need to meet.'

'Oh, I thought we'd talked about that already. I thought we'd agreed it wouldn't be necessary. At all.'

Nathan was still there then. Still listening.

'It's important,' he said. 'I swear. I wouldn't have rung if it wasn't. I need to see you. Now. And I'm sober, all right? Not like when I called you the other night.'

Silence. He pictured her face.

'OK.'

'The same place as before' he said. 'The Starlight.' Where they'd first talked. Down the road from Jack's flat.

'Fine. The incident room. I'll see you there in half an hour.'

Was Nathan in the room with her? Or was she watching the doorway, wary in case he returned? He pictured where her phone was in the hall. Where her bed was too. And the front door.

He hung up. Waved down a cab. Told the driver to take him

over to Warren Street. What the fuck did it all mean? What that heavy had said. Had Keira really OD'd? Somehow fucking drowned? Just like that? Out of the blue? Jesus, yes, it was possible. And shit, the cash he'd given her, she could have even spent that on whatever it was that had topped her. Or not. Or she hadn't bloody OD'd at all. Because that made sense too. Because if Tara had been killed, then why not Keira too? Or, fuck, was he just out of his depth? Because he couldn't make any sense of it at all.

He stared out the cab's window, feeling sick. They were cutting through Bayswater now, getting closer to her, to Sharon. So he was back then? Her fella. From wherever the hell he'd been . . . oh, yeah . . . Hong Kong. Meaning what? That if things hadn't already broken down good and proper between Frankie and her, then they would have done now. Forget her. Forget you and her. You're not going to see her about you. This is about Jack.

She was already waiting in the Starlight by the time he got there. Same table they'd sat at before. No other customers. She'd already ordered him a coffee. Milk, three sugars. She'd already half-finished hers.

'So what's with the *Janey* thing?' he said, sitting down.

An ice-breaker. Her face stayed hard as rock.

'It's my middle name, if you must know,' she said.

'What's wrong with Sharon?'

'Nothing. He just . . . Nathan . . . he doesn't like it. He thinks it's . . . It doesn't matter what he thinks,' she said. 'Listen. Why am I here?' She still hadn't taken off her coat.

'That girl you told me about . . . Star . . .'

Her eyebrows darted up. '*I* told *you* about?'

So she still thought it was him who'd put in that anonymous call to tell the cops that Star's DNA might prove a match to the condom from Jack's flat. Thought, but couldn't *prove*.

He didn't bite. 'Yeah,' he said, 'that's right. When you came round to mine.'

'What about her?' she said wearily.

Carefully does it. He had to pretend he'd spoken to Keira *after* Star had been found dead. Or Sharon would know he'd been lying when he'd denied knowing who Star was when she'd accused him of making that anonymous call.

'After you told me Star . . . Tara's name,' he said. 'I asked around. About who she might work for.'

'You've got no right. That's our job. Not yours.'

'Yeah, well I done it anyway.'

'Stav Christoforou,' said Sharon. 'That's who you're about to tell me she worked for.'

'That's right.'

'We ask questions too.'

'Yeah? Well I asked about who she hung out with as well. Who her friends were.'

'And?'

'And I found someone. Her best mate.'

Sharon shook her head. Her lips made a thin red line as she sipped at her coffee.

'What?' said Frankie. 'Girls like her don't have any friends?'

'I'm not saying that.'

'Then what *are* you saying?'

'That girls like her – and whoever they hang out with – will sometimes say anything if it will get them what they're after. Like money, or attention, or drugs . . .'

'So?'

'So if you're about to tell me that you've turned up some lead on who killed Tara Stevens and how this might prove your brother's innocence, all on the say-so of someone claiming to be

247

Tara's best mate, then you'll have to forgive me if I take it with a pinch of salt.'

'You take it with as much salt as you like, but this friend of Tara's I spoke to . . . what she told me was that Tara Stevens *did* go off with my brother that night . . .'

Sharon stared hard into the steam rising up off her coffee, her brow knitted in concentration.

'They got a match,' she said.

'For what?'

'The condom. The two sets of DNA . . . they matched Tara's and your brother's . . . And other tests they've done, on the semen, it proves they had intercourse that night.'

Bloody hell. He'd only gone and done it. He'd only gone and got the bloody cops to bloody well check it out, thanks to that call he'd put in. He nearly punched the fucking air.

'But that—'

'No,' Sharon cut him off. 'It still doesn't prove he didn't kill Susan Tilley. Even within the time frame that new information has given us, it's still possible for your brother to have gone out to her grandmother's house. Without Tara Stevens actually giving him an alibi, which she no longer can. Unless . . .'

'Unless?'

'What time did this *friend* of Tara's say your brother met up with Tara?'

'A few hours before Susan Tilley was killed.'

'So not at the same time?'

'No, but near enough at least to cast some doubt on where my brother might have been that night around that time.'

'And it's something she'll swear to, is it? This friend?'

'No.'

'No?' Sharon flared. 'Then why are we even—'

'Because she's dead.' He let it sink in. 'They fished her out of the river by Hammersmith this morning. She OD'd. At least that's what I've been told.'

'Was she a drug user?'

'Yeah.'

'A prostitute?'

Frankie nodded. 'Another one of Stav's girls. But that doesn't mean she OD'd . . . I mean, don't you find it a bit fucking suspicious? That two girls – one who was with Jack at some point that night, and the other one who knew she was – are now both bloody dead?'

'It could just be a coincidence . . .'

'And what about the fact that Star was found battered to death in her kitchen? Just the same as Susan Tilley's grandmother.'

'The wounds might have been superficially the same—'

'*Superficially*? They both had their heads caved in. I read it in the paper.'

'There's no proof that the weapon used was the same. In fact it's highly unlikely that it is because . . .'

'Because what?'

'Nothing.'

But it clearly wasn't nothing. She was blushing, embarrassed. Or angry with herself about what she'd been about to say.

'Tell me,' he said. 'It's about Jack, isn't it?'

'Well, I suppose you're going to see it on the news tomorrow anyway . . .'

'See *what*?'

'They found his car.'

'Whose?' His stomach lurched. 'Jack's?'

The same car he'd had since he'd passed his test. A Renault piggin' 5. The least gangster-ish car in the world. Frankie remembered him buying it. Or him having it *bought* for him anyhow. The old man hadn't been in a position to do it. So Frankie had.

Had used some cash he'd put aside for going to Ibiza with some old school mates. Hadn't mattered that he hadn't gone. His life had already moved on by then, hadn't it? What with him running the club. Him thinking he could just skip town and go partying in the sun for a week had been nothing but a fantasy. One he'd stamped on, hard.

'Where?' Frankie said.

'Yesterday morning. Near a pub over in Shepherd's Bush.'

'What pub?'

'The Andover.'

'They got any footage of it? From round there. Any cctv? Anything that shows whoever the bastard was who left it there? And when it was put there?' Was it *after* Jack was banged up?

She shook her head, then bit down on her lip. Oh, shit. There was worse to come.

'They found the murder weapon, Jack. A baseball bat. And her blood. Susan's blood. It was covered with it. So was the car. And . . .' Sharon looked down at the table '. . . her underwear, Frankie . . . the gusset torn from her . . . it was inside the glove compartment along with Jack's wallet . . .'

'And, what?' Frankie could hardly believe what he was hearing. 'That's meant to prove something, is it?' He scratched at his neck. He felt like his skin was on fire. A horrible image jumped into his head. Of Jack being there. Him doing *that*. No. *No*. He rubbed at his face. Don't you fucking believe that. Don't you even fucking think it.

'The car was locked, Frankie. There were no signs that anyone had broken in.'

'So what you're saying is that my brother is meant to have done all this, *then* driven back to London and parked his car miles away and made no attempt to clean it up? And instead he – what? Walked? *Walked*? Called a fucking cab? Somehow fucking made his way back home to his flat and then what? Had a half-arsed clean-up? Before falling-a-fucking-sleep? No. *No.* It doesn't make sense.' He stabbed his finger down hard against the table. 'It. Does. Not. Make. Sense.'

'Unless he was high.'

Which was still clearly the line the cops were sticking to.

'*Or.* Didn't. Bloody. Do. It.'

'I'm sorry, Frankie . . .'

'Not as bloody sorry as I am. Or Jack will be. When he ends up in prison for life for something he didn't fucking do.'

He wanted to shout, to scream at her, until she admitted that what he was saying was true. But it wasn't her fault. He knew that. Even now. Feeling like he wanted to smack someone in the face. She was just doing her job. Right? And risking her job too. Yeah. Breathe in. Breathe out. She's not the enemy. She's here, isn't she? Talking to you about Jack. She'd not just shut him out.

Think. Use your brain. Forget the bloody car. Nothing you can do about that. Concentrate on what you do know. Prove he's innocent some other way.

'What about how the killer got in?' he asked.

'Where?'

'Tilley's grandmother's house. And Star Stevens' flat too.'

'What about it?'

Stay wary. Don't give away that you were there that night at Tara's flat. Just stick to what you've read in the papers since.

'In both cases, the victims let the killer in, didn't they?' he said.

'Yes, but plenty of—'

'And at Star Stevens' flat there were flowers, weren't there?' He was on safe ground here. It had been mentioned in one of the papers.

'Yes, and one of the lines of enquiry we're pursuing is that whoever killed her was someone she was romantically linked to.'

'Romantically?'

'OK, a client. Someone who got obsessed with her. Who didn't want to share her. It wouldn't be the first time.'

'And what about at Susan Tilley's grandmother's house? Were there any flowers there?'

'No . . .' But something changed in her expression as she said it.

'What?'

'Nothing . . . no . . .' She shook her head, slowly, her eyes narrowing. 'I can't be certain . . .'

'*What?*'

'Petals,' she said. 'Yes . . . I remember . . . right there by the front door . . . near where Susan's grandmother was found . . . I'm sure I remember seeing something, yes, and thinking it odd . . .'

She looked frustrated. That she might have missed something. Meant she was listening to him too. Wasn't just dismissing what he was saying out of hand.

'Has she said anything yet?' Frankie said. 'The old lady. About what she saw?' About what he wanted to hear. About it not – *please God* – having been Jack. 'Because she might remember something about this too . . . about the flowers . . .'

'No. I'm sorry.' She'd guessed what he'd also been hoping to hear too. 'She's still too ill to talk. We've not been able to speak to her yet.'

There was still hope there. By God, there was.

'If someone did set up Jack,' Frankie said, 'and Tara was somehow involved, then they could have killed Tara and then Keira. To make sure they kept quiet about whatever else they knew.

To keep Jack from having an alibi. To make sure he still got the blame . . .'

Sharon said, 'This friend of Star's . . .'

'Keira.'

'Do you know her surname?'

Frankie shook his head.

'I'll look into it,' she said. 'Find out who got pulled out of the river. Find out how she died. Whoever does the autopsy . . . I'll make sure they're thorough . . . that they look for all possible causes, you understand?'

That they'd look to see if she'd been murdered. Yes. Frankie nodded. He got it.

She made a show of checking her watch. 'I'd better get going,' she said.

They stared at each other.

'Thanks,' he said. 'For coming. And for this. For what you're going to do next. I appreciate this.'

'That's OK. And this . . . asking questions that might need to be asked . . . it's part of my job.'

She meant work. Business. That that's why she was here. All right. Fine. He knew when not to push.

'Goodbye, Frankie,' she said.

He nodded. Watched her go. The light of the café's sign lit up her face all golden for a second as she walked underneath it. Made her look beautiful. Somehow perfect. Like a statue.

Go after her.

Make her stay.

Don't let her leave.

But it was already too late. She'd already gone.

38

Frankie found Xandra in the service alley at the back of the club the next day, clanking around in the early morning sun.

'What you doing?' he asked.

'Clearing out crap.' She chucked a broken toilet lid into one of the council bins.

'Where from?'

'The basement. The other storerooms down there. Thought I might as well. Paint's drying in mine. Nothing to do there.' She smiled. 'Why? What's the matter? Did I wake you up?'

'Yeah, something like that.'

He'd slept pretty well for him, a couple of nightmares aside. He'd gone to bed feeling down. Done in. Not just because of the madness of the last few days. Because of her. Sharon. Because her leaving him there sitting on his lonesome in the Starlight had left him feeling like shit cubed. More alone than he'd felt in years.

He took the empty wheelbarrow off Xandra, went in, got changed into his blue overalls and started loading it up. She got stuck in too. Hard worker. Good to have around. Slim was still a bit funny about her, mind. Had let slip to Frankie that a tenner had gone missing off one of the punters' tables the other night. Slim had asked her about it. Not *accused* her. Asked. But she'd just shrugged, apparently. Not *denied*. Not like a real thief would.

That's what Frankie reckoned. Slim, though, he still wasn't so sure.

Over the next hour, Frankie helped her clear out a fine selection of crapola from the club, filling three big council bins with smashed bottles, splintered cues, broken chairs, rusted paint tins, and brushes so stiff with varnish you could have slashed someone's face open with them.

A right mental thought, that. Frankie shook his head, lighting a cigarette as the two of them stood there in the alley having a break. Jesus. He stared up at the blue sky. All this madness with Jack . . . what he'd seen at Star's flat . . . that poor cow's face . . . it was doing his head in. Making him see shit that wasn't there. Seeping into him. Like some kind of fucking poison. Right down into his pores.

The bad dreams he'd had . . . he could still remember bits of them now. Stressy ones. Him scrabbling round the flat hunting for that gun . . . people pounding at the door. He blew smoke out. Get a grip. He needed to fight this shit. The F.E.A.R. Not give into it. But Christ, it was hard.

What Dougie had done to Mickey was a part of it. Done to his eye. Frankie kept thinking about what Mickey might have told him. About his chat with Frankie? Enough for the Hamiltons to pay Mo a call? Enough for Mo to then work out that Frankie had already done the same? Was he already halfway down the road to Shitsville without even knowing he'd set out?

Or worse . . . what if Mickey had told Dougie – and whoever else had been there with him doing the cutting – about the call Jack had got about that girl the day Susan Tilley had been offed? What if the Hamiltons made the same link to Stav that Frankie had? What then? Because, shit, if that happened, well, then everything started unravelling, didn't it? They might work out that Frankie had gone to see Tara. They might do their homework better than the pigs and find some way to prove it. Take down both James brothers together. Double the fucking revenge.

Frankie took another long drag on his fag. Quit your worrying. Panic's gonna get you nowhere. Nothing he could do about any of it. Nothing but wait. The same as with Jack. He was stuck. At a fucking impasse. Waiting to see if the old lady put Jack in the clear. Waiting for Sharon to get Keira a postmortem. Waiting to see if it turned up some connection between her and Star's death and the night she was with Jack. Waiting for Tommy Riley to try and get him word on this witness. Waiting on his next fucking move.

He ground out his cigarette. Spat on the ground. He hated it, feeling this powerless, this *weak*. Not who he was. Not what he was about.

'Right,' he said, turning to Xandra. 'What we were talking about yesterday . . . You got me that list?'

'Sure. Right here.' Xandra pulled out a folded piece of A4 from the pouch of her paint-spattered denim dungarees. She grinned. 'We really doing it then?'

'Yeah, might as well. Crack on, eh? Especially with you still dressed up like you're auditioning for Dexy's Midnight Runners.'

'Hah-hee-hah.' She handed him the piece of paper.

Her plan. Giving the whole place a makeover. A facelift from the basement up. Seeing as they already had a whole bunch of painting gear up and running, why not, eh? She looked well pleased. Probably because he was putting her sort of in charge. Best move, mind. He sucked at DIY.

Him chatting through his plans a couple of days ago for running a tournament here had given her the idea. When he'd got onto the subject of potential sponsors, Slim had pointed out that one of their first considerations would probably be how the place looked. And looking like it did, like a total khazi, might just put them off.

Xandra had then let slip that decorating had been her family's old business. Out of nowhere. Kapow. A personal piece of info. Just like that. Which had gone a fair way to explaining how she'd done such a good job of her own room here, of course. She'd not mentioned any of her family by name, though. Nothing about them at all. Maybe they were the problem? The reason she'd run away? He hadn't chased Sharon up for that social worker yet. Not sure how Xandra would take it even when he did.

'Right,' he told her now. 'I'll be back in an hour, then let's hit it, yeah?'

She nodded. Her eyes were twinkling in the sun. She lit another cigarette to hide her smile.

He read the list over on the way to the multi-story. The girl had nice hand-writing. Educated then. No surprise there. She was smart. Clearly knew a thing about commercial scale decorating too, judging by the amount of kit – power tools, brushes, turps, rollers, groundsheets, masking tape, sandpaper and paint – she'd written down here.

The Capri was hardly ideal for work of the picking-shit-up variety. But he managed to fit it all in after he'd done his shop down Wickes. Truth was he wanted to get every last second's worth of driving out of it before he sold it. Knowing it was going to pay for Jack's brief only made it feel even more precious.

He parked the Capri out the front of the club behind a freshly waxed black beemer and started unloading the gear from the back. Weird. He heard the clack of a ball being struck though the club's open door. Laughter too. It was well early for punters. No one ever tipped up much before eleven.

There were two of them inside. Big like barn doors, six footers. Suited. Both clocked him as he came in. He didn't recognise either of them. Something about the laid-bloody-back way they eyeballed him that rang alarm bells. Either cops or crooks. Bad news either way.

'Hey, Frankie,' called out Xandra.

She was kneeling in the corridor which led out past the bar to the back door, scraping away at the old flock wallpaper.

'Hi.' He shot her a frown, tilting his head a little to indicate the customers, as he carried the first set of bags over to her.

Xandra shrugged. Didn't look panicked, mind. Meaning they'd not caused any trouble. Yet. He put the bags down. She looked them over sceptically, *professionally*. He liked that. She was taking this shit seriously. Good thing too. Costing him another arm and a leg he already didn't have.

'That it?' she said.

'Nah, the rest's in the car.'

'Right.' She looked relieved. 'I've been thinking . . .' She turned her attention back to the floor and peeled the minging faded blue carpet a little way back from the skirting board. 'Look . . . You've got some nice boards under here. We could strip this off and give them a varnish. Make the place look a little bit more contemporary, eh?'

Contemporary? Nice. He smiled.

'You think that would look better, do you?'

'I know it would.'

'Fine.'

'It would smell better too. I don't know how many years people have been tramping back and forth across this carpet on their way to the toilet, but trust me, it's taken its toll. And it'll be cheaper to do the boards than buy new carpet. All we need is a decent floor sanding machine and some masks and we'll be able to do it ourselves.'

'OK,' he said. 'Sounds like a plan.'

Clack. Another ball being struck behind him. He pulled the receipt from Wickes and a pen from his pocket and quickly scribbled down Kind Regards' name and number and slipped it into Xandra's hand.

'I get any trouble with these two gibbons,' he said softly, handing it to her. 'You duck out the back and phone my lawyer and tell him to get round here pronto.'

She nodded, pocketing the piece of paper. Her face hardened. Ready for action.

He slowly – casually as he fucking could – turned and walked back through to the hall. Right. Let's get on with this. Find out who these two jokers are. Standing behind the bar, he cracked himself open a can of Coke.

'Can I get you gents anything?' he said.

The bloke who'd taken the last shot, and was in the process of lining up a long red, smiled slowly and laid his cue out on the table, before looking up. The older of the two. Slick black hair and grey stubble round his chin. Late forties.

'Frankie James?'

'Yeah?' Frankie's tone said it all: Who the fuck wants to know?

'You sure about that?' The man's voice was rough, street rough, commanding. He walked towards Frankie, eyes locked on him. His companion, ten years younger, stayed put, leaning up against the wall next to the door, oh so relaxed, but there was something deliberate too about the way the fucker stayed facing Frankie as well, watching him like a hawk, itching to see what went down.

'Of course I'm fucking sure,' Frankie said without a smile.

'In which case, I've been misinformed,' said the man.

'How's that?'

'I heard you were a sharp-dressed little bastard.'

Little? Frankie stared him down. 'Yeah? And who told you that?'

The man looked slowly round. 'I see you're tarting the place up?'

'That's right.'

He stared at Frankie's overalls. 'Having to do it yourself. I guess times must be hard.'

Frankie didn't like the way this guy was looking at him. Not one bit. Like he was something this guy had just scraped off his polished fucking brogue. Didn't like the way this conversation was going either. Like this guy was spoiling for a fight.

'Who are you? What do you want?' he said. Careful so the man didn't see him slowly reaching beneath the counter with his left hand for the cue.

'The name's Tam Jackson,' he said. His hand moved. Slowly, smoothly, *confidently*, into his jacket pocket. For what? Frankie's pulse raced. Images of cop shows and Westerns flashed into his mind. Oh, shit. Was that what this was? A hit? Had Dougie Hamilton sent this man to do what he'd not been able to do himself out there on the street?

Frankie gripped the cue, pulling it back out of its brackets, stepping back as he did. At the same time, the man's arm emerged back out of his jacket. But gripped in his hand wasn't the pistol or blade Frankie had half-expected, but a crisp white envelope. Frankie stared at it, then at the cue gripped in his hand, which was now in full view.

'That for me?' Frankie said.

'I could ask you the same thing,' said Tam, staring at the cue.

'I was just gonna have a little practice,' Frankie said.

Yeah, on my face, the man's expression answered with a wry smile. Frankie wasn't fooling him. At all. But this smooth fucker wasn't fooling Frankie either. Right there alongside the unwavering smile, he'd just glimpsed something else – a wariness, nerves.

He walked over and put the envelope down on the counter in front of Frankie, but kept his forefinger pressed down on it. Still his.

'A gift,' he said.

'From who?'

'You'll see.' His smile widened.

It . . . Frankie glanced down at the envelope. What the hell was in there? When he looked back up, he saw Tam was still staring at the cue Frankie had gripped in his hand.

'I might take you up on that game some time,' he said. 'But not today. Got too much shit on my plate to deal with already. And now . . .' he tapped the envelope firmly, before finally pulling his hand away '. . . so have you.'

He glanced past Frankie into the mirror behind the bar. Adjusted his tie. He took another look at Frankie's overalls, that same look of superiority and distaste crossing his face, and slowly shook his head.

'I knew your old man,' he said. 'Not well. But enough.'

'Enough for what?' Frankie said.

'To know he was the kind of man who'd do what he was told. When he was told it. And you're no different. No better than him. So just make sure you make the right choice. OK, kid?'

What the fuck? Who the fuck was this guy? Frankie felt the blood rush to his face. It must have shown. Tam's smile stretched for a second in delight. But before Frankie could say a word, he just turned. Just turned his fucking back on him. And walked. Real leisurely like. Back across the hall to the front door.

The other wanker, his backup, or minder, or whatever the fuck he was, held the door open for him, then nodded once, briefly at Frankie – like to tell him he'd be seeing him again and couldn't fucking wait – before following Jackson outside.

The door thumped shut behind them. All Frankie could hear then was the sound of his own beating heart.

'What the hell was that about?' Xandra asked, at his side.

How much had she heard? How much had she understood? How much did *he* understand? Shit, what the hell was in this envelope? He stared down at it. Still hadn't picked it up.

'Nothing,' he said. 'No one.'

'It didn't look like nothing. *He* didn't look like no one.'

She was staring at the envelope. 'Early Christmas card?'

'Maybe.'

'Or something about your brother?'

No flies on her. She'd guessed the same as him.

'Chuck us the car keys then,' she said. 'I'll go get the rest of the gear.'

Knew when to mind her own business then. He dug the keys out of his pocket. Held them up for her.

'Don't worry,' she told him, snatching them away. 'I won't nick it. I can't even drive.'

He watched her go. Then leant heavily on the bar and picked up the envelope. He stared. This was bad. What Tam had said. About this. Like it was going to somehow change his life. For better? Or worse?

He dug his finger in under the flap, prising it open, wondering who'd sealed it, whose dried spit he was touching now.

A single sheet of white paper inside. He took it out, unfolded it. A photocopy. Of what? A motorcycle courier docket. Some firm based out in Hounslow. Why the fuck had they just given him this?

Then he saw. The date. The same day Jack was meant to have killed Susan Tilley. And the time of the pickup. Less than half and hour before the time of her death. And the drop-off address

. . . out in Berkshire. The same place as Susan Tilley grandmother's house. Whoever this courier was, they'd gone there that night to deliver a parcel right around the time that Susan Tilley had been killed.

Which could mean only one thing. This courier had to be the cops' witness – the fucking liar or killer or whatever the fuck they were – who was going to swear in a court of law that Jack had been there and had murdered that girl. Meaning the geezers who'd just delivered it – Tam Jackson and his goon – they had to be working for Tommy Riley. He'd come up with the goods Frankie needed. Exactly like he'd said. Meaning Frankie now owed him that favour.

That much was settled now too.

39

Who was this bastard? That's all Frankie could think as he marched across Charing Cross Road.

The way it boiled down was this: either the courier was lying about what he'd seen, or Jack was lying about what he'd done. And Jack wasn't lying. Was he? No, he still had to believe that. Which meant the courier was. But why? Had they been paid? Or were they involved on some deeper level? Was it them who'd repeatedly swung that bat?

Frankie had changed back into his suit. Not because of what that flash bastard Tam Jackson had said. Frankie didn't give a shit about having to graft for a living. No, he'd got his suit on – a crappy old one, mind – because he needed to look like a cop.

He spotted the antique bookshop up ahead. An old-fashioned wooden sign above its glass double front read 'Ronald Chivenham, Dealer in Books of Antiquity'.

It might have been faster, of course, to ring up the courier company and give them the docket number off this photocopy he had in his pocket. Then see if he could get the name of the courier who'd made the delivery to Susan Tilley's grandmother's house. But he couldn't see them just giving up that information, let alone any contact details through which Frankie could then track the courier down. Not unless he told them he was police. But the cops would no doubt have already spoken to them about their star witness. Would have asked them to report any further suspicious enquiries made by anyone else. And the last thing Frankie wanted was this courier getting tipped off that someone else was trying to track him down.

So he'd come here instead. To the pickup address the courier had collected the parcel from that night. In easy walking distance from the club. He marched up and gave the door a firm-but-polite, cop-like knock, before pushing it open and stepping inside. A little brass bell rang out.

'I'll be with you in a minute,' a man's voice shouted from somewhere out back.

The place was a tip, but not an ugly one. Frankie had always liked books, not just reading them, but the feel of them too. It was one of the reasons he'd wanted to go to uni so much. Just to be there in some library surrounded by them. His mother had always read to him and Jack as kids. Jack had loved it too. Had been really into reading as a kid. Right up until their mum had gone missing. Where it had all gone wrong.

Frankie checked the walls and ceiling for cctv, the same as he'd done outside. Nothing. Good. If whoever owned this place sussed that he wasn't who he was about to claim he was, then at least they'd not then have his mugshot for the real cops to ID.

Could the shop owner be involved? In on whatever this was along with the courier and whatever other bastards had decided to set Jack up? He'd find out soon enough.

Footsteps.

'Hello, can I help you?'

A tall, grey-haired old geezer appeared through a doorway at the back of the shop. Posh accent. Serious-looking in an academic kind of way.

'Mister Chivenham?'

'Yes?' Chivenham peered uncertainly at Frankie through his half-moon specs.

'I'm Detective—' *Major*, he'd been about to say. The Prime Minster's name, the first name he'd thought of. Didn't have to.

'Ah, more police,' Chivenham interrupted. 'About that poor girl?'

'S'right.'

'It's dreadful, of course, completely dreadful, but I already told your colleagues all that I know.'

'If it's all right with you, I'd like to run through it one more time. Just to make sure there's nothing we missed.'

A kettle whistled out back.

'Very well. I was just fixing myself some tea. Would you like a cup yourself?'

'Why not?' said Frankie. 'Milk three sugars.'

'Biscuits?'

'Perfect.' He smiled. Every cop he'd ever met, they'd had an even sweeter tooth than him.

Chivenham nodded at his desk near the window. 'Make yourself comfortable. I'll be back in two ticks.'

Frankie sat down in one of the two big armchairs facing the desk. Well, this Chivenham hardly looked like a criminal mastermind, did he? More like a schoolteacher. And not from this decade either. More like the 1950s. Frankie couldn't think of anyone *less* likely to have been involved in Susan Tilley's murder.

As Chivenham whistled tunelessly out of sight, Frankie took out a notepad he'd picked up in Ryman's on the way over. Black and discreet. Like the one Sharon had pulled from her bag that night she'd collared him at Jack's. He bent its spine and flicked through it a few times to rough it up. Then flattened it down on a new page and pulled out a well-chewed biro that he'd got from the bar at the club.

Chivenham came back and placed a laden wooden tea tray on the desk between them.

'Shall I be mother?' he said, pouring milk into the two cups, before topping them up from the pot.

'Lovely,' said Frankie.

He stirred in three heaped teaspoons of sugar, then removed the courier docket from his pocket and smoothed it out on the table beside the silver tray.

'Ah, yes,' Chivenham said.

Meaning he'd clearly seen it before. Frankie had to be careful. He didn't know what the real cops would already have asked. Didn't want to go making him suspicious by repeating the same series of questions. Better talk a bit of shop first. Put him at his ease.

'How long have you worked here, Mister Chivenham?'

'Oh, well let me see. It must be nearly fourteen years. Yes, since 1981.'

'A wonderful place. You must be very proud.'

'Yes. I suppose I am.'

'And couriers are a regular part of your business?'

'Quite. Increasingly so.'

'And this particular courier . . .' Time to cut to the chase. '. . . what time were they called?'

The passive voice. Frankie's old English teacher would have been proud of him. He wasn't saying *who* might have called the courier at all. Was hoping Chivenham would be generous enough to give that away.

No dice.

'Eight o'clock,' the bookseller said. 'Just before closing time. It was late-night shopping that night, you see.' He offered Frankie a biscuit, before taking one himself. 'I had the book all parcelled up and ready. It was important it looked nice. It was to be a gift, you see. A wedding present for that poor girl.'

Who was the customer? Who ordered the book? That's all Frankie wanted to ask. Couldn't just come out and say it, though. Would look odd, because the cops would have done it already. Had to try another tack.

'And how much would a book like that cost, sir? If you don't mind my asking.' How was it paid for? Could that payment be chased?

'That edition of *The Count of Monte Cristo* isn't a particularly rare book,' Chivenham said. 'Although this one was in very good condition, the same as with all my stock. A hundred and twenty pounds was the price we agreed.'

We . . . him and whoever had bought it. Whoever had told him which address it needed sending to. Whoever was involved in Susan Tilley's murder, who'd sent the witness there to lie.

'And remind me, sir,' said Frankie, 'the customer paid for this by . . .' Frankie picked up his notebook, keeping its pages hidden from Chivenham, and made a show of flicking slowly back through it, as if referring to other notes he already had.

'Well, it's like I told the lady detective who came round . . .'

'Mmm-huh?' Frankie didn't look up. Lady detective? Did he mean Sharon? Had it been her who'd been interviewing him?

'They paid in cash,' Chivenham said.

Meaning there'd be no bank details to trace, not like with a credit card or cheque. Bollocks.

'And all above board, you understand,' added Chivenham. 'I'm scrupulous with my accounts. Everything's right there in my ledger.'

'Absolutely, sir. Of course. And a regular customer, was he?' *He* . . . Again, Frankie made a show of consulting his notes. Sharon would have asked too.

'No. Never seen him before. Or since. A friend of the girl's family,' he said.

'And the description you gave to my colleague?'

'Yes,' said Chivenham. 'A white man . . . middle-aged . . . Nothing particularly distinguishable about him.' Chivenham took off his glasses, rubbing at the bridge of his nose. 'My glasses, you see. I really should get a new pair. Oh, there was one thing, I remember. A cravat. He was wearing a burgundy cravat. I only noticed it because I haven't seen anyone wearing one in such a long time.'

A cravat. Frankie wrote it down.

'This courier company . . .' Frankie tapped the docket with his forefinger. '. . . you called them up yourself, sir, did you?'

'Yes.' He glanced at the notebook. He'd obviously mentioned this before as well.

But Frankie still couldn't see it, how the courier had got this gig to collect this book and take it out to the property, thereby giving him a perfect cover for being there. Unless this Chivenham was in on it too. But he still couldn't believe that.

'Any reason for using this particular firm for this particular job?' he said. 'One of the regular companies you use?'

'Well, no,' said Chivenham. 'Actually now you come to mention it, I'd never even heard of the firm before this.'

From the way he said it, it was obvious he'd not told the cops. Maybe they hadn't been looking too deep, thinking that in Jack they already had their man.

'Actually, it was his idea,' Chivenham said. 'The customer's. He gave me their card. He said he knew they delivered out that way. Where the girl's grandmother lived. And they'd be able to get it there for later that evening when someone would be at the house to take delivery.'

Bingo. The perfect way to sneak their man in as a witness. But who was the customer? Chivenham didn't know. Only one way to find out. From the bastard courier himself.

'This courier . . .' Frankie said '. . . the description you gave my colleague . . .' He feigned checking his notepad again.

'Yes, sorry about that, but at least it wasn't my eyesight to blame this time . . .' Chivenham pressed his hands together awkwardly. 'It's just these chaps all look the same, don't you know, with their helmets and leathers on. They hardly look human at all.'

In-human would cover this one just fine.

'But there was one thing . . .' Chivenham said.

'Being.'

'His accent. It didn't sound . . . British . . .'

'What then?'

'Eastern . . . Eastern European . . . I'm sorry, but I can't be any more specific than that.'

Frankie made a show of writing it down. 'No, thank you, sir. You've been very helpful . . . very helpful indeed.'

40

Frankie checked the *A–Z* on the Capri's passenger seat as he waited at the lights. Blur were twanging their latest on the radio. Some tune from *Parklife*.

Cockneys. Mockneys. Frankie wasn't even sure what he was himself any more. Just the same old him? Or now some kind of bloody detective? Or maybe he'd just lost the plot entirely somewhere along the line?

The radio's drumbeat smacked him hard in the chest. The courier firm was only a couple of streets away.

Still not sure how he was going to play it. Pretend to be a cop again? He'd done all right with the book dealer. But could he pull it off twice? No way on earth was he just going to walk into the courier firm's office and find the actual courier sitting there waiting. He'd have to persuade whoever was there to hand over the contact details instead.

All well and good – so long as whoever ran the desk there fell for Frankie's fake cop act. But what if they didn't? And called the cops? The same if he spooked them by coming on too heavy. Then the witness would end up not just anonymous, but in witness protection. Assuming he wasn't already. In which case any address Frankie managed to get today would be useless anyhow.

His other option was just scoping the place now, then coming back later. Burglary.

The lights turned green and he joined the slow-moving tail-back of traffic on the other side of the crossroads. A contraflow. Road works. Fucking London, eh? Still, he might as well enjoy the ride while he still could. Six potential punters lined up to have a dekko next week. He patted the steering wheel. Was going to miss the old girl when she was gone.

He sighed. Fuck, he was knackered. He'd called in at Wandsworth on the way here. To see Jack. News about his shitty Renault having been found was already all over the tabloids and TV. The lot. The blood, the bat, the torn underwear. The red tops now had Jack painted not just as a murderer, unborn baby killer and beater, but a perv too.

Jack had been a wreck. Whatever swagger he'd tried putting on in front of Frankie the last time they'd met was now long gone. The perv shit made a difference. A *big* difference inside. Whatever protection Riley might have offered him from Hamilton's boys before, there were plenty of other prisoners – lifers who didn't give a shit – who'd now fancy having a crack at Jack too. To do their moral fucking duty for their country and their Queen.

'They're talking about sticking me on the nonce wing,' Jack had told Frankie. 'With the paedoes and the rapists. For my own protection. I've told them no. But I don't know, Frankie. I don't feel safe here. Not any more.'

The old man had got wind about the contents of Jack's car as well. He'd been next on Frankie's visiting list today, across town in Brixton. He'd not been happy either. The whole time they'd talked, he'd kept his knuckles clenched like he'd wanted to snap something or crush it. Most likely a neck.

He'd heard Frankie out. About how nobody, not even Jack, could be so stupid as to leave a weapon and blood right there in their car. Or walk fucking home. If you ignored what the cops said about Jack having been high, which Frankie reckoned just sounded like bullshit anyway, then none of this made any sense. More like this was a stitch-up, pure and simple. That's what he'd told the old man. He just hoped the old bastard believed him. Hated to think he might not. That would destroy both him and Jack.

Frankie turned into the street the courier firm was on. A suburban backwater. He drove past the address and pulled into a car park opposite, in front of a small parade of shops. Had a good nosey through the car windows. Only cctv he could spot this side of the street was above a Londis and that was pointing the other way.

OK, so let's hit it. The cop routine. A quick in and out. Keep it confident. And polite. The same as before. He pulled on a baseball cap and shades. Got out, locked the car and crossed the road. Headed for the courier office.

No cctv on show. Nice. He took off his shades and cap and tucked them into his jacket pockets. But the office's front door opened just as he reached it. A woman in her early forties came out, flipping the sign round to 'Back in 5 minutes'.

He noticed she didn't double lock the door, despite the keys hanging from her belt. He walked past, head down. He clocked a phone box ten yards away. Ducked inside and watched the woman head into a sandwich shop opposite. She had blonde hair, cut short. A cheap blue suit with some kind of corporate scarf round her neck.

A queue several people long snaked back from the sandwich shop's counter. Frankie pulled the courier docket from his pocket and rang the office number. No answer. No one in.

He had just minutes. He pulled his cap and shades back on and hurried back to the office door. Watching the shops opposite in the half-reflection of the office window, he took Sharon's business card from his suit pocket. Feel the quality. Expensively-thick, but flexible. Perfect.

He waited for a second when no one was passing, then slid the card up the doorframe to the tarnished Yale lock. Another sign of a misspent youth. He hadn't exactly ever been a pro, but he had broken into a few places in his time. Mainly for kicks, in his teens. For dares. Just to see if he could. Into school, to tag the halls. Or through open restaurant windows to nick booze. Stuff that could have got him a police record, but luckily never had. Looking back, all he felt was ashamed.

But he did still remember this. Him and his mates had used to practise on one of their dad's plumbing stores when he wasn't around. The trick was to apply pressure with the shoulder, allowing you to thread the card in between the door and the frame, then use another card – his own this time, an Amex, long maxed out – to prise back the locking mechanism until . . . Hey, presto. The lock popped.

He pulled on his gloves. Another disposable pair nicked from a garage forecourt on the way over. He turned the handle. Another glance in the window's half-reflection. The middle-aged blonde bird was still in the queue. Not looking at him. He stepped quickly into the courier office, shutting the door behind.

He felt a shiver down his spine: a buzz of fear, of being somewhere he wasn't allowed.

'Hello?' he called out. Just in case there was someone here.

No answer. This place was a tip. Stank of fag smoke. Just the one desk with a square grey IBM on it. He hurried over and checked out the screen. Good: the screensaver hadn't kicked in. Even better: not a new computer. He'd used one like this at school.

He scanned the named file folders laid out across the screen in a neat row: invoices, insurance, overheads, payroll, jobs . . .

He pulled out his photocopied docket again. The courier's signature was illegible, but the date and time were clear enough. He clicked the 'jobs' folder open. All neatly organised inside. He quickly scrolled down to the right date and opened the file. A Lotus spreadsheet. A list of the forty-six jobs for that day. He read down the postcodes. Only two pickups in W1. But two different couriers. One called Jones. One Baotic.

Baotic. What was it the bookseller had told him? About the courier's accent being East European. Well, that put this Jones out of the picture, right? But what about *Baotic*? Was that East European? Who fucking knew?

He checked his watch. Just crack on. Get the gen. You're running out of time. He checked out across the street again. Could just about make out the woman. At the front of the queue, being served. Arsewipes. How long did he have left before she got back? Minutes? Less?

He shut the folder and dragged the mouse back to the one labelled 'payroll'. Fuck. Hundreds of names. Maybe everyone who'd ever worked here. But all sorted alphabetically. He scrolled down . . . Ross Adams . . . Salvador Apellido . . . until Baotic was there.

Double clicking on the name file, Frankie's heart thumped. Baotic's employment details. The jobs he'd worked. The one in W1. But only a couple before that. His first one only a fucking week before. Meaning the wanker had only just started working here. How fucking convenient. Hadn't done another job either, since Susan Tilley had died.

Then gold dust. The shithead's address. Frankie snatched up a yellow Post-it from the block next to the keyboard and grabbed a biro from the pot beside. He started scrawling down the address – then felt the hairs on the back of his neck stand up.

Movement. He looked up. Fuck. The blonde. Already halfway

across the street. Ten seconds and she'd be here. Shit on a stick. What had he been thinking? He should have checked again before.

He double-clicked the mouse. Shut down the file. Too late to run. Somehow had to front this out. But how? He snatched up the Post-it. Stepped away from the desk. Would she have some way of checking which files had been recently accessed? Quick. Get away from the computer. The last thing he needed was her telling the cops that someone had come here snooping and looking for Baotic. He took another quick two steps. And fuck. His shades. He took them off. His jacket too. No way would a cop have walked in here uninvited.

She reached the door. Still hadn't seen him inside. She fumbled for her keys. He risked another step away from her desk. Then stopped as the door handle turned and the woman came in.

'Hi,' he said loudly, stepping forward, another whole pace from her computer.

She looked up, startled. Her takeaway soup carton slipped from her fingers. Her hand shot up to her mouth.

Frankie's quickly reached out.

'There, gotcha,' he said.

She stared in disbelief. He'd caught the soup carton. Just in time. Hadn't spilt a drop.

'Sorry,' he said with a smile. 'I didn't mean to startle you. Blimey, that was close.'

'But who . . .? How . . .?'

He pushed the carton into her hands. 'Oh, yeah, right, the door . . . it was open,' he said.

She looked from him to it and back again, like it might somehow be able to contradict what she must have suspected deep down was a lie. Frankie just kept smiling.

'Smells good,' he said. 'What is it? Chicken?'

'Er, ham and pea,' she said.

But she still wasn't buying it, him just being here. Not yet. He could see it in her eyes as they flicked to her desk, then the door. Keep her calm. Keep this contained. Quick. Give her a fucking good reason why you're here.

'Salvador,' he said.

'What?'

'Apellido.'

Her eyes widened in recognition of the name, the same one he'd just seen on her screen.

'Salv?'

'Yeah, right. Salv,' said Frankie, his smile widening once more. 'He told me I might find some work here.'

'Oh, well . . .' The woman's shoulders sagged with relief. She walked past Frankie to her desk. 'And how is he?' she asked.

'Great.'

'Still enjoying being back in Barcelona?'

Barcelona? 'Absolutely,' Frankie said. 'He couldn't be happier.'

'Right, well, first things first. Have you got a clean licence?'

'Oh, yeah,' Frankie told her, still smiling, sitting down. 'Clean as a whistle. I'm as honest as the day is long.'

41

Frankie got back to the club around three and checked in with Slim. All quiet on the Soho front. A healthy looking till too. A bunch of twenty-something lads on a stag weekend down from Edinburgh had come in after lunch. Had done about eight pints each. Nice.

Frankie had one himself. Just the one, mind. Needed his wits about him. He shot the breeze with Slim for a while. Xandra was out doing a food shop over on Berwick Street. Slim brought up that missing tenner again. Said someone else had complained about a missing fiver last night, as well, but they'd been pissed, he admitted, so who bloody knew?

Frankie told him not to worry and Slim tapped his nose and nodded at the floor, saying he wouldn't. He meant the loose tile there just under the fridge, where he hid the till key after hours. Something they'd both kept from Xandra. Even though Frankie felt more and more he now trusted her enough to know.

He had a quick catch-up with her when she got back. She was looking happy, and healthy. Had fixed up the kitchenette out back and had started making her own food. Not bad either. Frankie tucked into a bowl of macaroni cheese that she knocked up. Even Slim had to admit it wasn't half bad.

Frankie ducked out around four to a phone box over on

Shepherd Market. One down a dark alley, used by hookers for contacting johns. No cctv cameras in sight.

He made a quick call. To Aunty Sal and Trumpet Dave. Not real rellies. Old pals of his mum and dad's. He asked them how they were. Their kids as well. Around the same age as Jack and Frankie. Sal said how sorry they were about everything, about Jack. She said there was no way he'd done it. No fucking way at all.

Frankie called in a favour. They had a place down near Brighton. A holiday cottage. He told them he needed some time on his own. Just a couple of days. To recharge his batteries. Sal came good. Told him the cottage was empty for the next couple of weeks. He could stay as long as he liked.

Halfway down Poland Street on his way back the club, he spotted Snaresby. Too fucking late. The bastard had already spotted him too. He was parked up inches from the club. In a silver Saab. Too nice, too spenny for a cop. A straight cop anyhow.

'She's awake,' he said, as Frankie marched past. 'Properly awake and talking now.'

Frankie stopped dead in his tracks. The old woman. That's who he meant. Susan Tilley's gran.

Snaresby's shark eyes twinkled. 'I interviewed her earlier today.'

Frankie pictured Jack's face in the Visitors' Centre: the need, the raw fucking desperation in his eyes. But no, fuck it. Snaresby wasn't here for that. To give him good news. To tell him the old girl had put Jack in the clear. He was here because of bad news. To give him bloody grief.

'And?' Frankie couldn't stop himself from saying it.

'And the good news is . . . that she remembers the attack . . .'

Frankie felt sick. Sweet Jesus. He tried to read Snaresby's face.

Couldn't. Jesus. Please don't let her have ID'd Jack. Because if she has, then that means . . .

'But whoever attacked her, when she opened the door to him, he was wearing a balaclava,' he said.

'And did he?' Again Frankie couldn't stop himself asking. 'Did he take it off? Did she see his—'

'No.'

So she hadn't ID'd Jack. But, fuck it, she hadn't cleared him either. Frankie's whole body sagged. His one hope. Gone. Just one glimpse. That's all it would have taken. One glimpse of someone else's face. Not Jack's. Then this whole fucking horror show would have gone away.

'She doesn't even remember what colour her assailant's eyes were or even how tall he was,' Snaresby said. 'Considering what he did to her next . . . the brutality of the attack . . . it's hardly surprising, I suppose.'

Frankie saw his hands were shaking. Snaresby saw it too.

'Too much drink, son? It'll do that to you,' he said.

The stink of him. Frankie felt it wash right over him. The foul guff of Snaresby's aftershave. His dirty Old Spice or Brut.

'And that's it, is it?' Frankie said. 'Why you're here? Just to tell me she's not put my brother in the clear? Just to see my fucking face?'

'Oh, no, son,' Snaresby said, taking out his Marlboros and brass Zippo. 'You've got me all wrong. I'm not here to mock you. No, no, not at all. Quite the opposite, in fact. I'm here to help.'

'Yeah? And how the fuck d'you figure that?'

'Well, I just want you to get on with your own life, don't I? Don't want you clutching at straws.'

'Straws?' What the fuck was this wanker on about now?

'False hopes. Like this old lady or someone else somehow suddenly proving your little brother didn't do it. Because you can't go putting your whole life on hold for a fantasy like that, can you? Any more than you can for something equally unlikely . . . like your old man's appeal . . .'

'He's innocent too. They both fucking are.'

Snaresby tutted. He flicked his Zippo into life and sparked up a smoke. 'I mean, that's just it, you see, son. You're looking at all that . . . you know, really focussing in on it . . . when you should be, well . . . looking ahead . . . to your future . . .' He stretched out his spidery arms like he was conducting a fucking symphony. '. . . to here . . . to the club . . . to London . . . to everything you've got going . . . everything that's waiting for you further up the line . . .'

'And you expect me to believe that, do you? That you actually give a shit about me any more than you give a shit about my brother or old man?'

'I'm just a decent cop doing his job. And I've been doing it a fair old while. Long enough to know that just because there's a bad apple in a family – or in your case, two . . .' He blew smoke up into the air. '. . . doesn't mean you have to make it three. Doesn't mean you need to end up going down the same nasty little path as them. Because you're not like them, are you? Or at least you don't have to be. You can be someone else. Your own man.'

What was this? Why was this bastard doing this? Why was he taking the piss? Snaresby stared at him. Watched.

'Go fuck yourself,' Frankie said. 'You don't know anything about me. Or my family.'

He marched on into the club. Could still feel that bastard grinning. The toe-rag. The wanker. What the fuck was all that about? Why'd he tried winding him up like that? Just because he could? Because he thought it was funny? Because he hated him? For whatever the same fucked-up reason he hated the rest of Frankie's family? Or because he'd wanted to wind him up enough to get Frankie to hit him? For the pleasure of then being able to bang him up as well?

Well, fuck him sideways. He'd failed.

'What's the matter?' said Slim as Frankie reached the bar.

'Nothing. Nothing that a drink won't fix.'

His *own man*? That tosspot. Frankie poured himself a double vodka. Necked it. He stared across the club at the door. You think you fucking know me? Think a-fucking-gain. Tomorrow night. Oh, yes. We'll soon see who's the smart bastard out of us two.

That dumb fuck Snaresby didn't even know he'd got his prime witness's name.

42

'That woman. She rang,' Xandra told him as she joined them at the bar, a couple of stacks of glasses in her hands.

'Who?'

'The shouty one.'

'Oh, *her* . . .' She meant Sharon. Frankie had had enough of cops for one day. Even her. 'What did she want?'

'Just to call her back. Said it was important.'

About the old woman? Her waking up and not being able to clear Jack? Would have probably broken it to him a whole lot nicer than that piece of human shit outside.

'She made me promise,' said Xandra. 'That you'd call.'

She offered him the phone. He shook his head.

'As soon as you got in. Or she said she'd have to come round.'

He groaned. Because, really, what was the point? Who needed to hear shit news twice? But then he remembered. The last conversation they'd had. How they'd talked about how Susan Tilley and Tara Stevens had been killed. Both bludgeoned. And the petals. And Keira too. About how she'd told Frankie Jack had been with Tara and how knowing that might have got her killed.

Maybe this wasn't about the old woman at all? But the autopsy instead? What if they'd found signs of foul play?

He hurried up to the flat and called her. No joy at work. Tried her home. No boyfriend answering this time. Just her.

Half an hour later and he was pulling up outside the Starlight café. He was just slapping a parking ticket down on the Capri's dash, when he clocked her walking along the opposite pavement and ducking inside the caff.

He found himself smiling. Not just at the sight of her, though there was something about that too, the way she walked, even at a distance. No, more because he couldn't help remembering his mum's favourite movie. *Brief Encounter*. A black-and-white classic. The story of a man and woman whose love affair grew over a course of meetings in a jaded café not much different from this.

His smile faded. Mum was gone. A memory. Just like that stupid film. And nothing was growing between him and Sharon. Whatever connection they'd had had been cut. By her.

He joined her at the counter. She nodded. Didn't speak.

'And a coffee,' she told the guy serving. 'Milk, three sugars.'

They sat down opposite each other. The usual table. She stirred her tea.

'It looks different here in the daylight,' he said.

'Yeah.'

'Feels different too. Less like sneaking around.'

'It still wouldn't look good, us being seen together. Not for work.'

What was that meant to mean? That if they weren't here because of Jack, then that would somehow be fine?

'You look tired,' he said.

'Thanks.'

'I don't mean it like that. I just mean, you know, like you've been working hard.'

'I have.'

'And outside of work?'

She looked annoyed. Still didn't want him prying. About him. Her bloke. 'I meant your mother,' he lied, remembering her

284

Parkinson's, how sad she'd sounded when she'd talked about it, how bloody helpless too.

'Yeah,' she said. 'That. That and Nathan.'

Not him bringing it up, her boyfriend. Her.

'What's he done?'

The way she'd said it. Something was up.

'Nothing,' she said. 'Yet . . .' She sighed. 'He wants us to move.'

Us. 'Where?'

'Hong Kong.'

'Jesus. I thought he'd only just got back.' Frankie pictured her there, couldn't help himself. A million miles away.

'He's been offered a permanent position,' she said. 'A promotion. He's got contacts there. They know people in the police force too. He says they can find me a job. They need people in the run up to the handover.'

'The what?'

'Of the islands. To the Chinese.'

'Oh, yeah.' He'd read about it somewhere. Hadn't seemed important. Until now.

'Will you go?'

'I don't know. He says we don't have to. That he doesn't either. Not if I don't want us to.'

'And?' Don't do it. Tell him to leave, but don't go with him. Stay here in London. Where you belong. Near bloody me.

She lit a cigarette. 'Christ, I shouldn't be talking about this. To you of all people. I don't even know why I am.'

'And yet here we still are.'

She shook her head, then looked back at him. All serious. Hard. Her work face. Shutting him out of her life again.

'The reason why we're here,' she said.

'The old lady. I already know. Your boss called round to tell me in person.'

She looked surprised. Should he tell her how Snaresby had handled it? No. He'd only start swearing. Wouldn't be able to stop.

'About how she remembered opening the door,' he said, 'and seeing that bastard with a balaclava pulled down over his face . . . But her not remembering anything apart from that.'

'And the flowers?'

'What?'

'Did he tell you about the flowers? Because that's the first thing she saw. When she looked. They were obscuring his face. That's why she opened up the door fully to him, because she thought he was there because of the wedding the next day . . . just delivering flowers—'

'Meaning it could be the same person who killed Star . . .'

'*Could* . . . Or maybe this connection . . . it's just what we want to see . . .'

We? What did she mean? That she was finally coming round to his way of thinking too?

'But, listen,' she said. 'The reason I called you. It's not about the flowers . . . I spoke to the pathologist this morning,' she said.

'You mean about the autopsy? About Keira?'

'What you were told. About her. It was right. She drowned.'

Was that it? No. There was more. He could see it in her face.

'But there were also . . . There were wounds,' she said. 'Ligature marks . . . around her wrists . . .'

'Meaning what?'

'She'd been recently restrained . . .'

'Tied up?'

'Yes, but there's no proof this was against her will.'

Because she was a hooker. It might have just been part of a trick.

'There was also a laceration. One and a half inches long.

286

Just above her right cheekbone. But nothing that couldn't be accounted for by her falling in or being hauled out by the river police . . .'

Whatever it was she wasn't saying . . . he did the maths for himself. 'Or,' he said, 'someone could have hit her.'

'But even if that were so . . . it wouldn't even have been enough to knock her out . . .'

Meaning it was nothing like the batterings Susan Tilley and Tara Stevens had endured. Nothing to connect either of those deaths to this.

'You're certain?'

'Positive,' Sharon said. 'She was alive at the time of submersion.'

'How can you be sure?'

'From the chemical reaction that occurred when the water mixed with the air and mucus in her lungs. As the air was forced out under pressure, it produced a foam – that's what the pathologist found inside Keira. Which means she went in breathing.'

Not murdered and then dumped. 'So what are you saying did happen?'

'One possibility is suicide.'

'No.' Frankie didn't buy it. She'd been too switched on, too hard.

'There were high levels of alcohol in her system. Drugs as well. It's possible that she either killed herself, or that this was an accident.'

'No,' Frankie refused to believe this either. 'She was a junkie.' The one thing that bastard doorman at Stav's place had got right. 'She was used to drugs. Wasn't some first-timer who'd be unaware of their effects. You can't tell me she just somehow ended up beside the river and fell in.'

'With the cocktail she was on, I can't imagine she was exactly too switched on. She had high levels of both cocaine and GHB in her system. Enough to—'

'What?'

'Coke and GHB. Which means—'

'No, wait,' Frankie said.

'What?'

GHB. Where the fuck had he heard that before? Come on. Think. Then . . . Yes . . .

'It was Keira,' he said.

'What was?'

'When I spoke to her . . . when I met up with her, she told me that Star had some contact, some secret dealer . . . who'd been scoring her that, whatever the fuck it is, along with all kinds of stuff . . .'

'And?'

'And it's another coincidence, isn't it?' Frankie said. 'This GHB . . . first Star having some, then Keira being found dead after taking it. What is it exactly?'

'Exactly?'

He nodded.

'Gamma-Hydroxybutyric acid,' she said. 'A club drug. Class A. Causes a wide range of symptoms, from euphoria to dizziness . . .' She started counting off on her fingers, making Frankie think this was probably something she'd been tested on as part of her training. '. . . to disinhibition, nausea . . .'

Frankie remembered the congealed vomit on Jack's sheets, the stain on the floor.

Sharon continued, '. . . and amnesia, drowsiness and . . .'

She shut up herself before he even had time to butt in. Then stared at him. He knew what the fuck she was thinking. Because he was thinking the same bloody thing. What if it was GHB that Jack had taken that night? A massive dose of it? What if that was why he couldn't remember anything? Because he'd been suffering from amnesia? Brought on by that bloody drug?

'What does it look like?' he said.

'What?' She stared at him for a second, still reeling.

'The GHB. A powder? A pill?'

'Er . . . Either. Or a liquid.'

'Liquid?'

'Yes. It's soluble. A salt.' Her brow crumpled even further as she said it. 'There are some cases where it's been used as . . . as a date rape drug . . . because people don't remember, and because it's easy to put into . . . to dissolve in someone's drink . . .'

Frankie just stared.

'Which means Jack might have been drugged? Spiked?' he finally said. Was that what had happened? What if he'd not even known he was taking it? What if he'd been given it when he thought it was something else? Duped, doped and hung out to dry?

'It's possible. Yes.'

'Was he tested for it?'

'No, I mean he did agree to a blood test, but—'

'But what?'

'With Keira . . . the pathologist said she tested positive for it, but only because she'd died. Otherwise her body would have cleared it less than four hours after ingestion.'

'Meaning it didn't show up in Jack's test?'

'No. But it does show up in hair samples. For months. The pathologist told me that too.'

'So Jack can still be tested for it? To see if he took it?'

'Yes, but . . .'

'But what? That would prove—'

'No, Frankie. It wouldn't. It still wouldn't prove he didn't do it. We won't be able to prove from any hair test which night

289

he took it on, or how much. Someone . . . the prosecution . . . could just argue that he'd taken it recreationally . . . to get high.'

The way she said it, the way she'd distanced herself from it, from *them*, the prosecution, did this mean she *was* now on his side? On Jack's? Was she thinking the cops might just possibly have got it all fucking wrong?

'And it might not only be Jack,' he said. 'But her too,' he said. 'Keira. That's why she might have drowned, even though she'd still been breathing when she went in. Because the GHB had been used by someone else on her to get her wasted . . . proper wasted . . . And those marks on her wrists . . .' What was that word Sharon had just used? 'Those ligatures . . . after she'd been drugged, they could have tied her up, and then taken her there to the river, before cutting her free and rolling her in . . .'

'Again, Frankie, I'm sorry but there's—'

'No way of proving it. I know.'

But I don't need proof. Not now I *know*. Not now I know as well where that lying bastard of a witness lives.

Sharon checked her watch. Her face was full of doubt. About what? Jack? Or him? Nathan? Was she meant to be with him now?

She stood up. He did too.

'I'm going to feed this all back in,' she said. 'To the investigation. Not where I got it from. Just the thinking . . . the possibilities . . .'

She nodded. It felt like a promise. She turned to go. But then turned back. She leant across the table and kissed him on the cheek. He felt a lump in his throat. Like a fucking kid.

He watched her walk to the door and out. He thought back to the last time he'd watched her leave. He'd done nothing then, even though he'd wanted to. Couldn't follow her now either. What she was going to do next, it could save Jack's life.

But how long would it take her? Her talking to her people? Feeding all this back in? He pictured Snaresby. That bastard wanted his brother to rot. Or worse. He'd block her every step of the way.

He pictured Jack too. There in the prison. The people who wanted to do him harm. He was running out of time. Even if Sharon did somehow pull this out the bag . . . Jack might be already dead.

Frankie drained his coffee. He went out and got into his car. He took the Post-it note with Mario Baotic's address written on it from his pocket and held it tightly in the centre of his balled-up fist.

He couldn't just rely on Sharon sorting this for him. He still needed to sort it himself.

43

Frankie gazed out through the hire van's windscreen. At the Chinese takeaway on the corner. So close he could smell the spare ribs. Baotic – assuming the geezer he'd just followed here really was him – was still inside.

A cloudy night. Pitch black. Tip fucking top. Frankie already had his gloves on, his balaclava rolled up on the top of his head under his hoodie. Getting to be quite the habit, eh?

He'd parked up by the little metal gate that led into the park across which Baotic had taken a shortcut on his way here from his neat little suburban semi a couple of streets round the corner.

Frankie had been waiting for him to come out of there all fucking evening. Hadn't wanted to go barging in. Not like with Mo. Looked too big for just one person. Mind you, no telltale signs of kids outside. No bikes or basketball hoop in the yard. But still possible he had kids or a partner in there. Best to keep himself well clear of all that. He'd waited until the fucker had come out. He'd watched him kiss a woman goodbye. His girlfriend? Wife? A flash of short blonde hair. He'd watched him through the park, then pulled the van up here.

Look alert. Here he was now. Coming back with his little blue plastic takeaway bag. Heading for the park gate. Time for Frankie to make his move. He slid the pistol from under the seat and got out. Stuck the weapon down the back of his jeans and went to the back of the van. Opened the double doors, but not too fucking wide. The lights were off inside, but he could still make out the shapes on the floor: a sack, T-shirt, crowbar, padlock, chain and duct tape. The fucking works.

He waited, heart racing. He checked the road behind him and up ahead. Baotic was the only person in sight. He tugged his cap down low. Keep cool. Keep calm. Keep careful. Because if this bloke really had been out there when Susan Tilley had been murdered, if he really was in on it, then who was to say he wasn't some kind of fucking gangster himself? Might even have helped do it. Joined in with whatever fucker had already driven there in Jack's car.

He was real close now. Whistling. Just a couple more steps and . . . Frankie turned to face him . . . bollocks, he was big . . .

''Scuse me, mate,' he said.

The man's dark brown eyes narrowed.

'Me?' he said. 'What is it you want?'

Frankie's pulse raced. A heavy accent. East European. Just like bookseller had said.

'Oh, right, well you see, mate,' said Frankie, 'if you don't mind, can you just hold the door here a second, like, while I pull this parcel out?'

The man grunted something. Shit. What? Was he saying no? No, here he was. A good fucking citizen. He stepped in nice and close. Close-a-fucking-nuff.

Frankie grabbed him by the back of the neck with his left hand. Rabbit punched him well fucking hard in the gut with his right. Once. Twice. Nice. Doubled him up. Winded. Way too fast for the fucker to get a good look at his face.

Frankie kept his grip on him. Bundled him into the back of the van. Climbed in after him. Slammed him down hard on the floor.

He wedged the pistol's barrel into the side of Baotic's face. 'You say one fucking word and you're dead.'

Nada resistance. Frankie jerked his arms behind his back. Duct taped his wrists. Trussed him up like a turkey. Then gagged him, forcing a wodge of the T-shirt into his gob. Just enough to breathe. Not enough to choke.

He pulled the doors shut behind him and fumbled for the light. Got it on. More duct tape around Baotic's face. To stop him spitting out the gag. He hauled the sack over his torso and head. Wrapped the chain round him. Then padlocked the bastard to one of the metal struts on the side of the van.

Gotcha. You'd have to be fucking Houdini to get out of that.

He stuck the pistol back into his jeans. Got out the back of the van. Checked the street. A couple of teens loitering a hundred yards away. No one closer. So far so bloody good.

He drove south, careful to keep under the speed limit. Reckoned his ETA to Trumpet Dave's cottage down in East Sussex was about an hour. He put on a CD. *Dark Side of the Moon* by Pink Floyd. Had brought it because his old man had always used to chill to it around bedtime and it had always helped Frankie relax.

But half an hour later and he was still buzzing. Christ on a bike. This wasn't just wrong, or illegal. It was bang to rights full-on bloody mental.

Christ only knew what sort of time he'd get for this. Especially with this fucker being a cops' witness. Life. Had to be. They'd throw away the fucking key.

Too late to turn back now, mind. Didn't want to anyway. No matter how wrong this was officially, it felt right. Justified. And, yeah, fuck it. He lit another cigarette. No getting away from it. Something about all this that he *liked*. Same as when he'd seen how piss easy it was to shit up even a proper fucking villain like Mo. All it took was force. An effort of will. He still remembered how good it had felt to key that wanker's car.

He checked the rear view mirror. Saw himself staring back. Maybe this had always been in him. In his blood. Like them Bloodthirsty James Boys back in the day. A great big fucking King Kong chest beater of a gene right here inside him all this time. Just waiting to be fucking set free.

Was this what it was like for real gangsters? For the Rileys and Hamiltons of this world? For Shank friggin' Wilson? Was this what made people fear them? Not the fact they were evil, or psychopathic. Nothing as black and white as that. Just because they'd discovered that they could . . . be stronger . . . and control . . . and get whatever they wanted, just by terrorising another human being into giving it up?

Another half hour later and he hit the south coast. The cottage was up on a hillside just past Devil's Dyke. Middle of fucking nowhere. Frankie pulled up in the yard and got out. Total silence. No one in earshot, or gunshot. Not for fucking miles.

He'd used to come here as a kid sometimes with his mum and dad. Happy days. He turned back to face the van. Thought of Baotic inside. Something in him squirmed then. What? Doubt? Over what he was doing? Who he was being?

No, fuck that. No way you're backing out. This isn't about now. This is about the greater good. About Jack. This witness can do him for life. Or even just keep him inside for long enough not to matter. Just long enough for one of Hamilton's boys to do him.

Frankie flexed his fingers inside his gloves. He'd got one big advantage on the cops. Something else he'd worked out on his visit to Mo. Where the cops were trained to think like a criminal to catch one, Frankie could go one better – he could act like a criminal too.

Do whatever it took to get to the truth.

And he would.

44

'In two seconds, you're gonna tell me your fucking name.'

Frankie glared through the eyeholes of his balaclava at Baotic. At least he fucking prayed it was him. Dried blood all over him from when Frankie had jumped him in London. Now had him duct taped to a chair in the cottage. Had used the kitchen table to wedge him up tight up against the cooker.

Fuck, he looked scared.

Frankie jerked the bunched up T-shirt out of his gob. Watched him shudder like he was going to puke.

'Who . . . Who are—'

'No, motherfucker,' Frankie yelled. '*Your* fucking name. Tell me it now.'

'Mario.'

Well, thank fucking hell for that. At least he'd kidnapped the right man.

'Mario fucking *what*?'

'Baotic,' the man said.

Bayotitch? To rhyme with bitch. East European for sure. Russian? Was that what he was dealing with here? A Russian? Shit, what if he was some kind of Russian bloody gangster? Moving in on Hamilton's turf? Was that why Jack had been framed? Because some Ruski hood wanted the Hamiltons and Rileys at each other's throats?

'Who do you work for, bitch?' Frankie said.

'No one.'

'Liar.' Another smack in the gut. Already knew this one didn't like that. He let him get his breath back, then he asked him, 'Who?'

'No . . . please . . . I don't know . . .'

Frankie picked up the crowbar.

'You're not very quick on the uptake, are you? There's no point in you denying everything, because I already *know* what you've done.'

'I don't understa—'

Frankie brought the crowbar smashing down against the wall, just past Baotic's head.

'Oh. Yes. You. Fucking. Do.'

'Please . . .'

'Susan. Fucking. Tilley,' Frankie said.

Bing-fucking-go. Oh, yes. Right there. Blazing in Mario Baotic's eyes. This bastard was guilty as hell.

'Yeah, that's right,' Frankie said. 'Susan Tilley. And Jack James. You know that name as well.'

No denial. The bastard just started to shake.

'Ah, so now you see it,' Frankie said. 'How right royally screwed you are. Because I know what you've been doing. Talking to the cops. And even worse than just talking, you've been telling porkie pies.'

Baotic started to hyperventilate. What was he thinking? Where *were* the cops? Why weren't they protecting him? How the fuck had a nutter like Frankie tracked him down?

Frankie leant in close. Didn't hit him. Put down the crowbar. Took out a smoke and lit it off the gas cooker next to his head. Gave Baotic a nice, long look at the flame, before leaving his cigarette on the edge of the cooker, smoke curling up around Baotic's terrified face.

'You've got a very simple choice.' Frankie picked up his crowbar from the table. 'Either you tell me why you've been lying to the pigs right now, or I'm gonna break your fucking legs, then your arms, and then your fucking neck.'

'Please . . . no . . .' Tears welled up in Baotic's eyes. 'Please . . . believe me . . . I only do it . . . what he say . . .'

''Ello, 'ello.'

'*Who*?'

Tears. The fucker was crying now.

'Wilson,' he said. 'Mister Wilson.'

Wilson? Was this some kind of joke? Fucking hell. That cunt Shank Wilson was behind all this? He'd sent Baotic out there? But why? Was he behind the girl's murder as well? Or just covering up for someone else? Frankie remembered Wilson dragging Dougie Hamilton off him outside the Ambassador Club. Like he'd been doing Frankie a favour. That bastard had looked Frankie right in the eyes and had told him – *what*? That the best thing Frankie could do was disappear. That if he thought about pressing charges, he'd come back and *skin* him. That motherfucker. That motherfucker had been laughing in his face. He'd known Jack had been innocent all along.

'You work for him?' Frankie's said. 'That it? You one of Hamilton's fucking boys?'

'No . . . just things . . . just sometimes . . . just sometimes I do things for him . . .'

Frankie slowly shook his head. Things like lying about being a witness to something he wasn't. Because Wilson couldn't have used one of his own boys for that, could he? The cops would have rumbled that connection for sure.

'What did you do for him this time?' Frankie said. 'What did you really see?'

'I can't . . .' Baotic wept.

'Can.' Frankie hit him in the gut with the curved end of the crowbar. Hard as he could.

Breath hissed out of Baotic. Piss ran down his trousers onto the floor.

Frankie slapped the crowbar against his palm. 'I know for a fact that Jack James didn't do it,' he said. 'But I also know, because of the cctv that the cops have got, that you really *were* there at the same time as whoever drove in through those gates in Jack's car . . . Which means there were two of you there . . . So now you're gonna tell me . . . if the other fella wasn't Jack James . . . then who the fuck was it?'

Baotic's eyes stretched wide. He stared desperately at the door. Well, he could go swivel for it. Batman and Robin weren't coming here to save his sorry arse tonight.

'*Who?*' Frankie said. 'Who drove that car there? Who murdered that girl?'

Baotic tried to speak. Shaking too hard. His accent thickened. His words came out as whimpers and hisses. Made no sense.

'Or wasn't it just him who done it?' Frankie said. 'Was it you as well? One of your little favours for Wilson? Did you help him? Whoever it was who drove that car? Did you help him find that girl and her grandma? D'you help him finish them off?'

'No,' Baotic wailed.

Frankie gripped the crowbar with both hands and swung it back like a baseball bat, ready to let fly.

'Please. Anything,' Baotic screamed. 'I tell you anything you want to know.'

Jack leant in close. So close now he could see little red blood vessels bursting across the whites of Baotic's eyes. 'No, sunshine.

Not anything,' he said quietly. 'Just the truth. And nothing fucking but. You're gonna tell me what happened that night. All the details. All the names. You're gonna spill the fucking beans until there's nothing left inside the can.'

And he did. He started to talk. And once he started, he couldn't fucking stop. It all came out. How he'd done exactly what Shank Wilson had ordered. At exactly the time Wilson had said. He'd ridden out to Susan Tilley's grandmother's house to deliver the parcel he'd picked up from Chivenham's book shop after making sure he'd been sitting right there in the courier office when the collection request had come in. He'd driven his bike nice and slowly past the cctv camera at the end of the old lady's drive, which Wilson had already known was there. He'd then 'witnessed' what he'd been told to – namely that just after he'd got there, a man had come round the side of the house all covered in blood before pulling down his balaclava and getting into his car and racing away. A man he'd later positively ID'd as Jack James.

But he told Frankie what had really happened too. How he'd not seen this at all. How the real killer had still been there when he'd got there. How the real killer had walked round from the side of the house with a baseball bat in his hands, covered from head to foot in fresh blood.

'Who?' Frankie said.

'Wilson,' Baotic said. 'Shank Wilson. It was Shank Wilson who was there.'

Wilson. In. Fucking. Person. Frankie stared in disbelief.

'It was him who attacked the old lady and killed Susan Tilley?'

Baotic nodded.

'No one else?'

'No.'

But Jesus. Why the hell would he do that? Why would he have murdered his boss's daughter-in-law to be?

'Why?' Frankie said.

'I don't know. I vow it. I don't.'

Was he telling the truth? Yeah. Why not? Why the fuck would he hold back on this when he'd already given everything else up?

'What happened next?' Frankie said. 'After Wilson came from round the side of the house?'

'He smear blood all over the car,' Baotic said. 'Then change – his bloodied clothes . . . he place them inside a refuse bag and take them with him. But first he puts the bloodied balaclava back on . . .'

For the benefit of the cctv camera on the way back out. While Baotic then called the cops and told them his story.

And what then? Wilson must have driven back into London. And smeared those bloodied clothes all over Jack's flat and all over him too, as he'd lain there GHB'd out-for-the-fucking-count on his bed.

'And what about you?' Frankie asked Baotic, still swinging the crowbar slowly back and forth in his hands. 'Why did you do it? Why did you agree to accuse—' He stopped himself just in time. Had been about to say *my brother*. Would have given his own identity away. 'Why the fuck did you agree to accuse Jack James of murdering that girl?'

'He . . .' Boatic screwed up his eyes.

Frankie guessed what he couldn't say. 'Money? You bastard. You did it for money? How much? How much did Wilson pay?'

'Five. Five thousand.'

'Five measly fucking grand? To just stand there while some psycho murders a girl and batters her grandma half to death? To lie and put someone else in fucking prison for life?'

Tears ran down Baotic's face.

'It wasn't only . . .' he said.

'Only *what*?' Frankie pulled the crowbar back. It was all he could do not to just let fly.

'Money.'

'What else?' Frankie growled.

'He knows . . . Wilson . . . he knows other jobs I have done . . . for him . . .'

'What jobs?'

'Things that can send me to prison, deport me . . . and my wife, back to Bosnia . . . to where we . . . where we have no life . . . he has proof of things I do . . . it will only take one call . . .'

Blackmail. Blackmail and money. Belt and fucking braces. If the money wasn't enough to make this prick play ball, then there was always the added threat of turning him in.

But the biggest question of all was still left unanswered. Why had Hamilton's chief enforcer done it? Was he jealous of Dougie? Did he want her for himself? Was that it? Was he in love with her? Or had she turned him down? Or had he done it for money? Because he was batting for the other side? Secretly working for Riley or some other mob?

Frankie stared down at the sobbing wreck in front of him. His hands tightened on the crowbar. This piece of shit deserved it. Pain. Something to remember for the rest of his miserable life. He'd have gone to court, all right. He was terrified of Shank Wilson. He'd have done what he was told. No matter what the consequences were for Jack.

He still had the crowbar in his hands. No. Don't do it. Leave. Before you hurt him. This isn't the bastard you want. It's that motherfucker Wilson. He's behind this. He's the fucker with the answers. The cunt who needs to pay.

Frankie went outside. Lit a smoke. Inhale. Exhale. Right. OK. This is over. You got what you came here for: proof. Jack is fucking innocent. Jeee-zuz. Yes. Fucking yes. But now fucking what?

No point him just having Baotic tell him this, was there? Needed to get the bastard to tell the cops as well that it was Wilson who'd been pulling the bloody strings as well as swinging the bloody bat.

And God knew what else he'd got up to. Stav's brothel was affiliated to the Hamiltons. Meaning Wilson could have known Star. Could have paid her. Or blackmailed her. To slip Jack some GHB. To knock him and his memory out. So they could then set Jack up good and proper with all that blood.

Wilson could have then killed Star as well. To stop her from talking. Had it been him who'd lamped Frankie in her kitchen that night? Him delivering the flowers to get in, just like he'd done at the old lady's house? And what about poor Keira? Had he then murdered her too? Because she'd known too much?

No way would Frankie get Wilson to admit any of that. But the cops might. Once they'd nailed him for Susan Tilley's murder. Once they started looking into him. What else he'd been up to. What part he'd had in Tara and Keira's deaths.

But not Snaresby. Oh, no. He wasn't getting a sniff of this. Sharon. She'd listened. She'd tried to help. Was still trying. Well, it was time for some payback. Frankie was going to serve her Shank Wilson's head up on a plate.

But first things first. He had to make sure Baotic told Sharon exactly what he'd just told Frankie. Only problem being, Frankie wouldn't be there with a crowbar next time to help him remember it right.

He lit another cigarette. Stared up at the stars. Think, you fucker. *Think*.

Ten minutes later, he walked back inside. He ignored Baotic. Poured himself a drink. Had a little hum.

Then he turned to him and said, 'I'm gonna take you back to London tomorrow and cut you free. Then you're gonna turn yourself in. And tell the cops what you done and why you done it . . . But while you're telling them all that, you're gonna keep your fucking mouth shut about our little chat tonight . . . Got it?'

Baotic's whole body sagged. He wasn't going to die. He was going to make it out alive. It was all the bastard could do not to actually bloody smile. But Frankie saw something else too. Right there in the middle of his bloodshot eyes. How he was already thinking about how he could turn this situation round. Put one over on Frankie. Not do what he was told.

Well, not so fucking fast, my friend. Frankie twisted Baotic's chair round so he could see the sound system up on the kitchen top. A tape was turning in the deck. Its red record light was on.

'Don't even think about not showing,' Frankie warned. 'Because everything you just told me, I've got it on tape. The bit about Wilson being the killer . . . about you being there to pretend it was Jack James who done it instead . . . all that'll go right to the cops . . . to Sharon Granger . . . the same detective you're gonna hand yourself in to tomorrow . . . and, trust me, if you run, there won't be anywhere you can hide . . . not from Wilson or the cops . . .'

'Yes,' Baotic said. 'I will . . . whatever you tell me . . .'

But it was still there. In his eyes. This bastard was a survivor. Wouldn't have made it out of Bosnia otherwise. The threat of the recording might not be enough. Frankie didn't know if something like that would even hold up in court. Maybe Baotic was smarter than him. Maybe he already knew. Frankie needed to completely shut down any thoughts of a plan fucking B. Needed to make this prick understand that it wasn't Shank Wilson he needed to be afraid of, it was him.

'That's good to hear,' Frankie said. 'But in case you get any dumb ideas, there's something else I want you to think about. And that's your Mrs . . . Your wife . . .'

Ah. Better. His eyes didn't look so optimistic now.

'Your pretty little blonde wife,' Frankie said, remembering the woman he'd glimpsed at his door. 'Yeah, you see I've been watching her. And not just me. My associates. Where she goes. What she does. Who she knows. The fucking lot. But do you know what the really cool thing is?'

Baotic slowly shook his head.

'A couple of my associates are watching her right now. And will be all night. And tomorrow. And until I fucking tell them not to. Meaning if I don't hear from my contacts at the cop shop that you've been a good boy and have told Detective Granger the truth, then trust me, you're gonna find yourself single faster than you can say, *Who murdered my fucking wife?*' Frankie leant in. So close his mouth was touching Baotic's ear. 'And then, once we've finished with her, my friend, guess who's fucking next?'

45

The drive back up to London was murder the next day. It was pissing down. Good for what Frankie had planned, mind.

He dropped Mario Baotic off blindfold in the driving rain on a piece of waste ground round from West End Central Police Station. Told the wanker to wait there for five minutes with the blindfold on before handing himself in. Reminded him of the consequences if he fucked up. Told him one of his associates was already watching him.

Five minutes.

Then he was to get in there and do his bit.

Frankie drove off. Watched him in the wing mirror, just standing there waiting like a fucking ghost. Frankie headed back to the multi-storey where he kept the Capri. Top floor. Back corner. Nice and quiet. No cctv.

He'd got all the gear he needed for the clean-up already stashed. He scrubbed the back of the van. Wiped it down. Switched the plates back over from ones he'd unscrewed off of another van the day before. Then he bagged up his gear – the balaclava, gloves, crowbar, duct tape, chain and hoodie – and drove the van back to the hire yard up on Kensal Rise, ditching all the goodies in separate bins on the way.

All except the gun. It wasn't that he needed it. Didn't. Not now all this was over. Now Shank Wilson was going away, the

Hamiltons' hatred would be directed away from Frankie and Jack and onto Wilson instead.

But something still stopped him chucking the gun. Part worry that some other fucker might find it and use it on somebody. But a darker fear too. Could the cops tell from a gun whether it had been used in a crime before? He was pretty sure they could. He didn't believe the old man had ever actually used it. But some-one else might have, someone who'd asked him to look after it. And who knew what kind of shit storm might blow into town if it suddenly turned up now?

He got a cab home. Stashed the pistol in his mattress. Show-ered. Scrubbed himself. Got dressed. Nice and smart and clean. A different man. He put a call in to Riley from a public booth. Left a message. Nothing too explicit. Phones got bugged, didn't they? Especially people like Riley. Frankie said to tell him he'd 'acted on the new information provided' and was 'expecting to be able to share some very good news very soon'. He also asked him to take extra special care of the 'inside security work' they'd discussed. Meaning the last thing he wanted was Jack being done over in prison before news got out that he'd done nothing wrong.

Frankie popped into The Pillars of Hercules for a pint. Looking out across Soho, he pictured Tommy Riley's face the last time he'd seen him in St James. He'd be well chuffed with Wilson getting busted. The heat on him and his boys would get called off. And put on Hamilton's set-up instead.

But Frankie could still feel it, the pressure of that handshake. That favour that Riley would one day call in.

He wondered if Sharon would make the arrest herself. Perhaps she already had? Would she call him herself to let him know that Jack would soon be set free? He headed back to the club. Probably best be there. In case she called. He fancied playing a few frames too. Just to chill himself out.

The place was deserted, though. Nearly noon and no one had even opened the doors. The table covers were on. No sign of Slim or Xandra. For God's sake. He hated losing business. What the fuck were they on?

'Xandra,' he shouted.

Nothing. Shit. She must have overslept. He walked out back to knock on her door. Found a neatly written note taped to it. Slim's handwriting.

It read:

> DON'T BOTHER LOOKING. SHE'S GONE. SO'S THE KEY FOR THE TILL AND ALL THE MONEY THAT WAS IN IT. OVER £400. I HATE TO SAY I TOLD YOU SO, BUT WELL ... LIFE'S A BITCH

Frankie sighed. He opened the door and switched on the light. But no, no Xandra. Her bed was neatly made. But her bag was gone. Her trainers too. Missing from the window ledge where she kept them. Just like she'd never been fucking here.

Knackeredness. Bone deep. It ran him right over then. He locked up the club again and headed up to his flat. Then stopped. Halfway up the stairs. Because what the fuck? The door was wide open. There was no way he'd left it like that.

He turned and checked out the hallway door leading back out onto the street. Shit. It was ajar. The hairs on the back of his neck prickled. Burglars? Xandra? Had she done his flat over too?

He ran up the last remaining steps. And saw he hadn't just been burgled. His flat had been torn apart. He grabbed one of the old man's golf clubs – a sand wedge – from the bag by the door. Gripped its handle in both hands, remembering the weight of the crowbar last night as he'd screamed at Baotic again and again.

Any bastard still in here, they'd better fucking watch out.

The kitchen was empty. The living room, bathroom and spare room as well. Or not empty. More like full. Of smashed lamps, crockery, electronics. The same with the bedroom, his pillows and mattress had been slashed . . . Oh, fuck. He got down on his knees. But crap. The pistol. It was gone. The tin with the ammo in it too.

Dickhead. He should have chucked it. Or kept it where the old man had, behind those bloody bricks. Or never taken it out. It hadn't even been loaded and he probably hadn't even needed it to deal with Baotic at all.

Baotic . . .

Oh, no. No. No, no, no. Frankie's heart drummed. Him getting broken into now. Today of all days. No way. Uh-uh. This was too much of a coincidence.

He ran for the living room, his pulse hammering. He grabbed the phone and stabbed in the digits for Sharon's number. He already knew them by heart.

'Hello?' she answered.

'It's me, Frankie.'

'What is it? What's the matter? You sound—'

'Just answer me . . .' He was in a flap. Bollocks. Didn't know how to tell her, not without landing himself in it up to the neck. '. . . your witness . . . the courier . . .'

'I've already told you – *wait*,' she said. 'How the hell do you know that he's a cour—'

'Just tell me,' Frankie said. 'Has he changed his story? Has he told you Jack didn't do it? Has he—'

Nothing. She said nothing. Shit. Baotic. That motherfucker. He'd called Frankie's bluff. He hadn't bloody handed himself in.

He'd done one. A runner. He'd got the fuck out. But gone where?

Frankie slammed down the phone. Look at the fucking state of this place. Whoever had come here hadn't just been looking for him. They'd been searching for something. Not the pistol. It couldn't just be that. That was just something they'd found. No. Only one thing it could be. The tape. The tape with Baotic's confession on it.

But how? How could Baotic have known to come here? How could he have known it was Frankie who'd abducted him last night? He'd not shown his face. There was nothing he'd said that could have given him away.

Not unless . . . Fuck . . . Not unless Baotic had gone to someone else instead, someone who'd connected the dots, someone who'd already known that Frankie was out to clear Jack's name, someone who'd be screwed as much as Baotic was by what Baotic told them was on that tape.

A creak. Oh, shit. Frankie already knew. Without even fucking turning. It was Shank Wilson. He was here.

46

'Wakey-wakey, rise and shine.'

What . . .? Hissing. Frankie heard hissing. There. Then gone. Where was he? In bed? Dreaming? Drunk. Cold. So cold. Move. Can't. Help. Call out. Shout. Can't. Movedammitjustdoit. No. Nothing. Someone. Help. Me. Please. Pleeeease.

'That's right. And it's back up to the surface you come. Being underwater. That's what people say it feels like when they've been chloroformed and coshed. Some people don't come back at all, of course, haḥ-hah. But it looks like we've got lucky with you . . .'

Coshed and chloroformed? A memory. Frankie's living room. Someone had grabbed him. Someone had—

Wilson . . .

Frankie tried forcing his eyes open. No. Everything stayed black. He blinked. Couldn't. Something there. Had he been blindfolded? Taped. A sickly sweet smell. In his nostrils. In his mouth.

You're alive. Alive. Don't panic. He hasn't killed you yet. Try moving. Again. No. He felt his arms, clamped to his sides. His knees and ankles were locked together too. He tried shouting again. Twisted his jaw. Couldn't. No good. Gagged too tightly. Could barely manage a moan.

'Don't bother struggling,' the voice said.

Wilson's. Definitely Wilson's.

'You'll only piss me off even more than you already have.'

A rush of blood to Frankie's stomach. Like he was going to puke. Or shit himself. Or just fucking explode. But no. Not that. He'd just been lifted. Quickly. Up. By how many people? Two. Yes. Two pairs of hands. Was it Baotic? Was that who was here helping Shank Wilson now?

Back down. Oh, Christ . . . onto, *into* what? Something cold and hard. Behind his back and his head. Wood? Was he in some kind of a box? A thud. Above. A lid? Had it just been closed? Oh, Jesus wept. Was it a coffin? Was he being buried fucking alive?

Break out. Got to. Now. Do it. He tried smashing his head against whatever he was inside. Too tightly trussed up. Couldn't even squirm. He tried to shout again. Tried to scream. Could only growl through his gritted teeth.

'Shut it,' Wilson's muffled voice said.

That cunt . . . that fucker . . . he was still here then? Frankie hadn't been left here. Abandoned. In this . . . In whatever this was.

A lurch. Moving. He was being lifted again. Inside whatever the fuck this container was. Being carried. A crunch of footsteps. Ten . . . twenty. Then they stopped.

A pause. A creak. One he recognised. Yes. The back door of the Ambassador. Shit. They were carrying him out into the service alley. Then where? Please. Christ. Let someone see. Please. Do it now. Someone look. Over here.

More footsteps. Ten . . . thirty . . . then another lurch . . . a change of direction? Must have reached the end of the alley. A car horn blared. Somewhere close. Were they out on the street? Where were they taking him? What the fuck were they going to do with him when they got him there?

Another hundred steps, two hundred. Then traffic. Then

quieter. Just footsteps. Then they slowed. Another noise he recognised: the scraping of a warehouse door. A warehouse? Fuck. Not good. Not good. Grunted, muffled orders. Whose? Wilson's? More doors opening. Closing. He tilted, slid inside the container. Christ, where were they taking him? Down. Into what? A basement? Double, triple, fucking shit. This was not going to end well.

The lid. Cold air. Hands grabbed him. Dug under him. Hauled him up. He tried struggling. Smack. Pain. Laughter. Someone had just punched him in the face. He felt himself being twisted into a sitting position. Onto something. A chair? Then shrieking. More duct tape. Being wrapped tight around him.

No way could he fight his way physically out of here. If he didn't manage to talk his way out, he was dead.

47

Bright light. Frankie's blindfold was torn from his eyes. He winced, tried to twist away. But something – some*one* – grabbed him by the throat. He couldn't breathe. He stared into the light. He tried to scream. Nothing.

'Shouting's not gonna do you any good, is it, sunshine? Because guess what? There's no one near to fucking hear. You should have paid more attention to that little note I left you in the club. You should have backed off when you still had the chance.'

Wilson? *Was* it Wilson? Frankie couldn't tell. Not for sure. Too much echo. That chloroform . . . had it fucked his hearing? Was that it? Or something else . . . where they were . . . underground. He thought of all the buildings near the club. Hundreds had basements. Could be any one. Somewhere no one could hear him scream.

Crack. More pain. Another punch. Fucking hell. His jaw. Whoever had hold of his throat, they let go. He tried to throw himself sideways. No dice. This chair he was taped to . . . it was fixed to the floor.

The light shining into his eyes, it suddenly raced backwards. He blinked. Tried to see. And there – yes, there, right in front of him – a man. The light was a torch. Whoever was there, they were holding it. It swung right, then rapidly in. Smashed him hard in the face. Jesus. White pain. Worse than before.

Whoever was there, they started to laugh. 'That's better. Saves me throwing a bucket of iced water at you, doesn't it? Not that I don't want to, you understand. It's just the fucking faff of having to go all the way upstairs to fill a bucket and bring it back down.'

Upstairs. Frankie's eyes were starting to focus. He slowly looked around. Yeah, he was downstairs, all right. Way down. Somewhere bloody horrible too. Somewhere ancient. Industrial. A spaghetti of pipes on the ceiling. A single bare bulb. A puddle of light beneath. Steep stairs leading up to the right. And to his left? Oh, sweet Jesus . . .

The courier. Baotic. Or what was left of him. His face was one big bruise, his eyes nothing more than purple slits.

'That's right. Take a good fucking look,' the voice said. 'People say that time travel's impossible. But it's not and I can prove it. Because that's your future, right there.'

Bile leapt up in Frankie's throat. Had Wilson beaten Baotic to death? It looked that way. But if Baotic was here, then who the hell had helped Wilson carry him?

'It's good to finally see you again face to face, Frankie,' Wilson said, lowering the torch so that Frankie could look at him properly. 'I didn't think it would come to this, me having to deal with you personally, like. But you know what? Now that it has, I've got to admit it: I'm really fucking glad.'

You. Fucking. Psycho. Bastard. Piece. Of. Shit. Wilson was dressed in a blue boiler suit with a flash of red at its collar. A silk cravat. Fuck. Just what the bookseller had said.

He shot Frankie a toothy grin. Then crossed over to a trestle table set against the wall and took off his cravat and folded it neatly there – before stripping off his boiler suit and boots and laying them out folded beside it. He scratched lazily at his underpants. Then began humming what sounded horribly like an old Kylie Minogue hit. He pulled on a blood-spattered white tracksuit, black rubber wellies and a pair of latex surgical gloves.

Shit. He's going to fucking kill you. He's going to tear you apart. Stall him. Get him talking. But how? He couldn't even move his fucking lips. Don't give up. Think. Yes. Two sets of hands. Someone else knows you're here. Someone who might not be as bat-shit crazy as him. Or someone might have seen him carting you out of the club. Xandra. Maybe she changed her mind? Came back guiltily with the cash? Please, fuck, yes. She might have followed you. Called the cops. Yes. Don't give up. You're going to be OK.

Oh Jesus, Christ – *what the fuck was that?*

A scraping. A hiss. A croak. To his left. Frankie tried throwing himself right. Got nowhere. He turned. He looked. The courier. Christ. He was looking right back at him through his hideously swollen eyelids. Bloody hell. The fucker was still alive.

'That him?' Wilson asked Baotic. 'That the little twat who kidnapped you last night?'

Baotic nodded once, so heavy it looked like his head might fall off.

Frankie growled at him through his gag. You fucking liar. You never saw me. You lying piece of fucking shit.

'Thought so.' Wilson winked at Frankie and tapped his temple. 'Brains, you see. I've got a whole fucking head full of them.' He nodded at Baotic. 'A right fucking mess, ain't he?' Wilson's look turned to one of pure hatred as he stared into Frankie's eyes. 'But not as big a fucking mess as you've made of everything, my lad.'

Frankie saw the punch coming this time. Braced himself. Pointless. Did him no good. He heard the crack of his nose breaking. Blood filled his mouth. He started choking. Wilson leant in and ripped the duct tape from his mouth. He smiled as Frankie sputtered, gasping for air.

'Now, now, we don't want you drowning in your own claret, do we?' he said. 'Or at least not yet.'

'Fuck you,' Frankie said. He spat as hard as he could at Wilson. Hit him too. A nice fat gob of spit and blood. Right on the motherfucker's chest.

Good. Decision fucking made. Only one he had. No point in trying to wriggle out of this. Wilson had him at his mercy. And he had no fucking mercy. Unless Frankie played this perfectly – unless he convinced this total fucking nutter that he wasn't afraid of him, and that he still had some cards up his sleeve – he was going to die down here. And soon.

'Good,' said Wilson. 'You've still got a bit of spirit left in you. It'll make this all the more fun.'

Fun?

Wilson hit him again. Frankie's head snapped back.

Frankie sucked in air. Breathe bloody through it. This is just sparring. Just down the gym. You hold your strength. You pray. You wait. You pray and you wait for your chance.

'You see, you deserve everything you're gonna get,' Wilson told him. 'For interfering, right from the start. Right from the moment you decided to start snooping round your brother's flat . . .'

The cigarette in the parked car outside Jack's building . . . Not a cop. Wilson. Him watching. Even back then.

'But most of all,' Wilson said, 'for messing with my witness. For putting stupid ideas in his head about handing himself over to the cops. I mean, it's just as fucking well he's more scared of me than he is of you. Or he really might have done what you fucking told him.'

Wilson stepped in even closer. He cocked his head to one side and stared into Frankie's eyes.

'So where is it?' he said.

'What?'

'The recording of my boy here confessing that I paid him to say he'd seen your stupid cunt of a brother killing young Miss Tilley.' His dark eyes glinted. 'Because then, my little Bosnian friend here, he can go back to being my witness again. Because look at him. He's learned his lesson proper this time. From here on in, he's going to do exactly what he's told.'

The recording . . . This was it. The only card Frankie had left to play.

'It's somewhere safe,' he said.

'Yeah, but where? You see, I've already looked through your poxy little flat and I couldn't find it there. Where is it? Somewhere hidden in the club?'

'No. Somewhere you won't ever find it. And if anything happens to me, I've left instructions for who it's to go to . . .'

Wilson held up his blood-drenched hand. 'Yeah, and blah, blah, blah, they'll then take it to the pigs, am I right?' He grinned. 'You've been watching too many fucking movies, son. You see, you *are* going to tell me where it is, because I'm gonna fucking well torture you rotten until you do.'

'If I give you that recording, you'll kill me,' Frankie said. 'You'll have no reason to keep me around.'

Wilson's eyes narrowed.

'Meaning I fucking well won't,' Frankie said. 'I'll go to my grave not telling you, and then the person I've given it to *will* give it to the cops. And then we'll see who gets the last laugh, because then you'll be fucked.'

Frankie braced himself. Waited for the punch.

'Stop,' a voice called out.

48

Wilson lowered his fist. His face reddened with anger, but he did as he'd been told: he stepped aside.

Someone else walked into the room. Jesus. Shit. Him? Yes. Terence fucking Hamilton. Wearing a blue boiler suit, the same as Wilson had been. Like he was some kind of manual worker. Bloody hell. Was it Hamilton who'd helped carry him here? Was it him who was working with Wilson? No. No bloody way. It didn't make any sense.

'You?'

'Funny, ain't it?' Hamilton said, staring into Frankie's eyes. 'The person behind it all is the person the cops are least likely to suspect.'

'But—'

'Yeah, exactly. But why the fuck would Terence Hamilton have done that? Why the fuck would he ruin his own son's life by having someone murder his future wife? I bet if you told any number of coppers that, they'd laugh in your face. Because it doesn't make any sense, right?'

Hamilton continued to stare until Frankie realised his last question wasn't rhetorical.

'No,' he said. 'It doesn't.'

Hamilton sighed. His skin was pale as ivory. Heavy black shadows circled his eyes.

'I did try putting him off the whole idea, you understand,' he said, 'but he never was a good listener.'

Did he mean Wilson? Wilson had wanted to kill Susan Tilley and Terence Hamilton had just let him?

'But Dougie's stubborn, see?' Hamilton said. 'Gets it off his mother.' His lips peeled back over his teeth. 'That was a joke,' he said. 'Laugh.'

Frankie couldn't. He just gawped. Couldn't believe what he was hearing.

'He told you to fucking laugh,' Shank Wilson barked, stepping in quickly and punching Frankie in the side of the head.

Bastard. Frankie heard his tooth crack. Pain ripped through his mouth. The wanker. He spat bits of tooth mixed with blood onto his lap.

'All right, all right,' Hamilton said, waving Wilson away, 'give him some air, Shank. Get back over there and have yourself a smoke.'

Wilson sniffed, rolling his shoulders like a boxer between rounds. Not done with Frankie yet. Not by a long fucking stretch. But he was a good attack dog. Did what he was told.

'You've not got kids, have you, son?' Hamilton said. 'And I don't suppose you ever will now. But I'll tell you something: becoming a father, especially to a boy, it changes everything. You start thinking, not just about yourself, but other people. And not just about the here and now, but the future too. And it can be nice all that planning. But do you know what the worst bit is?'

'What?'

'Someone threatening to take it all away.'

Who? Here right now, Frankie couldn't think of anyone either brave or bleeding stupid enough to ever want to do that.

'Of course, she didn't mean to, I suppose,' Hamilton said.

She?

'But then they got this plan into their little heads, didn't they? About moving away. To America. To be near *her* family. Her aunts and uncles. And to be *pro bono* this and *pro bono* that, and to la-de-dah change the world for the better and to change him too, my boy, into something he was never meant to be, some sort of crusading lawyer . . . To leave all this . . .' Hamilton gestured round the freezing basement, like it was Shangri-bloody-La. '. . . every fucking single thing I've ever worked for . . . to leave all this . . . and me . . . behind . . .'

Frankie just stared. This fucking lunatic. He wasn't kidding. He'd done all this . . . had her killed . . . to stop his son *leaving*? He'd murdered his own son's fiancée for *that*?

'I mean, if they'd just wanted to go out for a bit,' Hamilton said, 'then OK, fine, that would have been all well and dandy. Because I'm a patient man, see? I could have waited a few years. And worked on him. On his common sense. And his true loyalties. Until he'd come back. With or without her. To *take* what was rightfully his. To *be* who he rightfully is. But that's just it. I ain't got a couple of years. Not any more. I needed him back in the fold – and fast.'

The way he said it. This last bit. Yeah. That and the colour of his fucking skin. Frankie suddenly got it. What this was really all about.

'That's right,' Hamilton said, reading his mind. 'I'm dying. Fucking cancer. Would you believe it? I've been stabbed twice, shot once and beaten within an inch of my life, and nothing could stop me. But this will. It'll fucking kill me. Doc says I'll be lucky if I see another Christmas.'

Oh, yeah, Frankie got it all right. Hamilton was just doing what any businessman would: appointing a successor. Only Terence Hamilton was a fucking psycho. If getting the right man for the job meant murdering people who got in the way, then so be it. That was just business too.

'What's the best way to make someone an enforcer?' Hamilton asked. 'Fill him with hate. Her getting murdered, stripped, defiled . . . in what oh-so-transparently appeared to be a revenge attack by Riley for the murder of one of his boys . . . that was more than enough to make Dougie the man he now is . . . a torturer . . . a killer . . . someone capable of beating another man to death and then dumping his body by the side of the road . . .'

He meant the pimp the cops had found murdered by that bin, the one with the knickers rammed down his throat. Dougie Hamilton had done that? Terence stared at Frankie, his eyes blazing. With what? Fucking hell. With pride.

'And I tell you this, son: once you start down that path, it's hard to turn back. And even harder to turn your back on your family ever again. And that's what's happened to him, to my boy. He's part of it now. Part of this. He's committed. To who we are. To what our family is and will continue to be . . . long after I've gone.'

'Why Jack?' Frankie said.

'Why do you fucking think? Because I needed someone framed for the murder. And framed good, so there'd be no doubt in Dougie's mind that her murderer had been caught.' His dark eyes glittered. 'Otherwise he'd never stop looking, would he? And if he'd looked long enough and hard enough, he might even have ended up looking at me.'

'But why my brother? It could have been anyone.'

'Because he was a perfect fucking fit. And not exactly the sharpest tool in the box. Stupid enough to get caught for that ruck in the Atlantic with my boys, which meant the cops knew he was working for Riley. But not just that. Everything. I swear, after Shank here had battered Danny Kale to get the whole ball rolling, then me and him sat down to work out who to frame, and your brother stood out a mile.'

So Danny Kale, the first of Riley's boys who'd been murdered over a month ago, had been nothing but a ruse, to make Susan Tilley's murder look like a proper revenge killing to both Dougie Hamilton and the cops.

'He ticked all our boxes, didn't he, Shank? He's a known druggie with a thing for hookers. Which made it dead easy for us. For that slag to pick him up and fuck him and get him wasted on a nice little cocktail of coke and GHB . . . enough so as he wouldn't remember a fucking thing . . . Easy for her to keep him there all curled up in his flat like a little baby and then call Shank and let him in when he called round . . .'

Frankie saw it. He saw it all. Wilson would have taken Jack's car keys and, with Dougie Hamilton already safely under his father's watchful gaze in a Soho restaurant on his stag night, he'd have driven out to Susan Tilley's grandmother's place to batter her and murder her grand-daughter. Then later back to Jack's to smear more blood from his bagged-up clothes over everything there including Jack. With a few bottles of bleach and a bucket thrown in to make it look like Jack had tried cleaning up.

'So you set him up and then you told the cops where to find him,' Frankie said.

'That's right. He called the cops from right outside your brother's building. Then I called your brother from right outside the cop shop, the second I saw them come streaming out. It was just like down the dog track, us sending off our little hare before a pack of running dogs.'

Leaving Jack looking guilty as sin.

Hamilton smiled. The cunt was enjoying this, letting Frankie know exactly how well they'd stitched Jack up.

'And what about Star?' Frankie said. Just keep him talking.

Keep him talking and hope to fuck that someone really is on the way to help.

'Ah, yes. Little Tara Stevens,' Hamilton said. 'I fucked her once, you know. Right up the arse. You should have seen how wet it got her pussy. And a good girl she was for us on this too. All Shank here had to do was get Stav to put in a call to your brother, to tell him he had some nice new girl on his books. And then your brother, he came running, didn't he? Just like the naughty little perv that he is.' Hamilton shot a glance into the shadows. 'That said, as clever as we thought we were being, we nearly did fuck up, didn't we? Or rather, Shank did, didn't you, Shank?'

A grunt from the shadows.

'You see,' Hamilton said, 'he should have fucking topped her too that same night. Somewhere else. But he said he didn't need to, because he'd already paid her off and had told her he'd kill her kid back in Liverpool if she ever shot her mouth off. But he was wrong. Weren't you, Shank?'

No answer. Hamilton pursed his lips, staring at Frankie.

'You can never trust a whore, son,' he said. 'Which is what I told him. She was a loose end that needed tying up.'

'It was you,' Frankie said, twisting his head and peering into the gloom. 'At her flat that night. You killed her.'

'That's right,' said Hamilton. 'I sent Shank round to deliver her some flowers.'

'He tried to kill me too,' Frankie said.

Wilson barked out a laugh. 'If I'd wanted you fucking dead, you already would be.'

'What then? Were you planning on framing me for Star's murder?'

Frankie remembered Star's twisted body.

'I did think about it,' Wilson said, stepping back into the

light. 'But it would have been too messy, getting you involved as well as your brother. It might have confused what's already a nice tight shut case for putting him away. And all manner of questions might have been asked if the cops had connected Star to your brother. They might even have worked out that he'd met her round at Stav's that night, and someone there might have mentioned the kind of gear she'd been carrying, and even found out who it was who'd given it her . . .'

Wilson meant the GHB. He'd supplied it.

'Of course, I thought about killing you too,' Wilson said, 'once I saw who it was I'd knocked out. But then I'd have had to get rid of your body. Couldn't exactly have left you there, or that would have muddied up the whole case as well.'

'So why call the cops?' Frankie asked. 'Why tip them off to go to Star's apartment?'

Wilson smiled. 'I didn't. I nearly shat it when I read about the filth turning up in the papers and that they'd nearly caught someone too.'

Meaning someone else must have called them. Who? Frankie thought back. That crack in the door of that flat down the corridor. The click of its lock as it had closed. Must have been the neighbour who'd dialled 999. Must have heard something.

'Of course it did make us wonder what the hell you were doing in her flat in the first place,' Hamilton said. 'Or rather it would have, if you hadn't let slip how you made the connection between your brother and Star in the first place.'

Frankie's mind reeled backwards. He remembered standing there outside Star's door . . . he'd called out her name, and Keira, he'd called out hers too . . . he'd said he was her friend.

'Keira,' Shank said.

Oh, Jesus. It was his fault. He'd led them right to her.

'The poor thing drowned,' Hamilton said.

'You murdered her. There was GHB in her blood. Ligature marks on her wrists. You—'

'Now how the fuck would someone like you know something like that?' Hamilton snapped.

Shit. Frankie kicked himself. He'd said too much. About the autopsy. Only one way he could have found out that.

'This cunt's been talking to the filth.' Hamilton turned on Shank. 'I told you it was a mistake to use the same drug on her that you used to dope Jack . . .' He glared at Frankie. 'But even if you have been talking out of school . . . even if the cops have made that connection . . . the one between your brother and Susan Tilley and all that blood is still so much more compelling than that . . .'

Hamilton still believed Jack would end up convicted then. He spat on the floor right in front of Frankie's feet.

'Fucking kill him,' he told Shank. 'Use the gun you found in his flat. And don't fuck around. Just shoot him in the head.'

Wilson marched over to the table and picked up the pistol. He started walking back.

'Wait," Frankie said. 'You do that and—'

'And *what*?' said Hamilton. 'That tape you left – *if* you left it, which I doubt – it'll go to the cops. Yeah, you already said. But you know what? Even if I did believe you that you've left instructions for someone to hand it in, I'm still prepared to risk it. With you being dead and no longer around to even back up your conversation with Baotic here, and without him confessing now to shit, which he won't, that tape won't stand up either.'

'It'll still cost you your witness,' Frankie said. 'There's no way the cops will be able to use him, not after hearing that.'

'Maybe so,' said Hamilton. 'But again, so what? There's still all that forensics, isn't there? All pointing at your brother. Enough to put him away.'

Was he bluffing? Was he really prepared to risk it? Frankie couldn't fucking tell. Shank Wilson was easier to read, though. His dark eyes were sparkling with excitement. No doubt what was about to happen next. Frankie James was about to get shot. He raised the pistol.

'Who said I'm planning on sending it to the cops anyway?' Frankie said.

Silence. Wilson was still aiming the gun at Frankie's head. Unwavering. Like he'd done it before a million times. An exe-fucking-cutioner's stance.

'You what?' Hamilton said.

'It's Dougie,' said Frankie. 'Dougie's the one that tape will be going to.'

Hamilton's pale face flushed. He stepped forward. He grabbed Frankie by the throat.

'You fucking *what*?' he roared.

Smile. Yeah, that's right, you bastard. Frankie eyeballed the motherfucker. Give it all you've fucking got, son. Grin. Let this bastard know it's you who's got him by the balls. Not the other fucking way around.

'How long do you think it's going to take a bright boy like Dougie to figure out that a mutt like Wilson here only ever does what he's been ordered?' Frankie said. 'That he only ever does what he'd been told to by his boss?'

'He's bluffing,' Wilson said.

'Yeah,' Terence said, but already Frankie could feel his grip slackening. 'Yeah.'

Hamilton let go. He stepped back.

'Shall I do him?' Wilson said.

'No.' Hamilton pulled a pair of transparent surgical gloves from his pocket and snapped them on. 'The amount of trouble this one's caused me . . . him fucking daring to talk about my

327

boy . . . I'm gonna fucking well do him myself.'

Wilson nodded. He lowered the gun and pressed it into Hamilton's hand. He waited for him to shoot, but instead Hamilton stepped forward. Without warning, he pistol-whipped Frankie across the side of his head.

Frankie's head lolled. He saw red. Vomit shot up his throat and spurted from his mouth.

'But first I'm gonna have myself a bit of fun with him,' Hamilton said.

Frankie's ears were ringing. He couldn't see properly. He felt like someone had stuck a knife right into his brain.

'Whatever you say, boss,' Wilson said.

'Go wait upstairs,' Hamilton told him, putting the gun in his right pocket and taking out a Stanley knife from his left. 'I might be some time, and I don't want to be fucking disturbed.'

49

Hamilton stared. The motherfucker hardly even blinked. Wilson peeled off his blood-stained clothing and boots. Got changed back into his boiler suit. Humming that Kylie song again. *I Should Be So Lucky*. The sick fucking prick.

Baotic was whimpering. Softly. Like a dog having a dream. Was he unconscious? Having a seizure? Frankie couldn't bear to look at him. Not just because of the state he was in. Because he now knew how Baotic must have felt last night when Frankie had been terrifying the shit out of him.

Frankie knew it. No one was coming. In a minute the pain would start. He wouldn't be able to think. He pictured his mum. Dad. Jack. Sharon too. Slim and Kind Regards and Xandra. He'd bloody blown it, hadn't he? Had screwed up royally. He thought he'd been so clever. But he hadn't. He'd relaxed. He'd thought this was all over. Thought he'd won. What a prize-winning fucking dick.

He stared down at the brickwork between his shoes. It was already spattered with blood. Nothing compared with what Hamilton had planned for him now, mind. He hoped it would be quick. Knew it wouldn't. Hamilton had just had his only son's wife-to-be beaten to death. How much worse was he going to make Frankie suffer now?

The light dimmed. Someone stood in front of him. Two black boots together side-by-side.

'Shame we didn't get a camera set up.' Wilson. 'I get the feeling it's gonna be one hell of a show.' He reached out and cupped Frankie's chin. Forced him to look up. 'It's been a pleasure getting to know you,' he said. His dark eyebrows bobbed. 'And that foxy female detective you've been seeing? The one you've probably been talking to an' all . . . Don't you worry about her. I'll make sure to pay her a little visit in a few months' time to give her one from you.'

'You cunt.'

Frankie jerked his head back, shaking himself free. How did Wilson know about Sharon? Fuck. Jack's flat. If Wilson had been there watching, he'd have seen them leaving together too.

'You bastard. Leave her alone, or—'

'Or what?' Wilson laughed. 'Or fucking nothing. It's over, kid. You're dead.'

He turned and walked up the steps. His footsteps faded and then they were gone.

Silence. A terrible pressure started building up in Frankie's skull. Like any second now it might crack. Hamilton hadn't moved. The Stanley knife's tooth glinted in his hand.

Frankie stared back down at his shoes. He started to shake. Couldn't help it. Be brave. Remember who you are. Don't beg. Don't make this any more fun for this bastard than it already is. Fuck him. Fuck him to hell.

'Say, for example,' Hamilton said, 'you are telling the truth, and this recording of yours *is* set to be delivered to my son . . . what would it take for you not to send it?'

What? Frankie nearly puked again. Had he just heard right? Don't look up. Don't let him see how fucking desperate you are. Don't let him know you'd already given up. He might not be joking. He might mean it. He might really still want that recording. This might not be over. Not yet.

'Justice,' Frankie said through gritted teeth.

He waited for the sudden flash of movement. The blade scything through the air. The beginning of the fucking end. Hamilton's hand didn't move.

'How noble,' he said. 'For that junkie little brother of yours?'

'My junkie little brother who's innocent of all this,' Frankie said. And justice for her. For Susan Tilley. And her grandmother too. And for Tara and Keira as well.

Again Frankie waited for the blade. Again it didn't come.

'And what if I can give you your justice?' Hamilton said. 'Give you Susan's killer? Give him to the cops as well? So that your brother gets off?'

Frankie looked up. He couldn't help himself. He had to see Hamilton's face. To see if this was all some kind of sick joke.

'You'd give up Wilson?'

'Maybe. To protect my son.'

From you. From what you really are. From the ugly fucking truth.

Frankie stared into Hamilton's eyes, trying to read him. And this time, yes, he saw something less hard, less certain, than before. He was a bastard all right, but he was still human. Just. And his son. His weakness. He didn't want to lose him. Knew he would if he ever found out what he'd done.

This is it. Your fucking card. Play it right. Hamilton was every bit as guilty as Wilson for the murders. He'd given the orders. But getting Wilson . . . saving Jack . . . walking out of here a-fucking-live . . . fuck yeah, that would be a start.

'If you can do that,' Frankie said, 'then that recording, I swear to you now, it'll never see the light of day.'

Hamilton watched him. 'Oh, don't you worry about that. He'll confess.'

But how? Why? But what the hell did it really matter? Hamilton would have his ways. God only knew what else he had on Wilson, what other threats he could bring to bear.

'But I tell you this now,' Hamilton warned, 'if that recording ever does surface . . . for whatever reason . . . if my son ever gets to hear one word of it . . . I will have you and your brother and everyone you've ever loved painfully wiped from the face of this planet.' Hamilton took the pistol from his pocket. 'And this gun . . .' he said, crouching down and pressing its butt into the palm of Frankie's taped-up right hand, pointing it away and forcing his fingertips tightly round it and onto its trigger. ' . . . it'll go straight to the cops with your prints all over it, and you'll be nicked for this murder.'

Frankie just stared as Hamilton took the gun away. He didn't understand. 'What murder?' he said.

'This one.'

Hamilton pointed the pistol at Frankie's head, then turned and shot Mario Baotic in the face.

Baotic didn't even twitch. His head slumped forwards. Blood trickled out of a hole in his temple. Onto the floor.

'Whu-whu—' Frankie tried to talk. Couldn't.

'Whu-whu-why?' Hamilton asked. 'Whu-whu-why did I kill him?' He stared at Frankie with contempt. 'Because he's no fucking use to me now, is he? He's nothing but another loose end.'

The scumbag. The wanker. He just did whatever he wanted. Whatever he fucking well pleased. If Frankie had a hold of that blade . . . of that gun . . . he'd slash him to ribbons . . . he'd shoot the fucker dead.

'Someone will come and cut you loose in the morning,' Hamilton said. 'But until then, you just think on it, on what I've just said. And if for even one second, son, you consider double-crossing me, then you just take another look at our friend Mister Baotic there. Because trust me: he'll look positively pretty compared with you, if you ever think about fucking me around.'

50

'Holy fuck, Frankie. What the hell happened to you?' Xandra said.

She meant his face. The severe bloody mess Shank Wilson and Terence Hamilton had made of it. The swelling had gone down since last night. But he was no oil painting.

Two of Hamilton's goons had come first thing this morning. Both wearing masks. He'd not seen their faces. They'd taken Baotic, or what was left of him. God only knew where.

They'd come back for Frankie an hour later. They'd blind-folded him and had put him back in whatever box he'd been brought there in. He'd been driven across town and cut loose round the back of an abandoned warehouse in Shoreditch.

'Sweet Jesus.'

Frankie turned to see Slim coming in through the front door. He looked horrified.

'All right?' Frankie said.

'Well, I was going to say I had a God-awful hangover,' Slim said, 'but I look a hell of a lot better than you. You need me to call someone? Like maybe the police?'

'Nah. I'll be fine.' Frankie turned back to Xandra. 'But what about you, eh? How come you're back? I thought you'd be half-way to Honolulu by now.'

'Ah, yes. You mean with all that money I stole . . .'

She was smiling. Slim was too. Slim was blushing as well.

'Something you both need to tell me?' Frankie said.

Slim laughed. 'There's been a little bit of a mix-up,' he said.

'Though I did take some money,' Xandra said.

'Thirty quid,' Slim said. 'Half of the pay she was owed.'

'I needed it for a train. To go and visit someone,' Xandra said.

What the hell was going on? Why were they both still smiling?

'And the rest of it?' Frankie said. How much was it Slim had told him had gone? Four hundred quid.

'Tucked safely away in a box of tiles down in the cellar,' she said.

Slim nodded. 'Where her note said it would be.'

Frankie put his hands up. 'All right, will one of you just tell me what the hell this is all about?'

Slim explained. Xandra had taken it upon herself to go visit the shelter she'd stayed in when she'd first got to London. Before things had gone properly tits up for her and she'd ended up on the street. There'd been a couple of volunteers there who'd really tried helping her. She'd wanted to let them know she was doing OK. There'd been a letter waiting there for her too. From an aunty she'd written to when she'd been staying there, who lived over in Croydon. Someone she'd always liked as a kid. It had said she was sick. In a hospice. Was dying.

'I'm sorry,' she told Frankie now. 'I should have asked. Before taking it. It's just I panicked. I came back here to get my pay. But you weren't here. And Slim wasn't. And, well, I knew where you both kept the key.' Her turn to blush. 'Only then I broke it, didn't I? Trying to shut it. And I didn't want to just leave the rest of the cash in there then. Which is why I hid it and wrote the note, saying it was somewhere safe, and where I'd gone.'

'I found it down the side of the fridge, the note,' Slim said.

'After . . . well, you know . . . after I wrote my own note, telling you she'd done a runner . . . telling you she was a thief . . .'

Frankie shook his head. Christ, it hurt even to do that.

'Bloody hell,' he said. 'Well I'm glad it's all sorted out now.' He nodded at Xandra. 'And I'm glad you're back.'

Slim produced an envelope of cash from one pocket. A key from another. 'New spare,' he said.

'And where you planning on keeping that now?' Frankie asked.

Slim patted Xandra on the back. 'Same place I kept the other one,' he said. 'So we all know where it is.'

'Right,' Frankie said. 'Well, I'm glad that's all sorted. But if you don't mind, I'm going to have to duck upstairs. I need a bloody kip.'

'Ah, well maybe you'd best prepare yourself first,' Xandra warned him. 'Because there's one more little surprise coming your way.'

She looked up at the ceiling.

'What?' Frankie said. It couldn't be Hamilton, or why would he have set him free? Wilson? Shit, was that bastard on the loose again? No, letting other people know he was coming, that wasn't Wilson's style.

'It's her,' Xandra said. 'Your friendly neighbourhood policewoman.'

'Sharon?'

'I had to let her in. She said she'd get a warrant if I didn't. She's been up there over an hour already. I get the feeling she'll wait there all year.'

Shit. He'd called her, hadn't he? Just before Wilson had knocked him out. He'd called her and let slip he knew who her witness was. Or what he was. A courier. Her now dead witness. Jesus, would Hamilton have dumped his body? Had it already turned up? What the hell was he going to tell Sharon? How was he going to explain he'd known anything about her witness at all?

'You want me to come up with you?' Xandra offered.

'To protect me?'

'She looks pretty pissed off. And worried too,' Xandra said. 'And I can't blame her, the state your flat's in . . .'

Where Wilson had done it over. Bollocks. He'd forgotten about that too. He walked over to the sink behind the bar and stuck his mouth over the tap and turned it on. He gulped down fresh water. Tried washing the worst of the dried blood off his face.

'It's all right,' he said. 'I'll deal with it. With her.'

But as he trudged upstairs, he really didn't fucking know how.

The flat's hallway was tidy, was tidi*er*. The bedroom too. Had Sharon done it? No, forget that. More like Xandra. Or Slim. Jesus, he hadn't even asked her how things had gone with her aunt. He was useless, exhausted. His brain was fried. How the hell was he going to cope with Sharon?

'Well, at least you're still alive.'

It was her. Standing in the living-room doorway. Blocking it, her arms crossed. She must have heard him coming up the stairs.

'I can explain,' he said.

'I sincerely doubt that.'

Her fists were bunched. The whites of her knuckles showed. She was furious. He could see that. But shocked as well. By how messed up he looked.

'Who did that to you?'

Frankie didn't answer. He had no answer to give.

'I said *who*?'

'It doesn't matter. It's over,' he said.

But was it this time? Really? Please, fucking yes. Let that be true.

'And what about Mario Baotic?' she snapped. 'I suppose you know nothing about him either?'

'Never heard of him.'

'He was our witness. The same one you somehow miraculously knew was a courier.'

Was . . .

She stared at him, waiting for him to speak. Nothing he could say. Not without incriminating himself. Or Hamilton. Nothing that wouldn't result in him and everyone he'd ever cared for, including her, ending up dead.

'So that's it?' She looked like she was going to explode. 'You're just going to stand there and say nothing?'

He desperately wanted to tell her that everything, well some things, were going to be OK. That Jack's innocence was going to be proved. That at least the killer of Susan Tilley, and Keira and Star, was going to pay for what he'd done.

'He's dead,' Sharon said. 'Baotic. They found him two hours ago. Shot in the head.'

She waited. Let the silence rage.

'He'd been beaten . . . tortured . . .' She glared at Frankie's face. 'Like you . . .'

An accusation. She knew he knew so much more than he was letting on. Him and Baotic were connected. She'd sussed it. Did she think they'd been beaten up by the same person? Her eyes said as much. The same as they were clearly now asking him how come he was alive and Baotic was dead.

Frankie thought about Baotic's wife. His little house. Had she been told yet? Had she identified the body? Or had Hamilton left ID on him, so he'd be identified that much more quickly?

Just to get Jack out quicker? To complete his part of the deal?

'And he's not the only one,' Sharon said.

'The only what?'

'One who's dead . . .'

What was she talking about? Surely Hamilton would have called Dougie and the rest of his dogs off? Wouldn't have sanctioned them killing any more of Riley's men? Not now.

Another, even more horrible, thought occurred to him.

'You mean the old lady? Susan Tilley's grandmother?'

'No, she's much better.'

'Then who?' he asked.

'Wilson. Shank Wilson.'

'What?'

She spotted it right away, the surprise on his face. No matter how hard he tried to swallow it back down.

'Suicide,' she told him, watching him like a hawk. 'He was found in a warehouse last night after an anonymous tip-off, with photos of Susan Tilley, and a signed, typed confession by his side. Blew his head off with a shotgun.'

Frankie felt the room sway. Only just managed to keep his cool. To not lurch sideways. So that was the kind of confession Terence Hamilton had meant. One that could never be challenged, because its 'confessor' was already dead. He'd clearly decided that whatever leverage he might have had on Wilson, it hadn't been enough to bend him to his will. So he'd broken him instead. He'd shot him and had then planted that confession on him.

'The confession detailed how Wilson had tried to persuade Susan Tilley to run away with him,' Sharon said, 'because he was obsessed with her, but then when she refused him, he decided to kill her to punish her and in case she told Dougie what he'd planned . . . and it said how he'd then blackmailed Baotic to

338

go there and claim it was your brother who'd done it . . . and everything else that he'd done to frame Jack . . . including Baotic and the two girls he killed to cover up what he'd done.'

Frankie's mouth had gone dry. She was still staring at him, still watching. Say something. Anything to make her stop thinking you already know. Be how you're meant to be. Like you've just heard someone's confessed to the crime they arrested Jack for. Look happy, for fuck's sake. *Be* happy. This is what you wanted. You've got Jack off. The rest of it . . . Star, Keira and Baotic, they're not your fault. You did what you had to. You did the best you could.

'He's innocent, then,' he said. 'Jack . . .'

'If what Shank Wilson says is true.'

'What do you mean, *if*?'

'Well, do you buy it?' she asked. 'That someone like him, his boss's Rottweiller . . . that someone that loyal would have betrayed him like this?'

She knew. She *knew* this wasn't right. That something about it stank. But . . . he stared into her eyes . . . she didn't know what, did she? And wouldn't either. Not unless he told her. Not as long as he kept his gob shut.

'I don't give a fuck about Hamilton,' he said. 'Or Wilson. All I care about is Jack. And the fact you've now got to set him free.'

If she'd been furious with him before, it was nothing compared with the hatred that now blazed in her eyes. Why? Because she'd been proved wrong? No, he didn't believe that. Not even now in the heat of the moment. She was a pro. This was something more primal than that. And simple. He realised what then. It was because he was lying to her. Because he'd shut her out.

'Listen,' he said, stepping forward, trying to sound like what he wasn't, a decent person, not a fucking lying scumbag who was just here pulling her strings.

339

Because he still wanted her. No getting away from it. He wanted her, and with everything that had happened with Jack – everything that had kept them apart – now sorted, he wanted to make things right between them. He didn't want her to leave. He didn't want her to go to Hong Kong.

But before he could get another word out, she shoved past him. He turned to try and stop her, but she was already at the flat's front door. She slammed it hard behind her. He heard her running down the stairs.

51

Frankie was drunk. Again. But at least this time he deserved it, right? The Ambassador Club was buzzing, it was rammed, without a snooker ball in sight. It was Jack's 'Welcome Home' party and everyone was here.

Jack and all his mates, most of them Riley's boys. Smoking and drinking and stuffing their faces from the buffets that covered the tables. Riley had sent carpenters over to fit a bunch of protective boards this morning. The food too. Only the best. From Fortnum & Mason's down on Piccadilly.

Frankie had thought twice about accepting it. But not for long. He was still skint and, no matter how creative Slim was with the Breville, there was only a finite number of toasties he could rattle off.

Riley had sent over another envelope today as well. Care of Tam bloody Jackson. But when Frankie had opened it, instead of finding a lead to a witness in a murder case, he'd found a bundle of cash. A grand. Enough to get everyone here nicely pissed.

Frankie poured himself another pint behind the bar. He'd not yet had a spirit, though the optics kept glinting at him every time he served anyone else. He turned up the stereo a notch. The Rolling Stones' 'You Can't Always Get What You Want'. Picked up a nice welcoming roar from the crowd. Frankie wished his dad was here to see this. His mum too.

And Sharon. He'd not forgotten her. He'd left her six messages since she'd stormed out. At home and at work. She'd not got back. He'd nearly called Snaresby's office too, to ask if he'd seen her. He'd been that desperate. But speaking to that bastard . . . nah, he couldn't face that yet. Even though he reckoned it was only a matter of time before their paths would cross again.

Had she already quit her job? Now that her case had collapsed? Was she even now packing for Hong Kong? Or did she just hate him? Never want to see him again? That's how it felt.

The club's front door swung open. Riley came in, flanked by Mackenzie Grew and Tam Jackson. Just about Riley's whole crew was gathered here now, something that would have been unthinkable even a couple of days ago, when the turf war between them and the Hamiltons was still in full swing.

But all that was over. For now. Since Shank Wilson's suicide and confession, Hamilton had gone to ground. His boys and Dougie too. And what must he think? Dougie. About everything he'd done since his fiancée's murder? Now that he'd found out she'd been killed by one of his own? Who would he be tomorrow? What kind of a man by next year?

Frankie pitied him for what had happened to him. And for who his prick of a father was. But he was glad too. That his own life and Jack's were no longer screwed.

And Riley . . . well, just look at the bastard . . . Riley obviously felt the same. His shining eyes locked on Frankie's. An invitation to join him. An order, of sorts.

'You all right here for a minute?' Frankie asked Xandra, picking up an open magnum of champagne.

'Sorted, boss,' she told him with a smile.

She was hardly recognisable from the waif who'd walked in here out of the storm that night. He'd even got round to bloody asking her about her trip to Croydon. It had gone well. Or as well as any visit to a hospice could. Her aunty had been happy she'd managed to find herself somewhere to call home. Frankie was glad it was here.

He took the fizz and four glasses with him, squeezing past Slim, Ash Crowther, 'Sea Breeze' Strinati and Kind Regards, who were all busy discussing the local lad, The Rocket, again and whether he might win the Masters for a second time. Hmm. Maybe there might be a way to lure him back here for an exhibition match. Even to help promote his tournament if he ever got it off the ground. Now that would be something to aim for, all right.

'You look pleased with yourself,' Riley said as Frankie reached him and laid out the four glasses on a table beside him.

'I am.' Frankie started to pour.

'And so you should be. I knew you had it in you. You got your brother out. You got the result you needed, the same one all of us did.'

Hamilton now being under close police scrutiny. With his ambitions neutralised for now. And Wilson gone forever. An added bonus there. For humanity as well as Riley. No bleeding doubt about that.

Frankie handed Riley a glass.

'One day, I'm gonna ask you for the details,' he said, leaning in.

But Frankie wouldn't tell him. Not the whole truth. Not about Hamilton's involvement. Not ever. No way could he ever risk it getting out that it had come from him.

'Cheers,' Frankie said. 'For your help. Not just with Jack, but with this.' He raised his glass to the room.

Frankie didn't mean the cash for the party and Riley knew it. Tam Jackson did too and he scowled. Because there'd been something else in that envelope he'd delivered. A note from

343

Listerman the Lawyer, telling Frankie his overdue rent had been settled by Mister Riley. The next three months as well. Payment for all that he'd done. The second good news Frankie had got from a lawyer this week. The other being that he'd got Jack cleared in time before they'd employed that trial lawyer. Meaning he'd still got his Capri.

Frankie handed Tam Jackson and Mackenzie Grew each a drink. Mackenzie told him thanks. Tam Jackson said nothing at all. Riley raised his glass in a toast.

'To brothers,' he said. 'Blood brothers and brothers-in-arms.'

The four of them clinked their glasses and drank.

'To brothers,' Frankie said, under his breath.

Riley didn't hang around for much longer. He left with Jackson and Grew. Frankie decided to call it a night himself not much after. He was still bloody knackered. He said his goodnights. Told Jack he'd swing by tomorrow to pick him up to go visit the old man. He left Xandra and Slim in charge as the party rolled on. He headed on up to the flat.

He spotted the brown A4 manila envelope on the mat the second he opened his flat's front door. He stared at it. Didn't pick it up. Who was it from? How the fuck had it got here? He looked back down the stairs at the door leading out onto the street. It was shut. Didn't look like anyone had broken in.

He knelt down and opened the envelope. Reaching inside, he took a single colour photograph out. It showed the old man. In his prison uniform. His hair was cut exactly the same as the last time Frankie had seen him. Meaning this had to have been taken in the last few weeks. No, sod that. More like days. That same small shaving cut was right there on the old man's cheek. Exactly where Frankie had seen it on his last visit.

Frankie's heart drummed. He turned the photo over. A message in block capitals read:

I MIGHT NOT BE HERE FOREVER, BUT I'LL ALWAYS
HAVE EYES ON YOU

From Hamilton. About the tape. About how even when he was dead, if Frankie ever broke his promise and gave it to Dougie, or dared let fucking slip to anyone the real truth about what had happened – then Terence Hamilton still had people who'd get to Frankie, who'd get to the old man as well.

Frankie rocked back on his heels, shaking his head. The sick joke was, of course, he couldn't have given Dougie the tape even if he'd wanted. Because there *was* no bloody tape. Never had been. Not even in the cottage in Brighton. He'd just switched on the machine. Set its wheels turning. To make Baotic crap it. To get the bastard to do as he was told.

It was only when Shank Wilson had brought its existence up down there in that basement that Frankie had realised he might be able to use it to buy back his life. And he had.

He flinched, dropped the photo. The downstairs front doorbell had just buzzed. He stuffed the snap back into its envelope. Slipped it under the doormat. Then headed quickly downstairs.

Who now? Probably just someone trying to get into the club, right? The music through there was still pumping. But what if . . .? Yeah, why not? What if it was Sharon? What if she'd got his messages after all? What if she'd had a change of heart?

But it wasn't her. It was the blonde. Martha, or Megan, or Molly or May. The girl who'd left her phone number written in bright red lipstick on the mirror above the sink the day Jack had turned up all covered in blood.

Her bright eyes flashed at Frankie, all mock annoyance. 'You didn't call,' she said.

He looked her over. She was wearing a little black dress, wrapped tight around her. She looked every bit as fit as the first time he'd seen her in the 100 Club bar. He thought about Sharon. But this wasn't her. She wasn't here. Sharon Granger was gone.

'Then I suppose I'd better ask you upstairs,' he said.

She pressed herself up against him. Slipped her arms around his waist.

'First this,' she whispered, rising up on her tiptoes, before softly kissing him on the mouth.

It was only when they broke apart that Frankie saw her. Sharon. There on the other side of the street, next to a black cab that had just dropped her off.

'Wait!' he shouted.

But it was too late. She was already getting back into the cab. He pushed past the blonde and stepped out into the street. But the cab was already pulling away. And Sharon didn't look back.

He watched the cab's red tail lights fade into the night. He was an idiot. A fuck-up. Was he never going to learn? He stood there in the middle of his street, of his city, alone.

END